Sophia's Journey

Joyce Rickards Newcomb

Published by Christmas Lake Press 2023
www.christmaslakecreative.com

ISBN 978-1-960865-02-1

Interior layout by Daiana Marchesi

Dedication

For my family.
They have given me love and inspiration in abundance.
They are my True North.

For good or ill, storms will come.
Ominous signs forewarn.
The morning dawns red, the earth quiets, the sky darkens.
When the wind begins to roar westward
across Maryland's Eastern Shore,
Trees fall. The landscape changes.
Secrets are revealed.
Lives change.

Acknowledgments

Writing this book has not been a solitary endeavor. I have relied on guidance and encouragement from so many people, and I am grateful for their gifts of time, knowledge, and energy. The historians who recorded and interpreted events following the American Revolution laid the foundation for this book. Volunteers at Salisbury University's Nabb Research Center in Salisbury, MD, helped me understand the unique nature of the Delmarva Peninsula. Thanks also to Pam Sourelis, who first introduced me to the art of fiction.

I want to thank Sharon and Steve Fiffer, my mentors and staunch believers in the worth of this book. Cofounders of the Wesley Writers Workshops in Evanston. IL., they have created a safe place for writers to practice their craft, to hear their work read aloud, and to receive feedback from fellow writers. Thanks to Francie, Barb, Bill, Kendra, Sarah, Daphne, and Katy. Their comments saved me from many missteps.

I offer my heartfelt thanks in equal measure to Christmas Lake Press and its publisher, Tom Fiffer, whose enthusiasm for *Sophia's Journey* brought this book into being. He chose Julia Bobkoff as my editor. It was a perfect match. I will be forever grateful to Julia, not only for her prodigious editing skills but also for embracing my characters and their story. We sing the same song.

Most importantly, I thank my family. My sons Henry and Jim never doubted me but stood quietly by, having the wisdom to offer an opinion only when asked. My sister Carol Heitman Mazzocco took on the task of designing the book cover and drawing the map of Records Landing and Marshtown. Her skill and patience are truly appreciated.

And I thank you, the reader. Without my readers this book would just be a doorstop.

Table of Contents

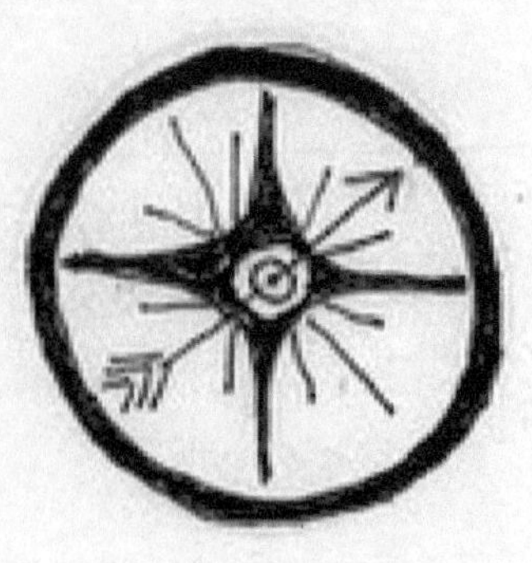

Pocomoke River
Tobacco Shed
Old C
Orchard
Great House
Cook House
Chicken Coop
Barn

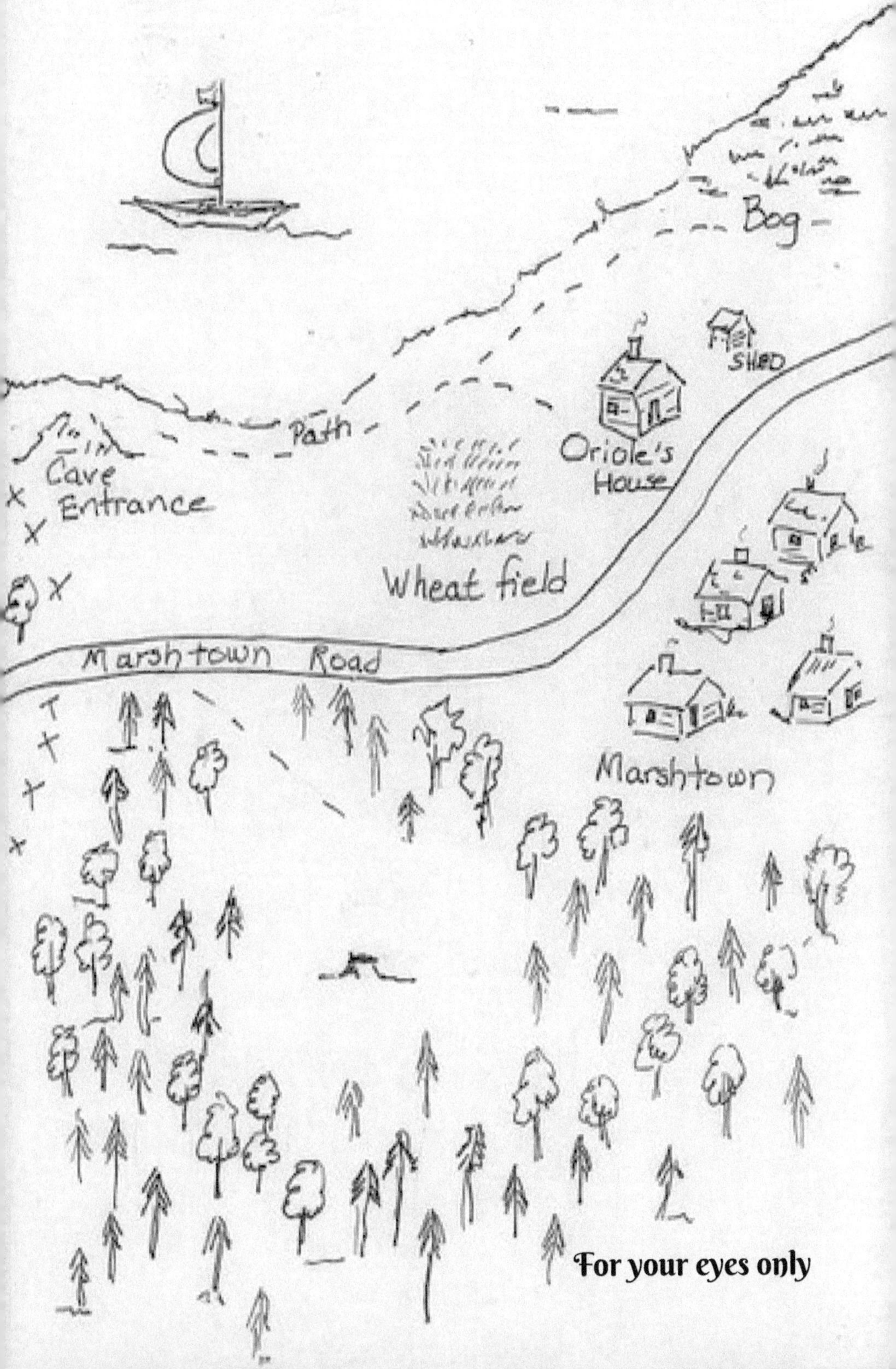

Bog
Path
Oriole's House
Shed
Cave Entrance
Wheat field
Marshtown Road
Marshtown
For your eyes only

Gone

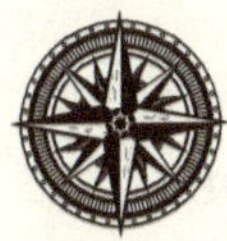

A Friday in Late October 1810

"Please, give this to Mother, tomorrow. No sooner," James implored, handing Sophia a sealed envelope. "I need time to get to the Chesapeake. No one, not Father, not even Uncle Caleb, will be able to find me once I am there. With the right wind, I'll reach Baltimore in no time at all."

How like you, Sophia thought, looking at the letter she clutched in her hand. How like you to escape Father's demands by bolting and leaving me to smooth things over. Only before she could speak her mind, James threw his arms around her. Calmed by the usual comfort his big hugs brought, Sophia stood still.

"Don't go," she begged. "It's foolhardy to sail up the bay alone. Who will spot the shoals?"

"Then pray for me," he said, stepping back. "Nothing you say will change my mind. Father neither. I am nearly fifteen, old enough to make my own way. Grandsire did."

Always impatient. And reckless, Sophia thought as she watched her tall, lanky twin leap aboard the shallop and cast off.

As if he heard her thoughts, James grinned, then gave her a smart salute before raising the sail. "Never fear, Phee," he shouted, calling her by her pet name. "I will return."

Wind filled the canvas, and the boat with James at the tiller moved away from the pier. The shallop cut through the Pocomoke's dark water as if it, too, were eager to leave. Moments before reaching the bend in the river, James, his left hand still on the tiller, turned back toward her and waved.

In her mind, Sophia could hear him saying in his newly deepened voice, "Off on a grand adventure!"

"Wait!" she called out. "Your hat! You forgot your hat!" But the wind had picked up, speeding the shallop forward. "God speed," she whispered as she watched her brother's sturdy boat disappear around the bend.

And just like that, he was gone.

Sophia blinked back tears. Along the riverbank cypress trees, their feathery needles now a rusty red, looked drab. The Pocomoke appeared darker, more the color of black tea. The river, the woods, even the plantation itself now seemed empty, and Sophia felt the pain of loneliness for the first time.

"May God keep you safe and bring you home again," she prayed, recognizing once again her twin's recklessness. Forgetting his hat was careless. It was probably hanging on a peg in the hallway. He'd need it on the Chesapeake where there was no shade. Worse, he had paid no heed to Grandsire's warning.

Remembering her beloved grandfather's counsel made her wince. Dead almost a year now, Grandsire always had carved time out for her whether it was to teach her draughts or the proper way to raise a sail, even if she would never command a ship.

She recollected a day when she and James had just turned twelve and they had been standing together on the deck of the *Rebel Ann*. Grandsire was teaching them the proper method for raising the mainsail.

"Never set sail on a Friday, though," Grandsire had said, looking directly at James. His blue eyes, usually twinkling with good cheer, were stern. "No journey begun on Friday has ever ended well. My crew would mutiny if I gave the order to hoist the mainsail."

Today is a Friday, Sophia thought. She lingered for a few minutes near the end of the long pier, hoping James would remember that warning and turn back. When he didn't appear, his chestnut curls blowing wildly about his face, she turned her back on the river. Tucking his letter inside her sleeve, she walked slowly toward Great House, her shoes crunching on the path of crushed oyster shells.

The white clapboard mansion with its tall windows and long front porch sat at the top of a gentle slope facing the Pocomoke. Centered on the roof was a square railed platform, called a widow's watch. From this vantage point, anyone brave enough to climb up the steep stairs could, with a spyglass, see who might be traveling past on the river. Sixty-six miles long, the river angled westward from the brooding Great Cypress Swamp in the north to the Chesapeake Bay. If the wind was right, it was a three days' sail to Baltimore. The Records' small plantation was far enough beyond Snow Hill to avoid any disturbance from the large sloops and schooners that sailed upriver to the city's busy shipping port.

Rivermen, usually hunters and fishermen, had used Great House as a landmark for the last fifty years. After the Revolution, they began saluting as they sailed their skiffs past. Sophia assumed the men were applauding her grandfather's uncanny ability to capture British ships, which had helped win the war. Even though he never said, Sophia believed Grandsire secretly appreciated the gesture.

Instead, when she had asked him why rivermen saluted, he said they were complimenting the fine house.

"I hired the same carpenters who built my ship to construct this house," he said with satisfaction. "Just like the Rebel Ann, it can withstand whatever the winds blow our way."

Sophia had been standing with Grandsire in the widow's watch when a riverman's salute prompted her question. She was ten years old. Grandsire had coaxed her up there to survey Records Landing from a new perspective. The whole of the plantation stretched below her. The river, pastures, woods, orchards, the cookhouse, the barn, even the path to Marshtown, she could see it all. "Now I know what birds see," she remembered saying as she hugged Grandsire in delight.

Looking at the house now, though, Sophia realized that it appeared shabby, as if Great House had lost its pride after Grandsire died. A new coat of paint would bring back its luster, she thought, knowing full well that Father would never hire anyone to paint the house. He refused to spend money on anything, saying President Jefferson's embargo was forcing planters to tighten their belts. Commerce with the British was essentially cut off.

Last month, he had called both her and James into his office to explain that their tutor would no longer be coming to Great House. In his next breath, he started lecturing James, saying it was time James apprenticed himself to the judge in Snow Hill. When James had outright refused, Father had launched into another speech, reminding James of his filial duties.

I don't know why Father persisted, she thought as she continued toward the house. Everyone in the household, right down to four-year-old Willie, knows that James loves the sea not the law. I can't even . . .

"Good morning, Miss Phee. What gets you up at this fine hour?"

Sophia stopped, suddenly aware of her surroundings and surprised to discover that, lost in thought, she had unwittingly veered off the path and headed to the cookhouse. Sally, her tight black curls covered by a bright blue kerchief, was standing by the door, wiping her hands on her apron, grinning.

Returning her greeting, Sophia shrugged and said with a little laugh, "I've heard this is the best time of day, always full of possibilities."

"Big storm coming."

"What makes you think that?"

"Look at the sky, child. It was on fire at dawn. You know what they say, 'Red sky in the morning, sailor take warning.'"

Sophia glanced up and frowned. A few ragged pink clouds, remnants of the fiery sunrise, moved across a violet sky. Little shivers of fear prickled the nape of her neck. Two bad omens in one day. She touched her sleeve to make sure James's letter was completely tucked away from notice. She had promised to keep his news secret. Besides, it wasn't too late. James could turn his boat about, turn back. After all, he never stuck with any idea for long. Father would forgive him, if not now, eventually. Sophia closed her eyes, willing her brother to return.

"Not like you to worry about storms," Sally said, her brown eyes full of questions.

Sophia's eyes flashed open. "I'm not worried."

What I am worried about right now is you, Sophia thought grimly.

Sally had been working at Records Landing for as long as Sophia could remember, certainly long enough to know that Sophia was habitually late for breakfast. Being awake, dressed, and walking up from the dock was more than out of the ordinary. It was obvious Sally was fishing for answers.

Sophia tried to divert her. "You don't seem alarmed, so why should I be?"

"Nothin' like a long walk in the morning to chase away worrisome thoughts. But I guess you know that."

Sophia didn't respond.

"Well, I best stir up the embers and get breakfast cookin'. There'll be biscuits soon."

"I know a little brother who will be happy about that! I'm off to the barn to milk Ginger. It's a little surprise for Faith."

When Sally chuckled, Sophia grinned. Her elder sister's lack of enthusiasm about chores before breakfast had become the subject of much good-natured teasing. The only reason Faith had insisted on doing the morning milking was because she had a beau who often came calling in the late afternoon.

At Records Landing everyone had chores, even Willie, whose job was to help Sally, although Sophia thought her little brother did more eating than helping, especially if molasses cookies were involved.

"Nothing prospers without hard work," Father would say when assigning chores. Unlike so many other planters on the Eastern Shore, he had never owned a slave. Sally lived with her family down the road in Marshtown. She walked to Great House every day but Sunday to cook and help with the housekeeping chores. Father paid her. Some folks in Worchester County called the Records family abolitionists, nearly spitting out the word as though abolition was an abomination. Father wasn't one to start an argument but if called out as an abolitionist, he always said, "We Americans fought the Revolution so that *all* men would be free. Slavery is the abomination."

He is right, Sophia thought, picturing the slave auction she had witnessed last year in Baltimore. She could not erase from her mind the image of a boy, no older than one of Sally's children, being led away from his weeping mother. Sophia shuddered, remembering his anguished wail. She thumped the milking stool down beside the Jersey cow.

"An abomination! Isn't that so, Ginger?" she muttered, stroking the cow's brown flank. "Everyone should be free to make their own decisions. Even sons."

The cow turned her head toward Sophia as if in agreement.

Most days, Sophia found the rhythmic sound of milk splashing into the wooden bucket relaxing. Today, however, she couldn't shake the feeling that James was in danger. Even in the best of weather sailing a small boat on the Chesapeake had its risks, risks she had ticked off on her fingers for James's benefit at dawn.

"First,'" she had said, touching her index finger, "lightning. The water is wide. There is no protection. Second," she touched her middle finger, "high winds. They could shred your sails. Worse, you could capsize. Third, you are alone. No one would know if you were in trouble. Fourth, pirates. Don't laugh. There are thieves lurking on the bay. They'd take that boat you love so much or worse." She had closed her fist and smacked it into her other hand hard enough to make a loud clap.

He merely smiled.

"This beauty is yar," he said, slapping the boat's smooth gunnel. "Grandsire and I designed it. I named it. *Freedom* is smaller than most shallops but that makes it easier to navigate. With only one mast, not two, I can sail it anywhere, just not to the ocean."

And so, she agreed to keep his secret until the next day. Now she wished she hadn't.

"James is making a mistake," she told Ginger. The cow munched her hay.

⚓

The brunt of the storm hit six hours later. Gale force winds began buffeting Great House and Sophia had run upstairs to shutter the windows.

As she struggled against the wind, Sophia kept repeating, "Stay safe, get to shore, forget your boat," willing her brother to hear her. Sometimes, even when apart, each twin understood what the other was thinking. Later, after the fact, they would tell each other, "I just knew," and then laugh about it.

But today is no laughing matter, Sophia thought. Father should be here, not in Snow Hill. He'd find a way to bring James home. Except if Father were here, if he hadn't insisted that James clerk for the judge, he wouldn't need to go looking. James would be safe.

"Fiddlesticks!" she shouted as the wind tried to snatch a shutter out of her hand. "I never should have promised," she muttered, bolting the final shutters closed with a loud clang.

Climbing onto the tall four-poster she shared with Faith, Sophia rested her head on her knees and worried about the right and wrong of keeping secrets.

She was still sitting there when she heard James shout her name. Over the roar of the hurricane, she heard, "Phee! Phee!" The call was so urgent that she scrambled off the bed and ran to the window, opening the shutters to the mercy of the wind. She hoped to see him standing at the base of the magnolia tree. He wasn't there.

"James!" she screamed as if expecting an answer. All she heard was the punishing rain and howling wind.

"Mother!" Sophia cried as she raced down the stairs. "Something terrible has happened to James!"

She found Mother sitting in the drawing room calmly waiting out the storm. Mother's only concession had been to move from the chair by the window to one by the table in the middle of the room where she continued to knit by candlelight. Her face looked unlined in its soft glow.

"Good gracious, Phee. Lower your voice," Mother whispered with just a trace of a Scottish accent. "You know James is with Father in Snow Hill. Father has a court case this morning. The two of them will find safe harbor there." She nodded toward the daybed where Willie slept oblivious to what was happening. One small arm dangled over the edge; the other he had tucked beneath a feather pillow.

"That boy can sleep though anything," Mother said and smiled fondly. She put down her knitting. "Unlike you, Sophia. I think the storm has pricked your imagination."

"No, No. I am not being fanciful." Sophia walked to her mother and handed her the letter.

"What's this?"

"James wanted you to have it. He walked home from Snow Hill before sunrise," Sophia fought back tears.

"Walked twenty miles? Through the night? Where is he now?"

"Gone. He told me to give you the letter. Tomorrow."

Mother looked at the square creamy envelope with *Mother* scrawled across the front. "That scalawag," she said turning it over to break the seal only to find the wax had already cracked. She slid the note out.

"Has he run off to Marshtown?"

Sophia shook her head. If only he had, she thought.

Marshtown had always been their safe harbor. Whenever she or James got into trouble, they would run there, to Oriole's cabin. Once their nanny, Oriole remained a trusted confidante. "Let's talk it out," Oriole would say in her soothing Jamaican accent. "Always set things to right before that old sun sets."

"No, not to Marshtown. Not this time." Sophia told her mother. "James took the little shallop. He's gone."

"Oh, no." Mother held the letter close to her heart. She looked toward the shuttered windows then down at her idle hands. She sighed. Raising her head, she held the letter out to Sophia.

"You read it," she said softly. "I don't have my spectacles. I cannot make out his scrawl without them in this low light."

Pretending to scan the note she had already read, Sophia cleared her throat before beginning.

"Dear Mother," her voice quavered. She took a breath and went on.

"I have decided to follow Grandsire's example and follow the sea. I am sailing to Baltimore to enlist in the American Navy at Ft. McHenry. The sale of Grandsire's shallop (it is rightfully mine now) should cover the cost of uniforms and a sword with some left over. I feel it a fitting way to spend my inheritance. I think Grandsire would be pleased.

"Tell Father I am sorry to let him down. I would like to honor his wishes, but the thought of studying law suffocates me. He must know I will be a better sailor than a lawyer. Tell Faith to follow her heart. I know she is sweet on someone, and tell little Will I know he will make Father proud. He is the oldest boy at home now.

"I am giving this letter to Sophia to deliver. She understands why it is so important for me to leave. Don't worry about me. I will send you my address as soon as I know it. I hope you will write. I will keep you all in my prayers and hope that you will do the same for me. With love from your son James."

Mother's fair complexion had turned ashen. "Oh, dear Lord. What has he done?"

Sophia handed back the letter then sank to the floor beside her mother's chair. "I should have told you right away," she moaned.

"Don't worry," Mother murmured as she stroked wisps of tawny brown hair away from Sophia's face. "James may not be an eager scholar, but he is a fine sailor. He'll know what to do in this storm. He'll find a cove, drop the sail, and wait it out."

"You don't understand." Sophia bit her lower lip. "James needs help now. I heard him call."

Mother took Sophia's hand into hers. "Oh, Phee, maybe what you heard was your own fear." She pressed Sophia's hands together. "He's in God's hands now."

"What can I do?" Sophia said huskily before all the tears she had been choking back began to spill over and slide down her cheeks.

"You can pray," Mother said softly. "As soon as the storm ends, we'll search for him."

Sophia nodded. There was nothing left to say. She leaned her head against Mother's knee and closed her eyes. Outside wind and rain pounded against the house.

After a while, Willie woke. Rubbing the sleep from his eyes, he looked around. "Is it night? Did I miss dinner?"

"No," Mother said. "As your Grandsire would say, 'we are having a bit of a blow.' Nothing to worry about." She smiled as Willie climbed into her lap. She smoothed his hair and held him close.

"The only things wee children hunger for is food and love," she said more to herself than to Sophia. "It's only after they grow bigger that they hunger for other things." She sounded sad.

Mother began to croon a Scottish lullaby; one she had sung many times before.

"Blow the wind, blow," she sang. "Swift and low. Blow o'er the ocean . . ."

Sophia closed her eyes and listened to the familiar song about wind and oceans and freedom. Maybe, she thought, James is safe, scared but safe. And for the moment, her whole world seemed safe.

When the wind abruptly ceased, Mother rose and walked swiftly to the window, raising the sash and unbolting the shutters. Without turning, she told Sophia to fetch Faith and Sally from the cookhouse.

"Is it over?" Willie asked, hurrying to stand beside his mother.

She shook her head sadly and bolted the shutters closed.

"Not yet" she said. "We all will wait out the rest of storm together. Storms like these always have more to say."

2

Another Stormy Day

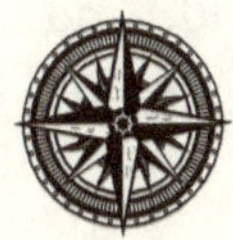

Six Months later

The white gander launched his attack when Sophia stomped around the corner of the house. China Boy had been napping beneath the magnolia. Startled awake, he came at her with his head lowered, hissing angrily.

"Shoo, shoo, you silly goose." Sophia snatched the mobcap off her head and flung it at him.

Turning his fury on the ruffled white cap, China Boy struck at it with his thick bill even before it landed.

"I'm not the enemy. It's Father you need to worry about."

China Boy halted his assault and began preening his wing feathers as if embarrassed by his mistake. Most days Sophia would have laughed. Today she muttered, "Stupid goose," as she stooped to pick up her cap. Setting it firmly on her head, she hurried toward the apple orchard and the road to Oriole's cabin.

A well-worn wagon track, known as the Marshtown road, ran directly through the center of the orchard then snaked through what once had been an ancient forest. Many sky-scraping pines had been felled and hauled away years ago to be become masts for English and French sailing vessels. Although some of the old trees remained, the forest was mostly a mix of second growth pine and hardwood.

Sophia walked quickly, blinking back tears as an overwhelming sense of loss swept over her. Will it never end, she wondered? First, Grandsire, then James, and now this. I should have known. Bad news always comes in threes. If Grandsire were living, he never would have allowed the plantation to be sold. And never to a Talcott.

"Fiddlesticks!" she yelped, stubbing her toe on a large branch lying in the road.

Could this day get any worse? Of course not. Father had already taken care of that. She sat down in the middle of the road, pulled off her shoe, and wiggled her big toe. No damage done, she decided, then eyed the offending obstacle. It was about four feet long and thick as her forearm.

Standing the branch upright as if it were a pole, she got back on her feet. The branch had a solid feel to it. The perfect walking stick. Breaking off the smaller branches, then smoothing the wood as best she could without a knife, Sophia brandished her new staff toward the sky.

"I won't go!"

At least I am not afraid to speak my mind, she thought, trying to justify her behavior at breakfast. Father's revelation was, was . . . she searched for the right word, settling on *detestable*. What he had done was vile and shameful. How unlike him, a stickler for honorable choices. Worse, he had acted pleased.

"I won't go!" she repeated, this time almost shouting.

The words reverberated through the woods, silencing the birds. In the stillness, Sophia heard a pig grunting.

She knew instantly—a Talcott hog was loose. Certainly not the first time those traitorous Talcotts had let hogs forage here. Hogs were nothing but trouble. Talcotts were nothing but trouble.

Sophia followed the sound to an old clearing not far from the road. There two shagbark hickories grew among the stumps of giant oaks cut down even before Grandsire had bought the land. A boar, dark gray with wiry black hairs bristling along his back, was snuffling around an old stump, foraging for nuts. The boar raised his head to stare directly at her. With an angry squeal, he moved toward her.

"Get!" Sophia shook her staff at him. "This is not your plantation. Not yet anyways."

The boar halted. His small eyes glittered as if lit from within. His jaws opened and shut with an ominous click. Judging from the length of his tusks, Sophia decided he probably hadn't been inside Talcott's pig lot for more than a year. Any man who raised pigs knew a boar's tusks had to be cut back at least twice a year to prevent him from injuring or killing whatever displeased him. Sophia didn't doubt for a minute that this boar had turned feral.

"Never go near a wild hog. They'd just as soon attack you as not," Father had warned when she was old enough to walk alone in the woods. It seems today I have no choice, Father, she thought.

"Get! Scram, you trespasser!" Sophia whacked her staff against a nearby stump in an attempt to scare him off. "If Grandsire were alive, he'd turn you into hams." She whacked the stump again.

The boar continued to stare at her. Sophia narrowed her eyes and took one step closer.

"No Talcott pig is going to grow fat on Records land," she warned. "There are consequences."

A year or two before the Revolution began, Grandsire had killed a Talcott pig for trespassing. He had shot it, butchered it, and was smoking the hams and bacon when the Worchester County sheriff showed up with his posse of Loyalists to arrest him. Unlike Mr. Talcott, Grandsire had refused to sign the loyalty oath pledging allegiance to the crown. A British magistrate found him guilty of theft and fined him 900 pounds of tobacco—nearly a year's crop.

Grandsire claimed the punishment was more for his political leanings than his actions.

Sophia shook her staff at the pig. "Shoo! Shoo! Shoo!"

The boar trotted away in the direction of Talcott land. She exhaled in relief; but at the edge of the clearing, he stopped. Whirling about, he scuffed the earth with his sharp hooves, kicking up puffs of grainy dirt. Then with a rumbling roar, he charged, tusks pointed right at her.

Clutching the folds of her skirt in her free hand, Sophia raced to the center of the clearing where there was a large stump as big as a wagon wheel and high enough, she hoped, to keep her safe. Unless the pig was a jumper. Shoving her staff toward the middle, she struggled to pull herself up. The edge, softened by rot, crumbled, and she lost her grip. In that moment, though, the boar paused to paw the ground again as if deciding his next move.

Sending a plea to Grandsire to keep her safe, Sophia leapt, throwing herself lengthwise across the stump's uneven surface. Never once taking her eyes away from the hog, she sat up and scooched her way over to the center.

The boar lunged at the stump and reared up. Scrambling to her feet, Sophia picked up her staff. Three short steps brought her close to the edge. Gripping the staff with both hands, she planted her feet and swung. The pig caught the staff in his jaws, pulling it from her grasp and snapping it in two. He splintered the pieces with his hooves.

Sophia froze. The boar stared up at her with incandescent eyes. Saliva tinged with blood dripped from his mouth. He shook his head violently from side to side, sending bloody droplets flying. Then, without a sound he turned away. He trotted out of the clearing and into the forest.

Sophia waited. She could feel her heart thumping against her ribs. He'll change his mind, she thought. He'll come after me. A sensible person would run, she told herself.

After her legs stopped trembling, after her breathing calmed, she thanked Grandsire for watching over her, then jumped down from the stump and walked toward the road. The chalky taste of fear stayed with her. Every so often, she looked over her shoulder to make sure the boar wasn't stalking her. He was never there and she wondered if he had left because Grandsire had intervened or because the pig had forgiven the attack.

One thing Sophia knew for certain—she had struck the pig because she was afraid he'd kill her. The blow had been meant to teach him a lesson: "Don't tread on me," she had yelled as she swung. Freedom was precious. Her own life was precious and she would fight to save it.

It wasn't that long ago that she'd been ready to give it all up. Right after James went missing, Sophia had prayed for God to end her life. When He hadn't answered, she had begged Oriole to give her a potion, anything to end her pain.

Oriole had walked away, leaving Sophia curled into a tight ball of grief in the majestic bed Grandsire had bequeathed to her and Faith.

When Oriole returned, perhaps later that day or perhaps another day, Sophia couldn't remember, she had brought a warm drink in one of Mother's thin china cups.

"Drink this. It will help you heal."

While Sophia sipped the sweet brew, Oriole told her the tea was made from the leaves and blue star-shaped flowers of the borage plant.

"It can ease sadness," she said. "Plants have powerful medicine."

Borage tea was very much on her mind today as Sophia emerged from the woods.

Ahead, just beyond a field of newly sprouted spring wheat, she could see Marshtown—a row of five log cabins, each with a blue door, each facing the road. Oriole's cabin was the one on the end nearest the marsh and set off from the others by a white picket fence. Behind the fence she saw a familiar flash of orange. Sophia began to run.

Oriole was chasing turkeys. Flapping her orange shawl about, she was attempting to herd a half dozen of the big birds into a small coop near the fence. She greeted Sophia with a wide smile.

"Glory be! You showed up just in time," she said, huffing a little. "Help me coop these gobblers."

Sophia couldn't help but laugh. Oriole's Jamaican accent always cheered her.

"Seems like I've been chasing animals all morning," Sophia said as she opened the gate. Fanning out her skirt, she began flapping it at a big tom that had run past Oriole. Between the two of them the turkeys were cooped within minutes.

"Thank goodness," Oriole said. "These barn-raised turkeys got no sense. They'll stand out in the rain with their beaks open 'til they drown. They're not a bit like their wild cousins."

Wrapping her shawl back around her shoulders, she smiled at Sophia. "What brings you here, child, with a bad storm brewing?"

"A storm?"

Oriole pointed eastward. A low line of black clouds was advancing over the woods. Behind them, massive gray thunderheads boiled upward.

"Get inside before it hits." Oriole waved the ends of her shawl at Sophia, who giggled.

Sophia was still smiling when she burst into the warm cabin. The air was heavy with the aroma of black bean soup. Her appetite, lost after Father's announcement, came roaring back. She glanced toward the hearth, hopeful that the caldron hanging over the low fire held enough soup for company.

The room was unusually dim for this time of day. Both windows were already shuttered against the storm. Looking around, Sophia found Oriole's grandchildren and two more youngsters at the other end of the room, away from the heat of the fire. They were sitting cross-legged on a rag rug, looking at her with expectant expressions.

"Did you bring us a sweet?" Jebediah, the oldest, asked as he scrambled to his feet. "Maybe Momma sent us a cookie or two?"

"Not today," Sophia said. "I left in a hurry. Maybe tomorrow. Your momma told me she's planning to bake up some molasses cookies." She cocked her head to one side. "Is that all the greeting I get, Jebbie? Where are the sweets. No how-de-do?"

She cracked a grin to let the ten-year-old know she was teasing him.

"We are all pleased to see you, Miss Phee. No foolin'," Jebediah said, grabbing her hand and leading her to where the other children were sitting.

She knelt down beside them. "And I am glad to see you all, too. Only no cookies today." She made a sad face, drawing down her mouth and wiping a fake tear away. "No time for any lessons either. I came to talk to Granny Oriole."

"That's all right," said six-year-old Fry, Jebediah's brother—only he said "wite," not having mastered his pronunciation of the letter *r*.

The two other children nodded in agreement. Becky and Summer lived down the road and were left in Oriole's care each day while their parents worked.

"You'd better stay." Jebediah told her. "Granny said to take cover. There's a fierce storm coming."

"Could blow us all away," Fry, said, opening his eyes wide.

"Only a thunder-maker." Oriole said. She had followed Sophia inside and was stirring the soup. "So, what brings you out on such a day?"

"I didn't know a storm was coming."

"I'm not believin' my ears. Captain Joseph's granddaughter payin' no heed to weather signs."

"I noticed," Sophia said. "I always do now," she added more grimily remembering the morning James had set sail. Neither of them had paid attention to the sky then.

"When I woke this morning, I saw the fiery sunrise. I guess Father's shocking announcement drove that warning from my head."

Sophia hesitated. Perhaps blurting out her news in front of the children was not the best idea. Rising, she smoothed her skirt and walked to the hearth to stand close to Oriole.

"Father came home from Baltimore last night," Sophia said. "This morning at breakfast, he told us Records Landing has been sold to the Talcotts."

Sophia paused, expecting her beloved nanny to react but Oriole said nothing, didn't even raise an eyebrow.

After a moment Sophia continued. "You have to understand. Sally had fixed us a sumptuous meal, just like Christmas morning. Mother had set out the good china. Father had insisted Willie join us at the table even though he's too young and still should be eating in the kitchen. Halfway through breakfast, Father, all full of smiles, stands and clinks his glass for attention. For a moment I thought he was going to tell us that he had good news about James. No. Father tells us that the plantation is sold and that we are moving to Ohio in a month. Ohio! It's on the other side of the mountains, a wilderness."

Oriole gently touched Sophia's cheek. "My, oh my," she said and looked away toward the hearth. "That's a lot of news to swallow at breakfast." She paused. "Or any time," she added softly.

"Think of it," Sophia said. "In a month we will be gone."

She straightened her shoulders and stared intently at Oriole.

"Everyone that is, but me," she said, her tone resolute. "I told Father so. Then I threw my napkin on the table and left. You should have seen the look Faith gave me. My big sister is such a Goody Two-Shoes she'd never defy Father. Even when he's wrong."

"Hush. Don't disrespect your father. He is a good man."

"There's more," Sophia whispered, glancing over at the children to see if they were listening. The two older boys were playing Paper-Scissors-Stone with noisy enthusiasm. Becky and Fry were looking on. Satisfied that their attention was elsewhere, she continued.

"Surely you have noticed," she said. "Father has changed. Ever since, since . . ." Sophia's voice trailed off. There was no need to go on. Oriole knew the story. She knew how Father had searched, not pausing to eat or sleep. For days he and Uncle Caleb had searched the river without ever finding James or any sign of a broken boat. That is until they reached the Chesapeake. There upon the shore near the mouth of the river were fragments of the shallop. The search ended. Father returned. He was carrying a broken plank with "Freedom" painted on it.

Taking a deep breath, Sophia gave Oriole a despairing glance. "When Father came home last night, he was not alone. A boy, older than James, came with him."

"A visitor?"

Sophia shook her head. "I met him this morning in the cookhouse. He was there when I came to see Sally. She was in a flurry stirring up biscuits and making sure the porridge didn't burn so she didn't have time to warn me."

"She does make the lightest, tastiest biscuits," Oriole said and smacked her lips. "Some of them biscuits would taste mighty good with our soup."

"This boy was no visitor," Sophia said, refusing to be steered into a discussion of biscuits. "And he scared me half to death when I saw him lurking in the cookhouse. He was wearing greasy leather clothes and a fur hat with a striped tail. That hat was made from a coonskin. I thought he was either a thief or a savage."

"You are quick to judge people, today," Oriole said.

"Humph. It's Father's doing. He brought that scruffy thief here. He ate breakfast with us at the table this morning in his dirty clothes. He sat in James's chair. At least he was hatless."

"So, it has come to this," Oriole said softly. "It's a stormy day to be sure." She eased herself down in a rocking chair and motioned to Sophia, who sank down on the hard-packed dirt floor beside her.

"The worst thing is . . ." Sophia paused, her voice now husky with unshed tears. "The worst thing is," she continued, "that when James comes home, we'll be gone."

"Pack your sorrow away, Phee. Have some soup with us this day and let the future take care of itself." Oriole reached for Sophia's right hand. It was an old game. She would plant a kiss in Sophia's palm and tell her to save the kiss for a time when she needed it. Only today Sophia's right palm was scraped raw in places.

"What happened here?"

"A pig," Sophia said dully. "I chased a wild boar with a thick branch. He ripped it out of my hands."

"That needs tending this minute." Oriole gave Sophia a fierce look. They both knew a cut tended too late had sickened Grandsire. He had died days later, his jaws locked shut.

Raising her voice, Oriole called Jebbie from his game to fetch some scraps of cotton shirting from her rag basket and her medicine kit, which was hanging on a peg near the door. She directed Sophia to get the lye soap from the cupboard and to wash those scrapes. Fresh water was in a basin on the plank table. Both followed her wishes without protest.

"Think about this," Oriole said as she spread a healing salve on the abrasions. "James may be gone, but you haven't lost him. Not here." She touched the center of Sophia's chest. "You haven't lost Grandsire neither. You will hold them in your heart forever. So there ain't no reason for you to go on fighting pigs or fathers. It's up to you to keep on with living and find the joy in it."

"But Father . . ." Sophia started to say.

"Hush," Oriole said softly. "Your father must have his reasons. It would be best to hear him out." She reached over to stroke Sophia's cheek. "One thing I know is that nothin' on God's green Earth lasts forever, and we all have to accept that."

She smiled but her eyes looked sad.

"Except love," she added. "Love lasts."

Outside the wind began to blow harder, rattling the shutters. Large drops of rain began to pellet the roof. The children crept closer to one another.

3

Oriole's Tale

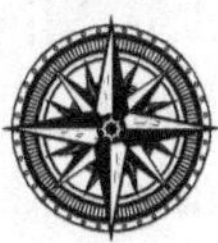

Rain lashed the cabin, thunder boomed, and the wind roared. A gust swirled down the chimney, sending a shower of sparks into the room and bringing Oriole to her feet. Quickly, she swept the glowing ash back into the fireplace.

"I'm scared," moaned Fry. Becky, not quite two, began to wail.

"Hush. It's just a thunder-maker." Oriole scooped up the toddler and carried her back to the rocker. The other children followed as if being close to Oriole would keep them safe.

"Tell the story, Grannie. Tell Summer and Becky about the big storm," Jebbie said, hugging his knees. "The one that blowed you here."

"Please, Grannie," Fry begged, crawling into Sophia's lap. She smiled and pulled him close.

"I'll keep you safe," she whispered, even as the wind reminded her of another storm, the one that took her brother.

"Must be more than sixty years ago," Oriole began. "I was just a bitty girl, about as old as Jebbie, here. Mama and me, we lived on a sugar plantation in Jamaica. Our master, he was a God-fearin' man. He prayed over us every morning afore he sent the field hands into the cane. Master lived in a big white house with pillars in the front. Mama and I worked in the kitchen house behind it. We ate the same food as Master and his family. Missus kept pieces of raw sugar cane in a jar, and she would give me some to suck on from time to time. Um, Um." Oriole smacked her lips, as though remembering the sweet taste.

"Don't matter though," she said, sitting straight up in the rocking chair so as to stare intently at the young ones. "When you're a slave, you ain't no better off than a dog. Might have a good master, might not. You got no say so in the matter."

"Yessum," the children murmured. Sophia sighed. Slavery was wrong. At least she and Father agreed on that.

"Go on," Summer said, his voice squeaking with excitement.

"Well, Sir," Oriole said, looking at Summer, "one day, a big sailing ship came into my master's cove. It was midday. The white folk were resting after dinner; the field hands working in the cane; Mama and I, washing dishes. One old black man was down on the pier, fishing. Ships came there to pick up the cane, but nobody knew this ship was coming."

"Pirates sneak up!" Jebbie announced. He scowled, trying to look fierce.

"That's right. Pirates." Oriole said. "They kilt the old man with one swipe of a cutlass. Then they came on up the hill to the big house. Master's son was reading in the library. He tried to stop 'em but they struck him down. Then they captured all the other white folk and locked 'em up in the root cellar. Marched 'em right by the place where Mama and me were hiding.

"We were in the kitchen pressed up against wall next to the cellar door. But the pirates passed us by on their way back to the big house. They tore through the house looking for treasure. You could hear 'em slashing and splintering furniture as they went. Later, I learned that they didn't find much, just some jewelry, a few pieces of silver, a little bit of coin, and some fancy clothes. Maybe that's why the two came back.

"One pirate yanked open the kitchen door and took my mama. The other snatched me. He was a big man, had to bend low just to get out the door. Outside, he slung me over his shoulder as though I was a sack of grain. I screamed and pounded his back with my fists. I bit him in the shoulder and kicked at him with my bare feet but he just held me tighter. He smelled like blood and salt and fire. For all I knew, he was the devil.

"The pirates put us in the hold. They put an iron bracelet around Mama's ankle and chained her to some other folk already there, white and black.

"The devil pirate set me down. 'No need to chain this little scrap of a girl. She can't hurt nobody,' he said. He grabbed my chin and turned my face toward a water barrel lashed to a post. 'You can fetch and carry. No need to waste crew's time on slaves.'

"He grabbed my wrist, shoved my hand up afore my face and then held his same hand close to mine. The little finger 'twas only a stump. 'Don't you cause no trouble, girl, or I'll cut your finger to match mine.'"

"No, no," Becky cried.

"No doubt about it. I was scared. No shame in that," Oriole continued, hugging Becky tight. "Mama put her free arm around me and held me close. My mama smelled so good. Like the vanilla bean. Even today if'n I smell vanilla, I think of my mama."

Oriole paused, saying all this rain was making her thirsty. Rain drummed on the roof of the cabin, the fire hissed as droplets racing down the chimney hit the hot ash, and the chair creaked as she rocked.

Jebediah scrambled up. Careful step by careful step, he brought Oriole the dipper filled to the brim. Slowly she sipped it dry before continuing with her story.

"Now, where was I?"

"The pirates took you," Jebbie prompted.

"Oh, yes. That's right. Even though I was in the belly of the ship, I could hear the captain shoutin' orders to cast off. 'Raise the foresail,' he commanded. Soon the ship began to move out of the cove and into the ocean. Right then, I knew I would never see Jamaica again.

"When night come, we heard the crew quarrelling. Angry about the poor haul, they were speculatin' 'bout the price we'd bring at the slave auction in a place called Maryland. If the winds held, Captain said, the ship would reach the colonies in a few days.

"Back then there was no United States," Oriole said, looking sternly at the semicircle of children around her chair. "England ruled this land."

The English are not done with us yet, Sophia thought. Father kept saying it was only a matter of time before there was another war.

A lightning bolt crashed to earth near the cabin. The children squealed. Sophia hugged Fry tight. He was wide awake, staring at Oriole, thumb stuck in his mouth.

"Hey," Sophia whispered, "you're too old for that."

"Un huh," Fry murmured, removing it. "Go on, Gwannie."

"Well, Fry, my chore was to bring cups of water to the folks in leg irons. The devil pirate, the one with the missing finger, he brought us hard biscuits once a day. If I soaked mine in water, the biscuit was easier to chew. The white boy chained next to my mother ate his that way."

Sophia smiled. This was the part she liked best, the part where Oriole and her grandfather met.

"Maybe just to pass the time or maybe just to keep our spirits up," Oriole said, "the boy kept predictin' we'd overcome this trouble. He told us he'd been 'prenticed as cabin boy on this very ship. When the pirates captured it, they kilt the captain and most of the crew. My new friend, you know who I mean, was chained. Seeing as the boy was white, the captain planned on selling my friend in Maryland, where he'd bring more money. Not as a slave, mind you, but as an indentured servant. Not the best thing to happen to a person, but better than being a slave. After seven years the indentured servant is freed. Once you are made a slave, you can never be free, so don't you let nobody snatch you." Oriole gave her audience a stern look.

"Yessum! "The boys nodded.

"What's a pirate ship look like, Grannie?" Jebbie asked. He seemed worried she was going to change the subject.

"Can't rightly tell you. In the hold it was always as dark as a starless night, and it smelled bad. Worse than an outhouse that ain't been limed. Only light we ever saw was when that devil pirate opened the hatch.

"Last time he opened it, the ship was rolling and pitching worse than ever. Folks not already sick were holding their sides and moaning."

Oriole paused. Outside rain continued to hammer the cabin. Lightning flashed, its light leaking in between the shutters. Thunder boomed. Inside there wasn't a sound.

"Well," she continued, "the devil pirate lurched down the stairs and into the hold. Didn't have no torch this time. Felt his way with his four-fingered hand until he found me. Grabbed me by the hair.

'Find me the white boy,' he snarled, or I'll snap your puny neck.'

"May the Lord forgive me, I did what he asked. He unchained Joseph, his name was Joseph, but you know that. The pirate took him on deck. All the way he was yellin' at Joseph, orderin' him to climb the main mast and untangle the rigging else he'd run him through.

"The hatch closed. After that, all I heard were moans and the slamming of waves against the ship. Moaning, banging and the thumping of my heart. I don't know how many hours passed before my mama told me to go.

"She whispered, 'Go. Get on deck.' Seawater was leaking into the hold from all over. She must have known the ship was sinking. Oh, I didn't want to go. I just clung to her. But she turned me round facing the stairs and gave me a hard push.

"I left. Had to feel my way, scramblin' along, trippin' over people. Hands reached out to guide me. Finally, I bumped against the rough steps. I climbed up and pushed against the hatch door. It was so heavy I could only raise it a foot or so, but the wind swooped down and yanked it open.

"That wind wanted me. I crouched down low and was saying my prayers to the Lord when a hand grabbed me round the shoulder. I screamed for I believed it was the Devil himself."

"Oh, Grannie, no!" moaned Summer. He was clutching Jebbie, who poked him in the ribs. "Hush up," he hissed.

"Yes sir, I figured I was a goner. I was so decided on dyin' I couldn't believe that it was my friend who grabbed me. If he spoke, I couldn't hear him. All I heard was the storm's mighty voice. Cold rain beat against me. Strong winds pushed me. Waves leaped onto the deck and tried to knock me down. Beyond, all I saw was a boiling white sea.

Joseph tied a rope around his waist and then around mine. We moved across the slanted deck together, leaning into the wind.

"I can't tell you how long we struggled or when we found the little boat tied to the stern. I can't even tell you how we got that boat into the sea. All I knows is that it happened.

As for the pirates, they were gone. They'd scuttled off in the jolly boat long before and left their prisoners behind. When I looked back to where the ship should be, it was gone, too.

"The waves were higher than pine trees, and the sky was the color of mud. Joseph and I huddled together on a plank seat in the middle of the boat. Afraid to move, I sat with one hand griping the seat, the other one clutching Joseph's shirt. That little boat just kept moving—up over jagged walls of water and down into deep troughs while the ocean roared and hissed. A monster waiting to swallow us.

"I prayed to the Good Lord to save us. Sometime toward morning the rain turned to a wet, stinging snow. We scooped it off the seat and put it in our mouths. We was so thirsty. That was the first snow I ever saw, and I figured it was Heaven sent.

"Joseph said the storm was called a nor'easter. He said nor'easters brought snow even in the spring. Still, he reckoned that the Lord had sent this snow. As I recollect, Joseph kept talking—he was a talker. I just closed my eyes to listen. Sometimes I slept but I never let go.

"Next thing I knew, the sun was shining. Our little boat was on top of a huge breaker wave rolling toward land. We were at its mercy. Didn't have no oars. Didn't know how to swim. The waves began to foam up. Our boat tipped forward.

"'Hang on,' Joseph yelled.

"The wave tumbled our boat with us clinging to it all the way to the shore. And that's how I came to America."

"Hallelujah," said Fry.

"Who's gonna hold this child while I stir the soup?" Oriole asked. Sophia nudged Fry out of her lap and took the sleeping child.

"Grannie, how'd you know you were in America?" Jebbie asked.

Oriole sipped a spoonful of soup.

"Um, um. Don't this taste good? Reminds me of Jamaica. Problem is folks don't grow black beans around here. I have to walk all the way to Snow Hill to buy these beans. Mebbe that's how I figured out I was in America. I had to walk twenty miles for a sack of beans."

4

The Widow's Garden

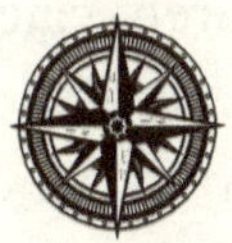

As heavy rain continued to pelt the cabin, the boys began to squirm. Jebediah poked Summer, who poked back harder. Sophia nudged the one closest to her with her foot and frowned.

Until this rain ends, we're as cooped up as Oriole's turkeys, she thought. She shifted Becky, now sound asleep in her lap. Heat from the fire combined with the toddler's warmth was making her uncomfortable.

"When can we eat, Gwannie? I think I'm gonna die," Fry said and flopped over on his side.

Oriole stirred the pot. "This soup needs to be thick enough to hold a spoon straight up."

Make that soon, Sophia prayed. The smell of the soup simmering on the hearth had sharpened her appetite.

Jebbie lay back, crossing his hands behind his head, almost bumping Summer, who grumbled, "Watch out."

"Please, Grannie," Jebbie said, "tell us about the pirate lady. You know, the one that found you on the beach."

"Jebbie, you do try a body's patience. Always wanting more." Oriole said, raising one eyebrow, her way of letting him know she was teasing. "Besides, what makes you think that lady was a pirate? I surely didn't know that, not for certain anyways."

The boys quickly wriggled around so they were facing Oriole. Sophia stifled a laugh. The boys' appetite for more of the tale seemed as voracious as hers was for soup.

"When that ocean tumbled me to the beach," Oriole said, "I was near drowned. Those big breaker waves had pushed me down and rolled me along so I could barely catch a breath. I lay on the sand gasping and spitting up mouthfuls of the salty sea. Joseph was nearby; the rope he'd tied around our waists during the storm still held us together. Over the booming of the waves, I could hear him choking and coughing.

"Then a voice above me said, 'Mercy, look what the ocean brought me.'

"I tried to see who was speaking, but my eyes were burning from the salt water, and the bright sun dazzled me. When I rubbed my eyes clear, I saw two bare feet first. I kept looking up, higher and higher. Those feet were attached to a tall, sturdy woman. Tallest woman I'd ever seen. Her skirts billowed behind her like sails. She stood stock still, her feet apart, her arms folded across her chest. Her skin was the color of honey and her brown hair was streaked with gold. As thick as a horse's mane it was. The wind blew it back away from her face so that I could see she was scowling. I wasn't sure if she was real or a demon come to throw me back into the sea. I dared not speak. I dared not move.

"Around her waist she'd tied a shimmery green sash. It held a long knife, a pirate's cutlass to be sure. She pulled it out, raised it high above her head."

Mimicking the woman, Oriole raised her long-handled spoon.

"Swoosh," she hissed, slashing downward with the spoon. "That blade whizzed down between Joseph and me, cuttin' that water-swollen rope as easy as you'd cut through soft butter. For all I knew that blade would split me next."

"Oh, oh," whimpered Fry, who was gazing wide-eyed at Oriole.

"Yes, indeedy," she said, walking over to Fry. "I was scared. My heart was thumping so loud I could scarcely hear. Maybe I did think she was a pirate.

"I must have screamed because the tall woman crouched down next to me. 'Hush,' she said and brushed my cheek with her hand. Just like this." Oriole leaned down to stroke Fry's cheek. Sighing, he looked up at her and smiled.

"When she touched me, my fear went away. Just like that!" Oriole snapped her fingers. "After the tall woman stood back up, she shouted as if she wanted the whole world to hear, 'Shame! Shame on you all!' The wind carried her words away. At the time, I thought she was scolding the pirates, but maybe not.

"She pulled Joseph to his feet, and when he was steady, she scooped me up in her arms as if I were no bigger than a baby. She carried me up the dune through tall sea grass to a high place where there was a grove of trees and a little stone house.

"Once we were inside, the house seemed so much bigger. Each wall had a large window. The shutters were thrown wide open and sunlight made the room as bright as all outdoors. Bunches of dried plants hung upside down from the rafters and the sweet smell of lavender met me at the door.

"Even though I was covered with sand and blood, the tall woman laid me on her big bed. For the first time since the four-fingered pirate took me, I felt safe. I closed my eyes. Next thing I knew, she was bathing my torn skin. It felt like my skin was on fire. While she worked, she kept murmuring, 'There, there. You'll be fine.' When she finished washing my cuts, she smoothed on an oil that soothed the burning, and she told me the oil would make me pretty again because it came from pretty flowers—orange and gold marigolds. That surprised me; no one had ever said I was pretty 'cept my mama.

"When the woman was finished, she wrapped me in a soft sheet and laid me on a pallet made with sweet smelling hay. As I lay there, the clean, sweet scent seemed to wrap around me too. I looked around for my friend. Joseph rested on another pallet near me. The woman was tending to his wounds. All the tightness in me eased."

Oriole walked back to the hearth, stirred the soup and declared it ready. She began ladling the stew-like mix of black beans, sweet potato, onions, and carrots into tin bowls, which she then put on the table. When all the bowls were filled, she beckoned. Each boy carried a bowl and pewter spoon to the rug, where he folded himself down into a sitting position without spilling a drop.

Sophia merely had to whisper "Soup's ready" in Becky's ear to wake her. Scrambling to her feet, she toddled to the table with Sophia right behind her. They sat side by side on the long bench. The boys cradled their steaming bowls between their knees and looked at Oriole, waiting.

"We thank God for this bounty," she said.

"Amen." The boys spoke in one voice and began to spoon soup into their mouths.

Oriole eased herself down beside Becky, putting a bowl of corn mush in front of her. When Becky turned down the corners of her mouth in disappointment, Oriole laughed.

"Won't be long afore you're spooning my soup, too" she said. "Black bean soup's too hot for your mouth right now." She offered Becky a spoonful of mush. "This will please you."

Conversation was put aside. The soft clank of metal spoons mingled pleasantly with the sound of the rain.

"We ate lots of soup on that island," Oriole said after a while, her voice soft with the memories. "Swallowing all that salty water made Joseph and me hot and cold with fever. The tall woman—we still didn't know her name—fed us clear soup and chamomile tea. After our fevers broke, she thickened the broth with arrowroot. 'Course I was too young to know that then. She taught me later.

"While we were getting better, she talked to us. Sometimes her voice sounded like a lullaby, and I'd drift off to sleep. When I'd wake, she'd still be talking. She told us about the island, called it a barrier island. She said a pirate once sailed his ship here to hide from the English ships and to bury treasure. She said her name was Widow Teach. Today, most folks around here tell tales about her husband. His name was Edward Teach. Only I didn't know who he was. Not then."

"I do," Jebediah said. "People called him Blackbeard because of his long black beard. He was the fiercest pirate ever."

"Well, that's so Jebbie," Oriole answered. "He came to a bad end. Still, Widow Teach, she never spoke about his business directly. Just said that she'd lived in a grand house in Charleston for a while until the townsfolk turned on her husband, and he'd gone back to a seafaring life. She didn't sound angry. In fact, I only heard her angry once and that was on a different subject. She said folks claimed her husband had married thirteen women before her. Each one had died or disappeared soon after the wedding. She was last, the 14th, and in a way, she had disappeared, too.

"She never said how she came to be on that island. Just that she never wanted to go back to the mainland. Folks, white and colored, came to her if they were sick because she knew about plants that made people well. They'd ring the bell down at the landing, and she would go down and tend to them. She never brought them to the house."

Oriole lowered her voice, and the boys leaned forward.

"One night, I woke to the sound of voices outside. I tiptoed to the window. Outside near the edge of the bluff, Widow Teach was arguing with a tall, thick man. There was a half-moon high in the sky. Even in the faint light I could see that his bushy black beard grew down to his waist. They was fussin' at one another, and the Widow Teach, she wasn't one to ease up on a fight. When they parted, I heard her say the word 'gold' before I ducked down and scrambled back to my pallet.

Next morning, when I woke, Widow Teach was sitting at her table sorting through a small pile of gold coins.

"Now, you're probably thinking that was Blackbeard's ghost come to pay his wife a visit. I don't know. Some folks say his ghost walks the shore looking for needy folk so as he can give them treasure. They say he is trying to make amends for his bloody deeds. It may be so. I can only say what I saw then."

Oriole picked up Becky and walked to the washstand.

"Mercy me, you're not the only one needing tending," she said, almost stepping into a puddle. Rainwater had seeped under the door. She sent Jebbie scurrying to fetch the bucket of sand by the hearth and empty it over the wet spot.

"You think the marsh is gonna fill up and wash over us?" Summer asked.

"Don't you fret, Summer. That marsh water is gonna stay right where it belongs. This rain will pass just like all things, good and bad, pass. Just like the days on that island passed until it was time to leave."

Once again, the storm was forgotten. Sophia moved to gather up the cups and spoons for washing but kept listening as intent as the boys. Oriole was coming to her favorite part, the widow's garden.

"You see," Oriole was saying, "Joseph recovered quicker than me. As soon as he was able, he chopped and stacked wood. He helped with the goats and even made a chair out of pine. It was a thing of beauty, and that way the three of us could sit in chairs at the same time.

"When I could finally walk without wobbling, I helped cook, although there was very little to do that way, not like when I helped my mama cook up a feast in Jamaica. In the early days I sat on a bench in front of the stone house. The widow gave me green willow branches so I could weave a basket. I wove carefully but I mostly looked at the ocean. I could hear the waves on the beach below. I could hear the gulls crying. Sometimes I cried along with them. I missed my mama so very much.

"Before too many days passed this way, the widow asked me to help in the garden. She had a large garden filled with plants I'd never seen before. As we weeded, she named each one and told me about its healing powers. Some were good for headaches, others for toothaches or curing fevers. One called 'burnet' stopped wounds from bleeding just like that." Oriole snapped her fingers.

Sophia gazed into the low fire. She knew how much missing someone hurt. In the glowing embers she could almost see the widow's sun-drenched garden. To her the widow's garden and the Garden of Eden were one and the same.

"What a wonder the widow's garden was," Oriole said. "Its narrow paths encouraged me to wander there. Plants with umbrella-like leaves grew next to tall plants covered with tiny white daisies. I learned to close my eyes and name a plant by the way it smelled. Why, a person could stay out there all day and just sniff. I walked in the garden every day, and little by little the ache in my heart eased."

Unable to be still any longer, Summer broke in once again, demanding to know why, if she was so happy there, she had left the island.

"Nothing is forever," Oriole told him. "One day, Widow Teach, Joseph, and me walked to a pine grove on the far side of the island where the wind always whispered through the trees. When we came here, the widow would bring her Bible and read to us.

"So, I was expecting a story that day," she said. "The widow read a little bit but then she closed the book and looked sad. She told Joseph that he must leave the island. He was old enough and strong enough to make it on his own. Our little boat, the one that brought us here, was patched. 'The dinghy's a seaworthy craft, one that doesn't require crew,' she told him. 'The girl must stay.'

"'No!' Joseph said, reaching for my hand. 'As God is my witness, I made a solemn oath during that terrible storm to always keep her safe.'

"But the widow stood firm. She told Joseph he wasn't capable of watching over a young girl. She said I needed a protection paper like the sailors carried. A paper that says I am free—one I didn't have.

"Then she said something else. 'Greedy men might take her and sell her the moment you shut your eyes. A young girl like her is easy to snatch.'"

Oriole had walked up behind Jebbie. She grabbed him by the shoulders just as she said 'snatch.'

"They snatch boys, too," she said in a low voice. "Don't you forget slavers are about! The widow warned Joseph. Now, I am warning you. Don't you go ramblin' into town by your lonesome!"

"Yessum," Jebbie replied and gave Summer a sheepish look. The two of them had snuck off to Snow Hill last week to take a peek at the tall ships harbored there.

"'Nuff said on that subject." Oriole gave Jebbie's shoulders a final squeeze. "I'm sure you young'uns all agree that Widow Teach was a wise woman."

"Un huh," the boys intoned.

"Well, she also gave Joseph something else—gold coins. Sovereigns. He tried to give them back, but she'd have none of that, saying the coins would buy his passage back to England or give him a start in the new world.

"Taking her hand and bowing low over it, just like a fine gentleman, he thanked her many times over and declared he'd never return to England.

"I was not surprised. One evening, as we were sipping our soup, he'd told us that his family—mama, papa and baby sister—had died of the sweating sickness, all dead within three days of each other. He had no other kin so he went down to the harbor where the sailing ships were and put his mark on an indenture paper. It was that or beg for food in the streets of Liverpool, where thieves would cut your throat for the shoes you were wearing." Oriole drew a finger across her throat.

Even though they knew Oriole's story by heart, the boys gasped in unison anyway.

Oriole smiled. "I don't imagine Widow Teach was much surprised by Joseph's decision to stay in America either," she continued. "Nor was she surprised when Joseph promised to come back for me. The widow already knew he was a man of his word.

"Then Joseph gave me the most curious look you ever did see. 'In all these days we've been together,' he said, 'you have never said your Christian name.'"

Oriole sighed, then she said, "Well, I looked down at my toes. I opened my mouth to say my name, but it stuck in my throat. My mama had been the last person to say my name. It was as if that name had gone down in the sea with her. I just looked at him with my mouth open and my eyes tearing up."

"I am sorry," Summer said. He looked as if he, too, was going to cry.

"Don't be sad," Oriole reassured him. "That's when Widow Teach named me. In less time than it takes to blink, she said, 'Her name is Oriole.' She pointed to a black and orange bird perched in a nearby pine tree. 'She is as pretty as that little bird over there, and she sings as sweet.' And that was that. Joseph left to make his own way. I became Oriole Teach. A lost girl with a new name and a new home."

Oriole settled herself in the rocker and then gestured for Sophia to come sit beside her.

"The widow and me, we worked side by side, gathering and drying plants." Oriole said. "We used our harvest to make remedies for aches, ills, and injuries. Each plant had a particular benefit, but you had to know what you were doing or you could cause harm."

Sophia looked down at the strips of cloth wrapped around her hands with a sense of pride, knowing that now she, too, could make the salve Oriole had used to heal the scrapes. Last fall in the dark days after James went missing, she remembered Oriole reaching out to hold both of her hands and then turning the palms upward. Oriole had uttered a soft *un huh,* a sound she often made when something pleased her. "Healing hands," she had declared. "Don't let them go to waste. You come to my cabin tomorrow to start your learning. Everything the widow taught me I will now teach you." That was six months ago. Now Sophia had a notebook filled with remedies made from plants.

As if Oriole knew what Sophia was thinking, she reached down and gently touched one of Sophia's hands before returning her gaze to the rapt audience clustered around her.

"Joseph," she said picking up the story, "true to his word, came back to the island a few years later. He didn't have papers. Said I didn't need 'em. Said I'd be safe because he was a landowner and a sea captain now. He was respectable. No sheriff would dare mess with him. The widow seemed satisfied.

"I was of two minds, you know. The widow had been good to me, and I truly loved her. Even so she urged me to leave. Said the island was for outcasts, not for seventeen-year-old girls. It was my time to go."

That's when you came here?" Fry asked.

"Uh-huh" Oriole waggled her finger. "Joseph, why, he wanted to build me a cabin on his land. That's when I put my foot down. No sir. I told him, thank you kindly but I'll buy my own land. I had the money. Widow Teach had given me some gold coins from time to time. 'Good pay for good work' is how she said it when she handed over those sovereigns. So, I bought this land. Joseph, well, he was stubborn. He insisted on building the cabin, and I let him. When it was done, I painted the door blue."

The boys all nodded their heads in approval. Blue was a powerful color.

"A blue door keeps the evil spirits out," Jebediah said emphatically. "If Blackbeard's ghost comes here looking for treasure, he'll not get in the door!"

"No, sir," Oriole agreed. "No thieving pirates can come in here." She closed her eyes.

The two older boys began to scuffle until Sophia crossly told them to find something better to do. "You're no better than pirates!" she concluded.

"Pirates," Jebediah repeated, his eyes lighting up with mischief. "I'll be Blackbeard. Summer, you be first mate. Let's capture Fry."

"Aargh," the two yelled in unison and swooped down on Fry, who squealed in mock terror. Soon all three were skulking around the cabin pretending to be on board a ship. Becky, clutching her rag doll, tried to run away from the boys, and tripped, skinning her knees on the plank floor. She began to cry and toddled over to Oriole, who sat the whimpering child in her lap.

Without a word being said, Sophia hurried to find the salve used earlier to sooth her own scrapes and smoothed it on Becky's knees. Quieted, the little girl leaned her head against Oriole's chest. Accompanied by the creak of the rocking chair and the soft drumming of the rain, Oriole began to sing, "Hush a bye baby, I pray you don't cry . . ."

Sophia studied Oriole's face, fixing every detail in her mind. The firelight cast shadows, darkening the hollows beneath her high cheekbones and deepening the lines by her eyes and on her cheeks. It was a beautiful face, and Sophia saw love and wisdom reflected there.

"Let me stay here with you," she said, blurting out her thoughts. "I can't bear to leave."

Oriole turned her head toward Sophia, resting her chin on Becky's soft curls. The little girl was contentedly sucking her thumb. Her doll had slipped from her grasp and lay beside the rocking chair.

"No," she said. "That would never do. No, it's your time to go."

"Then come with us. Come to Ohio."

"Honey Chile, I love you, always will. But my place is here. Who'll take care of these children if'n I'm gone? No. I'm old. My bones ache. But you're young. Most of your adventures lie ahead." Shifting Becky to one side, she held out her free hand to Sophia, who turned away.

"Now don't you get all huffy with me. 'Tis easy to see you're already angry with your daddy even though I 'spect you know he's doing what he thinks best for you all."

"He . . ." Sophia began.

"Hush!" Oriole held up her hand. "Your daddy is a good man. Don't you know, he's the one who brought me the freedom papers the widow said I needed. He's the one that got me the deed that says I own this land. I got 'em in a strongbox in a hidey hole 'neath these boards." She kicked the planks beneath her chair.

"Your grandsire and I had an understanding. But your Daddy, he can read really good, and he knows the law. He gave me the paper and said, 'Now you are free in the eyes of the law.' He told me to hold on to that paper, no matter what."

Oriole lowered her hand and tousled Becky's tight curls. "I'm a free woman. My child Sally and these children are free because of your Daddy. I got their papers, too. I won't hear a word against your daddy."

Sophia slumped forward and rested her head on her arms. There was nothing more to say. She felt her disappointment well up into her eyes and spill down her cheeks.

Suddenly anxious to leave, Sophia got to her feet. It must be midafternoon, she thought. I will have upset Mother. The storm must have made me lose track of time. Opening the shutters she saw the sky had lightened although a light rain continued to fall. Still, she reminded herself a little bit of rain never hurt anybody. She had to get home.

Pausing to pick up Becky's fallen doll, she dusted off the black cloth where a face should be. She smiled, remembering her confusion the first time she had seen the doll. "It's not finished," she had said. Sophia's own doll had painted blue eyes, a small nose, and smiling red lips. Oriole had explained some people believed that if a doll had a face, it already had been given a spirit. If a doll had no face than a child could give it her own feelings of joy or sadness.

"I think I need a faceless doll," Sophia said as she handed it back to Becky before leaning down to hug Oriole. "I must leave. I'm afraid I've caused enough upset at home for one day."

"Don't you fret. Everything's gonna be all right."

As Sophia stepped over the mound of wet sand, there was a loud rap on the door. Fry, who was fiddling with the latch, squealed and scrambled backwards. Jebbie leaped to hide behind Sophia's skirts while Summer scurried to safety beside Oriole.

"Who be there?" Oriole asked in her boldest voice. Then more softly she said, "Pirates don't knock. Lift the latch."

Sophia pushed the latch upwards.

The door swung open. A tall figure wearing a hat stood in the doorway.

"Pirate!" shrieked Fry.

"James!" Sophia gasped.

5

The Road Home

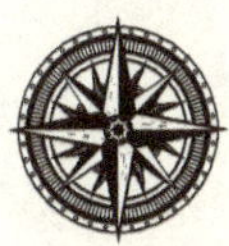

Whipping the sodden hat from his head, the visitor stood just outside the door. He appeared to be as startled as Sophia and the children.

"Begging your pardon," he said, clutching the brim with both hands. "Didn't mean to stir up trouble. Mr. Records sent me to fetch Miss Sophia."

"It's Miss Records to you!" Sophia said, feeling heat rushing to her cheeks. "This is the second time today, Mr. Harkness, that you've scared me nearly to death. Fry thought you were a brigand. And I thought… Well. It doesn't matter what I thought. Maybe you are a brigand."

Nathan looked perplexed. "Just doing what your father asked. I would have come sooner but a tree crashed down, almost hit the mule. He jumped back and sideways, getting himself all tangled in the traces. I had dickens of a time getting things straightened out. The tree was enormous. It'll take two men with a cross saw to clear the road. I had to leave the wagon on the other side."

While he talked, he kept rolling the hat brim tighter and tighter.

"Maybe you shouldn't be so jumpy," he said in a sharper tone.

"Maybe I wouldn't be, Mr. Harkness, if you weren't wearing my brother's hat. And," she said, looking him up and down, "his shirt and britches."

She reached out her hand. "Give me the hat before you ruin it completely." She snatched it from him. "Thief!"

"Land sakes, Child, invite that boy in 'fore he catches his death. He's wet to the bone." Oriole beckoned to Nathan.

Ducking his head, Nathan entered the cabin.

"Much obliged, Ma'am," he said. "I assure you I am neither a thief nor a pirate. I answer to Mr. Harkness but friendly folks call me, Nathan." He said and smiled.

"Humph," Sophia said, not in the least bit sorry she hadn't had the good manners to introduce him. She glowered as Oriole clucked over Nathan, hanging his coat in front of the fire, insisting he sit by the hearth and eat some soup before he went out again into the damp. The boys gathered round the stranger, staring solemnly and saying little. Becky clung tightly to Oriole's skirt.

Sophia pulled open the door. "I'll be outside," she muttered, her brother's hat clutched in her hand. As she paced back and forth on the small porch, she could hear the boys, no longer muted by shyness, plying the newcomer with questions: "Where was you from?" "What is Ohio like?" "Did you have to fight with Savages?"

Apparently, everyone is having a good time without me, she thought. I should just leave. The rain has ended. There is no reason to stay.

Still, she lingered, with myriad questions swirling in her head, the most pressing being who was this boy and why did Father hire him.

By the time Nathan joined her on the porch, his coat was nearly dry. He handed her Oriole's shawl.

"Oriole thought this might help keep the chill at bay," he said.

"Mrs. Teach to you," Sophia said. Taking the shawl, she stomped off the porch.

The yard was littered with branches and dotted with puddles so the two had to make their way across it carefully. Small clumps of dirt clung to their shoes by the time they reached the gate where the mule was tied.

"Where's the wagon?" Sophia asked. She was holding the hem of her skirt above her ankles away from the mud. This was her second-best gown and, since her encounter with the pig, already had suffered some wear and tear.

"I left it behind," Nathan said, untying the mule.

"Without the wagon, there is no reason you shouldn't ride on ahead. I can take myself home. It's not as if I don't know the way." Sophia said and without waiting for an answer started off down the road.

Nathan just shrugged. Leading the mule, he muttered, "She a mite touchy," as he caught up with Sophia.

After a while he said," you wouldn't get as muddy if you rode. You can ride, can't you?"

She gave him a haughty glance and kept walking. The bare field beside the road, the dark line of trees ahead and the low gray sky above seemed to mirror Sophia's bleak frame of mind. Puddles dotted the wagon track for as far as Sophia could see. With her skirt gathered in one hand and her brother's hat clutched in the other, she stepped over the puddles until she came to one the size of a small pond. There she halted, wondering if she should chance leaping over it or if she should take off her shoes and wade through it.

Nathan, who had been following several paces behind, led the mule up beside her.

"Can't you wait until I get across before you start splashing through?"

"Here's a better idea," he said as he scooped her up and plunked her down sideways on the mule's back.

After her initial gasp, the best she could manage was a "Well, I never."

"No need to thank me." Nathan sounded amused.

"I have no intention of that."

"You would be better off riding."

"My wellbeing is no concern of yours. I can take care of myself!"

"Suit yourself, Miss Records," Nathan said and led the mule forward.

Sophia noticed with some satisfaction that the muddy water nearly reached the top of his boots.

As soon as the mule reached drier ground, Sophia slid off and walked quickly toward the woods, trying to distance herself from Nathan.

To send this newcomer, no, worse, this interloper, to haul me back home is humiliating, she thought. Father might as well have said, "My daughter has no more sense than a lost sheep. She is too dimwitted to find her way back, so you'd better fetch her."

Sophia slapped her brother's hat against her skirt. One thing is certain, she decided: Nathan Harkness needs to be set straight.

Stopping, she turned back to face him. "First off," she said, "You should know that I am perfectly capable of getting from one place to another without assistance."

Nathan halted the mule. "So it seems."

With the toe of his scuffed riding boot, he dislodged a stone in the road and kicked it to the side of the road before staring back at her.

"Surely, you must know that running off like you did upset your ma," he said. "Worse, when she saw the storm brewing, she worried you'd come to harm. I think your pa sent me after you more to ease her mind than to rescue you. It's easy to see that storms upset her."

"My brother was lost in a storm," she said sharply. "He was on the river when a bad storm came up. He simply hasn't had time to write. Or maybe he did, and the letter got lost. Letters get lost all the time. He'll be back here, though. You can bet on that." Sophia gave him a hard look, daring him to say different.

"Well," Nathan said in a soft drawl, "I hope you're right."

"I know I'm right! Except now when he returns, we will be gone."

Whirling back toward the trees, Sophia started walking again. Nathan shouted after her. Something about downed trees. She shrugged it off. What did it matter that the storm had caused havoc in the woods? If the road was a tangle of fallen branches, she didn't need him to help her clear the way.

When she didn't hear the mule clopping along behind her, however, she slowed her pace. Turning back, she saw Nathan and the mule hadn't made much progress. Nathan was standing in the middle of the road. He had dropped the long reins and was pulling the bridle with both hands to get the mule to walk forward. The mule had other ideas. With his neck outstretched and his front legs braced, he was slowly lowering his hindquarters. Sophia let out a shout of laughter. There was no way Nathan was going to get that animal to move unless he knew the secret.

"You've got to hold on to his left ear," she shouted. "Twist it a little. Not enough to hurt, just enough to get his full attention. Talk to him. His name is King George, by the way. Tell him he's handsome. Tell him you admire him. Tell him he'll be home soon."

Nathan nodded briefly without taking his eyes off the mule. "Words we'd all like to hear," he muttered.

"And gather up those reins. You'll be in a real fix if he steps on one and snaps it!" Sophia didn't wait to see if Nathan followed her advice, so she missed his mock salute.

Entering the forest, she quickly understood his earlier warning. Here the scent of pine overpowered the smell of wet earth. A snarl of branches and tree limbs crisscrossed the road. Destruction was everywhere. Tossing smaller branches aside and stepping around bigger ones, she kept walking. No use waiting, she thought. King George seems to be in a mood. I must get home. The sooner I face Father the better.

My best approach, she thought, is with reason. I will point out that moving away from civilization is the same as throwing away my education, an education that he deemed important and paid dearly for. As Mother says, "Waste not, want not." It's best for all concerned that I stay behind. If not at Records Landing, then perhaps with the Reverend and his family in Snow Hill. Even though we are not Anglicans anymore, the Reverend doesn't seem to hold us any ill will for becoming Methodists. A pity the Methodist preacher doesn't stay in one place. Sophia sighed and kept walking.

Or, she thought a few minutes later, I could board with the judge's family in Snow Hill. Father has praised my handwriting; says I have a good hand. I could help out by copying documents, earn my keep that way.

Immersed in devising the best argument, Sophia blundered into a wall of branches. A massive old-growth pine, felled in the storm, barricaded the road. Thick branches broken by the fall were now jagged spears. Stepping back, she realized that she had missed serious harm to an eye by inches.

Maybe, Sophia thought, touching the branch's sharp tip, we won't be able to survive so far away from the Eastern Shore. It's a long, difficult journey. Who knows what we could encounter crossing the mountains? Our very lives will be at stake. Why is Father so willing to risk everything?

She shivered. A new wind, a cold wind, came whistling through the pines. It tugged at Oriole's orange shawl and sprayed Sophia with rain droplets. She pulled the shawl tight around her shoulders. In the distance, a bird was calling, fretting over its lost nest. Sophia ached with the loneliness of loss.

She was still standing beside the tree when Nathan got there, the reluctant mule in tow.

"I had no idea that a storm could do this," she said softly. "Where were you when the tree fell?"

"Over there," he pointed to the abandoned wagon, about twenty feet down the road on the other side of the tree. "I think that's why King George keeps balking. He's afraid another one will fall."

"You were so close. That tree could have killed you both!"

"But it didn't. I ain't no ghost if that what's worrying you." Nathan gave her a funny little half smile. He seemed amused.

"Don't be silly," she snapped.

"Well, I thank you for your concern." His drawl seemed to thicken.

"Are you making fun of me?"

"Nope. Now, can you get yourself over that tree or do I have to boost you?"

"I'll manage." Her tone was snippy. She plunked her brother's hat on top of her mobcap.

Using one of the lower branches as a step stool, Sophia was able to sit on the trunk and swing her legs to the other side. She would have made it unscathed except that her hem caught on a splintered limb. Yanking the skirt free, she heard a ripping sound. She grimaced and slid down the other side only to land in a mud puddle.

So much for Faith's advice, Sophia thought sourly, remembering what her sister had said before breakfast.

"Change into something nicer than that old brown homespun you're wearing," Faith had said. "You look as scruffy as a molting hen. Wear the green calico. It's more in fashion. Besides it makes your eyes look pretty. A girl should always try to look her best."

Well, if wearing mud were the fashion, I'd be the best-dressed girl at the ball, Sophia thought. She hoisted herself into the wagon and began examining the damage—a small tear in the bodice from her encounter with the pig and a long tear in the hem from the splintered branch. The skirt was soaked all the way around the bottom and splashed with mud halfway up to her knees. Not ready for the ragbag yet, but definitely not my second-best dress anymore, she decided. As for the shoes, the thick brocade was pulling away from the sole. For the second time that day, she wished she'd worn her moccasins.

Sophia watched Nathan lead King George around the fallen tree. Every few feet the mule planted his feet and let out a high squeaky protest. The bray always made Sophia giggle. God surely had a sense of humor, giving that ornery beast such a puny voice.

Taking off her brother's hat, she scrutinized it. James would be furious. The crown sagged and the brim drooped. She knocked it against the wagon to shake the water off. Not even a year old and certainly the worse for wear, she thought, remembering the time when James bought it. The peddler had called it a carriage hat, saying that the style was the height of fashion in Baltimore. James had paid him five United States dollars, money he had earned from trapping foxes and selling the hides.

A lot of animals died for this hat, Sophia thought as she fingered the brim. She remembered the peddler saying that a hatter needed fur from the underbellies of ten beaver pelts in order to make it. "Like wool felt, only better," he had promised. "Totally waterproof."

Not totally, she thought. The only things not soaked are the feathers. In her mind Sophia saw her brother pluck those two tail feathers from the wild turkey he'd shot earlier that morning, before the peddler had stopped by with his wagonload of wares. James had secured the feathers beneath the hat's headband.

"Now I'm really macaroni," he had crowed as he placed the carriage hat at a jaunty angle on his head. Whistling *Yankee Doodle*, he had strutted around her. *Yankee Doodle went to town a-riding on a pony, stuck a feather in his cap and called it Macaroni.* Until, in a sweeping gesture, he had doffed his hat and bowed low before her. What a jester. He could always make her laugh.

"Hey!" Nathan's call abruptly brought her back to the present. "Can you give me a hand?"

One glance told her King George now was refusing to back between the shafts of the wagon.

"Please, just give him some of that sweet talk while I pull the wagon forward." Nathan sounded exasperated.

Sophia answered with a sugary insincere smile before saying just as sweetly, "Can't imagine why Father would send someone to fetch me who doesn't know how to harness a mule to a wagon."

Nathan sighed. "Just talk to the mule."

"Happy to oblige."

Stowing the hat beneath the plank seat, she jumped down and began whispering in King George's ear.

As soon as the mule was hitched, Nathan swung himself up and onto the wagon seat in one easy motion. He reached over to give Sophia a hand. Ignoring the gesture, she climbed up and seated herself with what she hoped was some grace.

"What are you staring at?" she asked crossly, smoothing her skirt.

"I was just thinking you remind me of something."

"What?"

"A puma."

"Never heard of it. What is it?"

"Some folks call it a mountain lion. It's a big cat, bigger than you, and it's one mean critter."

"You're saying I look like a mean old critter."

"No. I'm just saying you remind me of one. Because of your green eyes and your tawny brown hair. I meant it as a compliment. A puma's real pretty you, know. Just dangerous."

"Well, I never." Sophia could feel her cheeks redden. Hastily, she leaned down to retrieve the hat.

As she fiddled with the feathers, she studied Nathan out of the corner of her eye. There was a watchfulness about him. His wide-set gray eyes seemed guarded as though he was hiding something. Most likely, a cautious fellow, she thought. If it weren't for that small bump midway down his nose, he 'd be handsome. He probably broke his nose in a fight, she guessed. All in all, though, better looking than most, Sophia decided.

Earlier today, when Nathan had surprised her in the cookhouse before breakfast, she had thought he was a ruffian up to no good. He had been dressed in trail-worn buckskins and had a hatchet thrust through his belt. Now, dressed in a linen shirt and cloth trousers, he was not so alarming.

The wind blew harder, showering them both with cold droplets.

Sophia fingered the hat and then thrust it toward him. "Here. You might as well wear it. It will keep your head dry."

Nathan gave her a quizzical look.

"Go on, take it. You're the one who took it in the first place."

He shook his head, no.

"Suit yourself." She laid the hat on the seat between them.

"I am not a thief," he said, keeping his gaze fixed on the mule's ears. "Your mother gave it to me along with the clothes I'm wearing. Not a good fit, I am afraid. A bit too short and snug. Your mother took my measure. She said that there were more clothes packed away and that she'd alter a shirt and trousers to fit me right away." He turned away as if to look at something deep in the woods.

Sophia was sure she saw his ruddy complexion deepen.

"I never had no one fuss over me like that before," he said without looking at her. "Those buckskins are the only clothes I own."

Sophia felt a twinge of guilt.

"Mother's quite clever with a needle," she said in a more civil tone. "She worked for a seamstress in Baltimore before she married." She hesitated before adding, "She didn't mean for you to keep the hat, did she?"

"I thought she did. She said I'd have need of a good hat with a brim. I suspect my coonskin looks strange to folks around here. I took that hat to please her."

"Humph." Sophia's resentment flared. She snatched the hat off the seat and held it in her lap. "Mother never should have given it away. Besides, I don't suspect it fits you either. Your head's too big."

Nathan didn't answer. With a slap of the reins, he again clucked to the mule to pick up the pace. King George willingly moved up to a fast trot.

They traveled in silence. Sophia had to hold on to the seat with her free hand as the small wagon jolted along the uneven road. She wished she could stop being so prickly. Still, even if she could manage a pleasant conversation with this perplexing person, she had no idea what to say.

Nathan broke the silence. "I didn't mean to startle you back there at the cabin. You looked as if you had seen a ghost. How long has your brother been gone?"

"Since October." Sophia pulled the shawl close around her, more for comfort than for warmth. "The hat, the clothes, they're his."

"Your father told me he drowned."

"Father doesn't know that for certain. James was sailing his shallop to the Chesapeake when the storm, probably a hurricane, hit. My Uncle Caleb and Father searched along the river for days. They found his boat broken apart. They never found James."

Sophia looked down at the hat.

"It was my fault."

"That seems unlikely."

Sophia's eyes fill with tears. "You don't understand." She said, her voice, husky with emotion. "My brother and Father didn't see eye to eye. James left because he couldn't agree to Father's demands. And because . . . because I couldn't convince him to stay. Truth be told, deep down I wanted him to leave, to show Father he couldn't always have his way."

Sophia took a deep breath and fiddled with the brim of the hat. After a moment, she said, "I should have been the one lost in the storm, not James. Our family would be better off."

"That's a strange thing to say." Nathan pulled back on the reins, slowing the mule.

"Not so strange. Girls don't matter as much. Father had big plans for my brother. And whenever James refused to go along with those plans, Father would ask me to step in." Sophia looked over at Nathan.

"You look skeptical, Mr. Harkness," she said. "Let me explain. Father hired a tutor to groom James for the law. Only when James groused about it, Father encouraged me to study alongside him, probably to shame him into becoming a more serious student. My sister Faith, like most girls, had quit her studies when she was ten. But he told me because I loved book learning so much I should continue my studies. He said I could help James through the rough spots."

Sophia swallowed. Sometimes, she thought, words keep pouring out of my mouth long after I should have stopped talking.

"I don't know if this means much," Nathan said. "But on the way here, your father spoke of you with such pride. He said you were—his words mind you—remarkable."

The mule stopped abruptly. Another, smaller tree had fallen across the road Nathan didn't seem in a hurry to move it. Sophia shrugged and gave him a sad smile.

"I guess that means a lot. Father's not one to lavish praise."

Nathan continued to sit in the wagon as if waiting for her to say more until Sophia grumbled, "If we are ever going to get home, you better clear the road."

He handed her the reins and climbed down. Using the same small hatchet Sophia had seen earlier, he made the road passable with a few well-directed hits. Back in the wagon, he reclaimed the reins and urged the mule forward.

King George began to trot. Sophia gripped the rough board seat with both hands to keep from sliding. Today's heavy rain had carved a shallow gully along one side of the road so that the wagon kept tipping slightly to the right. Sophia looked over at Nathan. He was looking straight ahead.

"Take care. These washouts could crack a wheel or snap an axel."

"I know what I am doing, Miss Records."

"I hope so."

They traveled in silence until she said, "James isn't dead. I would know. He and I, we can tell each other things without talking. I'd feel an emptiness if he were gone and I don't."

Sophia hunched forward, her eyes on the mule.

"I've always wanted a brother," Nathan said quietly. "Never thought about the hurt of losing one."

Sophia smoothed the turkey feathers. "Where is your family?"

Nathan shrugged. "Don't have one. My parents are dead. I don't even know the day or the month I was born. At least I know the year and the place—1793, Philadelphia."

"Oh, my stars. I am so sorry."

"It's been a long time now. I was just a baby when the yellow fever took them, or so I was told at the orphanage."

"How terrible." Sophia swallowed. Oriole was right, she thought, when she told me I was too quick to judge. It's true I judge people too harshly.

She turned toward him, wanting to apologize for her rudeness earlier but not wanting to interrupt.

"Many children became orphans that year," Nathan was saying, his tone flat, matter of fact. "They say thousands of Philadelphians died that year. Still, I wonder sometimes what my life would be like if my parents had lived, if they had fled the city like others did. Then, I wonder why I was spared."

The wagon jolted to a stop. Another thick branch lay across the road. Nathan jumped down.

Sophia shook her skirt, hoping to rid it of the mud caked to the hem. Disaster is like mud, she thought. It leaves stains difficult to scrub away. How hard it must be not to have a family.

"I ought to come back here with an axe. Lots of good firewood just lying around," Nathan said climbing up to the plank seat. Although instead of urging the mule forward, he sat back, holding the reins loosely and letting the mule graze on the brown grass between the wagon ruts.

"You are not as uppity as I thought you'd be," he said as he urged the mule forward with a slap of the reins.

Sophia uttered an embarrassed laugh.

"Is that a compliment?"

"No, I mean, yes, I guess," Nathan said. "I thought a planter's daughter like you wouldn't give me the time of day."

He gave Sophia a searching look, making her wonder what he was hoping to see. Trust perhaps.

Sophia pulled the orange shawl tight. Sitting on a wagon seat and talking with a boy she hardly knew seemed strangely private as though they were alone in a secret world.

"Not so high class, Mr. Harkness. As daughters of an abolitionist, Faith and I are not part of the leisure class. Money seems to be a bit tight these days, so Father doesn't hire much help. Faith and I help out around the plantation and are happy to do it." She turned slightly to look him square in the face. "What about you? At what age did you leave the orphanage?"

"When I was five," he said, "A man claiming to be my uncle came for me. The way I see it, there were too many mouths to feed and not enough healthy people to care for us orphans, so the director started giving children away with very few questions asked. As it turned out, this 'uncle' didn't have the best intention."

Nathan's sour expression revealed his resentment. He lifted the reins and clucked to King George, who grabbed one last bite before raising his head to amble along.

"That's it? You can't end there. What happened?"

Nathan gave her a little half smile.

"Ain't much more to tell. Uncle Jack, that's what he wanted to be called, took in orphans by pretending to be kin. He took only boys who were orphaned young. Boys who couldn't remember their families. He kept five of us at his place so we could help with the cotton. When one died, he went traveling, got another. We were cheap labor."

"That's slavery!"

Nathan shrugged in a hopeless way that implied some folks have no choice.

"You may have guessed," he said, "This so-called uncle lived in cotton country. One of our chores was to pick seeds out of the cotton. The first day I got there, Uncle Jack gave me a large tin cup. He told me to fill it to the top with cotton seeds. Each one of us had a cup and after a day's work in the fields, each of us had to fill his cup before climbing to the loft to sleep."

As Sophia listened, her sympathy for Nathan strengthened. It never had occurred to her that another's life could be so harsh, so unloving. She'd always known the date of her birth, and she'd always known who her kin were. She lived in a safe, comfortable house. There were rules to be sure but they were fair. Nathan was telling her about a world she didn't know existed. And because she didn't know what to say, she patted his arm.

Again, he gave her that little half smile, as if disparaging himself.

"That's all in the past," he said. "I left that place. I was sent on an errand one day and I just kept walking."

"Where did you go?"

"Here and there. Like I said, I just started walking. After some wrong turns, a year or two later I ended up at the place where three rivers meet—the Ohio, the Monongahela, and the Allegheny." The strange sounding words rolled off his tongue.

It was almost musical, Sophia thought. And intriguing. "The Ohio river is named after the state?" she asked.

"No," he said. "I think an Algonquian tribe gave the river its name. Americans called the state after the river."

"I know nothing about the wilderness," Sophia said. "You know about it first-hand."

Nathan grinned. "When I got to the town where the rivers meet—it's called Pittsburgh—I had traveled a lot of miles, and I thought I knew a thing or two. Only I didn't."

Sophia regarded him silently, wondering how he had ended up here with her on this muddy road to Records Landing.

As if he knew her thoughts, Nathan said, "If it wasn't for your father, I'd still be working for a nasty bloke, a Conestoga wagon master. I'd be loading freight, shoveling manure, and washing enormous wagon wheels."

Frowning, Sophia asked, "Why not leave his employ?"

"Not easily done," Nathan said. When Sophia gave him a quizzical look, he explained that the wagon master had played him for a fool, telling him he must sign a paper in order to be hired on as second man on the freight run from Pittsburgh to Baltimore.

"I didn't take the time to find out what was writ," he said. "I put my mark on what turned out to be indenture papers. When I demanded to be released, the wagon master threatened to drag me before the magistrate. We were arguing outside the courthouse, when my luck began to change. Your father stepped in. He was on his way into the courtroom when he overheard us. He came to my defense. He convinced that scoundrel to tear up my indenture. Some money changed hands. Afterwards your father told me if I helped his family remove to Ohio, he'd consider the debt paid. I jumped at the offer. He said it was a gentleman's agreement. I'd never been called a gentleman before."

By now, the wagon had rumbled through the old growth forest and was entering a hickory grove near the edge of the woods. King George let out a wheezy bray and began pulling at the bit.

"Almost home," Sophia said with a twinge of regret. The urgency to get home had been replaced with dread.

"Just how angry is my father?" She clutched the hat. Nathan shrugged. Sophia felt her face tighten. She didn't want him misjudging Father. "Don't get the wrong idea. He's not like that Uncle Jack. Father's never laid a hand on me. He only gave James a switching once, but I was the one who deserved it."

Nathan chuckled. "How did you manage to pin the blame on your brother?"

"Not a laughing matter, Mr. Harkness." Sophia said, bothered that he thought so little of her integrity. "Father caught me riding his precious white mare, Pearl."

"If you were riding, why did your father punish James?"

"Because it was his idea." Sophia looked down at the hat. "James was full of ideas." Sophia drew in a deep breath and exhaled sharply before continuing. "He made life exciting."

She turned to look directly at Nathan. She wanted him to understand the situation, not think her the type to step aside and let someone else take the blame and the punishment.

"Father cherishes Pearl, Elijah's Pearl to be exact. She has won him many races. No one is allowed to ride her but him, certainly not me. Worse I was riding Pearl bareback. Ladies ride sidesaddle, and Father expects his daughters to act like ladies."

Sophia tilted her chin upward, a mischievous glint in her eyes. "There is no denying I loved riding the mare. I hid an old pair of James's britches in the hollow of an old oak so that every time Pearl was turned out into the far pasture, I could steal a ride. James would come, too. He never rode, just urged me on. Then, one day Father showed up."

Sophia's mouth curved downward. "I can still hear him. One thunderous word, 'Halt!' As soon as my feet hit the ground, he ordered me back to Great House. Nothing more. But as I set off running, I could hear Father shouting at James. scolding him for not using the brains God gave him. Saying I could have been killed."

Nathan didn't seem impressed by the escapade. "Well, God looks after the foolish," is all he said, which irked her.

"What about you?" she snapped. "What's the worst thing you ever did?"

"Aha! Curious just like a puma."

"Not that again," she said under her breath, surprised to be only mildly irritated. Obviously calling her some kind of mountain cat amused him for some reason.

Sophia slumped down in the seat. The wagon had reached the orchard. "Just how much trouble am I in?" she asked in a small voice.

"I can't rightly say. Your father seemed more disappointed than angry. I guess that's for you to find out."

They fell silent. Sophia wanted to thank him for telling her about Uncle Jack but she didn't know how to say it. She wanted to apologize for acting so quarrelsome along the way but didn't want to bring that subject up either. Then in a moment of inspiration, she offered him the hat.

"Please, she said, "It's yours. At least for now."

Nathan raised his eyebrows. Sophia thought he looked truly astonished.

"No," he said. "I don't want people thinking me to be someone I ain't."

"Please. As a favor to me. Consider it a peace offering."

Nathan smiled.

"Thank you," he said gravely and took the hat. After smoothing the brim to his liking, he put it on his head before driving the wagon to the carriageway in front of the main house. No one was in sight. A bay horse, one Sophia had never seen before, was tied to the iron hitching post. Someone seeking father's legal advice no doubt, she reasoned.

Dropping the reins, Nathan leaped to the ground, and walked to her side of the wagon. He held out his hand.

You have arrived safely, Miss Records," he said.

Sophia smiled. "Thank you for seeing me home, Mr. Harkness" she said and, taking his hand, stepped down with as much grace as she could muster.

"It was a pleasure, Miss Records" he said, tipping the hat. "Although, I answer best to Nathan."

Sophia felt her cheeks redden. "Friends call me Phee."

"Then Phee it is," he called back as he led King George toward the barn.

6

Confrontations

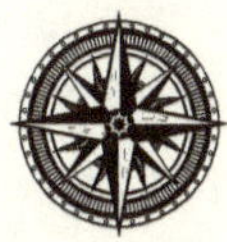

Before Sophia could slip inside, Willie came barreling out of the front door, almost knocking her down. The avid expression on his round face told her he was bursting with information. Willie's blue eyes, so like Grandsire's, sparkled with anticipation.

"Slow down, mister! What's your hurry?" She reached down to hold him by his lean shoulders and gave him a puzzled look. He seemed more grown up than when she had left this morning. Willie squirmed away. He straightened, looking very much like a small commander with a message to deliver.

"You're in trouble, Phee. Mama told me to tell you to go to your room and wait for her."

"She knows I'm home?"

"I told her. She's had me looking out the window forever. She told me to tell you . . ."

"I know, I know."

"No, you don't. Father's in his office with someone important, and Mother said he is not to be disturbed. I gotta go. Mr. Harkness promised to take me fishing." Willie grinned up at her. "I'm glad you're back, Phee," he said and raced off toward the barn.

Sophia stared after him. He is different, she thought, then realized he was wearing britches. Since when did Mother say he could stop wearing baby dresses? He had been fussing about those dresses ever since he turned four last November. 'Not yet,' Mother always said, 'wait just a little longer.' What had made her change her mind, Sophia wondered, turning toward the thick oak door.

A snarling bear glared at her. She stroked its nose, now shiny from years of rubbing. When Sophia was small, Grandsire had held her up to examine the brass knocker, telling her not to be afraid, saying that the fearsome bear stood guard to keep everyone inside the house from harm. Sophia had stroked the bear's nose to say thank you. It had become a habit.

Not even you can protect me today, she thought as she opened the door. The harm has already been done. She closed the door softly. Removing her sodden shoes, she tiptoed down the hall and up the stairs to the bed chamber she shared with Faith. It was empty—not a surprise. Controversy always made Faith squirm. No doubt she had volunteered to work in the wool room. Carding wool was a sure way to stay in Mother's good graces.

Sophia fell backward onto the tall four-poster bed that dominated the room. The featherbed's downy softness was as reassuring as a hug from Grandsire. He had bequeathed it and the six drawer chest to both girls. Now as Sophia lay there listening for her mother's approach, she wondered what Grandsire would advise her to say. Probably, to speak the truth.

Hearing a soft knock, Sophia slipped off the bed. It had to be Mother. Faith would barge right in. Mother's knock was her way of saying, "Have you collected yourself? Are you ready to talk to me?" And Sophia appreciated the courtesy.

"Come in, please," Sophia said with more conviction than she felt.

Mother opened the door and stepped inside. She stopped just beyond the threshold, where she waited, silently.

Her reticence was disconcerting. At first Sophia couldn't think of what to say. Then she could only think of things she knew her mother would want to hear like, "Father's right. I made a mistake," or "I didn't mean it. I want to go to Ohio."

What she finally said was "Forgive me. I didn't mean to worry you." At least that was true.

"Instead of celebrating our news, you cause concern." Mother said. She seemed disappointed rather than angry.

"I am truly sorry. I meant no harm."

"Running away never settles a disagreement. You should hear your father out."

"Father's mind is made up. I have no say in the matter."

"Children sometimes misjudge their parents. Sometimes to their peril." Mother's voice quavered as though she was holding back tears.

Sophia's resolve to stand her ground crumbled. She walked the few steps across the room to her mother, who opened her arms. They hugged each other tightly before Mother gently pushed her away and reached up to stroke some strands of damp hair away from Sophia's face.

"I am glad you are home," she whispered, "When the storm came upon us so suddenly, I thought I might have lost you, too. That I couldn't bear."

Ashamed, Sophia looked away. She had an ever-present memory of her mother sitting in the parlor, the Bible open on her lap, waiting for James to come home. Had Mother been waiting for her the same way?

She stepped back to put more space between them. Standing this close to Mother seemed awkward, unnatural. Sophia had grown so fast this winter that she was still surprised when forced to lower her gaze in order to meet her mother's.

"I want to stay here," Sophia said, willing herself not to sound belligerent but failing. "I can't imagine why Father wants to leave this place. Grandsire would never allow it."

"Again, you assume. Grandsire put great trust in your father's decisions. I believe he would be pleased that your father has decided to make our home in Ohio where the land is fertile. The venture is promising."

"Aren't you afraid? Don't you think about what happened when you came to Baltimore from Scotland? Your parents didn't survive."

"We were ill prepared. There were so many adjustments that first year—different food, harsh living conditions, and worst of all strange diseases. The Hardening they call it. Our family won't face that in Ohio."

"What about the red Indians? Maybe they don't want us there. We could be killed, if not by savages, then by wild animals, like…" she hesitated, trying to think of the most dangerous animal imaginable. "Pumas!"

Mother gave an exasperated sigh. "Pumas? Whatever they are, it doesn't matter. Like it or not, we are leaving."

Not me, Sophia thought. Had Mother forgotten about James? Someone had to stay behind for his sake. What if after finding his way home, he found Talcotts living in Great House? No, someone has to be here.

Sophia turned away. Bringing up James would only start a different argument. Mother and Father had as good as buried her brother months ago. These days, they rarely spoke his name let alone expressed any hope of his survival.

Walking to the window, she looked down toward the river. Nathan and Willie were standing at the end of the long pier, fishing. Willie was laughing.

"Since when did Willie start wearing britches?"

"Since today." Mother said, joining Sophia at the window. "Father suggested it. Willie's pleased as punch. He jumped up from his chair when Father suggested it and shouted, 'Hooray. Now I am a big boy!'"

Mother smiled fondly. "As soon as breakfast ended, I shortened an old pair James wore when he was a little older than Willie. I'll sew up a new pair before we leave. Father brought bolts of tabbinet and broadcloth from Baltimore. He wants you girls to have new gowns suitable for traveling. I am to engage Mrs. Crampton to help me. She's a fine seamstress."

"My staying here will save you some trouble."

Mother exhaled loudly. "Sophia, that is just enough! I can't believe that a daughter of mine is acting so mulish. Headstrong behavior does not become a young lady. Sometimes I think that all those books Father encourages you to read have affected your mind."

This was an old argument. Sophia retreated to the bed and sat stiffly on the edge, ankles crossed demurely even though her feet didn't quite reach floor.

"God made woman to be man's companion," Mother continued. "It says so in the Bible. She is to bear and to forbear. Really, Sophia, you must learn to hold your tongue. Model your behavior after Faith's. I have heard no complaints from her. "

There was no use arguing. Sophia looked glumly down at her dress muddied from the road.

"I'll try harder," she said, knowing she wouldn't.

"Good," Mother said and smiled. "Now hurry and tidy up. Just look at yourself. Your gown is filthy. And torn. It needs immediate attention. Remember the proverb . . ."

"A stitch in time saves nine." Sophia finished the saying with just the slightest glimmer of a smile. Mother was always quoting little bits of wisdom, she thought. Mother quotes Benjamin Franklin more than she quotes the Bible.

Loosening the laces of her bodice, Sophia pulled the damp gown over her head, then untied her petticoat and handed both to her mother before leaning forward to give her a kiss on the cheek.

"I am truly sorry I worried you. I didn't think . . ."

"That is the problem, Phee," Mother said with a look of pure exasperation.

"You don't always think!" Her tone was crisp.

Folding the soiled garments over her arm with a muttered "tsk, tsk," Mother walked to the door only to pause once again at the threshold as if she had just remembered something. She turned back to face Sophia.

"When you've freshened up," she said, "your father wants to speak with you. He'll be in his office. But, if the door is closed, don't interrupt. Come back later."

"Yes, Mother," Sophia said with a quick curtsey. So, I've earned a double scolding, she thought.

The front door banged open.

"I caught a fish," Willie shouted. "It's a big one! Nathan got two. Come, see. I've got 'em right here."

"Don't bring those smelly fish in the house!" Mother cried as she rushed down the stairs. "My goodness, Willie, those are fine fish. We'll ask Sally to cook them for supper." She whisked the boy and the fish outside.

Mother cannot abide a mess, Sophia thought. I wonder how she will take to dusty travel.

With messes and the hardening on her mind, Sophia walked to the washstand. For once, Faith had left water in the pitcher. Sophia poured some into the porcelain washbasin then lathered up a washcloth with a bar of Pears soap.

It smells like a summer garden, she thought, as she washed her arms and scrubbed dirt from beneath her nails before putting the basin on the floor to wash off her feet. After rubbing herself dry with a rough linen cloth, she took a faded blue calico gown from a peg on the wall and slipped it on over her shift. Not that she had much choice, she either could wear this hand-me-down from Faith, the brown homespun, or her best gown.

Twisting first one way then the other, she considered her appearance as reflected in the square looking glass that hung above the washstand. The dress simply didn't suit her. The bodice felt much too tight across her chest. She turned sideways to check the seams. I'm going to bust out of this before long, she thought. Standing on her tiptoes, she tried to see her hem and failing, climbed onto the bed to get a better look.

The dress is too short, she thought. It should be headed for the rag bag. I must have grown three inches over the winter. I bet I'm taller than James. Only he must be taller, too.

Slipping down from the bed, she began to brush the tangles out of her waist-long hair. Tugging on a streak of blonde, she wondered if pumas were brown or blonde. Whatever color, though, they had to be ferocious. Peering into the looking glass, she snarled, then decided she didn't look dangerous, just silly. The freckles sprinkled across the bridge of her nose didn't help. A puma with freckles, ridiculous.

Nothing is right, she thought, brushing her hair with long, hard strokes. If James had stayed, we wouldn't be leaving. Silently she hurled accusations at her twin. "You should have faced Father. You should have told him the truth, that you were born to be a sailor. It was cowardly to sneak off. This is all your fault!" Shaken by the depth of her anger, Sophia turned away from the looking glass.

"Everything is all wrong," she grumbled as she pulled on clean stockings then searched unsuccessfully for her moccasins but could find only one. "Oh, fiddle! I'll just go shoeless."

Moments later, Sophia, her hair now smoothed and tied back with a yellow ribbon, stood at the top of the stairs while she dithered about tactics. There were some rules that should never be broken: Daughters do not talk back; they always show respect; and they never question their father's decisions. Except, Sophia told herself, I wasn't talking back this morning. I was just speaking my mind. Father is always talking about the rights of man. Well, I believe daughters have rights, too!

Trying to ignore the queasy feeling in her stomach, she walked down the stairs the way she imagined Marie Antoinette would have walked from the Bastille to the guillotine, her head held high and her step firm. The story of the doomed queen was a favorite of hers; and even though she disapproved of royalty, Sophia doubted that she would have stood with the crowd heckling the young French queen about to be beheaded.

Now as she descended to face her own fate, she mouthed Marie Antoinette's famous words: "Courage! I have shown it for years; think you now I shall lose it at the moment my sufferings are to end?" Only I should change the words, Sophia thought. It should be, "Now my suffering is about to begin." Not that Sophia believed Father's punishment would be severe. What she dreaded most was hearing the reproach in his voice.

On the low landing, Sophia halted. No one was around to observe her queenly descent. Behind the stair-wall she could hear Willie chattering away and her mother's murmured response. The long hall was empty. The thick paneled door to the parlor was closed, the front door shut tight. Late afternoon sunlight streamed through the tall narrow window at the west end of the hallway, illuminating the wide corridor all the way to her father's office door at the east end. It, too, was closed.

Sophia was about to retrace her steps when the door opened. Father and a taller, younger man with dark hair came out, still engrossed in conversation as they walked toward the front door.

Sophia froze. She recognized the man immediately. This is impossible, she thought. Why would someone so famous come here? Please, God, don't let Father rebuke me in front of Stephen Decatur. A captain, and now a commodore!

Although Sophia knew she was staring goggle eyed, she couldn't help herself. A real American hero, here. A commodore in the United States Navy here in her house. Everyone on the Eastern Shore was talking about him, praising him for defeating the Barbary pirates, not once but twice! And if she wanted to hear a hair-raising tale of the victories, her Uncle Caleb was happy to tell her. He had been there, fought alongside Stephen Decatur.

The first time Sophia had seen the commodore, she and James had been at a gathering in Snow Hill, standing in a crowd cheering when someone nearby remarked that Captain Decatur was hot tempered and prone to dueling. As far as Sophia was concerned, those qualities only proved that Stephen Decatur was the bravest man to be born in Maryland. Uncle Caleb concurred.

"Please, God, don't let the commodore see me," Sophia now prayed. But even as she offered up her silent plea, Father spoke.

"Phee! I'm glad you're home safe. Commodore, I'd like you meet my daughter, Sophia. She, too, is an admirer of yours." Father motioned to Sophia to join them.

Reluctantly she descended the few steps and walked down the hall to stand beside her father. She curtsied stiffly hoping neither would notice her ill-fitting clothes or her stocking feet.

The commodore took her hand and bowed his head slightly.

"I am pleased to meet you."

Sophia, certain she appeared childish and awkward, willed the floorboards to split open so she could fall into the cellar below. She gulped, then stammered, "the pleasure is mine."

The rest of the encounter was a blur. All she remembered was that when Father suggested she wait in his office, she had fled without saying "Goodbye."

Standing by the tall, narrow window in Father's office, rehashing her inelegant behavior, Sophia watched the commodore and Father walk down the carriageway to the hitching post where the bay horse was tied. Even out of uniform Commodore Decatur had a commanding presence, she decided. What business could such a man have with Father, she wondered. But nothing came to mind.

She smoothed her dress in the hope that she didn't look as silly as she thought she did and then spent the next few minutes chastising herself. *Why is it that I always make a mess of things? If only I had taken a little more time to find my moccasins. If only I had brought this dress to Mother for alterations when she asked weeks ago. I am such a juggins.*

She watched as her father gave a farewell salute to the commodore, who tipped his hat and turned his horse toward the lane leading to the main road. Father stood there for a few minutes, looking toward the barn before turning back toward the house. He seemed in no hurry to talk to her.

It made Sophia wonder if Father might have some misgivings about leaving. Normally, once Father made up his mind, nothing on Heaven or Earth could change it. *Maybe, this time,* she thought, crossing her fingers, *once he's heard my arguments, he will reconsider.*

She looked around the small square room. Wide double doors closed off the office from the drawing room. Father's desk, a tall mahogany secretary, was strategically placed on the front wall beside the window. When seated there, Father could see out front window or lean back and see through the side window without leaving his chair. The desk was the helm of the plantation.

Today the long-paneled doors of the secretary were open, revealing three rows of books bound in rich leathers and tooled in gold. Sophia ran her fingers along the spines. The books were treasures that enlivened long winter evenings. She had read most of them, even the first two volumes of Blackstone's *Commentaries*. The only book missing from the shelves was the Bible. It lay open on a table in the west parlor where the family always gathered after supper to hear Sophia or Faith read a chapter aloud each night.

I would benefit from reading a passage on repentance right now, Sophia thought as she sank into the office's one comfortable chair, a large wingback. Crossing her stocking feet at the ankles, she waited for the scolding that was sure to come. Minutes later, she heard boots clomping along the hallway then silence, followed by a long deep sigh. Sophia wondered if Father dreaded confronting her as much as she dreaded facing him.

"So!" Father said, opening the door. "You have come to apologize."

Rising to face him, Sophia smiled slightly but there was no happiness in it. She had intended to apologize for rushing off. Now, however, upon hearing what she considered to be an order, she changed her mind and lifted her chin in defiance. The only sound was the ticking of the hall clock.

"I assume by your silence, you are unrepentant," Father said, his tone mild. Sophia looked at him askance, her expression softening. She had expected a stern lecture on filial obedience.

"Can I also assume you are determined to stay in Maryland?"

"Yes."

With a deep sigh, Father turned his gaze to the scene outside the side window. Somewhere near the barn, the cow mooed impatiently, letting everyone know milking time was approaching. Neither Sophia nor Father remarked on it.

By now, the room was mostly in shadow. Father walked to the double doors and opened them, bringing light and air into the smaller room.

The drawing room was empty. The dining table had been cleared. With the leaves removed, it was now circular. Beyond it the wide sweep of the brick hearth was totally in view. The fire had burned down to a few glowing ashes. Father took three logs from the lidded wood box beside the hearth and laid them atop the ashes. With a few puffs from the bellows, he coaxed a small flame to life.

Sophia remained standing in front of the wing chair. A prisoner in the dock, she thought as she waited for her sentence.

Apparently satisfied the logs would catch fire, Father walked back into his office and pulled back the desk chair, turning it toward Sophia.

"I asked you to come here not to scold you but to explain. Be so kind as to listen to what I have to say."

Despite his conciliatory tone, Sophia remained wary. Father was good at persuading people to do things they didn't want to do. Her mind was made up, and no amount of talk was going to change that. It is so obvious, she thought crossly. James won't know how to find us.

"Will you listen to the facts instead of jumping to ill-informed conclusions?" Father continued. "Come over here. There is no need for us to shout at one another." He beckoned to her.

Taking a deep breath, Sophia walked slowly across the floor to stand beside him. This morning he had looked happy, pleased to tell everyone the news about a new home in Ohio. Now he looked worried. The crease between his eyebrows had deepened. Sophia noticed for the first time that his sideburns were turning grey.

Imprisoning her right hand between his large square ones, Father looked intently at her face. "Why? Why are you so angry with me?"

Sophia returned his gaze with a fixed determination."

"Clearly," she began, "it's not my place to question your decisions, but in all frankness, I think you are making a mistake."

When Father didn't react to the criticism, she took a deep breath and continued. "This is our home. I don't see any reason to abandon everything we love for. . . how did you say it this morning? For an adventure. For the chance to begin a new life in a new state." Realizing she had gone too far, moving from frankness to disrespect, Sophia lowered her gaze. "Do your worst, she said. "Mete out the proper punishment for a disobedient child. Whip me and be done with it."

"What?" Her father gave a shout of laughter before he added, "What makes you think I would? I've never raised a hand to you."

"You whipped James!" She flushed with humiliation. Couldn't Father ever take her seriously!

"Please, Sophia, I wasn't laughing at you," he said, holding her hand a little tighter. "The thought is just so preposterous. I don't believe in whipping children. Despite what tale James may have told, I never whipped your brother. Perhaps if I had, he would still be alive today."

Father dropped her hand and looked away. He cleared his throat.

"Maybe I was too easy on James," he said. "He was headstrong. And, just like you, he made impetuous, emotional decisions. He broke rules. He never should have taken the shallop out alone."

"He didn't know there was a hurricane coming." Sophia said, automatically leaping to her twin's defense. "And you weren't there to stop him!"

Sophia looked stricken. The words had slipped out unintended.

"Is that how you feel? Is that why you are so angry?"

"No." Sophia turned away, trying to blink away tears. When she looked back, she saw his misery. His face was flushed, his eyes moist.

"I know it's not your fault," she said with a catch in her voice. It's mine. I could have stopped him. I didn't try hard enough." Tears ran unchecked down her cheeks.

Father took out his wide linen handkerchief and handed it to her then steered her toward the chair. She dropped limply onto the seat. Father crouched down beside her.

"It's not your fault, Sophia. Blame the river, blame the storm if you must, but do not blame yourself. The wind was too much for the sail; the dark water hid a snag; the boat capsized. James couldn't hold on. The river swept him away. That is the sad truth."

Sophia pressed the wadded handkerchief to her mouth and gave a shuddering sigh.

"You don't know for sure. We must not leave here not if James is trying to get back to us."

"Be reasonable, Phee. There is no use waiting around, expecting that someday he'll come walking into the yard whistling 'Yankee Doodle.' Don't let false hope hold you back. You must get on with your life."

"I can't. Everyone says I'll get over it. Is that ever possible? Have you? Has Mother? Willie still cries out for James at night. Sometime I see Faith staring out at the river with this sad expression on her face. None of us has gotten over it. That's the truth."

"A sad truth."

"It's too much to lose," she said. "James, Grandsire, and now Great House. By selling Records Landing you have let Grandsire down." Sophia glared at her father in disapproval.

"What do you mean?" He seemed perplexed.

"Grandsire told me the Talcott men have schemed for years to acquire this plantation. Except that was a prize, he said, they would never win."

With a wry smile, Father stood and walked over to the side window. "Come here, Phee. Look out the window. What do you see?"

Sophia walked back to the window. "I see the barn and beyond it the tobacco shed. I see the pier and the kitchen garden, the cookhouse, then the chicken coop and beyond it the orchard."

"A tobacco shed full of tobacco that we haven't been able to sell because of Jefferson's embargo, a barn with little hay because that same tobacco crop has soured the land, and an old house that cries out for repair. Not much of a prize these days. Selling was a necessary decision, a final decision and not one made lightly. There's no turning back." He cleared his throat. "Now," he said gruffly, "you need to make a decision. Your Mother and I have discussed this and we are in agreement. You are old enough to determine where you will live."

Sophia regarded her father warily. "I don't understand."

"We are asking you to choose to either come with us to Ohio or to remain in Maryland. If you decide to stay behind, you will go to Baltimore to live with my brother's family. Your cousin Sarah is attending an academy in Baltimore as a day student. This is an opportunity for you to further your education and I would be happy to pay your tuition there."

"You mean stay behind without you?"

Her father nodded

Sophia closed her eyes. Going away to school! It was what she daydreamed about—not studying with a tutor but attending an academy with other scholars, a place with many teachers and hundreds of books. Something few girls ever were allowed to do.

Father interrupted her thoughts. "You don't have to decide this minute,'" he said. "Think about which road will point you toward happiness. I must have your answer preferably before your aunt and uncle arrive here in three weeks. We leave for Ohio in a month."

"I decide?" Sophia repeated, sounding dubious.

Father stooped down and kissed her on the forehead. She felt a rush of gratitude but, looking up at him, she saw the lingering sadness in his eyes.

"I must add," he said with an attempt at a smile, "that I hope you will come with us. Our family's future lies in the West. Our Republic's future lies there, too. Still, if you believe you must remain in Maryland, your mother and I will understand."

He held out his hands, pulling Sophia to her feet and walked with her to the office door. Stepping into the hall, she hesitated but Father had already closed the door.

"How," she wondered, "How will I know if the decision I make is the right one? Whichever one I make, I am sure to disappoint someone."

Unwelcome Guests

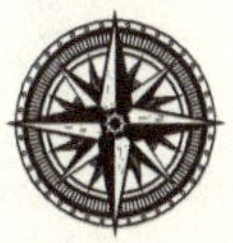

"*Come, butter, come; come, butter, come,*" Sophia chanted as she plunged the wood dasher up and down. She sat on a bench outside the cookhouse and steadied the tall butter churn between her knees. Even though the morning was cool, the repetitive motion kept her warm. Although usually soothing, as it allowed her time to dream, today her thoughts were churning along with the cream.

Four precious days gone already, she told herself, trying not to panic. Whatever decision I make, my whole life will change. On the one hand if I stay behind, I will abandon my family; on the other hand, if I go to Ohio, I will abandon any hope of seeing my brother again. Father has put me in a terrible spot.

Sophia pushed the dasher down. Thunk.

Still, Father is allowing me to choose. She pulled the dasher up. Chunk.

Fiddlesticks, whatever I do, I hurt someone, she muttered and began chanting the old rhyme again, hoping to banish her thoughts.

> *Come, butter, come; come, butter, come.*
> *Peter stands at the gate*

Waiting for his buttered cake.
Come, butter, come.

Only her thoughts kept returning to her dilemma. Everything is happening too fast! Mr. Talcott should stay away from here until we're gone. With a wry smile, Sophia altered the rhyme.

Come, butter, come,
Mr. Talcott's at the gate,
Waiting for our house to take.
Come, butter, come.

She sang her sassy version over and over to the soft rhythmic thunk-chunk of churn and dasher until butter formed. After pouring the leftover watery milk into a blue speckled stoneware pitcher marked buttermilk, she scraped the soft creamy spread, now a pale yellow, into a crock.

The entire household knew that Mr. Talcott was coming in person to examine the house. He had sent a letter, hand delivered by his slave Jacob two days ago, saying that he would be arriving Tuesday afternoon at two o'clock sharp. Sophia, along with the rest of the family, had been sitting in the parlor listening to Father read scripture when Jacob rapped on the side door, the one that Sally used to bring in their meal from the cookhouse. Father seemed annoyed at the interruption but read the letter on the spot because Jacob kept shifting his hat from one hand to the other, obviously in a hurry to return to his master with an answer.

"Tell Mr. Talcott that Mrs. Records will receive him, as I will be away on business," he had said, escorting Jacob to the door.

"Leave it to Mr. Talcott to wait until Sunday to tell us," Mother had snapped as soon as the door closed. "Of course, it has to be Tuesday, the one day you will be away. I think he planned it that way!"

"It can't be helped," Father shrugged. "He is within his rights and he can't hide behind his land agent forever. There's no point in stirring the pot. I'm sure you and the girls can handle the situation."

"No doubt," Mother had replied. She had slapped her hands on her knees and then given Sophia and Faith a stern look.

"Tomorrow," she said, "I want this house made ship shape, shined from top to bottom. No cobwebs in the corners, no dust under the beds. I can't imagine where that man will not poke his nose!"

After breakfast the next morning, the siege on household dirt began. Mother handed Sophia and Faith brooms. "Start sweeping," she said with a smile, followed by a favorite quote: "Energy and persistence conquer all things." Both girls sighed. There was no use arguing when Mother evoked Benjamin Franklin.

Surprisingly the day went smoothly. Father secluded himself in his office away from Mother's campaign, saying that because court would be in session tomorrow, he needed to double-check his brief if he was going to successfully argue his client's case.

Sally delayed washday until Tuesday to join forces with Mother.

Together they had taken down the heavy brocade drapes in both the parlor and the drawing room and given them a good shaking before moving on to dust and polish every stick of furniture downstairs with beeswax. As soon as Sophia and Faith finished sweeping out all the rooms, Mother set them to washing the tall windows on the first floor with vinegar and water. She even recruited Nathan to help. Standing on a ladder, he washed away the smoky grime outside, while the girls cleaned the thick wavy glass inside. Sophia kept trying to make Nathan laugh by making faces at him but all she got was an occasional smile. Faith, never one to shirk, stuck to her task so the job got done before the sun went down. Mother seemed satisfied with the results.

"It's not a spring house cleaning," she had said, "but it will have to do."

That was yesterday.

Today, Mother kept finding more tasks for the girls. After the noon meal, a thrown-together affair of hot porridge and thick slices of day-old bread slathered with the freshly churned butter, Mother had one more request. Sophia and Faith were to watch for their visitor while she saw to it that Willie studied his letters.

"You can pass the time by working on your samplers," she said.

"I wonder if there ever was a time when Mother just sat still with nothing to do," Faith whispered to Sophia.

Sophia laughed. "Probably never. She's a firm believer in idle hands being the devil's tools. Still, if we are going to watch for that horrible man, we might as well be comfortable."

In the hall, the tall case clock chimed the hour. Mr. Talcott was to arrive by two o'clock. They had a whole sixty minutes to themselves.

With very little coaxing Sophia convinced Faith to help her lug a chair from the parlor into Father's office and place it by the tall front window, then shove its mate next to it. From here Sophia pointed out, they had a good view of the carriage way.

"Can you keep a secret?" Faith whispered after they were settled and had begun stitching.

Sophia put aside her sampler. The leaves on her apple tree looked diseased. She needed to rip out half the stiches and start over. Such a bother.

"Why do you want to know?" She gave her sister a teasing glance.

Faith was bent over her sampler, squinting at the tiny even stitches that outlined Great House. She would benefit from spectacles, Sophia thought. To refuse them for fear of spoiling her looks was pure vanity.

Faith stopped sewing and looked up. "First tell me if you can keep a secret." Faith sounded eager to confide.

"Secrets?" Sophia smiled. She knew how to keep them. After all, Grandsire had trusted her with his. She had discovered Grandsire's hidey-hole three years ago. Grandsire had sworn her to secrecy, saying it was important that no one learn about the existence of the underground room. She had never told a soul, not even James.

"You needn't worry. I am trustworthy," Sophia said.

Faith bit her lip apprehensively, as if reconsidering whether or not to continue, then blurted out her news.

"Mr. Mueller is going to ask Father for my hand."

She paused as if waiting for Sophia to respond. But Sophia merely raised a questioning eyebrow.

"Tomorrow," Faith said with emphasis. "He is going to ask Father tomorrow." She looked pleadingly at Sophia. "You mustn't breathe a word."

"Oh, La!" Sophia said. She took a hold of Faith's hands. The two girls stared at each other, the one with joy, the other with astonishment.

"What makes you so certain?" Sophia finally asked.

Faith smiled and gave Sophia one of those you're-too-young-to-understand looks. "Remember when Zach, I mean Mr. Mueller, and I went walking after Sunday meeting? You know, two weeks ago when the preacher was in town? Mr. Mueller and I were in that pretty little grove of trees by the river when he told me, all bashful like, that he wanted to ask Father for permission to marry me. That is, if I was willing."

"And you agreed?"

Faith nodded and squeezed Sophia's hands tightly.

"How can this happen?" Sophia asked in disbelief. "You are not of age and besides we are going to Ohio in less than a month."

"I know, Isn't it wonderful?" Faith said. "A whole group will be traveling together. If you hadn't run off the other day, you'd know that. The Muellers and two other families are going. The minister, too. Zach—Mr. Mueller—and I plan to marry in Ohio! We'll be the first ones wed in our new little town."

I should have known something was brewing, Sophia told herself. Faith has been so cheerful lately, so full of smiles and giggles. And here I thought she was excited about the journey to Ohio.

Faith shook her hands loose from Sophia's grasp and looked down at the sampler in her lap. She picked at a loose thread. Her checks were flaming.

Speaking so low that Sophia had to lean forward to hear, Faith confided that when she had said "yes," Mr. Mueller had pulled her close and kissed her square on the mouth.

"I kissed him back," Faith said, eyes shining. "His mouth tasted so sweet."

"Sneaking off with Mr. Mueller. Worse, kissing him. And saying yes to marriage before Father had agreed to it," Sophia said, ticking off Faith's lapses.

"Keep your voice down."

"It's a good secret but that's all it is," Sophia whispered. "You know Father will never agree. I can hear him now," she cleared her throat and fixed her eyes on Faith, trying to imitate Father. "He'll say, 'Be reasonable, Faith. Mr. Mueller's not much older than you. He has no prospects. Marriage, I am afraid that is not possible right now.'"

Faith looked pleadingly at Sophia. "If Mother or Father say anything to you, please back me up. They listen to your opinions. I am sure you agree that Mr. Mueller and I should wed. We are both hardworking, perfectly matched. We can set up housekeeping in Ohio and start our married life together there." She smiled, her face flushed with happiness.

Thoughtfully, Sophia regarded her sister. Faith's sleek dark brown hair was pulled back into a bun hidden beneath her ruffled cap. Short wisps that Mother called scolding locks had escaped and now trailed delicately down her pale neck. She looks beguiling, Sophia decided. Being in love suits her.

For months now, ever since that huge man (Sophia privately called him the German giant) had bowed low over Faith's hand and asked her to dance the reel with him at the summer social, Sophia had listened to her sister describe the many merits of Mr. Zachariah Mueller. Night after night, before falling asleep, Faith would tell and retell how kind he was and smart. When he looked at her, she said she could feel her heart do cartwheels.

Most nights Sophia had just listened, although once she felt compelled by honesty to point out that the only topic that she had heard Faith's precious German talk about was the importance of rotating crops and dosing sheep—that is, when he talked at all. He never had an amusing story to tell. He never talked about books he had read. Politics didn't seem to interest him. He was neither here nor there. Perhaps worst of all, he seemed desperately lacking in a sense of humor.

"Not everybody has to be a political thinker or laugh at silly jokes," Faith had said, quick to defend her suitor.

Sophia had just rolled her eyes and muttered "dull, dull, dull."

"Humph!" had been Faith's reply as she flopped over on her side and then treated Sophia coldly the next day.

Now Sophia wondered how her sister had sped from those midnight whispers to marriage talk. In fact, ever since Father's announcement last week, Faith had not mentioned Zachariah's name once. Apparently, Faith could keep a secret, too.

"Soon I will be the mistress of my own house. It's everything I've ever wanted," Faith said.

"I guess that depends on Father," Sophia replied and raised her crossed fingers.

The crunch of wheels on the carriage way cut the conversation short.

"Drat! He's here already," Sophia exclaimed as she hastily slid her needle into the linen backing of her sampler and tucked it into her sewing basket.

Both girls peered out the window. A small sleek open carriage pulled by two cream-colored horses stopped at the hitching post. A man stepped down from the carriage. His companion, a woman dressed in dark clothing and wearing a plumed hat remained seated.

Sophia looked at Faith. Arching her eyebrows, she said in a lofty tone, "A phaeton! Apparently, Mr. Talcott's come up in the world."

"So it seems," Faith said. "You let him in, Phee. I'll go see what's keeping Mother. Surely Will's done copying his letters by now."

"Coward. You're the one who wants to be mistress of a house."

"Not today and not this house." Faith tossed her sampler on the chair and dashed out of the room.

Sophia sighed. It would serve the man right if no one answered the door, she thought. We didn't invite him nor would we. Everyone on the Eastern Shore knows the Records and Talcotts simply don't get along. He should know he's not welcome.

Mr. Talcott, though, was demanding to be seen. He was thumping the brass knocker with such force that the sound reverberated loudly through the whole downstairs.

Too bad the bear can't bite him, Sophia thought as she hurried to the door, and swung it open. A stout man of middling height brushed past her.

Unsettled, Sophia turned to face the rude guest. He was well dressed and clean-shaven like her father. But unlike Father, who had cut his hair short, Mr. Talcott still wore his hair in a queue. There was a rank odor about the man, causing Sophia to wonder if he held to the old belief that bathing during winter caused illness.

Mr. Talcott eyed her coldly. "Mr. Records was told to expect me," he said and, removing his tall black hat, handed it to her as if she were a serving girl.

In her head Sophia heard her mother murmuring, "Mind your manners, young lady."

Controlling her irritation, Sophia spoke in an even tone, "My father is away on business. My mother will see you in his stead." She looked down at the fashionable topper she was holding before adding, "I don't believe we have been introduced. I am Miss Sophia Records."

"Indeed," he said. "It's a pity your father has his daughter performing tasks normally assigned to slaves."

"There are no slaves at Records Landing, Mr. Talcott."

"Then if you please, Miss Records, inform your mother that I have arrived."

"There is no need. She is aware. And will join you shortly. Her instructions were that, if you arrived early, you should wait in the drawing room. It's just down the hall, through that open door and then through the French doors to your left. You'll see that those doors separate two rooms, a drawing room and a parlor. The parlor is reserved for more important occasions."

Sophia smiled then added, "I will just see to your hat." She gave him a quizzical look, "Will your companion be joining us?"

"No. She prefers to wait in the carriage."

Mr. Talcott turned abruptly, the coattails of his frock coat flapping as he strode down the hall. Sophia ducked into Father's office, walking through it to the drawing room and then closing the two wide paneled doors behind her. She placed the hat on the side table.

Seeing that Mr. Talcott was still standing in the parlor, she walked to the threshold between the two rooms and paused, resting her hand on one of the French doors. The glass panes in the elegant door gleamed. After yesterday's whirlwind cleaning not a trace of dust remained. Sophia regarded the man with the same attention she would give an unruly mule. He was surveying the room with a proprietary air.

Sophia invited him to join her in the drawing room but he lingered in the parlor, examining the carved mantle, the oil paintings, and the polished mahogany furniture. When he finally chose to accept Sophia's invitation, he pushed past her with a sour expression on his face and walked to the hearth. The fire had burned down but ashes still radiated heat.

"I don't like to be kept waiting," he said abruptly.

"I am afraid you arrived earlier than expected." Sophia said. "I am sure my mother will be down directly."

He gave her a disdainful glance. Mr. Talcott had a florid complexion that seemed to be chiseled with a permanent sneer. He did not wear his fine shirt with its lace jabot easily and now slid an index finger underneath the high collar. It looked to be a tight fit on his thick neck.

"Might I get you a glass of water, Mr. Talcott?"

"No."

"Perhaps you would like to sit by the window where it is cooler? "Sophia gestured toward a dainty, upholstered chair with wooden arms placed near the window. It looked to be too unsubstantial for a man of his bulk.

"No. I prefer to stand." Mr. Talcott planted his feet farther apart.

Suit yourself, Sophia thought and walked to the narrow door beside the hearth. She opened it to let in some air. Pulling a lavender scented handkerchief from her sleeve, she held it to her nose briefly then seated herself in the small armchair. Tucking the handkerchief away, she folded her hands demurely in her lap.

I've done my part, Sophia thought and kept still. The minutes ticked by.

"Tell me, Miss Records, are you happy about moving?" Mr. Talcott asked, breaking the silence.

"Yes." Sophia raised her chin slightly, unconsciously daring him to doubt her.

"Good. Such an uncivilized land, though."

"Perhaps, but a grand adventure for the brave."

"Indeed."

Mr. Talcott, apparently tired of waiting, began to wander around the room. He seemed particularly interested in doors.

"What's this one's purpose?" he asked shutting the side door, reopening it, then shutting it again.

"We call it the cook's door," Sophia said. "The path outside leads to the cookhouse."

Mr. Talcott nodded and moved on to Father's office doors.

"That's private," Sophia said. Mr. Talcott nodded but opened and closed the one of the doors anyway. He rattled the doorknob.

"The house needs work, but I think my daughter will be happy here. She ought to be, I paid a pretty penny for this ramshackle place."

Sophia bit her lip, holding back hot words.

Mr. Talcott seemed unaware of her resentment.

"This room seems sparsely furnished," he continued.

"Two chairs were moved to another room temporarily. They are usually beside the hearth. We take our meals here, so we need ample space to accommodate the dining table when it is expanded."

She looked toward the center of the room. Sally had put the room to rights after the noon meal by removing the table leaves and placing four tall-backed chairs around the now circular table. More tall-backed chairs were lined up against the wall opposite the hearth, two on either side the tall china cabinet.

"Only four of you dine here? I thought your family was larger." He frowned. "I forgot. You've had recent losses. A pity. The old man, your grandsire I believe, had lived beyond the three score and ten promised in the Bible. But the young boy, your twin, am I right? His death . . ."

"Not dead, missing." Sophia snapped, clenching her hands into fists.

"Oh? I had heard differently." Mr. Talcott appeared perplexed. "Yes, Death is hard to accept."

As if to change the subject, he walked over to the window where he fingered the heavy brocade curtain. "Nice," he said as though selecting goods from a Snow Hill draper.

"The fabric was imported from Paris," Sophia said, rising to her feet and stepping away.

"Of course, your Granddaddy did like fine things. Not that he ever paid for them, or so I've been told." He prowled around the room, stopping to examine a brass candlestick.

Sophia closed her eyes. "Please God," she prayed silently, "Get me out of here."

Her prayer was answered with a shriek.

"Help! Someone, help!!"

Sophia and Mr. Talcott nearly bumped heads in their haste to look out the window. Down by the barn a girl about Sophia's height was hopping up and down trying to dodge repeated attacks from China Boy. He was hissing and pecking at the frightened girl's ankles.

"It's Judith!" Mr. Talcott roared. "Get that vile creature away from my daughter."

Without a word, Sophia turned and hurried out the cook's door with Mr. Talcott close on her heels. She hitched up her skirts and began running across the lawn toward the screaming girl.

Wait 'til I get my hands on Willie, she thought. He must have let China Boy out of the coop. He's probably hiding behind the barn door laughing his head off. From the corner of her eye, she saw Sally running from the cookhouse waving a dishrag above her head like a soldier waving a battle flag. Try as she might, Sophia couldn't suppress a giggle.

Sophia got to Judith first.

"Stop screaming," she said sternly. "You're only making matters worse."

Judith kept on hollering. The gander made another thrust with his bill.

Uttering a soothing "tsk, tsk, tsk," Sophia picked up China Boy.

He struggled, whipping his head around to strike at her. Quickly, she pinned the squirming goose high up under her left arm. Then, snatching off her cap, she covered his head.

"It's all right. It's all right," she cooed. "That girl's not going to hurt your family." China Boy calmed under her touch.

She gave Judith a hard stare, fighting back the urge to laugh. The girl was a mess. Her bonnet with its long veil and ridiculous plume had slipped off to the side, giving her a lopsided look. It's a trespasser's just reward, Sophia thought, completely overlooking the fact that Judith was a guest.

Gulping back ragged sobs, the frightened girl was trying to speak but could only hiccup.

When Mr. Talcott arrived a minute later, he was out of breath and scowling.

"Why didn't you wait in the carriage like I told you?"

Judith cringed and backed away. She seemed as frightened of him as she had been of the goose.

"I got bored," she stammered. "I didn't mean to cause trouble. I just wanted to look around."

Clenching his fists, Mr. Talcott immediately turned on Sally, who had arrived a minute before him. "And you, Girl, why were you so slow getting here?"

That's no way to talk, Sophia thought. I'll let China Boy loose if he says another mean word.

The cook, though, acted as if she had not heard the man. Without a glance in his direction, she walked directly to Judith.

"Don't you worry, Miss. That goose can't do you no real harm. You come with me to the cookhouse, and I'll give you a cool glass of buttermilk."

Judith gave a shuddering sigh and looked toward at her father. When he gave a curt nod, she began to walk in the direction of the cookhouse with Sally bringing up the rear.

Mr. Talcott turned swiftly toward Sophia. "When I move into this place, the first thing I'll do is wring that goose's neck. Roast goose will be my very first meal."

Sophia hugged China Boy close. Not if I can help it, she thought. Swallowing her anger, she said, "The goose is merely guarding his nest, Mr. Talcott." She glanced toward the house to see her mother standing in the doorway. "I believe my mother can see you now."

Cradling the 20-pound goose in her arms, Sophia hurried to the coop, muttering to China Boy as she walked.

"Some people have no manners, snooping around another's place. Who does that Judith Talcott think she is? You have every right to protect your family. And so do I. Don't you worry. I won't let that odious man get his fingers around your neck. I just haven't figured out how yet. But I will."

She yanked open the slatted door of the coop and lowered the goose to the dirt floor. He waddled away, waggling his tail feathers and honking softly to China Girl, who was setting on a straw nest near the back. She answered with a series of low chuckles.

"You best stay put," Sophia called after the retreating gander before slamming the iron bolt shut.

It seems as if those people can do nothing but cause trouble, she thought. Someone ought to take the pig man down a peg or two. Mother may have insisted that I mind my manners with Mr. Talcott, but she never once said I must be polite to his daughter.

Scowling, Sophia veered toward the cookhouse. Judith needed to be taught a thing or two.

8

An Unlikely Alliance

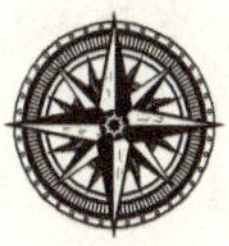

Judith was sitting on the log bench outside the cookhouse. She had straightened her bonnet and retied the veil but failed to tuck dark strands of hair, loosened during her skirmish with the goose, back into the bun coiled at the back of her head. Every so often she would raise the hem of her gray frock slightly, apparently looking for rips in her stockings and bruises along her shins. As Sophia neared, she straightened her skirt and folded her gloved hands primly in her lap.

She's as thin as smoke, Sophia thought, stopping in front of the unwanted visitor.

"Your goose tore my stocking."

"Maybe you'll think twice before putting your nose where it doesn't belong," Sophia snapped back. "Have you recovered? Your throat must be sore from all that screaming."

"Sorry I caused such a ruckus." Judith lowered her gaze. Surprisingly, she sounded remorseful.

Sophia hadn't expected an apology. Her expression softened slightly as she gave Judith a closer look. The delicate veil sewn to the brim of Judith's gray bonnet shadowed her face. Even so, Sophia could see two thick sausage curls curtaining Judith's cheeks. She'd probably be pretty if she'd pull that hair back, Sophia thought. She may wear the latest fashion in bonnets and dresses but that's as far as it goes. Faith could teach her a thing or two about making herself look attractive.

Judith looked up. Her dark brown eyes, fringed with thick dark lashes, peered earnestly at Sophia through the thin veil.

"I just wanted to look around, maybe get a peek at your father's famous mare," Judith said, eyes downward. "My father talks about that horse all the time. I swear he knows her bloodlines better than mine. If I didn't know better, I'd say he bought this old place just to own that horse." She sounded as if she found her statement oddly amusing.

"That's ridiculous. Pearl is not for sale." Sophia's voice took on a hard edge. "Father would never do that. Why, selling Pearl would be the same as selling a daughter."

"Fathers have been known to sell daughters. Not outright, perhaps, but by arrangement." Judith's voice was cold.

"Not *my* father."

"Maybe not, but I wouldn't bet on him keeping that horse. You see, my pa always gets what he wants. This plantation will be his soon. He's been talking about owning it for years."

"Seems to me you Talcotts are no better than pirates, taking whatever strikes your fancy." Sophia clenched her fists. Oh, how she wanted to slap that superior look off Judith's face.

Judith's eyes narrowed. "Look who's talking!" Her tone had turned scornful. "Everyone knows your grandsire was a pirate."

"Fiddlesticks! He was a privateer, fighting for American independence. Any educated person knows that!"

"Pirate, privateer, what's the difference. Seems to me your grandsire was nothing more than a common thief, one who stooped to stealing and butchering hogs." Judith jumped to her feet, almost treading on Sophia's toes.

Sophia glared at her, refusing to move. "First, there is a big difference," she snapped. "A pirate is a lawless cutthroat. A privateer is an honorable ship's captain fighting for his country. Second, you're putting blame where it doesn't belong." She took a deep breath, willing herself calm.

Then, as if she was speaking to an ignorant child, Sophia began to talk more slowly, enunciating every word. It was an old argument, one told and retold over the years. "*Your* grandsire was warned many times not to let his hogs root in our tobacco fields. That boar was trespassing. I'd say he got what was coming to him."

"Humph. I'd say *your* grandsire got what was coming to *him*. If you ask my pa, he'll tell you that Captain Records got off easy with just a fine."

"A fine of 900 pounds of tobacco. His whole crop! No pig, even a so-called prize boar, is worth that much." Sophia glared at Judith.

"Thieves pay a higher price. Now, step aside. You are blocking my way." Judith tried to push past Sophia. "One thing is for sure. Your brother James was a much nicer person than you."

"And how would you know?" Sophia scowled.

"Know what?"

"Know that James was nicer? Or anything about him." Sophia said. Her unspoken accusation—liar—hung in the air between them. There was no way that this dreadful girl could know her brother. He never would exchange pleasantries with a Talcott. But if he had, surely, he would have said so.

"We met by accident more than a year ago," Judith said. "I was riding through the woods between our plantations, and James was hunting a fox. He stepped out from some brush, startling my horse. I fell off."

She smiled. It was easy to see that she enjoyed the memory. "He was quite the gentleman," she said. "He caught my bay and brought him back. After he helped me mount, he continued to hold the reins. He kept apologizing."

"Really," Sophia said, her tone implying the opposite.

"He didn't know I was a Talcott. I didn't know he was a Records. Not at first. He said he hoped he'd be in the woods next time I fell, and then he actually doffed his hat. He was so proud of that hat." She hesitated. "He complimented me," Judith added softly. "Called me a comely lass."

"Only in your imagination. You never met him."

"But I did and we became friends. That first day, I told him I rode out most afternoons and that I'd come this way again tomorrow. The next day, he was there, leaning against an old oak. After that, we started meeting by the oak at least once a week. It wasn't until our third encounter that we discovered we were supposed to be enemies. We decided to keep our friendship secret."

"So you say." Sophia turned to leave.

Judith took hold of her arm, startling her. "Please, don't be angry. The reason I came today was not to look at your father's horse. I came to tell you I was sorry about James. I wanted to come sooner, but Pa wouldn't let me visit. Now that Pa is buying Records Landing—that's what you call this place, isn't it—I wanted to come and tell you I would make sure his grave was honored." She smiled sadly. "It seems I know a lot about tending graves."

"You have been misinformed. There is no grave for James. He is merely missing. There is no body to bury."

Sophia sank down on the bench, drained of energy. This was the second time today a Talcott had declared James dead. Such assertions raised doubts. How could she be so sure James had survived the storm?

As though she understood, Judith joined Sophia on the bench. Neither girl spoke. Sophia listened to the muffled clank of pans coming from the cookhouse and smelled the rich aroma of something spicy baking. A few sparrows searched the nearby ground for stray seeds, while overhead a red bird sang from his perch in the ancient magnolia tree.

After a minute, Judith asked, "You think James could be living?" She sounded eager for reassurance.

"Perhaps. One can only hope." Sophia shrugged. "Hope can be cruel. I never know if I should cry or sing."

"Life itself can be cruel," Judith said. "Less than a year ago, Mama called me her beauty; my two brothers teased me unmercifully, said I was taking on airs. They would strut around with a parasol pretending to be me. I used to get angry. Now I wish they would tease me. Only they died, Mama too. All dead from smallpox."

"Forgive me. I didn't realize it was your family." Sophia clutched the bench so hard her knuckles whitened. Why didn't Father tell me, she wondered, even though she knew her parents tried to shield her from frightening news. She had heard rumors in Snow Hill about a family infected with smallpox. When she had asked Father, he had said in a somber tone that the rumors were true. Except, he never named the family, saying only that she would be safe. She had been vaccinated whereas the other family had not. Three years ago, Father had insisted everyone in the household be inoculated as soon as he had learned about a vaccine. It had taken a lot of persuading before Mother agreed to the plan. It was scary. Each of them had developed a small fever and a bit of a rash but recovered quickly.

Looking over at Judith now, Sophia felt a wave of compassion. She wanted to apologize for being discourteous. Instead, she stayed mute, searching for the right words.

Judith stared down at her gloved hands. "My pa was away on a trip to England. Mother fell ill first, then my brothers," she said, almost whispering. "It was in midsummer, four months after I had met your brother. "

She turned to stare at Sophia as if daring her to say those meetings never happened. When Sophia murmured her sympathy, Judith took a deep breath and then continued, her voice devoid of emotion.

"My mother first complained of a fierce headache. Before long she was burning with fever. I nursed her as best I knew how. Our slave Kisha, she'd been infected as a child, helped. A week later Mother was covered with this hideous rash. Both my brothers developed the fever, then days later the pustules. Kisha and I did our best," she said, twisting her entwined fingers back and forth. "But we couldn't save them. Ben, our barn nigra, dug their graves and I buried them, even though by then I had a headache and fever. Then I developed the horrible rash. All I remember is shaking with cold and then burning with fever. Kisha nursed me through. By the time my pa showed up, driving that fancy carriage you see, I had recovered enough to greet him with the terrible news."

Sophia shook her head sadly. "I am so sorry for you," she murmured then frowned. "Why didn't Kisha run to Oriole for help."

"My family has no dealings with that woman."

As if to soften her sharp retort, Judith reached over to touch Sophia's arm. "I appreciate your sympathy, though," she said. "I'm all cried out now. After all, my mother and brothers are with the Lord in Heaven, and that is a far better place. James said as much. You see, after I was well and strong enough to ride again, I continued to meet your brother until…" Her voice trailed off.

"He was kind," she said after a minute. "I wish he hadn't left. But he had other plans."

"What did he tell you?" Sophia said, suddenly hopeful Judith might know something useful.

Just then Sally appeared at the cookhouse door. "I thought you young ladies might eat some of my molasses cookies," she said and approached, carrying a tin plate heaped with brown cookies glistening with sugar crystals.

Judith took one. "Still warm from the oven," she said and smiled her thanks.

"More buttermilk?" Sally asked, and when Judith shook her head, the cook picked up the empty glass speckled with tiny buttery globs. She left the plate of cookies on the bench between the two girls.

"Can you answer a question for me?" Sophia asked, picking up a cookie. "Why is your father so intent on owning this house? What's wrong with yours?"

Judith slumped and began fiddling with her bonnet strings. "Our house is not as fine as yours, a telescope house with rooms added as the family grew," she said. "Besides, Pa wants land on the river."

Judith lowered her voice. "Pa told me the house and the orchards will be mine. Great House is to be my dowry. It is all arranged. I am to marry a Mr. Dowling. But don't say anything. Please. The marriage banns won't be posted in church until this fall."

"You? Mistress of this house? You can't be much older than me." Sophia fell silent. Judith looked miserable. Faith been overjoyed when she told Sophia her news earlier.

"Why didn't you refuse?"

"Now that is a silly question," Judith muttered. "A girl's got no say in who she's going to marry. Pa seems pleased with the bargain. And, as he made very clear to me, my filial duty, his words, is to agree."

She made a face as if tasting something foul. "Mr. Dowling is older, in his thirties. He's a widower with two young children to raise," she said. "He needs a wife to tend them. With me married, Pa will be shed of me."

"Is that what you think?"

"It's what I know. He told me that his parental duty, again his words, is to provide for me until marriage. I have no illusions. No handsome planter's son will come knocking on our door asking to court me."

Sophia started to protest but Judith raised her hand.

"Look at me." Judith untied the wide gauze ribbons that held her bonnet in place and took off her hat. In the bright March sunlight,

Sophia saw that the skin along Judith's cheeks and forehead was discolored and deeply pitted.

"Pretty, huh?" Judith tugged at a lace glove, pulling it off. "I've got pox scars all over, even on my hands."

"Oh. I am so sorry," Sophia stammered.

"Don't be." Judith snapped as if stung by Sophia's pity. "At least my father has enough money to buy me a husband," she said with a haughty toss of her head before adding in a more sober tone, "I only hope I can manage a household as ably as your mother. Your slave seems so agreeable and such a good cook." Judith reached for another cookie.

"We have no slaves," Sophia said for the second time today. "Sally is a free woman. Father says no person can own another, that slavery is an abomination. When we need workers, we hire men from Marshtown."

"The rumors are true then. You are Abolitionists!" Judith said, her tone incredulous. "No wonder your father had to sell. Everybody knows a plantation can't make a profit without darkies."

"That's not true. Good farming practices bring profits, not slaves. No man should own another."

"Humph," Judith said with contempt. "Even the Bible says that the black man was born to be a slave."

"The Bible says no such thing," Sophia snapped, rising to her feet. "Can't you or your daddy read?"

"I reckon we can read as well as most. Maybe not as well as you with all your fancy learning. Pa says it's unnatural for girls to be schooled like boys. Says it gives them lofty ideas, makes them think they're as smart as men." Judith smoothed her bonnet's feathery plume before replacing the hat on her head and retying the ribbons.

"You best not be bringing slaves here. Grandsire will haunt you!"

"I'm not afraid of haunts," Judith said. "I am more afraid of stirring up trouble." She stood and, taking a deep breath, faced Sophia.

"Please," she said in a less heated tone, "I didn't come here to argue. I just wanted to talk to you about James. There's no need to tell your family about my friendship with him. Your parents might think him disloyal. Don't hurt your brother."

Sophia was considering her response when Willie rushed out of the barn shrieking with laughter and clutching the carriage hat. Nathan was in close pursuit.

"Give it back or I'll scalp you."

"No!" Willie kept running until he reached Sophia.

"Hide it," he panted, handing her the hat.

Without blinking, Sophia took it and held it behind her back.

"I don't believe it," Judith said. "Isn't that James's hat?"

"It's on loan to me," Nathan said as he approached the bench. "And," he added, "I want it back."

"I ain't got it." Willie said, now eyeing the cookies. He took two and held one out to Nathan.

"Which is it? A cookie or the hat?" Sophia asked, bringing the hat forward.

Nathan grinned. "Both," he said.

Taking the cookie with one hand, he reached for the hat with the other but at the last minute, Sophia pulled it away.

Shaking his head in mock exasperation, Nathan extended his hand again.

"If you please."

"Since you ask so nicely, of course." Sophia gave him the hat, which he promptly put on Willie's head. It slid down, covering Willie's eyes and ears. Everyone laughed. Even Judith.

Still grinning, Nathan took a hold of Willie's shoulders and turned him toward the barn. "We have work to finish, *Heleni*."

"Wait," Sophia said, catching hold of Willie's hand. "I do believe my manners are slipping," she said to Judith. "Let me introduce these ruffians. Meet, my brother William, the thief, and Mr. Nathan Harkness, the injured party."

Judith drew back as if to avoid any scrutiny.

"Hello," she said, addressing Willie before turning toward Nathan. Speaking in a less friendly tone, she asked, "*Heleni*, what kind of word is that?"

"It's Shawnee." Nathan said. "It means *man*. In Ohio, folks know what it means."

"Nathan is from Ohio." Sophia was quick to explain. "He is helping us out with chores on the plantation right now."

"I see." Judith's tone implied dismissal.

Nathan and Wille took the hint and, well supplied with cookies, walked back toward the barn.

"Your barn boy seems nice enough," Judith said, "although I am surprised you treat him as an equal. I am not used to being introduced to servants."

Before Sophia could challenge her, Judith hurried on to say, "Willie is darling, though. He reminds me of my youngest brother. Hal was mischievous, too. Full of energy." She paused and took a few faltering steps back to the bench. Sophia sat down beside her, wishing there was something she could say that could ease Judith's grief.

Lifting her veil, Judith dabbed at her cheeks. "My mama had such dreams for my brothers. Of course, my family believes . . ."

She breathed in sharply and then said with vehemence, "I mean Pa believes. He thinks England will reclaim the colonies. Mama thought so, too. After all, her father had been a titled Englishman. She wanted her boys to be among the gentry here. To ride fast horses, to live in grand houses, and to control vast estates. Others have done it. As for Pa, he was intent on making enough money so they could do that. He was not satisfied to remain a middling farmer like your family."

"And what about you? What did your mama dream for you?" Sophia asked, shrugging off Judith's arrogant remark.

Judith looked down at her gloved hands. "To marry well and to raise fat, healthy babies." She sighed and plucked at her damp handkerchief. "That's not going to happen, is it?"

She shook some crumbs from her skirt but instead of getting up to leave, as Sophia assumed, Judith lifted her veil to give Sophia an imploring look.

"I have no one to talk to anymore," she said. "No one who will listen and care. Not like your brother did." She reached for Sophia's hand as if seeking her friendship.

When Sophia didn't pull her hand away, Judith continued, "What I have to say, I have never told anyone, not even James. I beg you to never speak it to anyone, not to your sister or to your mother, not to another living soul."

Sophia nodded, even as she thought wearily, another secret. Secrets can weigh a person down, especially dark ones.

"When Pa came home and found Mama dead," Judith began, "he stormed about the house, cursing God for taking away everyone he ever loved. The one honest thing about Pa has always been his love for Mama. He had brought home a trunkful of new gowns from London. As soon as he got off the ship in Baltimore, he purchased that team of horses and that fancy carriage you see in the drive to surprise her. So, when he came home to discover that smallpox had killed what he loved most, he was inconsolable, shouting, saying that everything he had ever done, he had done for Mama, and now she was gone. He turned on our house slave Kisha, blaming her for letting Mama die. In the next instant, he ordered us to gather up everything, anything where the disease could be lurking—the bedclothes, the feather beds, Mama's dresses, the boys' shirts and britches, my gowns, my shifts even my stockings. He burned them outside on the front lawn. The stench of the feathers was stifling. Next, he ordered Kisha and Ben to scrub the house with lye soap. When he was satisfied with their work, he went inside and drank peach brandy until he could not stand."

As Judith spoke, she seemed to fade until she was no more substantial than a shadow. Now she gripped Sophia's hand even harder.

"Later that night, he had Kisha wake me. I stood before him in my new nightshift, one that Pa had bought for Mama. Pa was sprawled in his chair, his silver cup in hand. He told Kisha to pin up my hair and told me to lower my shift. Then he had me turn this way and that while he appraised me as if I were a slave on the auction block. He said my beauty was ruined, that my skin was so pitted that no man would want to look at me, let alone marry me unless he was desperate for money. He hurled his cup against the hearth. And then he wept."

Judith voice showed no emotion. If she hadn't been squeezing Sophia's hand so hard that it ached, Sophia would have thought Judith was reciting her catechism.

"Oh my God," Sophia whispered. "No father should . . ."

Touching Sophia's lips with a gloved finger, Judith hushed her,

"He was drunk," she said. "He has tried to make amends in his way. See, I wear my mother's fine clothes now, the ones he brought from England. They were never brought into the house until it was scrubbed clean. And he made Kisha a gift to me. Oh, don't look so horrified. You might find owning a personal servant pleasant. Someone to do your hair and bring you breakfast on a tray." She shrugged. "Now Pa has bought me a husband."

Sophia was silent. She needed time to think. That a father should act in such a hurtful, disrespectful manner was unimaginable to her. She wanted to tell Judith to rebel. But she had seen Judith cringe earlier and suspected Mr. Talcott was not reluctant to raise his hand to anyone who defied him.

As if he knew they were talking about him, Judith's father opened the cook's door.

"Judith!"

The girl dropped Sophia's hand and jumped to her feet. "Yes, Pa."

"Say goodbye to your little friend. We'll be leaving." He smiled at Sophia. It was a false smile, lacking in cordiality. Without waiting for a reply, he closed the door.

"I guess this is goodbye," Sophia said, realizing as she rose to stand beside Judith that she found this Talcott likeable. "I hope you will be happier than you imagine you will be."

"Perhaps," Judith said and smiled. "Please, walk with me. I have something to give you."

Side by side, they approached the shiny black carriage.

Judith opened the door. "Come sit with me," she said and pulled Sophia with her into the carriage.

"More secrets?" Sophia asked.

"Here," Judith thrust a book bound in green leather at her. The book looked familiar.

"I wanted to return this," Judith said. "James gave it to me the last time we met. He said I should read it because he could be another Robinson Crusoe. I didn't understand his meaning. James had told me after I read the book, I would understand that sometimes leaving a place was better than staying, no matter what might happen, even if meant being a castaway on a remote island for many years."

Sophia ran her hand over the book's smooth leather binding, remembering how James had loved the story. James, the boy who hated to read thick books, had read this one aloud to her and Faith. Then he had read again silently when he should have been studying. He was always quoting Robinson Crusoe and had acted out some of the island scenes. She was his Man Friday.

"I read the book twice," Judith continued. "Once when he lent it to me and once after I heard about the storm. I like to think he's on an island somewhere."

"Perhaps that's true," Sophia said, preparing to leave.

"Wait." Judith looked nervously out the small window. "There is something you should know."

Sophia turned back, puzzled.

"My Pa hates the folks in Marshtown."

"Why are you telling me this?"

"Because James was my friend. After I recovered from the pox and started riding again. I saw him. When I tried to hide my face, he told I should show my face proudly. My scars were proof I could survive. Sometimes when we met, we talked about our families. He was so proud of you; he said you were probably the smartest girl in Maryland. He even suggested I go see Oriole. He thought she had a salve that would diminish my scars. I've never dared go there. My father calls her a black witch and has forbidden me to step foot in Marshtown."

"She's not a witch. She was taught how to heal people. I could ask her for a salve."

"I'm not asking you to do that. I am warning you," she said, once again peering out the window. "I told you Pa drinks most evenings. Sometimes when he's in his cups, he rambles on about Marshtown. He suspects it was built on Records land, soon to be our land. He plans to drive off Oriole and her kind. Free nigras are a bad influence on slaves. He said if he can't chase them out, he'll find another way."

Judith leaned over Sophia to open the door. "You best go. Pa's coming. Your mama, too."

Sophia stepped down, out of the carriage.

"Just remember," Judith said in a whisper edged in steel. "Don't breathe a word of this to your family. You may be leaving Maryland but Pa could still make trouble. You should warn those Marshtown darkies, but if you say anything to your father or your uncles, I'll say you made it up. That it's all a lie."

Sophia had no reply. She stared at Judith, sitting primly with her bonnet and veil tied in place. A Talcott after all, Sophia thought. Friendly one minute, mean the next. Whatever had possessed her brother to befriend a Talcott?

As Mother and Mr. Talcott neared, Sophia hid the book in the folds of her skirt. Judith, all smiles, stepped out to be introduced and while Mother was expressing her sympathies to Judith, saying how sorry she was to learn about the terrible sickness and its dreadful cost, Sophia's mind kept rehashing Judith's warnings.

The parting of the Talcotts and the Records seemed pleasant enough until Mr. Talcott told Mother, he would be returning soon to speak to Father.

"It seems there are some matters that need to be settled, including my ownership of the white mare," he said. His words were clipped, his tone icy.

"I'm sure it's all a misunderstanding," Mother replied smoothly.

Extending her hand to Judith, she added, "Please do come again soon. I would be delighted to show you around. I understand you will be in charge of the household. Sally Teague, our housekeeper and cook, comes daily. You would be wise to retain her services. This little plantation runs smoothly because of her."

Sophia looked at Judith wondering how she would respond. Would she say Talcotts had no use for free black folk. Judith said nothing.

Sophia excused herself, and left, hugging *The Life and Strange Surprizing Adventures of Robinson Crusoe* close to her chest. She had a lot to think about.

9

The River Trail

The next morning, Faith shook Sophia awake as the hall clock was striking seven. "You are about to miss breakfast. I don't know how you could oversleep on the most important day of my life."

For a moment Sophia couldn't remember why this day was special. Then it all came rushing back: Faith's precious Mr. Mueller was coming to ask Father for permission to marry his daughter.

"Sorry," Sophia mumbled.

"You'd better hurry. Father gets impatient when we're late, and he must be in the best of moods today."

Sophia rolled out of bed and stumbled to the washbasin to splash the sleep from her eyes. She had stayed awake long past midnight, watching the pale quarter moon make its way across the sky while her thoughts contended in an endless tug of war.

The moon, the sun, even my family—almost everything moves west, she reasoned and, in the night, felt the pull to leave Maryland as she conjured up images of riding in a covered wagon, seeing real mountains, and floating down the mysterious Ohio River on a flat boat. She envisioned herself meeting every challenge of the wilderness trail, even pumas. Sophia wanted to be a pioneer.

Still, Judith's warning about Marshtown kept pulling her back. Even though Baltimore was many miles away, word of trouble would reach her faster there than if she were in Ohio. Surely, Uncle William could intervene. If she stayed behind, she would study at the academy she had heard so much about. And what about James? How could her parents abandon him? Back and forth those thoughts ranged, keeping sleep at bay.

"Sorry, sorry," she muttered to Faith. "I'll be down in a jiffy."

Minutes later, after Sally had rung the little silver bell calling the family to breakfast, Sophia hurried downstairs and slipped into her chair. Mother smiled. Father stood to say grace. The day had begun.

There was no idle chatter around the table today. Father and Nathan were discussing the number of barrels needed for packing household items. Faith was staring dreamily into space while Mother softly chastised Willie, who had already wolfed down his porridge and two buttermilk biscuits and was now eyeing Faith's untouched oatmeal. Sophia ate quickly, hoping to finish the meal without notice and be on her way.

No one seemed aware that she had missed her morning chores until Faith said, "You better thank your lucky stars for Mr. Harkness, Sophia. He let the chickens out of the coop and collected their eggs this morning." Faith had a faintly superior smirk on her face, as if trying to point out that she was the more responsible daughter. She didn't point out that Nathan had also milked Ginger.

Ignoring her and looking right at Nathan, Sophia mouthed the words, "Thank you."

Mother looked up. "Are you ill, Sophia? Generally, you are the early riser."

"No, no. Just had a hard time going to sleep last night."

"Oh?" Mother wrinkled her forehead.

Sophia squirmed. She had given her word never to tell her family about Mr. Talcott's plan. Still, she believed the threat was real. Oriole had to be told.

"May I be excused? I'll help Sally with the dishes. Then I'm off to see Oriole." Sophia pushed back her chair.

"Not so fast, young lady," Father said. "I want you to accompany Mr. Harkness to Snow Hill, show him the way to the cooper's shop."

"Oriole is expecting me, Father."

"You are spending too much time in Marshtown, "Mother said.

"Oriole's teaching me just as the Widow taught her. I have a small book filled with sketches of plants and how to use them as cures."

"You needn't bother. Mr. Franklin wrote a small book on how to cure ailments. I have found it quite helpful."

Sophia groaned inwardly. Apparently, there was no end to Benjamin Franklin's advice.

"I'll go with Mr. Harkness," Willie sang out.

"Don't talk with your mouth full," Mother said.

Sophia looked toward Nathan and thought he looked disappointed, as if he would miss her company. For a second, she was tempted to change her plans.

With an affable shrug, Father agreed. Nathan and Willie would drive the wagon to Snow Hill. Sophia would walk to Marshtown.

"I assume you will be spending some of your time with the children," Mother said. "If certain planters knew you were teaching those young ones their letters, there could be trouble. Sometimes Sally worries. As do I."

"Sally's children are free. The law only forbids slaves from learning to read and write," Sophia said crossly.

"Law or no law, many Marylanders act as if all people of color are slaves," Father said.

"Those people are just plain wrong!" Sophia pushed back her chair and began to gather the dishes, noisily stacking them on a wooden tray.

Walking out the side door, she saw that Sally had already lugged two steaming pots of water from the hearth to the weathered table outside the cookhouse.

"Bless you, Miss Phee. I surely could use a hand. If you'd just scrape any leftovers into the slop bucket, I'll get started." Sally plunged her hands into the soapy water. After washing each dish, she gently laid it in the pot of rinse water.

For a while the two of them worked in silence, Sally washing and rinsing, Sophia drying and stacking. Once in a while Sally would hum a little.

Finally, she said, "Is something bothering you, Honey?"

Sophia nodded. Giving Sally a sideways glance, she said, "I have to warn you about something, but you must not tell my parents. That would make things worse."

Sally stopped washing and turned her head to look Sophia straight in the eye. "Now, that's worrisome."

"Mr. Talcott is a dangerous man, Sally. Judith Talcott told me Marshtown won't be safe after we leave. You, the children, Oriole, all of you should come with us to Ohio."

"Don't you worry. You aren't telling me something I don't already know. That man is as treacherous as a wild boar. As for going to Ohio, I won't say that I haven't been tempted, Miss Phee. I don't know how your Mama is going to manage without me, but I am staying put."

When Sophia started to argue, Sally held up her palm.

"No, I will stay a Marylander. Have you forgotten? My husband is on a whaler for another year, He'll come home and then before long he'll go out again. The sea is in his blood." She shook her head as if to say what are you going to do with a man like that. "No, this place suits us best. As for my mama, wild horses couldn't move her."

"Mr. Talcott doesn't want free colored around this place."

"Honey, say no more. We colored know that being free has its problems. And you telling me about him ain't going to change nothing."

"But . . ."

"No, 'buts.' Now you run along. I can finish up here. I 'spect you have things to do. Just take the slops and feed the hog."

"But . . ."

Sally covered her ears with her soapy hands.

Sophia was halfway to the hog pen when Sally called out, "Remember, Miss Phee, hogs can be just as dangerous as those Talcotts. Especially hungry hogs. Don't you go in that pen! Pour the slop into the trough from outside the fence."

"As always," Sophia called back, annoyed that Sally was telling her something she already knew. She shrugged. And maybe Sally does know a thing or two about Mr. Talcott, she thought. I just hope she doesn't underestimate the trouble that is sure to come.

It was nearly nine o'clock by the time Sophia was ready to leave. Nathan and Willie were in the yard. King George was harnessed to the wagon and Nathan was boosting Willie up to the board seat just as Sophia came around from the front of the house.

"Wait," she called. "Father wrote down directions." She waved a piece of paper in their direction and hurried over. She handed the folded piece of paper to Nathan, who took it and tucked it into the waistband of his britches.

"Aren't you going to read it? You might have questions."

Nathan shrugged. "I'll figure it out." He swung himself up and onto the seat. "You'd best get going. You shouldn't waste your time talking to me." He sounded cool, disinterested.

"You best get going as well," she snapped, stung by his manner. Sometimes he was friendly, like on the ride home last week from Oriole's, and sometimes aloof, like now.

Nathan tipped his hat.

Turning toward the river, Sophia ignored him, pretending interest in a flat, smooth stone she spotted on the ground. It was a perfect skipper. Picking it up, she tossed it skyward a few times to determine its weight before walking out onto the pier. Behind her she heard Nathan cluck to the mule, then the clop of hooves and the rumble of wagon wheels. She didn't turn to wave goodbye. Instead, with a practiced snap of her wrist, she tossed the stone so that it skipped across the water eleven times before sinking. It was her best number. She grinned and turned to share her triumph but the yard was empty.

Gathering her skirts in her left hand, she hurried off the pier to make her way along the river's marshy edge until she came to a thick clump of dogwood. Carefully picking her way through the red-stemmed shrubs, she headed toward firmer ground.

The land she was walking on now looked the same as it had for hundreds of years. Grandsire had insisted that no one take an axe or spade to it.

He had told his family never to walk there, saying the land along the river was too dangerous. Quicksand sometimes lay hidden beneath fallen leaves. As far as Sophia knew, she and James were the only ones to disregard his warning. As usual, James had talked her into exploring this strip of wilderness.

We must have been about twelve, she thought, when we discovered the ancient trail. Looking around now, she saw a faint dip in the forest floor. A beech tree with a bowed trunk grew beside it. In the distance there was a similarly shaped beech; these strangely shaped trees marked a trail all the way to the great swamp. At least, that is what James claimed, saying he once walked the trail all the way. She wondered if he walked it alone. She wouldn't put it past him.

James never had second thoughts about embarking on dangerous escapades, Sophia thought with a wry smile, remembering his excitement when they first stumbled across the trail. Its discovery had been the perfect antidote for boredom. Neither she nor James had wanted to read the work their tutor had assigned. Snapping his book shut, James declared there was no reason to waste a pleasant day learning about the exploits of the ancient Greeks. Instead, they should do some real exploring. Sophia remembered agreeing with very little coaxing.

When they came across what appeared to be a foot path that day, James looked around cautiously. Even then she wondered if he had discovered it earlier and led her to it on purpose. He seemed to know a lot about it.

"This trail was used by savages," he whispered. "Some might still be here or, worse, smugglers or thieves. You never know."

James has always been a terrible tease, Sophia thought as she walked along the path. She remembered that she had given him a hard push that day, accusing him of making up stories just to scare her. He, of course, pushed her back, saying she was the storyteller, always trying to make things sound more exciting than they really were.

"And you don't?"

James had laughed.

Sophia sighed. Even now, her family accused her of having a wild imagination. It was a hard reputation to live down. She scuffed at damp leaves covering the trail. Even if I dared to tell Father about Mr. Talcott's plans, Father would think I was exaggerating. But if James were here to tell him, Father would take the threat seriously. No one had ever accused her twin of being fanciful, just lazy. He wasn't lazy though. Most of time he was just daydreaming about ships and sea battles or scouting the river for outlaws. He was smart about the things that mattered to him, like the history of Maryland and its early inhabitants.

"I know about these crooked trees," James had told her when they first saw them. "The Nanticoke tribe marked trails by using leather straps to tie down saplings growing near the path. Unable to grow straight, the trees became trail markers."

"See," he had said, pointing out a line of the strangely bent trees, spaced about an eighth of a mile apart. "That's a trail! Let's follow it. You never know what you'll find. If we look hard enough, we could find arrowheads."

He started off without waiting for her.

Sophia had been content to amble along the trail, more interested in finding wildflowers than arrowheads. Clumps of spring beauties had been blooming. Looking around now, she saw to her delight that small bursts of purple flowers dotted the forest floor; and she paused to pick a bouquet to bring to Oriole. Wrapping the flowers in wet leaves, she carefully tucked them into her scarred leather haversack, careful not to crush the blossoms.

I am glad I came this way, she thought. Spring always shows up along the river first.

"Stop fooling yourself, Sophia."

In her mind, she heard Grandsire's voice as clearly as if he were walking beside her. "You came here to sort things out."

Unconsciously, she nodded. It's true, she thought. Since when did I become the keeper of secrets? Faith's stolen kisses—that's an easy one to keep, after all she will be betrothed soon. But Judith's? That's a fearsome secret. Truly, it's more of a threat. I need to warn Oriole. Sally never will. I don't think Sally will have a second thought about the Talcotts coming to live at Records Landing. Until it's too late. Which brings me to the third secret, the one Grandsire entrusted me to keep. Sometimes a promise needs to be broken if it will keep the people you love safe. I have to go back to the place where that promise was made.

The land rose gradually until Sophia found herself walking along a high bank. She now had a good view of the Pocomoke. The river, which had been flowing to the south, angled west here. Below her, in the water, two large cypress trees, their smooth grey trunks skirted by bushes, grew several feet from the bank. They were far enough apart that a man could moor a dinghy there.

Those trees were landmarks Sophia knew well. She stopped, looked furtively around, then waited, listening for a rustle of leaves or the snap of a dead branch that would signal someone else was nearby. All she heard was blackbirds trilling their spring song and sparrows scuffling in the leaves. Still, she waited.

Sophia knew Grandsire had been right about the woods being a dangerous place. Records Landing was about thirty miles downstream from the Great Cypress Swamp, a place where Father, Uncle Caleb, and James sometimes went hunting. According to James, the river began in the swamp, which was a maze of streams fed by springs. The stream wound through peat bogs, cattails, marsh grass, and a forest of cypress. There were footpaths on the many small islands but solid ground often turned to quick mud. A person had to have his wits about him to survive not only the marsh but also the cottonmouths and, in the summer, hordes of mosquitoes. Even so, James had sworn, some folks lived there, most hiding from the law.

"They don't always stay," he had said. "Some come down river."

Remembering his words, Sophia felt a shiver of fear along her spine. The silence and isolation along this forgotten trail now felt oppressive, making it hard to breathe.

A shadow slid across the ground in front of her, making her jump. A bald eagle soared overhead. As Sophia watched, the bird abruptly folded its wings and plunged feet first into the river. Just as quickly the eagle rose, its great wings beating the air, a fish caught in its talons. The bird's harsh cry echoed along the river.

Sophia felt another tremor of fear. Did I made a mistake coming here? This time Grandsire is not waiting for me. If I fall or become trapped, no one will find me. She hesitated, looked back, then squared her shoulders and walked to the edge of the bluff.

10

Grandsire's Secret

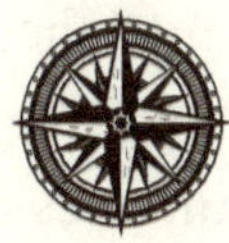

Sophia stood staring at the river.

"I'm here, Grandsire," she whispered.

Bunching up her skirts, she picked her way down from the bluff. The steep descent was a tangle of downed trees, exposed roots, and ropelike vines. Two feet from the river, she stopped. The earth was soft here; a person would leave tracks. She saw none. No one had come snooping around, at least not since the last rain.

Even though the other side of the river was just as wild, she knew she couldn't linger. A boat or canoe could come by at any time. How many times had Grandsire told her to keep this place secret? Too many times to count, she thought, answering her own question.

At the river's edge, a mound of twigs and cattail stems poked up above the amber water. A faint odor of musk told her the den was occupied. Muskrats must find this a good place to raise a family undisturbed, she thought, smiling. It was as secluded as it had been when she first came here three years ago.

That day, a water bird's nest built in a small tree beside the river below had caught her eye. Sophia had started down the bluff to get a closer look, tripped on a root, and gone sprawling, tumbling all the way to the river's edge. The fall knocked the breath out of her, making it impossible to shout for help. Besides, who would hear her? James was far ahead.

Still gasping for air, she had grasped a sturdy Virginia creeper vine and pulled herself to her feet. Holding to the vine, hand over hand she began to clamber up the steep slope. She had gone only a few feet when the plant became entangled in what appeared to be a large mat of vines. Thick tendrils twined themselves around nautical ropes fashioned into a net. What looked like rigging used on sailing ships had been turned into a curtain of vines meant to conceal.

Cautiously, Sophia had lifted up a corner of the curtain. Behind it she saw a cave, probably carved out by the river years ago. All of James's stories about the Great Swamp had immediately popped into her head. It could be a robber's lair. Clearly, someone didn't want this cave found. She told herself that any sensible person would turn away, crawl back up the slope. Instead, she remained rooted, staring at the wide opening. This cave might have been used by the Nanticoke, she speculated. One little peek inside wouldn't hurt. And, maybe, just maybe, there were arrowheads. Wouldn't that surprise James?

Pulling the curtain to one side, Sophia had stepped inside. The dark cave was deep and she felt a shiver of fear. Black widow spiders spun their ragged webs in such dark places. Cottonmouths often denned up in caves. Praying no such poisonous creatures lived here, Sophia inched her way toward a wall. The leafy curtain flopped back, blocking out the light.

"Oh, no," Sophia groaned loudly.

Before she could utter another word, a large hand grasped her shoulder, while the other pressed against her mouth.

"Be still," a familiar voice had whispered roughly. "It is only me."

Grandsire had taken away his hand and pulled her tight against his chest.

"There, there," he kept saying while he patted her back gently as if she were a small child who had awakened from a bad dream. "I didn't mean to scare you."

When she stopped trembling, he held her back from him and raised a finger to her lips.

"Sound carries a long way on the water, he said. "You've got a good set of lungs. If you shouted out, people up and down the river could hear you. No telling what would happen next. Folks might come poking around here. This place is hidden for a reason."

Stifling a nervous giggle, Sophia leaned against him. He put his arm around her and gave her shoulder a gentle squeeze.

But that was three years ago, Sophia reminded herself as she now stepped behind the vines. Grandsire will not be here to comfort me today.

"I miss you so much, Grandsire," she whispered huskily.

Ignoring the cave's moist chill, Sophia sat down on the hard-packed dirt just inside the opening. She hugged her knees close to her chest as she waited for her eyes to adjust to the dim interior. Always cautious, she listened for a scrape, a footfall, a rustle, any sound that would tell her she was not alone, and hearing none, relaxed. The hideout remained secret. Held tight by the quiet and the darkness, she closed her eyes, remembering Grandsire, his bright blue eyes, his silvery hair and trim white beard.

When she had first stumbled upon the hideout, after she had recovered from her fright, Grandsire had explained that the cave was in fact an antechamber, the entrance to a tunnel that he and his crew had dug during the early days of the Revolution.

"The river is shaped like an oxbow here," he had said, "so this spot, where we are sitting now, is about a quarter mile from that tumbled-down log cabin."

He had squeezed her hand and whispered as one conspirator to another, "Beneath that old cabin is a root cellar. This tunnel goes to that cellar. During the Revolution, cannon, muskets, powder, lead, even food—any cargo my crew and I removed from captured British ships—we stored here. Later, in the dark of another night, we would reload those captured munitions onto American vessels for transport to Washington's army. The British never discovered us, although they sent scouts up and down the river. The day may come when the tunnel and my old storeroom will be useful again. Until then, no one must know about it, not even James."

He had squeezed her hand again, more firmly this time. "You must keep my secret."

And she had. But today she knew that was no longer possible, not if she were to keep Oriole and her family safe. She gritted her teeth in anger. Those Talcotts!

No one knows about this tunnel or what it leads to, she thought. If Mr. Talcott tries to take the land or burn the little village, this could be a place of refuge.

She leaned against the earthen wall and closed her eyes. Just for a minute, she told herself. Last night's lost hours of sleep had left her tired.

She couldn't say when she detected the faint scent of tobacco. Someone was in the tunnel. Scrambling to her feet, Sophia turned to flee.

"Phee, come back here."

Sophia stopped short. Turning back, she stared into the darkness hardly daring to breathe.

Several yards further down the tunnel she perceived a faint glow. Moving closer, she saw Grandsire sitting cross-legged on the tunnel floor, his clay pipe gripped in his teeth. Beside him, a small oil lantern shed a circle of light. He patted the earth near him, inviting her to sit. She felt numb.

"You are scaring me again."

He chuckled. "Nothing is as bad as it seems at first glance."

She folded herself down beside him, her thoughts racing: His voice sounds the same. He doesn't look any different, the same white beard, the same kind eyes. Surely, I am imagining this. You see, James, you were right. I am the fanciful one.

Grandsire cleared his throat a couple of times, as he often did before he wanted to tell her something important. He took a long pull on his pipe.

"There are a few things you need to know," he said. "You've got some backwards thinking going on. Sooner or later, everyone dies. But that's the last thing a person does. The first thing is being born. However, the most important thing a person does is striving to live a good and useful life."

"I don't know what to do. Father says I must decide where I want to be—in Baltimore with Uncle William and his family or in Ohio with my family."

"Show me your palm."

Mystified, Sophia held out her right hand, palm up. He pointed to a deep crease.

"That's your lifeline. See how it curves down below your thumb? That means you should live for many years. See the shorter lines that cross it. Those indicate turning points. Make the right decision, you will live a long time. Make a reckless or ill-advised decision, you will alter the course of your life, perhaps shorten it."

Sophia stared intently at her hand. "How will I know what's right?" Her voice quavered, knowing too well that her twin had already made a reckless choice.

"Pursue whatever brings you the greatest joy," Grandsire said. "Your father has given you the opportunity to decide your own best path."

Sophia nodded in agreement. She kept staring down at her palm as if an answer was written there. When she looked back up, her grandfather was gone. The tunnel was dark. Once again, she was sitting near the cave opening.

Sophia felt off balance. If I told Mother, Sophia decided, she would say there are no such things as ghosts, that I dreamed about Grandsire because I missed him. Perhaps, she thought. Still, if Grandsire's spirit is about, I wonder what he would do if he knew Mr. Talcott's plan to steal the land Marshtown was built on.

Oriole! Sophia stiffened. Time was slipping away. She had come here to revisit the tunnel, not to find Grandsire. With or without his wisdom, this tunnel could be a refuge only if it was safe and not on the verge of collapse.

Reaching into her haversack, Sophia pulled out a small brass tinderbox and a thick candle. One thing was certain, if she was going to examine the tunnel, she needed light. One sharp tap of flint on flint sparked some of the tinder into flame. When the candle lit, she snapped the box lid shut.

Holding the burning candle away from her skirt, she scrambled to her feet. At the back of the wide entrance, deep in the shadows was the tunnel. She walked slowly, examining the earthen walls. Every foot or so, curved ribs dismantled from captured ships shored up the walls and ceiling to keep dirt from crumbling down into the tunnel.

Sophia walked in deeper. Something brushed against her face, making her heart leap. Nothing but a cobweb, but she had almost dropped the candle. Oh fiddlesticks, she thought, steadying herself against the wall. Something half buried in the dirt floor glinted in the candlelight. With her free hand she reached down and dusted it off. The hard, round object fit in her palm. She gasped—Grandsire's gold pocket compass!

She ran her finger over the initials *JR* engraved on the lid. Grandsire had promised that one day it would be hers. Only the compass had not been found among his belongings. Clicking the lid open, she saw to her delight the miniature oil portrait of her grandmother, Ann. Thank goodness, she thought, the damp of the cave has not destroyed the painting.

"Two peas in a pod," Grandsire always had said when he showed her the portrait, and Sophia would study the painting, forever curious to see this look-alike who had died before she was born. Her grandmother's hair was the color of golden sand. Ringlets, swept up with tortoise shell combs, were partially hidden by a tiny lace cap. Little wisps, scolding locks, curled around the side of her long white neck. Her startling green eyes seemed full of laughter. Sophia thought her very beautiful.

"I will never look like that." She had told Grandsire once.

"Not yet, but you will. More important, you have my Ann's courage."

Now as she studied the painting, Sophia recalled the story about her grandmother confronting a redcoat during the Revolution. There he stood in the barn a musket in one hand, in the other a rope looped around the milk cow's neck. According to Father, it was Grandmother Ann's withering glare that frightened off the soldier, not the loaded pistol she was carrying. If my grandmother could scare off the enemy, Sophia thought, maybe I can too.

"Thank you, Grandsire," she whispered.

She clicked the lid shut and slid the compass into her haversack before, standing a little straighter, she continued down the tunnel toward the cellar. As she walked, Sophia could see the tunnel was sound. Stopping short before a closed door, she grasped the handle. Don't be locked, she prayed and tugged. It didn't budge. Taking a deep breath, she yanked again.

With a raspy complaint, the thick wooden door opened.

Sophia hesitated. This was her first visit to Grandsire's secret lair in nearly a year. Before, whenever she opened the door, the room was bright with lantern light. Grandsire, pipe clamped between his teeth, would be reading or engraving a detailed map of the Chesapeake on a whale tooth. He always greeted her with a grin. "What took you so long?" he would say.

And she would wonder how he managed to overtake her without being seen so as to be there to greet her. Once, when she asked him, he merely shook his head.

"I will always be a step or two ahead of you, Phee," he said.

When Grandsire had failed to wake up one morning last July, Sophia no longer had a reason to come, not until now. Spiders had been busy during her absence. Fragile webs as intricate as Grandsire's scrimshaw curtained the doorway. She brushed them aside.

The room smelled musty as if a family of field mice had moved in and set up housekeeping. Otherwise, it appeared untouched. It was sparsely furnished. A pine bookcase stretched along one wall. It held Grandsire's well-thumbed copies of *Marine Atlas of the Northern Coast*, The *Nautical Almanac*, and *American Nautical Navigator;* an inkwell; a quill; a sheaf of paper; an hourglass; and an assortment of tools for carving. In the middle of another wall, there was a crude pine cupboard, empty except for a basket of shriveled up apples. Two oil lanterns, a jug of whale oil, and a coil of rope lay beside an old seaman's trunk.

The small table and two cane-backed chairs were still in the center of the room. An ivory game board was set up on the table as if waiting for Sophia and Grandsire to begin a game of draughts. It was Grandsire's favorite game and he gave no quarter.

"This is a game of wits, not chance," Grandsire would say before they started. "Always be at least two moves ahead of your opponent," he'd counsel, then grin and jump two of Sophia's unprotected men. "You can learn a lot from this old game. The English may have played it first, but we Americans play it better."

Walking over to the table, she slid a checker one square forward. Right now, I am one move ahead of Mr. Talcott, she thought. When I tell Oriole about this place, I'll be two ahead. She advanced the checker another square and grinned. Looking up, she almost expected to see her grandfather. But the room was empty.

Sophia began to make mental notes of what she would need to turn the cellar into a hideout again. Get rid of the mice and sweep out the spiders. Bring jugs of fresh water and sacks of food for the cupboard—beef jerky, cheese, and, to sweeten things up, peach preserves.

The problem was how to get the needed supplies here without drawing attention. If Grandsire was like a muskrat, as people said, there had to be another entrance, one closer to Great House. She remembered his telling her about a root cellar. Perhaps the old cabin held a secret or two. Muskrats always have more than one way to escape a burrow. She held the candle high, close to the celling, looking for a way out.

Hot wax dripped on her fingers and she dropped the candle, now almost a nub. The flame flickered out. I've been here too long, Sophia thought. Down here there is no way to determine the time. Oriole will be worried.

Making her way to the door, she closed it behind her and, grasping the handrail, made her way forward. At the entrance, she listened before pulling aside the curtain of vines. A crow was cawing in the distance, nothing more. Still, she waited, her eyes dazzled by the bright sunlight. The sun was high in the sky. There was still time to get to Oriole's and be home before milking. Sophia began to climb back to the trail.

11

The Truth About Salvation

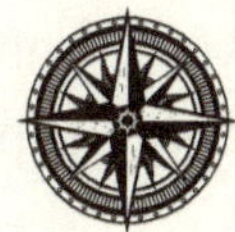

By the time Sophia approached the cluster of log houses, she was limping slightly. A wild tangle of fallen branches and downed trees had forced her to leave the ancient trail. Fearful of losing her bearings, she had kept close to the river, pushing aside the feathery pine boughs that slapped at her face and arms until the river seemed to lose itself in the peat bog near Marshtown. She had made her way back to the marked trail. It turned east, skirting the bog, but seemed to end in a dense thicket of tall, thorny bushes.

Grandsire probably planted these shrubs to discourage people from coming this way, Sophia thought. Well, Grandsire, you succeeded. If I didn't have to get to Oriole's, I'd go back. She was trying to thread her way through the hawthorns when she felt a stab of pain in her heel.

Balancing on one foot, she discovered a long thorn sticking out from the sole of her moccasin. She yanked it out. Can these woods get anymore dreadful? Apparently so, she decided, spotting a wood tick on her sleeve. She flicked it off and then stopped to shake her hair furiously. I'll never come this way again, she vowed and hurried on, favoring her sore foot. Ahead, she could see the weathered gray cabin. Its stone chimney had a feathery plume of smoke.

A few minutes later, as she rounded the corner of the cabin, Sophia spotted Oriole sitting on a bench next to the blue door, a basket of dried herbs beside her.

"Thank the Good Lord you're safe!" Oriole said, getting to her feet and opening her arms to give Sophia a quick hug.

Sophia returned the hug then untied the orange shawl she had knotted around her waist and held it out to Oriole, who smiled as she draped the shawl around her shoulders.

"I thought it might be another me comin' around the house," Oriole said, her brown eyes twinkling with suppressed mirth.

"I am sorry to be late, but . . ."

"Be sorry inside. You look all tuckered out."

As she stepped inside, Sophia sniffed the air appreciatively. "Something smells delicious." She limped over to the hearth to gaze into the cast iron post, placed on a trivet above glowing ashes. "I am so hungry I could eat a chicken with its feathers still attached."

"I guess it's fortunate then that I done saved you some of that stew. No feathers, though."

Sophia giggled and looked around. The cabin seemed unusually quiet.

"Where are the children?"

"I sent them down the road to keep Chloe company," Oriole said. "You know her, the blacksmith's pretty little wife who was helping your mother in the wool room. Chloe is expecting a baby any day now."

"Fiddlesticks! I could have looked after the children if I had come sooner, taken the road. Instead, I came along the river. So much has happened . . ." Sophia's voice trailed off. Reaching into the haversack, she pulled out the slightly wilted bouquet of spring beauties and handed it to Oriole.

Oriole made a clicking sound with her tongue. "These grow in the wild place," she said. "A dangerous place to be picking flowers."

"I had to go there. Mr. Talcott . . ."

"Hush. Sit yourself down, Miss Phee. Right there in my rocker. Rest that sore foot. And for pity's sake, take off those wet moccasins. Good or bad, a tale doesn't tell well on an empty stomach."

"But . . ."

"Sit down. Missy."

Sophia huffed and flopped down in Oriole's chair. It rocked backwards, almost tipping her out. Clutching the chair arms, she frantically leaned forward to regain her balance. If Mother were here, Sophia thought, she would say, "Whatever begins in anger ends in shame."

And she'd be right. Sophia closed her eyes and began to rock. The chair's steady creak was punctuated by an occasional pop from the hearth fire as one of the smoldering logs exploded.

"Lots of good chicken bits in the gravy," Oriole said as she handed Sophia a wooden bowl and a pewter spoon. "No bones to worry about. I fished those out beforehand. Don't want none of my sweet babies choking on bones. And no need to pout," she added. "It spoils the taste."

Sophia balanced the bowl on her knees and began to eat. The rich dish of savory potato, carrot, and chicken filled her with comfort. For the first time since she and Judith had talked yesterday, Sophia began to feel hopeful. Oriole had a way of making things right, even tea, she thought as she watched Oriole.

She had set the kettle to boil on its hook over the fire and then crumbled some dried flowers into a red clay teapot. When the copper kettle began to steam, she poured boiling water over the crushed petals and draped a thick cloth over the pot. While the tea steeped, she spooned honey into two red cups, adding a pinch of brown powder to one of them.

"So, you've seen that old Muskrat, Captain Joseph," she said.

Sophia nearly choked on a mouthful of stew. "How do you know I saw Grandsire?"

"Sometimes people have a look about them if they've seen a duppie. You've been along the river. Wouldn't surprise me none to learn your grandsire's spirit was hanging around down there, looking out for you," Oriole said, handing Sophia a steaming cup of tea.

Cradling the cup in her hands, Sophia leaned forward to breathe in the cinnamon scent before taking a sip. The tea tasted sweet, exotic. As she savored it, she gazed at Oriole. The woman had an uncanny ability to understand people's thoughts. Once a handful of townspeople had accused her of witchcraft. Grandsire had squelched that contention by standing up during a prayer meeting one Sunday to say such talk was spiteful nonsense. Oriole was a skillful midwife, nothing more, nothing less.

When the deacon had said, "Amen to that, Brother," the congregation had echoed faintly, "Amen." If some women gossiped about Oriole using magic to heal folks after that, they only whispered amongst themselves.

It's strange how people make up stories to cloak the truth, Sophia thought.

Oriole pulled the three-legged stool nearer to the rocker, fetched her tea, and sat down. "Tell me what you saw child," she said quietly.

Sophia leaned toward her. "I might have seen him but it may have been only a dream," she said under her breath.

"Good duppies always dream you."

Sophia gave Oriole a puzzled look.

"Not all duppies are bad. The good ones visit those they love in dreams," Oriole said. "I believe your grandsire wasn't ready to leave. Death took him by surprise."

Sophia nodded in agreement. Grandsire had gone to bed ill one night expecting to wake up the next morning, but for him the next day had never come.

"Can a good one still cause trouble?"

"Lawd have mercy, child. Your grandsire wouldn't harm a hair on your head."

"I know. I just saw him, talked to him. At least I think I did. I was hoping maybe he could make life unpleasant for Mr. Talcott. That man is evil." Sophia wrinkled her brow. "Grandsire said . . ."

"Hush. What your grandsire said is only for you to know."

Oriole got to her feet, putting her teacup on the stool, and reached down for the soggy moccasins. She stuffed each with rags pulled from a scrap bag before placing the pair several inches away from the hearth.

"Fire's no friend to leather."

"Oriole, please don't fuss. Grandsire had a secret . . ."

The old woman frowned. "Hush," she repeated. "And don't look so down in the mouth. Secrets ain't fit for folks like me. Who knows when the Lord will call me to glory? If you insist on tellin' someone, tell Jebbie," she said firmly. "Now let me take a look at that sore foot."

By now, the sun was shining directly through the west window. Oriole moved the stool into the sunlight. Then, resting Sophia's injured foot on the stool, Oriole gently pushed against the heel with her thumb.

"Ouch. It hurts right there," Sophia pointed to the sore spot.

"Just as I 'spected. You stepped on a thorn. The tip broke off in your foot. A quick soak in cider vinegar will draw the splinter out."

She pulled a dented copper basin from the bottom of a pine cupboard and placed it in front of the hearth beside her stool. Fetching a large jug from the cupboard, she poured a cup of vinegar into the basin then water from the kettle she had heated to make tea.

"We'll let that cool some," she said, "I don't want to add to your hurt." After refilling their teacups, she sat back down on the stool.

"I don't mean to spoil your tale," she said, "but it's best you tell Jebbie. Smart as a whip that boy. He'll turn eleven in June. Old enough to be a field hand but meant for better things." She shook her head. "You already taught him to cipher and to read. No telling what that boy can learn."

Oriole squeezed Sophia's knee firmly as if to underline the importance of her words. "You tell Jebbie."

Sophia looked down. There was no use arguing further.

"And speaking about learning," Oriole said, "I am wondering if you brought your book."

Sophia leaned down to retrieve the journal from the scarred leather haversack. Except when her fingers brushed against Grandsire's compass, she pulled it out instead.

"Look what I found."

Oriole's brown eyes widened slightly. "Well I'll be. Wherever did you find it?"

"In the tunnel."

Oriole didn't ask what tunnel or even raise her eyebrows. She just sipped her tea.

"You know!" Sophia cried.

"Your Grandsire spoke of it once, that's all. I've never seen that place, and I don't want to. One day I might be forced to tell where it is." Pursing her lips, Oriole turned to stare into the fire. After a minute, she said quietly, "Your grandsire was a good man. Truth be told, though, he had a way of ignoring laws. He always said, 'No one should obey the law of the land if it is contrary to the law of God.'"

Sophia started to protest, to say Grandsire wasn't one to break the law, but Oriole just smiled and shook her head.

"My, oh, my, he must be pleased you found his compass. He always said you should have it, said you had the adventurous spirit. A compass will keep you from getting lost." She paused to take another sip of tea. "Joseph always has had a way of giving what's needed. He surely knew what to give me."

"Your papers."

"No, no. Your daddy did that. He's the lawyer. Your grandsire gave me something better . . ." she stopped abruptly and stared directly at Sophia. Her look was stern. "Now this is for your ears alone. Ain't nobody's business but mine and Sally's."

Sophia nodded, thinking, *more secrets. It seems everyone has a secret.*

"Joseph gave Sally to me."

Sophia's eyes filled with shock and disbelief.

"Grandsire . . ."

"Ain't what you think. Just hear me out. I know what some say, all because Sally's skin is lighter than mine. Joseph was my friend. He was not Sally's father any more than I'm her mother." Oriole stood up. "Now you change places with me. My old bones are beginning to ache. You set on the stool and soak that foot. The water is cool enough now."

Sophia put her now empty cup down beside the chair and changed places, obediently slipping her foot into the warm bath. The light in the cabin was fading. The sun, now shining through the trees, cast long shadows along the cabin wall. The hearth fire had burned down to silent embers. Even the birds were still and Sophia felt as if the earth was holding its breath, waiting to hear.

"Contrary to what some say, I was married once," Oriole began softly. "I was late to jump the broom, and my fine man lived only a brief time after. When the Revolution began, he became a soldier. He said that freedom and justice for all were beliefs worth fighting for. A Redcoat shot him dead two months after he signed up."

When Sophia cried out in dismay, Oriole just smiled sadly at her and continued.

"He's with the Lord now, and I'll soon join him. We never had a child. How I hungered for a child to love, to raise, but I just didn't have the heart to remarry. At the time, only two other families lived near. Yours and the Talcotts. I stayed pretty much to myself, growing my herbs and healing folks when asked. I had my garden, some chickens and a few goats. Most everything else I got from the peddler. Every once in a while, I walked to town; so, when I showed up with a baby one day, everyone assumed that she was mine. I never said different. As far as I was concerned, Sally was my child."

Oriole crossed her arms tightly in front of her as if she felt a chill. Her voice deepened.

"The war was in its fourth year when my Sally comed along. Your grandsire was at sea, fighting the English. He captured what he thought was a merchant ship. Instead he found about twenty Africans in chains." Oriole shuddered, and Sophia knew she was remembering her childhood. "One of the twenty was a woman. She was big with child. Joseph learned that one of the sailors had thrown her down for pleasure more than once. She was carrying his baby."

Seeing the lines of sorrow in Oriole's face, Sophia reached over to put her hand on Oriole's knee.

"I am so sorry," she whispered.

"It's terrible in one way, wonderful in another," Oriole explained, her tone again composed. "Your grandsire had no use for slavery; you know that. He sailed the captured ship to Baltimore. Now it was the English who were in chains. The Africans didn't understand the war but they hated the English and were eager to fight. They joined Washington's army. Your grandsire brought the woman to me. Of course she had no papers."

The fire gave a loud pop, making Sophia jump. Oriole just kept rocking.

"The woman stayed with me for about a month and half. We didn't understand each other's talk; we spoke in other ways. She was beautiful but so very sad. A few days after I helped her give birth, she hanged herself. Out there." Oriole gestured toward the window and beyond to the woods.

Sophia groaned softly. Oriole reached up to touch her face.

"It's sad, yes. But her baby lived. And when she first smiled at me, I knew that this child was my salvation. And that's what I named her, Salvation. There's no comprehending the ways of the Lord." Oriole bowed her head and was silent.

Sophia twisted her fingers together and stared at them. "There's no shame in this," she whispered. "Why does it matter if folks find out?"

"Some might say Sally's a slave's daughter, that she ain't got rights. Darkies in Maryland best be careful. Even free ones." She shook herself as a dog might shake water off his coat and stood, swaying slightly. "But that's no never mind to us today. We got some work to do here."

Sophia reached out to steady her. Oriole took her arm, patting it.

"What's important today is that you leave here knowing the truth. Gossips have long tongues. I won't have you thinking your grandsire wasn't righteous." She smiled broadly at Sophia. "You know how your grandsire liked secrets. He told me Sally's birth should be our little secret, that it was better for Sally if folks believed she was my child. If some wanted to believe that he was the father, well, that was all right with him."

Arm in arm, the two walked to the table. Oriole picked up a few sprigs of what appeared to be dried fern leaves with button-like flowers.

"Chamomile," she said. "Some call it pineapple weed. The dried flowers made your tea. It helps calm nerves and bring down fevers." She frowned. "Do you plan on writing this down?"

Hastily retrieving the book from the haversack, Sophia sat down on a narrow bench in front of the table, where a quill and ink awaited her. Opening to the bookmarked blank page, she wrote, "Camomeal," spelling it as best she could.

When she first began this Book of Simples months ago, Sophia had determined that it should have two sections. In the first she named the plant, then described it, its uses, and where it grew. Often, she would sketch a leaf to help her identify the plant. In the second part, she listed diseases—everything from ship's fever and sore throats to stomach ailments and worms. She described the symptoms and the remedies—herbal teas, infusions, salves, and poultices. A red silk ribbon separated the two sections. Now, with her head bent over the page, she wrote as quickly as possible in the first part: "When brewing tea, use about a handful of the dried flowers for every cup of water. Steep ten minutes."

Oriole spoke of the herb with reverence. Calling it the queen of healing plants, she explained that chamomile not only healed people, but also helped any kind of plant growing near it to fight disease. Her face fairly glowed as she described a field of blooming chamomile.

"It's pretty as a bright green rug with small golden circles woven in."

After refilling the teacups, Oriole pulled the stool close to the table and was watching Sophia sketch a sprig of the dainty plant.

"Always pick chamomile in the summer when it's blooming. Hang the plants upside down in a dark place. My little shed has no windows for that very reason. Now, the flowers, if fresh, have a different use. First grind up the blossoms; next mix the powder into an oil—flaxseed or, better yet, olive oil, if'n you can find it. Lastly stir the mix into beeswax to make a salve. It will heal skin miseries."

Sophia gave Oriole a glum look. "I told Miss Talcott to come see you." Sophia said, thinking about the girl's scarred face. "I meant to tell you earlier. Her face is marked with the pox. Her cheeks are red and bumpy. I hope I wasn't wrong to tell her."

"I can help some, ease the redness. The pits won't go away but the pox marks won't be as noticeable. You were right to tell her. That's why you'll be a good healer. Help folks best you can, not judge 'em."

"Even when they want to do you harm," Sophia said glumly. "Mr. Talcott is up to no good. Miss Talcott warned me that he plans to shutter Marshtown. Run you off, to use her words."

Oriole laughed. "Dat man best be careful," she said. "My mama always said, 'Spit in de sky, de spit fall in your eye'."

When Sophia gave her a confused look, Oriole said, "Just another way of saying, what trouble you wish for others, will bring trouble on you."

"Then," Sophia said, "Mr. Talcott is surely headed for trouble."

12

The Nature of Chamomile

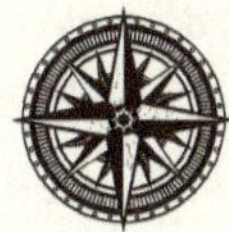

Even as afternoon shadows lengthened, Sophia remained at the plank table, writing the uses for chamomile in her Book of Simples.

"Chamomile to soothe, cinnamon to chase away a cold, honey to fortify, Oriole reminded her. "Everything I used to make your tea."

Sophia wrote slowly, taking care not to blot the page. After a while she put down her quill and pushed the book aside.

"What's the use? I'll be gone before you can teach me everything that I should know about making remedies." She rested her elbows on the plank table and cupped her chin in her hands. "Besides, who will believe me if I say a teaspoon or two of chamomile tea will cure a baby's colic? I am just a girl."

Oriole was mashing boiled sweet potatoes for pie. She smiled. "Sounds to me like you're just tuckered out."

"No, I'm not tired of this." She gestured toward the feather pen, the inkwell, and the open book. "I'm tired of worrying about what might happen after we're gone, especially to you and Marshtown."

"Land sakes, child. There's no need for that. I have met trouble head on before."

"But I told Miss Talcott to come here. Now I am afraid she'll bring trouble with her."

"Marshtown is no secret."

Oriole walked over and placed her hands on Sophia's shoulders. Sophia sighed and felt the tension in her shoulders ease.

"Mother doesn't approve, you know."

Oriole gave her an odd look.

"Mother didn't say it in so many words but I think she believes I come here to escape spinning wool into yarn. She wants me to concentrate on what she calls the womanly arts, like cooking and dressmaking. This morning she implied that we need only to follow Benjamin Franklin's advice to stay well."

Oriole gave a low, slow chuckle, making Sophia giggle in spite of her bad mood.

"Now, you know your mama only wants what's best for you," Oriole said. "Seems to me you're worried that she'll turn all her attention on you now that Faith has a fine man wooing her. Next time your mama asks about our lessons, you just say that it doesn't hurt to know how to make a sick husband well."

Sophia picked up the pen.

Still talking, Oriole went back to making pie. "Some folks believe if you scatter chamomile petals on a newborn baby, the child will have a sunny nature."

"That sounds like magic," Sophia said. "Mother would never approve."

"Might be magic, but I like to think that it's chamomile's soothing nature that stays with that child all his days," Oriole said, dusting flour off her hands. "There now, isn't that a pretty pie?"

She laid her palm along the side of the brick oven beside the fireplace. "Hot enough," she said. She was sliding the pie into in the oven when Jebbie came bursting into the cabin.

"Come quick! It's Miz Chloe. She told me to fetch you."

Instead of scolding him for shouting, Oriole said, "Catch your breath, Jebbie, then tell me what's happened." Her voice was soothing, and Sophia, who had jumped up, ready to run, sank back down on the bench.

Jebbie took a couple of deep breaths and began again. "Just like you asked me, I'm helping Miz Chloe mind the children. Miz Chloe was baking molasses cookies, when . . ." He gulped. "Oh Gawd, those cookies must be burned by now."

Sophia bit her lip to keep from smiling. Apparently, no matter what the situation, Jebbie was always mindful of sweets.

Oriole just nodded. "Go on. Where's Miz Chloe?"

"In the cabin. Sitting on the floor with her knees drawed up to her chin. The childrens are squatted down next to her, just looking at her. First, she is standing by the oven, waiting for those cookies, then she lets out a little yelp like a puppy makes, grabs her belly and sits right down on the floor. And she says, 'Tell Granny Oriole to come quick."

Oriole clapped her hands together with joy. "Sounds like Miz Chloe's baby is fixin' to be born." She went to the cupboard, took out her battered case of remedies, and then walked purposefully to the door, pausing at the threshold.

Jebbie was watching her with big round eyes. "You gotta hurry, Granny."

"Don't you worry none. Most babies take their own sweet time. Jebbie, you should sit a spell. Miz Sophia will slice you a piece of my sweet tater pie as soon as it's done."

Sophia sprang to her feet again, almost knocking over the bench.

Oriole smiled at her. "Slow down. That's pie's gotta bake first. I am going to need you to stay a while."

Sophia nodded, even though she knew she'd be late for chores. Faith will be furious if she has to do the milking twice today, she thought. Sophia was wondering how to appease her sister when she heard Oriole tell Jebbie that, as soon as he had enjoyed his pie, he was to trot on down to the Records' cookhouse and fetch his mother home. He was to say that Miss Sophia was here and that she'd be lending Oriole a hand 'til his mama came.

Sophia's eyes widened in disbelief, knowing that if she stayed, she would cause a scandal. Only older, married women were present at birthings. Surely, Oriole knew that. Mother already disapproved of her spending so much time here but this situation could end the lessons. No matter, Sophia thought. I'll face Mother's displeasure later.

If Oriole noticed Sophia's apprehension, she ignored it. Instead, she issued a string of orders before going out the door. Sophia was to bank the fire and take the pie from the oven as soon as it was baked— it should be done before too long—and let it set some before slicing a piece for Jebbie. She was to bring the pie and the ragbag to Miz Chloe's cabin. She knew the one. It was the second to last in the row of cabins along the road.

Later, when Sophia hurried down the rutted dirt road, she had no trouble finding the right cabin because the children were clustered around it. Summer and Fry were trying to peek through a crack in the shutters while Becky was sitting in front of the closed door, clutching her doll and looking worried. Before stepping around her, Sophia paused to pat Becky gently on the shoulder and whisper that there was sweet tater pie for supper. Becky's face brightened.

Once inside the cabin, Sophia hesitated. With the shutters closed, the only light came from the mound of glowing ash in the fireplace. The room was warm and strangely quiet so she flinched when Oriole spoke.

"Shut the door, child. Ain't nothing to be scared of. Miz Chloe is going to have her baby sooner than expected is all. Babies, you know, have a mind of their own."

Sophia wasn't sure if Oriole was trying to sooth her or Chloe. As her eyes adjusted to the dim light, she saw Oriole standing by the girl, who had been resting on a thin pallet and now raised herself to a sitting position. Sophia gave her a timid wave, remembering the first time they had met. Chloe had been all smiley and giggly then. Now she looked anxious.

Chloe had come to Marshtown last year in the company of Ulysses, a giant of a man who worked as a blacksmith in Snow Hill. He had lived alone in this cabin until then. Everyone knew that Oriole had insisted he and Chloe jump the broom before going to housekeeping, and they were happy to do it. They might have waited six months or more before the traveling preacher had showed up to marry them.

Their broom ceremony had been joyful. Everyone from Marshtown was there as well as James, Grandsire, and herself. The guests had formed a large circle around Chloe and Ulysses, clapping and singing while bride and groom both held the broomstick and together swept the ground all around the circle. Then Ulysses laid the broom on the ground in the center of the circle. Next Grandsire gave a speech about marriage. When he finished, Chloe and Ulysses joined hands and jumped over the broom. After much merriment and apple cider toasts, Oriole had served burgoo stew for the crowd. Sophia realized it was the last happy gathering she had shared with James and Grandsire.

"Don't stand there wool gathering, Miss Sophia." Oriole sounded impatient. "I need you to string a line from here to there." She pointed toward the bottom of two rafters. "So as to make a blanket wall. This woman needs her privacy. There's a rope in my bag. Blankets are in the six-board chest."

Jolted by Oriole's no-nonsense tone, Sophia quickly complied. The cabin walls were low enough that she could touch the roof beam where it met the wall just by standing on her tiptoes and reaching up. There she felt an iron hook. She found another on a beam near the opposite wall. It was easy to tie the rope and pull it tight across the room. She draped the length of the blanket over the line and secured it with wooden pins. It wasn't long enough to go wall to wall, but it hid the pallet and gave Chloe and Oriole the privacy they needed.

"Thank you," Chloe said huskily as Sophia turned to leave the tiny room. "I appreciate you stopping by."

Sophia smiled and stood a little taller. "I'll be staying a while. Until Sally comes." She couldn't keep the pride from her voice. She was beginning to feel confident. After all she had helped with the lambing just a few weeks ago. Delivering babies shouldn't be much different.

It wasn't long before she revised her thinking. Sophia was amazed at all the work having a baby caused. Besides building up the fire, boiling water, making tea, feeding the children, and fetching things Oriole needed like almond oil and nettle tonic, she learned to make a pot of thick gruel laced with some rum procured from Oriole's satchel. The gruel and the tonic, Oriole explained, would help Chloe regain her strength after her baby was born. For now, Chloe should only sip water or raspberry tea.

Throughout the late afternoon, Oriole was in and out of the blanket room, chatting with the children or supervising the cooking before returning to Chloe. She kept a basin of hot water in the room and, each time it cooled, she asked Sophia to empty the basin and refill it with water from the steaming kettle. Oriole would then add several drops of rose oil. The rising steam filled the small chamber with the smell of summer roses.

Only Chloe didn't always stay in that sweet-smelling room. Oriole kept encouraging her to move about, saying that walking hastened things along. Twice, when Chloe walked outside, Oriole gestured for Sophia to go with her. At first Sophia kept a firm grip on the girl's arm until Chloe began giggling softly.

"What?" Sophia asked, mystified, as she didn't see anything funny. "Is the baby tickling you?"

"Oh, Lawdy. No." Chloe shook her head and grinned widely at Sophia. "It's you. You make me laugh. I'm not some fragile old lady. You act like I'm gonna break in two."

Sophia let go of Chloe's arm, embarrassed. "It's not that. It's just that . . ." She looked at Chloe in confusion before blurting out, "I thought that having a baby made you weak. Aren't you hurting?"

Chloe flashed another toothy grin. "Oh, Lawdy, it surely doesn't tickle. Not when I get those pains." She laughed a little before saying in more serious tone, "When those pains come, I just think about the baby. I wonder if'n I'll have a boy or a girl, and I pray to the Lord. I pray that my baby be strong enough to withstand living."

Sophia realized for the first time how resolute Chloe was—not the silly, laughing girl she was last June or the quiet, subdued girl she was when Mother was teaching her to weave cloth.

"Oriole will take good care of you and your baby," Sophia said.

Chloe nodded. "I know. Ulysses will, too. He be so proud, always patting my belly and whispering to the baby there how much he will love him, as if that baby could hear."

Then without warning, she grasped Sophia's hand, squeezing it so hard Sophia cried out. Releasing her grip, Chloe gave a little rueful smile. "It seems I am a bit weak in the knees after all. We best go inside." She held out her arm. "Miz Sophia, please help me back to bed."

Sophia took hold of Chloe's arm. "My family calls me Phee. I wish you would, too."

Chloe nodded.

Later as the sky began to darken into dusk, Sophia began to worry. The children were tired and cranky. They needed to be in their own beds. She had run out of stories to tell and every scrap of pie had been eaten. She wished Sally would hurry. What could possibly be keeping her, and how, dear Lord, could she ever explain herself to Mother?

So, when Sally huffed into the cabin a few minutes later, a heavily laden basket on her arm, Sophia blurted out, "Thank God, salvation," before remembering Salvation was the cook's true name. She giggled softly. Oriole had chosen the right name.

The boys must have thought Sally had come to rescue them as well. They scrambled to their feet, shouting "Huzzah, Mama's here!" Only Becky, who was asleep in Sophia's lap, was unaware.

"Tut, Tut. You'd think I'd been gone a fortnight." Sally's round face glowed as she smiled fondly at her welcoming party. With Summer and Fry clinging to her skirts, she looked over their heads toward Sophia, asking about Chloe.

All Sophia could tell her was that she had heard Chloe whimper more with less rest time in between. Before she could ask about Mother's state of mind, Oriole poked her head around the blanket wall.

"Sally! Things are moving along right smartly for a first baby. I need you here."

Sophia looked up expectantly only to be disappointed when Oriole told her that her task was to make a fresh mattress for Chloe to lie on after the baby was born. She and the two little boys were to go to Oriole's barn and pull some hay from the loft.

"Make sure it's sweet smelling," Oriole cautioned. "And mix in some lavender. You'll find some in the herb shed. And, Sophia, you carry the tin lantern. Take care those boys don't kick it over and start a fire."

"The ticking's already been stitched together." Sally added. "It's in the six-board chest."

"Can't I do that later?" Sophia asked. She didn't want to be stuffing a mattress when the baby was born.

"Hush," Sally murmured as she stooped down to pick up Becky, who murmured sleepily, "Mama?"

"Hush," Sally said again. "Your mama will be comin' soon."

Pulling off her shawl, Sally laid it on the ground away from the fire and wrapped the sleepy child in it. "Now you stay put," she whispered. "I got my eye on you." She shooed the two boys out the door. "And you, too!" She turned to Sophia, who was getting slowly to her feet.

"Don't look so sour-faced, Phee. Everything is rush, rush with the baby coming now. Soon as you finish, send those boys to bed. Jebbie's at Oriole's cabin now. He'll look out for them. You come back here. Chloe's little baby ought to meet the young lady who's been helping his mama."

"Thank you." Sophia felt tears well up in her eyes. At least Sally understood. Abruptly, she turned to dash the tears away, not wanting to seem like a baby herself.

Appearing not to notice, Sally kept right on talking. "When you get back here, you can unpack what your mother sent." She pointed to the large willow basket she had set on the table.

"Mother?" Sophia sounded thunderstruck. "Mother sent some things? She knows I'm here? Helping?"

Sally chuckled. "The only person this baby hasn't fooled is your mother. She had a whole basket of things prepared. When I told her Jebbie'd come to fetch me home, she handed it to me, said to tell Chloe she was praying for her and the child."

"Did she say anything about me?"

"No, but I overheard her tell your father to ride to Snow Hill and tell Ulysses about the baby coming, and then ride here. He was to bring you home directly."

At that moment, Chloe cried out and Sally hurried behind the blanket wall.

This was not the time to dither. There was too much to be done to worry about Mother's state of mind. Sophia pulled the mattress cover from the trunk. As she raced out the door, she heard Oriole call out.

"You leave that mattress in the shed. It's too bulky for you to carry. One of the neighbors will bring it. And make sure those boys don't knock over the lantern."

The little boys were helpful, more so than Sophia had imagined. As they pulled down handfuls of good, sweet hay without the usual horseplay, she stuffed the ticking, taking care to make the stuffing as even and as firmly packed as possible. Every so often she would add sprigs of lavender. Finally, Sophia stitched the plump mattress shut with some thick thread, only pricking her finger twice.

When she returned to the cabin, Sally and Oriole were both crowded into the little room behind the blanket. Sophia placed the lantern on the table and then immediately began unloading the basket. She put the food—a small wheel of cheese plus jars of raspberry preserves, apple jelly, and pickled green beans—in the cupboard. The tiny clothes she stacked on the table. Mother had knit a cap, dress, and booties out of fine white wool. At the bottom of the basket were three small blankets made out of blue flannel and eight cloth diapers.

As Sophia laid the diapers on the table, she heard Chloe cry out.

"Lawdy, Lawdy, when is this going to end?"

Sophia couldn't help moaning herself even as she heard Oriole say in her soothing way, "Take heart, girl. You are almost done. Hold Sally's hands tight. Now, push. Push hard. Real hard. That's right. One more time."

Chloe gave one of those loud puppy-like yelps, and the next thing Sophia heard was the high thin wail of a newborn child.

"Hallelujah!" Oriole and Sally chorused. "Ain't he a fine one."

Sophia began to clap. She wanted to run outside and tell the world but she was afraid she'd miss something.

Moments later, when Oriole walked into the room cradling the child in her arms, all Sophia could say was "Oh my, oh my."

"Lookee here, Sophia, Chloe has a fine son. Never mind that he's a little messy. That's just birth blood. He's fine. The mother's fine." Oriole looked sharply at Sophia. "And if you take a deep breath, you'll be fine, too. Right now, this baby needs to be cleaned up."

Oriole kept talking as she tested the water in the basin with her elbow, explaining the water had to be the right temperature. "If'n you can't feel the water with your elbow, it be just right." Oriole's words washed over Sophia as the water in the basin washed over the tiny child. Both calmed.

Sophia gazed at the baby with wonder. Of course, she had seen her brothers after they were born, but that was later, after they had been bathed and swaddled. Everything about this newly born child was astonishing. His long dark eye lashes, his soft curly hair, his tiny nose, his hungry mouth. Each little finger had a tiny perfect nail. As she watched Oriole gently wipe him clean with a soft cloth, she thought, here is a true miracle, and she smiled and cooed at him as if he were her own.

After Oriole had dried him and wrapped him in one of the flannel blankets, she carefully laid the boy in Sophia's arms.

"Welcome," she whispered, and proudly brought him to Chloe, who reached out her arms to receive him.

Later that night as Sophia rode home, seated sideways behind her father, she leaned her head wearily against his back and clutched the sleeve of his frock coat. Riding pillion always made her feel as if she'd slip off even though Father kept the mare to a slow walk. There is no dance to Pearl's step tonight, Sophia thought. She must be tired, too. Snow Hill was at least twenty miles from the plantation, the trip back to Marshtown was no shorter and we've another mile to go.

Still, as sleepy as she was, Sophia kept thinking about the joy in Ulysses's face when he raced into the cabin and learned he was the father of a baby boy. With his face creased in smiles, Ulysses had carried the baby outside to show him to his neighbors who had come with small gifts of food. Already the biggest man Sophia had ever seen, tonight she thought he had stood even taller. He seemed so proud.

"Abraham," he had told them. "We will call him Abraham."

"Were you as happy as Ulysses when James was born?" Sophia asked dreamily.

Father stopped Pearl and turned in the saddle. "Happier," he said emphatically. "I was pleased to have a son, of course. But your mother also presented me with a twin, you. Your mother and I were twice blessed."

"Was Oriole there?"

"The doctor from Snow Hill was there but I believe Oriole stopped by. The doctor wasn't pleased but your mother was glad she was there."

"Did you sprinkle us with chamomile?"

"What?" Father moved uneasily in the saddle. "I wouldn't know about that. You'd have to ask your mother."

Probably not, Sophia thought and then remembered the handful of petals she had tied in a scrap of cloth and put in her haversack. In all the excitement she had forgotten to sprinkle them on Abraham. She hoped that tomorrow wouldn't be too late to ensure that he had a happy life.

13

Tit for Tat

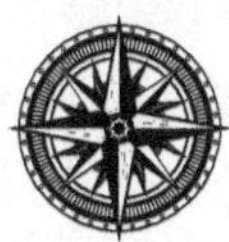

Nudge, nudge. Sophia groaned, rolled over and opened her eyes. Faith was standing beside the bed. Even in the half-light of dawn, Sophia could see her sister's wide smile.

"It's not time for morning chores yet," Sophia mumbled into her pillow before sitting up. She giggled. "Look at me. I could run out to the coop right now."

Still fully clothed, she remembered falling into bed, too tired to change into her nightdress. No doubt, she thought, I have some explaining to do. She gave Faith a penitent look. "I'm sorry about last night but . . ."

"Oh, never mind that," Faith said. Taking a deep breath, she placed her hand over her heart in dramatic fashion and said grandly "*I am betrothed.*"

"What?" Sophia blinked twice to make sure this was really Faith and not some aberration in a strange dream.

"Father consented!"

"Never." Sophia flopped back down.

"He did. I wanted to tell you last night. I propped myself up in bed to wait but you came home so late I was asleep. I can't believe I fell asleep. Father said we have to delay our plans until I am seventeen but that's not far off. Just think in a few short months I will be Mrs. Zachariah Mueller, mistress of my own home. I'll do as I wish not as I'm told."

As Sophia lay on her back, trying to absorb the news, she studied Faith's radiant face and wondered what had changed her parents' minds. Mother and Father were both against early marriages. In fact, Mother was always saying, "Enjoy your girlhood. Don't be in a rush to become a wife."

"Say something. Aren't you happy for me?"

"Of course, I am. It's wonderful news." Sophia sat up again, pulled her knees up to her chest, and rested her chin on them. Still contemplating her sister, she decided that being engaged must change a person. Faith's flushed cheeks and wide smile had transformed her into a beauty. Even more amazing, her normally taciturn sister now plunked herself down on the bed to chat.

"Phee," Faith grasped Sophia's hand and gave her a pleading look. Sophia looked at her warily. Faith was up to something.

"Phee," she said again in a wheedling tone. "I need to ask a favor. I know Grandsire bequeathed this bed and the chest of drawers to us both. But, Father suggested, with your consent, of course, that they could be part of my dowry."

Sophia drew in her breath and held it, curtailing a quick and angry answer.

"After all," Faith said, "I am the oldest. Grandsire wasn't thinking properly. We can't share this furniture after I'm married. Father said he would provide you with a bed and chest when you marry. Don't look so shocked. That's what he said. You can ask him." Faith gave her a pleading look.

Sophia shrugged, furious that Father had suggested such a thing without first talking to her. Not that carved mahogany bedsteads and elegant six-drawer chests were that important to her. What was important was both pieces had been bequeathed to her and Faith.

"I'll think about it, "Sophia finally answered. "I thought Father wasn't transporting any furniture to Ohio."

Faith smiled. "That won't be a problem. Father said even though there will be no room in our wagon, Zach's father might be willing to haul both. Dismantled, the bed doesn't take much space."

She patted the bed in a proprietary way. "Giving me your half would be such a generous gift. I would never forget your kindness."

Sophia frowned as she appraised her sister's pleading look. Faith always seemed to want more than her share.

"You know," she said slowly, thinking out loud, "Father plans to sell most of the furniture at auction. We could sell our bed and chest, then divide the money."

Even as she spoke, Sophia realized she really didn't want to sell Grandsire's gifts. Resting her forehead on her knees, she mumbled into the quilt, "Oh, go ahead, take them."

If Faith recognized Sophia' s ungracious tone, she didn't let on. "Thank you. Phee," she crowed. "Both?"

When Sophia confirmed it with a nod, Faith squealed with happiness. Then, instead of scrambling off the bed as soon as she got what she wanted, Faith stayed put. She prattled on and on about how wonderful Zachariah Mueller was. She praised his farming ability and his precise ways. Practically swooning over his German accent, declaring it manly, Faith said she found his parents' old-world ways charming. It was "Zach thinks this" or "Zach did that" until Sophia wondered if the Zach that Faith was talking about was the same stocky fellow who came calling almost every week. That Zachariah Mueller seemed tongue-tied.

"We have kissed," Faith whispered. Her cheeks flamed red.

"I know. You already told me."

"Not just that once. Many times. Not chaste kisses either. When he holds me close and kisses me hard, sometimes I think I am tipsy on love."

Sophia chuckled. Without a doubt Faith had been bitten by that love bug Oriole was always warning about. Imagine, my obedient sister disobeying the rules of proper behavior.

She really loves him, Sophia decided. Thankfully Faith hadn't said "yes" to the first person who proposed only because she wanted to be married, as Sophia had feared she might. Faith had admitted many times to being terrified of spinsterhood. Being considered an old maid was a fate Sophia rarely considered but was one that Mother often cautioned against. Mother always ended her warning with the promise that Father would select a proper husband for each daughter, an arrangement that bothered Sophia. As far as she was concerned, being told whom to marry was no different than Father choosing a stud for his beloved mare. Thank goodness, Faith had found a proper suitor on her own. Sophia beamed happily at her sister.

Before long, though, Faith's marriage talk became too much to bear so early in the morning. Sophia tried to turn the conversation to baby Abraham, but Faith shook her head vehemently from side to side.

"I don't want to hear about it," she said. "Mother was as stormy as a thunder cloud after she heard you were in attendance. She is afraid such a lapse of judgment, her words not mine, will hurt your chances for marrying well. I can't believe you stayed! It's simply not proper."

Sophia was about to defend herself when the hall clock chimed the hour. Both girls scrambled out of the bed.

"It must be seven o'clock!" Sophia said. "I'll hardly have time to make myself presentable before breakfast."

Faith, full of good cheer, offered to do all the morning chores if Sophia would return the favor in the evening. She would be visiting the Muellers later with Mother and Father. "Marriage details," she said.

As Sophia scrubbed herself clean and changed into a fresh frock, she kept laughing softly to herself. Being betrothed, as Faith put it, had not changed her sister that much. With Faith everything was always tit for tat. Perhaps sleeping in Grandsire's bed for the next twenty years would help her develop a more generous spirit. After all Grandsire had been a generous man.

14

Rights and Wrongs

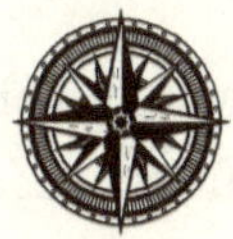

Breakfast was quieter than usual with Nathan and Willie absent. They had eaten earlier in the cookhouse so this morning there were only four at the table. Sophia wondered if Mother had planned it this way. All through the meal she fidgeted, waiting for a scolding. Instead, Father asked her to be his law clerk, saying she had a legible hand and that he needed someone to copy a dozen or so land deeds and wills. All had to be copied and distributed before the family left for Ohio.

Sophia gave him a startled look. Father had never asked for her help in this way. Pleased, she sat a little taller in her chair.

"You will be my good right hand while I am away," he said.

"Away?" Sophia raised her eyebrows. "I don't understand. What's happened?" She half rose from her chair, her face shimmering with hope. "Has James been found? Are you going to bring him home?"

"No, nothing like that." Father said wearily. "If only that were the case. More bad news I am afraid. Yesterday I received word that some clerk is refusing to give me the title to our land in Ohio." He cleared his throat, glancing at Mother as if to reassure her that all would be well.

"There is no other way around it," he said. "I must leave for Washington City today, right after breakfast. Apparently, some scalawag has challenged my right to the bounty land. It's not right you know. Congress awarded that land warrant to my father for his service during the Revolution. To him and his heirs. Those acres now belong to me!" He slammed his fist down on the table hard enough to make the dishes rattle. Sophia stared at her father in surprise. He usually controlled his temper.

"Elijah, there is no need to get so worked up about it," Mother said. "The land is rightful yours. You just need to provide the proof that you are the rightful heir."

"Well, its damned inconvenient to be away from here but I need to set things right and to pick up the deed myself." He gazed sternly at Sophia and then at Faith. "That means you girls must work doubly hard to help your mother. She knows what to pack up and what to leave behind."

"We can't possibly . . ." Sophia started to say but another fierce look from Father stopped her.

"You can do anything you put your mind to, "he said more softly, once again looking right at Mother. "Besides, more help will arrive soon."

Sophia gave him a questioning look.

"Didn't I say? Uncle William will be arriving before long."

"And Aunt Polly, as well?" Sophia asked. When Father nodded, she muttered, "some help she'll be."

Father frowned, folded his napkin, put it by his plate, pushed his chair back from the table, and stood, a clear indication that breakfast was over. Walking over to stand behind Sophia's chair, he grasped her shoulders and gave them a gentle squeeze.

"I am depending on you, Phee," he said. "Besides the packing, Faith will have her hands full helping your mother sort things out in the wool room now that Chloe has a newborn to care for. You will be helping me by copying deeds. I don't want you worrying your mother by running off to Marshtown."

"Both of you girls," he added, looking directly at Faith, "must stay close to home."

Sophia glanced across the table at her sister, who was blushing furiously. It was easy to see that Faith knew Father's remark meant no unchaperoned strolls with Zach Mueller, betrothed or not.

"But you mustn't leave today," Faith blurted. "Have you forgotten? We are to call on the Muellers. They are expecting us. We are going to discuss the wedding."

A look of regret passed across Father's face. "I am sorry, Faith. I truly am, but I must go. That piece of land in Ohio is our future."

"What about my future? What will the Muellers think?" Faith was close to tears.

"Faith, you and I will visit the Muellers today," Mother said. Her tone was pleasant enough but there was a firmness to it that discouraged further argument.

"I am sure they will understand," she said. "After all they are farmers, too. They know the value of land. We have plenty of time to work out the details of your marriage."

"Don't worry, Elijah," she added. "We'll manage. The girls are always helpful and now we have Nathan to look after the stock and do the heavy work."

"True," Father said. "That boy has proved to be a Godsend. Besides, my brother and Polly will be arriving in a few days. I left William a note—it's on the hall table—asking that he and Polly stay until my return. They can help with the packing."

Mother made a face. "If they must," she said. She sounded resigned.

An hour later Father was ready to leave. Nathan had groomed Pearl until her milky white coat gleamed. After saddling her, he brought the mare around to the front of the house where the family waited with Father beside the mounting block.

"Such a pretty girl," Mother said, and stroked Pearl's neck.

"As are you," Father said. Tipping up her chin, he kissed her.

Faith nudged Sophia. "Shocking," she whispered. Both girls laughed softly. Mother had told them more than once such public displays of affection were unmannerly.

"Elijah! You mustn't," Mother whispered, but Father touched his finger to her lips.

"Hush," he said. "Everything will be fine." Then he kissed her again.

He was heading the mare toward the road when he abruptly pulled back on the reins as if he had forgotten something and turned in the saddle.

"I am confident that we will all travel to Baltimore in a few weeks' time. From there, we board the stage to Cumberland, then on to Ohio in a covered wagon. The adventure of a lifetime!"

With a wave of his hat, he urged the mare into a fast trot.

Sophia stood with her mother and sister on the front porch until Father was out of sight. But Willie, barefoot as usual, ran down the carriage way, shouting "Goodbye, Goodbye," until Nathan caught up with him and led the little boy back to his mother.

Pulling Willie to her, Mother hugged him tight, then ruffled his hair playfully before turning him loose. "Now you are the man of the house until Father returns," she said. "Act accordingly."

"That's Phee's, job," Willie said, grasping Sophia's hand. "She always knows what to do. She can be the man of the house."

Everyone except Sophia laughed.

Later sitting at Father's desk, Sophia wondered if Mr. Talcott was the scalawag who had caused trouble with the deed. It certainly was a possibility.

Sophia sighed, looking at the pile of documents to be copied. There would be no visit to Marshtown today.

She gazed around the room. If, as Mother said, the kitchen hearth was the heart of the plantation, then this small room was its mind. She sat straighter. Sitting here at Father's tall mahogany secretary made her feel important. She glanced upward at the shelves of books stored behind glass doors. Father's thick law books and the tall plantation ledgers were crowded together on the first shelf. The two remaining shelves held more pleasant reading—the dog-eared copy *of Robinson Crusoe*, now back in its rightful place, plus two dozen other books bound in smooth leather. Three folios of William Shakespeare's plays leaned against Pilgrim's *Progress* and scuffed volumes of poetry by John Donne, Robert Burns, and William Wordsworth stood next to Benjamin Franklin's prized autobiography, with Thomas Paine's pamphlet *Common Sense* wedged between.

Sophia had read everything on the shelves except for the ledgers and law books. She pulled down the first volume of *Blackstone's Commentaries on the Laws of England* and began leafing through it. Today, she thought, I will begin my lessons in law. I should be the lawyer, not James. She shrugged. As if that could ever happen. Women were not allowed to practice law. She replaced the book.

Turning to the matter at hand, she regarded her task. Father had set out a pile of documents to her left and placed a stack of vellum to her right. Sophia placed the top sheet of the creamy paper in front of her and smoothed it. Father always bought the best stock, she thought. Taking a pen from the small collection of goose and turkey quills Father kept in a battered pewter cup, she sighed again, this time with exasperation. The nub of the pen was worn as was the next. Her third choice, a white quill, hadn't been shaped yet.

"Oh, fiddlesticks," she said and began rummaging through the secretary's shallow center drawer for a penknife. When she found it, she discovered it was too dull to cut through the quill's shaft.

Now she was truly annoyed. Finding the whetstone in the same drawer, she began sharping the little blade but pressed too hard, almost breaking the tip. "Haste makes waste," she reminded herself, examining the blade. It was undamaged and felt sharp enough to shape a nib.

Placing the quill on the thick desk blotter, Sophia made two diagonal cuts, one on each side of the feather's shaft to make a broad point. Then, holding the quill firmly in place with her left thumb, she slit the shaft down the center. The blade bit into the tip of her thumb.

"Fiddlesticks, Fiddlesticks," she grumbled and pressed her forefinger against the injured tip to stop the bleeding.

This assignment is not beginning well, she thought, as she dipped the quill into the brass inkwell. The nub seemed to hold too much ink. If she pressed too hard, she could easily blot the paper. No inkblots, her father had said. She wiped away the excess ink and then, finally, began to write, being careful to hold her injured thumb away from the paper. Nothing is as easy as it seems, she thought.

When nooning time came, she ate alone. The rest of the family had left midmorning to visit the Muellers. Nathan, who was clearing fallen tree limbs from the Marshtown road, either hadn't noticed the time or hadn't wanted to walk all the way back to Great House for a meal. Sophia nibbled at Sally's stew and cornbread and quickly got back to work.

Before long, her hand was aching. Being Father's law clerk was not as fascinating as Sophia had imagined it to be. The work was exacting. No word could be omitted. Father had asked her to make two copies of each document. All the land deeds were written in language so similar that the names and particulars often confused her. She had to read each sentence at least twice to make sure she had written the correct words.

No wonder James had run from such a fate, she thought and leaned back in the chair. Lacing her fingers together, she raised her hands high above her head as far as her arms would reach and held them there. The stretch helped. She returned her attention to the desk, noticing that the stack of documents didn't seem to have dwindled significantly. She sighed. Her hand still ached. Apparently, the most she had to show for her labors was an injured thumb and ink-stained fingers. The middle and index fingers on her right hand were so black now that she feared no amount a scrubbing would clean them. Wearily, she pulled another document from the pile, a will this time.

In the name of God, Amen. The thirtyeth day of December, Anno Domini one thousand eight hundred and eleven. I Samuel Crown of Worcester County in the state of Maryland, being sick and weak of body but of perfect mind and memory, thanks be given unto God for His mercy, Splat

"Fiddlesticks!" Sophia looked at the splotch of ink spoiling the writing. She had pressed too hard on the nib. Crumbling up the page and throwing it away would be wasteful. With a little effort, she could correct her mistake.

She reached for the fine sand Father kept in a ginger jar and sprinkled it on the blot to draw up most of the ink. She would have to scrape off the rest with the pen knife. But when she looked in the drawer, she couldn't find it. She hunted around the desk then re-examined the drawer. No knife. Puzzled, she pulled the drawer all the way out. It looked too short for the space. She felt inside the square that held the drawer. As she brushed her fingers along the sides, she felt a gap at the back. That board was at least an inch too short. Maybe the knife was lodged behind it. As she wondered how to remove the board, she felt something hard like a nail head along near the top. She pushed it sideways and heard a faint click. The board dropped down, revealing another compartment. Inside this compartment, a stack of documents.

Never stopping to consider that she was snooping or that the documents hidden there were of a very private nature, she pulled them out. Rifling through the stack, she could see that most were land deeds, some quite old. Mixed amongst the deeds was a will. Wills were always interesting to read.

It began just as the will she was copying began except the date on this one was 1809 and it began, *I Joseph Records . . .* Sophia's eyes widened. She was holding Grandsire's last will and testament. Quickly scanning to what she called the bequeaths, she began to read:

Im primes, I give and bequeath unto my beloved elder son William my plantation Records Landing, including all its buildings and any harvest stored therein.

"This cannot be!"

"Grandsire, you gave Records Landing to the wrong son," she muttered. Sophia wanted to crumble the document into a ball and burn it. How could Grandsire be so heartless? The plantation should belong to Father. He's the one who ran it, she thought. Uncle William has no interest in farming. He is a merchant with a fine house in Baltimore. She glared at the will as if it were the enemy before, with a sigh, she resumed reading.

To my beloved son Elijah, I give and bequeath the bounty land in Ohio, his pick of my tools, the milk cow, and the long wool sheep along with my thanks for his good oversight of my land. In addition, I leave him the mahogany secretary, the dining table and chairs, and the brass door knocker.

The brass door knocker! What good is that, Sophia thought angrily, without a house or door for that matter?

To my beloved son Caleb, who has my love of the sea, I give and bequeath the schooner, the Rebel Ann.

"Finally, Grandsire," she muttered aloud, "A good decision. Uncle Caleb deserves the schooner."

Sophia read through all the bequeaths, written in what appeared to be Father's careful script. The oil portraits of Grandsire and Grandmama went to her Aunt Polly, along with the silver tea service and the tall case clock. Her mother was given the loom, the spinning wheel and Grandmama's pearl necklace. Willie was to receive Grandsire's gold watch when he reached adulthood and she, Sophia, was indeed the rightful owner of his gold compass. Some of the bequeaths she already knew—the shallop went to James, the four-poster bed, its linens, and the mahogany chest to her and Faith. Nothing new there. Then, toward the end she read that Uncle William was named executor. He was, first and foremost, to pay Grandsire's debts. Grandsire's signature. written in his familiar, bold hand, appeared at the end of the will.

Sophia sank back in the desk chair, staring blankly at the will. Had Grandsire lost his mind?

"Miss Phee, can I talk to you?"

Sophia looked up, startled. Jebbie was standing in the hall doorway.

"Granny said I was to talk to you," he said.

Sophia nodded. She gestured toward the wingback chair. "Make yourself to home."

Jebbie walked to the window instead. He peered outside as if expecting trouble.

"Is something wrong?"

"No'm, maybe," he mumbled.

Squaring his shoulders, he turned to face Sophia. "Granny told me to come see you after Pig Man came by our cabin this morning."

Sophia sat upright. "Mr. Talcott?"

"Yessum. He didn't pay me no never mind. Not Miz Chloe neither. He just talked to Granny but I was right there. I heard everything. He said she must sell her land to him and she said, no. He kept demanding, louder and louder. Granny kept saying, no. She didn't shout but she had this look on her face."

Jebbie pressed his lips into a firm straight line and narrowed his eyes. "Like that," he said.

Sophia smiled grimly. She had seen that look a time or two. "Go on," she said. "What happened next?"

"Pig Man stomped off the porch and walked out to the gate where his big horse was tied. As soon as he mounted, he yanked on the bit so hard the horse reared up. Pig Man shouted something, sounded like, 'Stubborn folks pay dearly in the end.' Then he spurred his horse into a gallop. That horse had his ears flat against his head. He doesn't like Pig Man any more than I do." Jebbie hugged his arms to his chest and shivered. "That man is up to no good. Least that's what Granny said."

Sophia glanced down at the document still on the desk. Surely Grandsire never realized what his will might set in motion. Best it had never seen the light of day, she thought, gathering all the hidden documents together and replacing them in their niche.

Jebbie had resumed his watch at the window. His anxious expression made Sophia uneasy. Yesterday Oriole had covered her ears when Sophia tried to tell her about the tunnel. "You tell Jebbie," she had said.

Rising, Sophia joined the boy at the window.

"Listen, Jebbie. My grandsire had a secret," she began softly. She ended her tale by saying, "If Mr. Talcott starts trouble, take the children and hide there."

Picking up the quill, she drew a map of the old trail beside the river on a sheet of Father's paper. Her drawing showed the trail trees and the bend in the river. She told him where the opening was but didn't mark it down.

"You understand this place must remain secret?" she said. "Don't tell anybody. Not even your mama. If too many folks know a secret, it's not a secret anymore."

She blotted the ink. "Follow the trail, memorize the way as you walk, and then burn the map in the fireplace when you get home tonight."

Jebbie stared at her, his eyes big and round. He nodded in a slow, solemn way, as if he were saying "Amen" in church.

"And there's something else," Sophia whispered. "There may be another way in. Grandsire told me the room at the end of the tunnel is underneath the old cabin at the edge of the orchard. I think there might be an entrance there."

Jebbie kept gazing intently at her but said nothing.

"*And*" Sophia added, "I think we should find it. Right now." She grasped Jebbie's shoulder and turned him toward the door."

"You go first," she said. "Act like you're hunting dried-up apples for the hog. I'll be along. It could be that one of the hens is missing. Who knows, she might be in the orchard."

Sophia winked. Jebbie grinned. She knew he was ready for the hunt.

"Now go," she said and gave him a little push. She watched from the window as he raced across the yard only to be stopped by his mama. Sally called to him from the cookhouse door. Apparently, she wanted him to do something because he kept flapping his arms and pointing toward the big house.

Sophia closed her eyes and prayed: "Don't tell your mother, Jebbie."

It looked like Sally won the argument because Jebbie grabbed a bucket and hurried to the springhouse. She stepped back inside the kitchen house only to walk outside minutes later carrying an empty burlap bag, a canteen, and a basket covered with a white napkin. She waited on the bench until Jebbie returned, lugging the heavy bucket. She filled the canteen and then put it in the basket. She handed Jebbie the empty bag, kissed him on the forehead, and walked off toward the orchard and the road to Marshtown.

Jebbie turned to face the office window and bowed low from the waist. He was grinning. Sophia exhaled, surprised that she had been holding her breath.

Apparently, Sally was none the wiser and out of the way. Jebbie has a talent for play-acting, she decided.

Sophia looked at her stained fingers and sighed. On the desk, there was only a slender pile of finished work stacked alongside the documents still to be copied. Stopping now would delay her even more than her previous snooping had. Sophia knew she would need another two days to finish her assigned task.

Realizing that she would have to figure out a way to explain her slow progress, she sighed again. Nothing I am doing is straightforward, she thought, ticking off the misdeeds on her fingers: Abiding by Judith's wishes not to reveal Mr. Talcott's treacherous plans, snooping in Father desk, reading Grandsire's will. Sometimes what appears wrong can be right, she told herself. Straightening her shoulders, she capped the inkwell, returned the quill to the pewter cup, and walked out of the office.

15

In the Apple Orchard

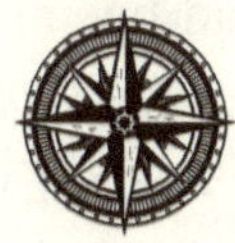

Calling out, "chick-a-chick-a-chick," Sophia walked toward the orchard, although no one was around to notice except Jebbie. He was poking into the bushes outside of the old cabin much like a hound puppy would when trying to find a scent. The burlap bag was about a quarter full of apples.

"Where did your mama go?" Sophia asked, worried Sally might be back soon.

"Oh, she wanted me to take Mr. Harkness something to eat. He's chopping up those blown down trees. Mama said he hadn't come back here for dinner and a man working that hard shouldn't miss a meal. So, I told Mama you needed me for important work. And she said, 'Well, in that case, I'll do it.' She didn't seem too put out about it."

Sophia smiled. Jebbie was always so earnest. "You're persuasive," she said and turned to face the cabin. "Have you looked inside?"

"I ain't goin' in there," he said. "There might be a duppie."

"It's just an old cabin. No duppies there," Sophia assured him. She had no intention of telling Jebbie it was quite possible that Grandsire's spirit might be nearby. She didn't want Jebbie or anyone else to talk about Grandsire the way they talked about the usual ghosts on the

Eastern Shore, the ones who rose from the mist to scare horses or who snatched sheets off clotheslines or who soured milk.

"Come on," she said a little too loudly and walked briskly through what had once been a doorway. Inside the afternoon sun was shining through the bare roof beams, creating a shifting pattern of light and shadow on the hard-packed dirt floor. The wooden shingles that once kept the cabin dry inside were now on the cookhouse roof. In fact, most of the one-room cabin had been scavenged for parts. One door and the cabin windows, frame and all, were gone, leaving rough-sawn empty squares in the thick log walls. Even the bricks from the hearth had been removed. The cabin reminded Sophia of a storm-wrecked ship left to rot on the shore.

"Ain't nothing here," said Jebbie, who had followed her in.

Sophia shook her head. "I'm not so sure. No puzzle worth solving is easy. Grandsire was a muskrat at heart. He would never let himself be trapped in a room with only one exit. See, even this little cabin has two doors."

A particularly strong gust of wind swooshed in through the roof, snatching Sophia's mobcap, and blowing it toward the second door.

"Oh, fiddlesticks," she said as she chased after it. She stopped short at the door. It seemed strange that one perfectly good door remained. She lifted the latch. Its iron hinges squawked loudly as Sophia pulled the door open and stepped onto a porch. The porch stretched from one end of the cabin to a woodbin near the opposite end. Not far from the door was a rocking chair. It was a pleasant spot to sit and had a good view of the woods that ran wild down to the river.

Sophia paused. For a minute she was six again seeing her grandsire sitting there on the old porch, smoking his pipe, and sipping peach brandy.

"Why are you out here all alone, Grandsire?" she had asked.

"Just enjoying the sunset and watching the wind."

"You can't see wind."

"Sure, you can. On land, trees show you the wind. At sea, the waves show you. Even when the ocean is calm, the lightest breeze will ruffle the water, telling you where the wind is coming from. When you watch for the signs, you can see lots of things that seem invisible."

Now a wind gust set the chair to rocking.

"Who be rocking that chair?" Jebbie said in a quavery voice. He had come up behind Sophia and was peeking past her.

Sophia grinned and quickly sat down in the weathered rocker. "Must be me," she said.

"You be careful, Miss Phee. You might be sitting on a duppie."

"Don't be silly, Jebbie. Now, you look around and tell me what you see."

"I see a big woodbin at the end of the porch. That's all I see, 'cept you in the chair and the plank floor." He walked over to the bin. The top was almost waist high.

"You are going to have to grow some more to fetch wood from the bottom of that bin," Sophia said.

Jebbie lifted the lid and leaned it against the log wall.

"Nah, I'd just jump inside." He hoisted himself up to sit on the edge. Sophia heard a soft thump.

"Whoa. The bottom's a long way from the top." Jebbie hollered. "You alright?"

"Yessum. Surprised is all."

Something's not right. Sophia thought. She walked over to the bin to get a better look. The porch floor ended at the bin so that instead of sitting on the planking, the woodbin was based on the ground. The proportions are all wrong, she thought, yanking open the lid to peer inside. The bin is too deep for practical use.

Just then Jebbie squealed.

"What is it, Jebbie? Spiders, snakes."

"I found something," he shouted, holding up what looked like a gold coin.

"Lucky you. Hold on to that," Sophia said but she thought it strange. People don't usually leave valuable coins in a woodbin. Nothing about this bin seemed right.

I wonder, she mused. Grandsire might have lost . . .

Then it clicked. Gathering her skirt in one hand, she sat sideways on the edge of the bin, swung her legs over and dropped down the few feet to the bottom. The floor, planked like the porch, was littered with wood scraps.

Crouching down, she felt along the floor, her fingers searching for something her eyes could not see in the dim light. Embedded in a plank near one side of the bin, she felt what she had hoped to find. An iron ring the size of her fist. She pulled at it. Part of the floor moved upward.

"This is it, Jebbie," she said in a hoarse whisper. "A trap door, a hatch. Of course. How like Grandsire. This is the way in!"

Jebbie was standing behind her, his back pressed against the front of the bin. He was holding the coin tight in his fist.

"I don't think we should go down there. You don't know what might be hiding in that place. I think we should go back to the house. Mama might be back."

"Faint heart never won fair maid."

"Huh?"

"I said don't be afraid."

"It's dark down there. We don't have no light."

"I'll go down. You be the look out."

Sophia tugged the hatch door wide open. It moved easily on its hinges. Unlike the old cabin's remaining door, someone had kept these hinges well oiled. In the faint light, Sophia saw stairs leading into inky darkness.

With her hand pressed against the earthen wall for balance, Sophia started down, feeling out each stair with her foot before putting her weight on it. The stairs creaked a bit but seemed sound. She tried not to think about spiders, but when a cobweb brushed across her face, she let out a muffled cry.

"You alright?" Jebbie asked in a quavery voice. He inched closer to the opening, sending bits of dried bark and dust floating down to settle on Sophia.

She sneezed a couple of times before answering.

"I'm fine. Just fine. You wait there, though. Don't leave me alone. And keep your voice down."

Sophia had counted seven stairs so far. As she felt around for the next one, she found she had reached the bottom. The problem now was that the stairs seemed simply to end. There was nowhere to go. The small space at the bottom of the hatchway seemed to be closing in on her, making it hard to breathe. She leaned against the wall in front of her. It moved slightly.

In that instant she knew. An image of Grandsire's secret room flashed into her mind. The cupboard, nearly empty, pushed against one of the walls. Of course. It hid the entrance. This wall was made of wood. She pushed it. The wall moved.

"Come on down, Jebbie," she shouted. "See what I've found."

"No, no. You come up," he called back in a loud whisper. "I heard someone ride through the orchard. It sounds like a horse stopped near the house."

Holding her skirt to one side, Sophia dashed up the hatchway. No one was expected. Mother, Faith, and Willie had planned to return close to suppertime. Besides, they took the wagon. It couldn't be them. Sally might have returned, but she was on foot. No matter who it is, Sophia thought, I need to be at Great House, not in a woodbin.

Scrambling up and out of the woodbin was no easy matter. Once on her feet, she reached back to help Jebbie. Then she closed the lid.

"Do I look like I've been inside a woodbin?" she asked shaking her skirts.

"You're dusty."

Sophia shook the folds of her gown more vigorously, then took off her mobcap and shook that too.

"Better?" she asked, settling the cap back on her head.

"Your cap's crooked."

She laughed. "You're better than a looking glass," she said and adjusted the cap. "Better now?"

Jebbie nodded. "You're forgettin' somethin'," he said in a solemn tone and opened his fist. The gold coin lay in his palm. He looked at it in such a loving way that Sophia couldn't keep from smiling.

"This belongs to you," he said and thrust the coin at her.

Examining it, she saw an image of King George and the date 1776. She drew in her breath, then gently closed Jebbie's hand over the coin.

"It's a British guinea, Jebbie," she said softly. "And it's yours. Finders, keepers."

Jebbie's eyes widened.

"You never know when you are going to need a guinea," she said. "Keep it safe."

"I will," he said.

"Now, let's go see who's come calling."

Sophia heard the knocker's loud, repetitive rapping as she picked her way through the tall weeds that grew along the cabin wall. Someone was expecting her to be at home. Someone was bringing news. Maybe it was about James.

Picking up her skirts, Sophia dashed through the orchard toward Great House, but at the road she stopped short. A long-legged bay horse with one white stocking was tied to the hitching post. Judith Talcott in her elaborate bonnet was standing at the front door.

"Quick go back to the cabin and grab that sack of apples," she told Jebbie. "You've got some pretending to do and I need to find out why Miss Talcott is banging on our door before she knocks it down."

16

What's Coming Down the Road

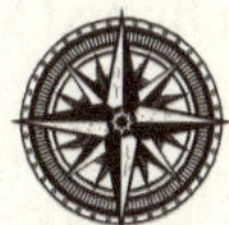

Dressed in a light gray riding habit with the veiled gray bonnet pulled tight over her dark curls, Judith could have been a pale replica of her mother. The difference was the noise she was making. Sophia doubted that the late Mrs. Talcott would ever have had the audacity to clang the front door knocker with such astonishing force. Sophia was sure she saw sparks.

"Take pity on our door. I am coming."

Turning, Judith waved. Then stealthy as a shadow, she opened the door and slipped inside the house.

"Can you believe that?" Sophia muttered to Jebbie, who had caught up, the apple sack slung over his back. "Some people have no manners. She doesn't live here yet!"

But then I shouldn't be surprised, she thought. After all she is the Pig Man's daughter.

Sophia was still seething when she swept into the hall a minute or so later with Jebbie in tow. Nor did her disposition improve when she discovered Judith standing in Father's office, peering out the side window, much like Jebbie had earlier in the afternoon.

"Is the view of the orchard better from inside the house?" Sophia asked, not even trying to hide her annoyance.

"You never know what might be coming down the road. Like that goose of yours." Judith said without turning from the window.

"What brings you to Great House?" Sophia asked coldly as she walked over to the secretary to determine if Judith had been snooping. The drawers were closed, the documents to be copied undisturbed

"When I was last here, your mother invited me to return when I had more time. She said she wanted to tell me about the house. Things she thought I should know." Judith turned away from the window to look at Sophia.

"When no one answered the door, I was afraid you were gone," Judith added. "Where were you?"

"Out hunting chickens," Sophia said flatly.

"And apples," Jebbie said, holding up his sack, a wide grin on his face.

"And apples," Sophia echoed. She smiled at the boy. He was really good at pretending. How could anyone stay angry with Jebbie around.

"I am afraid you came all the way here for nothing," Sophia continued in a more pleasant tone and then preceded to explain that Father was away on business. The rest of the family was at Mueller's place and wouldn't be back until late.

"Marriage plans," Sophia said. "My sister and the Mueller's son, Zachariah. You can't imagine how giddy Faith is now that Father has agreed to the match." Sophia rolled her eyes to convey her sister's temporary lunacy.

"Oh. How nice." Even the veil could not hide the other girl's sour expression.

Instantly recognizing her mistake, Sophia stammered out a quick "I'm sorry." She hadn't meant to be cruel. She knew there was no love in Judith's impending marriage, only duty.

"Have you met Jebediah?" she asked in a rush. "Jebbie, this is Miss Talcott."

"Please to meet you, Miss Talcott." Jebbie made a little bow.

Judith frowned. "Don't you have some place to be, boy?"

"Yessum," Jebbie said, looking down at his feet.

"Look at me when you speak, boy," Judith snapped.

"Well, I never," Sophia said without raising her voice. "Apparently, Jebbie, Miss Talcott is saying in an impolite way that she needs a word with me privately. Now might be a good time to feed those apples to the hog."

As Jebbie started to walk out the door, Sophia said more loudly, "Be careful. Hogs can be mean, just like some people."

"Yessum, Miz Phee," Jebbie said in an exaggerated way and marched outside, the apple sack slung over his shoulder.

"That boy's sassy. He'd best watch his step when I'm mistress here."

Sophia gave Judith a hard look. "Around here we speak respectfully to everyone," she said. "I suspect Jebbie won't be in a hurry to help out when you're living here."

"He'll do as I say."

"Jebbie's no slave," Sophia said, her tone clipped. "You forget."

"Colored is colored. Slave or free." Judith turned toward the window. She stood there surveying the orchard for a minute or two before facing Sophia again.

"I am afraid I have started off on the wrong foot," she said. "Please, let's begin again. When I was out riding, I saw your cook Sally on the road, talking to that white boy who works here. When she told me that you were the only one to home, I rode directly here. So, you see, I didn't come to see the house. I came to talk you."

Sophia felt a trickle of alarm. "And why was that?"

"If things were different, if I hadn't gotten sick, if James were still here, we might someday have become family, sisters-in-law."

Judith paused. "Regardless of who are our fathers are," she added, emphasizing every word. "Whatever you may think of me, I was, am, your brother's friend. And in the spirit of that friendship, I think we need to talk."

Sophia drew in her breath sharply. With a curt nod, she ushered Judith into the parlor and sat her in the armchair near the hearth. A fire had been laid but was unlit and Sophia left it that way. Picking up one of the straight chairs, she placed it so that it faced Judith and then sat down, folding her hands primly in her lap.

"I am listening," she said, then waited without further comment for Judith to begin. Sophia had no intention of acting eager. Whatever Judith had to say, it couldn't be that important anyway.

Judith leaned back in the chair and closed her eyes briefly before sitting upright and loosening her bonnet strings. She gazed around, a wistful look on her face.

"Our parlor is not near as pretty as this one," she said, smoothing her riding skirt, although it didn't need smoothing. "Will you be moving the furniture to Ohio?"

"No. Some of the pieces my uncles are taking; the rest are to be sold."

Sophia looked at the room so elegantly furnished by Grandsire years ago. The thought of selling even one chair made her miserable.

"I must tell my pa."

"Is that why you came today? To appraise the furniture?"

Judith shook her head. She reached into the elaborately embroidered pocket she wore tied around her waist, pulled out a folded sheet of paper and handed it to Sophia.

"Pa has a stack of these," she said. "He is always on the lookout for fugitives."

Sophia unfolded the handbill. Placing it on her lap, she began flattening out the creases with her palm. The first thing she noticed was the inky portrait.

"Why bring me this?" she asked as a knot of fear began to grow in her belly.

The headline in large black letters screamed: "RUNAWAY $50 REWARD." Underneath was the sketch of a young black woman's face which bore a striking resemblance to Chloe. Worse, beneath the drawing, a paragraph described a woman very much like the blacksmith's wife, even the names were the same:

Ran away on the 10th of January, 1810, from my plantation PLEASANT LAND in Prince George's County, Maryland, a NEGRO WOMAN, named CHLOE TYLER. She is of a copper color, 18 years of age, rather a pleasant countenance, slender and well made, has a short, quiet walk, and stammers very much when she speaks. She has a thick scar from the bite of a dog on her right leg. The bite was cauterized to prevent hydrophobia. She has free relatives in Washington City. I will give $50 if she is taken in Prince George's County and $100 elsewhere. In either case she must be delivered to my manager, Mr. Covington Jones, or secured in jail so that he can re-claim her.

—H. L. Woods

Chloe might be that runaway, Sophia realized. She often stammered when she was nervous. As for the scar, that was unknown. Chloe wore a long dress so her bare legs were never exposed.

"I have never seen this person."

Sophia handed the paper back to Judith. "If you are trying to find her, I am afraid your trip has been wasted."

"No, you don't understand. I am not Pa's spy. I wanted you to know that Pa thinks he saw her this morning in Marshtown. She was sitting in a rocking chair at Oriole's and holding a tiny baby."

Judith leaned toward Sophia. "I am not trying to cause trouble," she said, looking around the room once more. "What I have to say is for you alone. No one else is around? Not the cook or that boy Jebbie?"

"No one," Sophia said, now anxious to hear what the other girl had to say.

Squaring her shoulders, Judith sat up straighter. Then, surprisingly, she removed her bonnet, exposing her pock-scarred face. It was as if Judith was saying, I have nothing to hide. Sophia moved her chair closer. The hall clock was chiming the hour as the older girl leaned forward. She spoke softly about what had happened at the Talcott plantation that morning, saying that her Pa had rushed back from Marshtown in an agitated state. His poor horse was so lathered up that the stableman had to walk him for an hour before the horse was cool enough to be stabled.

"As soon as Pa came in the house," Judith said, lowering her voice even further, "he started shouting for Mr. Dowling. That man is living at our house now. Him and his two noisy children."

By the sour look on Judith's face, Sophia didn't need reminding that Mr. Dowling was the man Mr. Talcott had chosen to marry his daughter.

"That no-account man would murder his own mother for money," Judith added before going on with the story.

According to Judith, she had watched from the doorway while her pa had flipped through the handbills advertising fugitive slaves until he found the one that he believed described the woman he had seen in Marshtown. He told Mr. Dowling the woman had been holding a newborn child, so that turning her over to the law might bring even more money than the reward poster offered.

"It gets worse," she said, pressing her hands together as if praying for forgiveness. "For an uneducated man, Mr. Dowling must know every law concerning runaways in Maryland. Right off the top of his head, he quoted a law passed by the Maryland legislature in 1796. That law sets a fine of $300 on free Negros convicted of forging freedom papers for slaves. The law doesn't apply to white men, Sophia—not that your father would forge papers—but it does apply to anyone in Marshtown who supplied a runaway with freedom papers."

"No one in Marshtown would forge papers," Sophia said. "Nor does anyone in Marshtown have the money to pay such a steep fine."

"Please," said Judith, "hear me out. This is the worst part."

Sophia nodded. Outwardly her expression was impassive. Inwardly she was seething.

"Mr. Dowling told Pa that the law specified that any free negro convicted of forging papers who was unable to pay the fine could be sold into slavery to pay off the debt."

Judith cleared her throat. "Pa clapped Mr. Dowling on the shoulder, saying 'Two birds, one stone! We will collect the reward and clear those darkies out of Marshtown. What a stroke of good fortune.'"

"A terrible mistake has been made," Sophia said, trying to keep the alarm out of her voice. Except, knowing the Talcott family's history of profiting from false accusations, Sophia believed everyone in Marshtown was in danger, certainly Chloe, Abraham, and Ulysses, perhaps, even Oriole. Something Oriole had said yesterday now came to mind.

"Babies need to be wrapped tight," Oriole had murmured as she swaddled Chloe's son, wrapping him up so that only his little face showed. "Babies need to get used to freedom a little bit at a time—just like slaves who break free."

At the time, Sophia had been too swept up in the excitement of Abraham's birth to think about Oriole's words. Now she was worried that Chloe really was the runaway described in the poster. Nobody knew exactly where she had come from, just that Ulysses had brought her to Marshtown early last year. When Chloe came to Great House to help spin wool into yarn, if any visitors stopped by, Mother always shut the doors to the wool room, leaving the girl alone to work uninterrupted. Or at least, that is what Sophia had thought at the time.

"Father would never permit such a travesty of justice," she now said with conviction. She balled up her fists as if ready to fight Mr. Talcott herself. "Father would represent Chloe before the magistrate in Snow Hill."

"He won't have the chance. Pa plans to forestall that possibility until your family leaves Maryland."

Judith refolded the handbill and returned it to her pocket, then picked up her bonnet.

"He has big plans, you know," she added. "Everyone in Marshtown should start carrying their papers at all times. Even that young boy, Jebbie. Right now, those people travel freely along the road. No one stops them on the Marshtown road and asks to see their papers so Pa is hiring patrollers from Virginia to keep an eye on things. Any white man can stop any black man for any reason and demand to see his papers but a patroller . . ."

Her voice trailed off. Patrollers were well known to be bullies. She settled the bonnet on her head and retied the gray ribbons tightly under her chin.

"I can't be gone too long," she said, standing. "I keep expecting Mr. Dowling to show up here at any minute. He tries to keep track of my whereabouts. Even so, I had to chance coming here."

Standing, Sophia grasped Judith's arm. "Why? Why come here?"

"Because . . ." Judith's gaze wavered. "Because soon Great House will be mine and I don't want trouble. Because I thought maybe you could convince those people to sell their land to Pa, move someplace else. My pa, like a lot of other plantation owners, believes free coloreds incite slaves to run off. He doesn't want any free coloreds living nearby. It's bad for his business. Pa says runaways are nothing more than thieves, thieves stealing themselves."

Sophia cleared her throat. "I guess I should thank you. It sounds as if you took a risk coming here." She gave Judith a speculative glance. "Does your father confide in you? Is that how you know his feelings?"

"No. I hear things," Judith said and brushed Sophia's hand away. "Unlike Pa and some of his friends, I don't think of you as the enemy. I thought you should know. There are stories, you know, stories about how your father and grandfather have helped runaways disappear.

Maybe in the marsh, maybe aboard your uncle's ship. But somehow, they just vanish."

"That's malicious gossip."

Judith shrugged. "Be that as it may, I overheard Pa say to Mr. Dowling that if Elijah Records interfered with their plans in any way, he would see to it—and these were his exact words—he would 'see to it that the high and mighty Elijah Records rots in jail for felonious acts.' Sophia, you are a lawyer's daughter. You must know that helping fugitives escape is a crime."

The clock chimed five. Judith leapt to her feet. "I have been here too long," she said. "Please, tell your mother I will come back another time." She smiled and extended her hand as if what had just been said had not happened, as if all the two of them had talked about was the weather.

Sophia walked with her to the front door.

Stepping outside, Judith said, "At the very least, you must tell those Marshtown darkies to be careful. Pa will be posting at least one patroller on the Marshtown road."

Halfway down the walk, she turned back to wave goodbye.

Judith acts as if we're the best of friends, Sophia thought, watching Judith struggle to mount her horse, who refused to stand still so that after a few minutes, Sophia felt obliged to call out to Jebbie. He came to Judith's aid slowly, scuffing his feet in the dirt as he ambled over from the cookhouse, a sulky expression on his face.

Once Judith mounted, Sophia closed the door. Such an unpredictable girl, she thought. Judith says she fears for the folks in Marshtown and yet she can't treat a boy from Marshtown with the respect he deserves. Is such a person trustworthy? After all, Judith is a Talcott.

A Question of Law

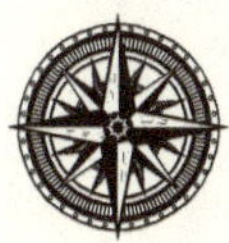

Judith's words haunted Sophia. Even though she tried to put her worry aside as she copied the wills and land deeds, Sophia began making mistakes, copying the same line twice or confusing the names of buyer and seller.

This will never do, she thought, as she crumpled up yet another sheet of spoiled paper before tossing it to the floor to join its fellows. She pushed her chair away from the desk in annoyance and began gathering up the flawed documents. These she threw, one by one, into the smoldering fire. It flared, hungry for the wasted vellum.

Hothead, she thought. That is what James used to call me. He said, one day my temper would flare and I would go up in smoke.

Well, James, you might go up in smoke, too, if you knew what Pig Man is scheming. And Judith, for all I know, is his accomplice. How well did you really know her? Can she be trusted? I really need to talk to you.

For a moment, Sophia felt the same intense pain she had suffered when James had first gone missing. Turning, she walked back to the desk and sank down on the chair. Sometimes losing her twin became a weight almost too heavy to bear. Pressing her fist to her mouth, she willed herself not to cry.

Sophia was sitting there still unable to pick up a pen when Mother walked into the office a few minutes later. Putting her hands on Sophia's shoulders, Mother gently rubbed the tightness away.

"I think you have done enough," Mother said. "You've been at this task for two days now. There are only a few documents left. You can finish up another day."

Sophia turned sideways in the chair. "I've made some mistakes," she said. "Wasted some paper."

Mother shrugged. "Everyone makes mistakes," she said. "What you need is a change of scenery."

Sophia gave her mother a speculative glance. "Father often talks to you about his cases. May I ask you something, something about the law?"

"I pick up bits and pieces. I hope this doesn't mean you are aspiring to be a lawyer. That's men's work."

Sophia wrinkled her nose in distaste. "After all this work, I would never even consider that job. I just have a question about certain laws."

"In that case, I will try."

"Is it true that the laws for white people and colored are different, even if the colored folk are free?

Mother crossed her arms. "Why do you want to know?"

"No reason. I just wondered if it were true?"

Mother sighed. "It's true," she said. "Certain laws exist because Maryland permits slavery and slaves are considered property. There are even special laws to protect slave holders from loss of this property."

"People aren't property."

"You and I know that but try telling people like the Talcotts."

"And is it true that any white man can stop any colored man and demand to see his papers?"

"Yes."

Despite noticing that the questions upset her mother, Sophia persisted. "Father says Ohio is a free state."

Mother nodded.

"Still, if a white man helped a slave escape in Maryland and the slave was caught in Ohio, would the man who helped the slave go to jail?"

"Really, Sophia. Don't pester me with questions. As I said, I only know bits and pieces of the law, things your father has told me. But it stands to reason that since slaves are considered property, then, yes, the white man would go to jail if convicted."

"Women, too?"

"Women, too. What's this all about, Sophia. Are you planning on breaking the law?"

"No. Just curious." She looked down at her ink-stained fingers. "You can't have me sitting here all day surrounded by law books and then be surprised that I start wondering about the law."

"Well, in that case, you are granted a reprieve. I need all hands on deck, as your grandsire would say. Uncle William has sent word that he and Aunt Polly are coming sooner than expected." Mother held up a crumpled letter. "This came off the packet ship from Baltimore yesterday. I received it courtesy of Mr. Harkness. William writes that he and your aunt will arrive by carriage, so we needn't arrange for anyone to meet them on the dock at Snow Hill. He explains that he will be collecting the tall case clock, and the oil paintings plus a few of the things we plan to leave behind."

Sophia groaned softly. "I will miss the sound of the clock. As for the paintings . . ." she trailed off before saying, "How will I recall my grandparents' faces?"

Mother sighed. It was an old argument, what to leave and what to take. She touched the center of Sophia's chest gently.

"Here," Mother said. "You will always carry them here. In your heart." Stiffening, she added in a no-nonsense tone, "Uncle William also informed me they plan to remain here to help us close down the plantation."

"I can't imagine Aunt Polly being any help at all. She just wants to make sure we don't take anything she wants."

"Sophia, really. You must respect your elders," Mother said before adding under her breath, "Even if they put on airs or come too soon."

Sophia wrinkled her nose.

Mother continued. "I want you to show Mr. Harkness the way to Uncle Caleb's cabin first thing in the morning. Sally needs oysters for the welcome dinner."

"I suppose this means the water way." Sophia turned her face toward the secretary and began fiddling with the documents. She hadn't set foot in any one of the small boats since James had left.

"It is the fastest way," Mother said and squeezed Sophia's shoulders gently. "The river is safe, Sophia. You have been traveling on it since you were a baby. You know every turn it makes."

Silence. Then Mother said more briskly, "If you don't fight this new fear of yours, you will be landlocked forever." She pulled Sophia to her feet. "Now, go stretch your legs. You have been at this work far too long."

18

Uncle Caleb's Cabin

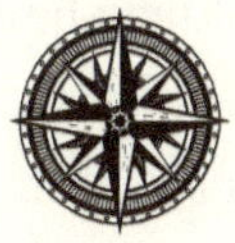

Sophia stared at the river, scanning the murky brown water for snags, sunken logs that could ram the canoe, capsizing it. She knew she must stay alert. Even though she knew the Pocomoke's every twist and turn, the river was always changing.

"Don't be afraid of it, but always respect it," Grandsire had warned when he first showed her how to read the river.

Now, kneeling close to the front of the canoe, Sophia rested her paddle across the triangular bow. Cool gusts of wind brushed past her face and tugged at the red ribbon she had used to bind her thick braid. Despite Mother's urging, she was hatless. The sunbonnet lay in the bow, where she had stowed it as soon as she and Nathan were out of sight of the dock.

She twisted around to smile pleasantly at him. Kneeling in the stern, Nathan was facing the bow with his knees placed far enough apart so that he could steady the canoe by shifting his weight. He wore James's hat tipped forward, shading his face, so that his expression was as hard to read as the river. He seemed so distant these days. Maybe this trip to Uncle Caleb's would help make them better friends.

"Dress up a little," Faith had told her last night. "If you want Nathan to pay attention to you, charm him. Just smile your sweetest smile and look him in the eye. Then cast your eyes downward and flutter your eyelashes a little. And always make him feel important. Men like to feel important."

Last night, Sophia had laughed and called her sister a "silly goose;" but now, looking at Nathan as he muscled the canoe swiftly forward with each firm stroke of his paddle, she thought she might give Faith's advice a try.

"I'm glad Mother could spare you. It's a nice day to be on the river," she ventured.

"Aye."

Sophia sighed. Just as Faith had already intimated, Nathan was going to be a tough nut to crack. Maybe she should just give up and just take pleasure in the day. She raised her face toward the sky, enjoying the sun's warmth. The wind brought the faint smell of the ocean and left a taste of salt on her lips.

Closing her eyes, she thought about oysters. Mother wanted two small barrels of them as she was planning oyster stew for tomorrow's dinner.

"We might as well enjoy our Maryland oysters," Mother had said. "It will be a long time, if ever, before we have them again."

Recalling her mother's wistful tone, Sophia wondered if there were oysters in Ohio. She looked back at Nathan. He seemed quite sure of himself as he propelled the small craft swiftly forward through the current.

"Do people eat oysters in Ohio?"

Nathan shook his head. "Clams. They are tasty."

"I wager oysters taste better."

Nathan shrugged. "Shouldn't you be watching the river?

"The river's high. The current's strong," she shot back, staring intently at him. Then, she looked down and fluttered her eyelashes.

"You got something in your eye?"

"No!"

So much for Faith's advice, she thought and felt heat radiating from her cheeks. Blushing is a curse, she thought. Turning toward the bow, she began to paddle. With each strong, straight stroke, she inhaled deeply. A minute or two later she felt better. It was easier to breathe out here, she decided. Easier to think, too. The persistent slap of water against the bow was soothing, unlike home these days.

The whole place had been a flurry of activity ever since Father's announcement. Faith's marriage proposal had only added to the turmoil. Mother and Faith were sorting through household items, determining what to take and what to leave behind. Any duplicate kitchen items were Faith's if the Muellers had space in their wagon. Most of the furniture was to be sold.

"We'll bring our tools, the cooking pots, clothes and, of course, the books. There is little room on the wagon for more," Father had declared that first night. "We can make what we need in Ohio."

"You can't make bone china, Mr. Records," Mother had responded. "We will bring the china."

Father had looked at her, raising one eyebrow.

"If I pack the dishes in wool batting, just as my mother did in Scotland, the china will make the trip across the mountains with nary a chip."

She had hesitated before adding in a no-nonsense tone, "And the feather beds. I have it on good authority from Mrs. Briggs that there are no feathers in Ohio. Her brother relocated to Ohio just last year, and his family is making do with straw. I draw the line at straw."

Sophia chuckled, remembering her sister's astonished expression. Neither she nor Faith had heard Mother openly dispute Father except for the time he had brought home the French bathtub. That time Father had prevailed despite Mother's contention that bathing would bring on illness. Now the whole family one by one bathed in the copper tub on a regular basis. Today, however, Mother prevailed.

Raising his hands in surrender, Father said, "Agreed. The feather beds and the china will go on the wagon."

"Hey," Nathan shouted from the stern, abruptly bringing Sophia back to the present. "Is that a snag?"

Alarmed, Sophia looked for any telltale ripples or swirls.

"All's well." She shouted back.

"Aye."

Sophia huffed, exhaling her annoyance at his short answer. Nathan was a puzzle. He had seemed talkative, friendly even, when he had brought her home from Oriole's after the storm. Since then, he had become more taciturn.

Oh, he was pleasant enough, she thought. He always smiled and tipped his hat—James's hat really—when she greeted him, but at meals he never addressed her or Faith. She had tried plying him with questions about Ohio but he always deferred to Father. Faith said he was shy. Sophia wasn't so sure.

She twisted around and gave Nathan what she hoped was her most winsome smile.

"Is the Pocomoke as pretty as the Ohio River?"

"It's hard to say. They're different."

Annoyed, Sophia splashed some water at him with her paddle. He ducked and splashed her back. The canoe rolled slightly. Sophia gasped and grabbed the gunwales, tearing one of her fingernails.

"You're not funny," she stormed. "We could have capsized."

"Sorry."

With two quick strokes, Nathan steadied the canoe.

"Perhaps we should move closer to the riverbank. The current is not so strong there," Sophia said, trying to keep the fear out of her voice.

Nathan nodded and steered the canoe nearer to land, The river was flowing through a swampy area, where bald cypress once grew. Years ago slaves had felled and skinned the trees, floating the massive trunks downriver to be cut into boards and shingles at the Snow Hill lumber mill. Water-swollen stumps and half-submerged snarls of tree limbs remained.

The canoe scraped against a large branch, barely visible above the water line.

"Turn starboard!" Sophia shouted as she stabbed at the obstacle with her paddle. Shoving the canoe away, she spotted a telltale ripple two feet in front of the boat.

"Snag! Dead ahead," she yelled, knowing that a jagged stump could rip a hole in their canoe. She began frantically backpaddling against the current.

"Paddle up!"

Surprised, she looked back. Nathan was holding his blade firm, slowing the boat. Fighting the current required all of his strength, and she saw his knuckles whitened as he thrust the wide blade of his paddle sideways away from the canoe. It veered sharply away.

Sophia gulped. Fear shivered up her spine. Only Nathan's quick reactions had saved them from being swamped or worse. Her throat tightened, making it hard to breathe. Did drowning hurt?

Sophia had never even thought about it before James disappeared on the river. Now, as she nibbled at the sharp edges of her broken nail, she imagined falling into the river, being dragged down by her clothes, fighting to resurface. Her lungs would beg for air until, unable to hold her breath any longer, she felt water rush in.

Greedily Sophia breathed in the river air, trying to ease the feeling of suffocation.

"Thanks. You saved us from a wetting," she said as soon as she was able. Her voice sounded strained, but Nathan didn't seem to notice.

"It was nothing." He spoke matter-of-factly as though he hadn't been even slightly alarmed. "You might as well stow your paddle. The current's so strong all I need do is keep the canoe pointed in the right direction." He patted the side of the canoe lovingly. "She's yar."

"Actually, I prefer a bateau." Sophia spoke sharply, miffed that he didn't need her help.

"Why?"

"It's not so tippy."

Nathan grinned. Slowly he shifted his weight from one foot to the other, making the canoe wobble. "You mean like this?"

"Stop it!"

"'Fraid of getting wet?"

"No!" Sophia snapped.

"Hey, you started it back there when you splashed me."

"And I could finish it, too."

"I 'spec you could," was Nathan's only reply, again in that annoying emotionless tone.

Sophia shrugged off the comment. He finally starts talking, she told herself, and I start an argument. What's the matter with me?

The capricious March wind began to play with her hair ribbon again, and she hunched down to protect herself from its bite. Nathan began to whistle. The high sweet sound of "Oh Susannah" seemed to harmonize with a blackbird's trill while the resonance of ripples lapping against the sides of the canoe added to the symphony. Unable to resist the tune, Sophia joined in, singing the words softly. "Oh, Susanna! Oh, don't you cry for me . . ."

For the moment she was content. The Pocomoke and its tributaries were as familiar to her as streets and avenues were to town dwellers. Her signposts were landmarks—an outcropping of rocks or a leaning tree. Keeping an eye out for Hunger Creek, Sophia noticed that the shrubbery and the trees along the riverbank were greener than a week ago. Time seemed to be swirling by faster than the current.

"There," Sophia called out minutes later, interrupting the song. "See that dead oak? That's just before you turn into the creek."

Backpaddling against the current again, Nathan swung the prow into the creek's frothy mouth. Then with strong, steady strokes he propelled the canoe through the turbulence. Admiring his seemingly effortless skill, Sophia wondered where he learned to handle a canoe so well. In many ways he handled it better than James. And Nathan didn't act as if he would take chances just for the thrill of it.

The little creek ran eastward toward the ocean, winding first through freshly plowed fields and then through woods. Because of the recent storm, the stream ran high. Sophia felt herself relax. There was no need for a lookout now. Sophia fished around for her bonnet. Turning to face Nathan, she rested her back against the bow.

She gave him a little smile, hoping to patch things up. "You're going to like Uncle Caleb. He's my father's younger brother. He's captain of the *Rebel Ann*. She was my grandsire's schooner. When Uncle Caleb is not at sea, he fishes the oyster beds near here."

"Ain't important whether I like him or not."

"Oh, honestly, Mr. Harkness."

His taciturn manner made her stomach churn. Apparently there's no way to carry on a conversation with this boy. Still, Mother always said that sugar attracted more flies than vinegar, Sophia thought.

"Look, I am sorry I got mad at you for rocking the boat. I get jumpy."

"I didn't mean nothing by it. I know how to keep a boat from turning turtle."

The remark struck Sophia as conceited.

"I 'spec you do," she said, mimicking his earlier remark.

This time, Nathan seemed to take offence. He tugged his hat lower over his brow and looked away.

Sophia stared out at the passing countryside and sighed. Nathan was hopeless.

The landscape was changing. Hunger Creek now flowed through a brackish marsh where coarse grasses grew. Home to a multitude of birds, the marsh was full of activity and sound. Overhead a few black-headed gulls hung suspended in the sky as though watching for intruders. Their mewing cries were as familiar to Sophia as the sound of the sea wind. Except for the sound of water lapping against the canoe and the cry of the gulls, the marsh was silent, as though it was holding its breath until the intruders had passed through.

Sophia gazed about in renewed wonder. This was her world. Along the grassy banks, bright yellow birds darted about looking for dried seed heads. A redwing holding dried grass in its beak flew by. A large turtle, sunning on a log, dropped into the creek with a faint plop. A great blue heron, pausing in its search for soft-shelled crabs, flapped its grey wings and, uttering a high barking cry, took flight, its long legs dangling. Nearby an ibis, high-stepping along the creek bed stopped to stare at the two travelers before resuming its hunt for minnows.

Nathan let out a low whistle of astonishment.

"Never seen a purple bird like that before. This place is pretty."

"I love the marsh." Sophia's voice caught. "I can't imagine any place more beautiful."

"Ohio is beautiful in its own way," Nathan said as he pushed up the brim of his hat. "It's hilly compared to here, and the forest is so thick with huge trees that in summer the leaves block the sunlight. There, summers are shady and cool. The woods are full of critters. Deer, bear, even a wooly cow-like beast folks call a buffalo. In Ohio, if a man knows how to hunt, he will never go hungry."

Sophia could hear the pride in his voice. "You make it sound like an Eden," she said with as much enthusiasm as she could muster even as she wondered if there were snakes in this Eden as well.

"I like sun," she blurted out loud.

Nathan laughed. "Well, I never said I didn't."

Before she could think up a reply, Sophia spotted Uncle Caleb's landing.

"There it is!" She pointed to a short-weathered pier nearly hidden in the tall marsh grass. Leaning down, she pulled off her bothersome shoes, suggesting that Nathan go barefoot, too.

"Over that hill lies the bay. On the far side is the barrier island called Assateague Island. It lies between the bay and the ocean. Anyway, this beach is no place for shoes." She wiggled her toes in anticipation of walking barefoot in the sand.

As soon as the canoe slid alongside the dock, Sophia scrambled out and secured the canoe to a piling with the bowline. Impatient to see her uncle, she stood at the beginning of the path, shifting her weight from one foot to the other while waiting for Nathan, who was slower to step onto the dock and tie up the stern. When he started unloading the small barrels, Sophia couldn't stand it any longer. "I'll just run ahead and let Uncle Caleb know we're here. Unless, of course, you need a hand."

Nathan straightened and looked at her, a little half smile on his face. "You go on, Miss Records. I'll be along directly."

"Why don't you call me 'Phee'? I thought we'd settled that."

"Don't want to show disrespect."

"I appreciate that. I truly do, but friends don't need to be so formal."

Nathan grinned. "So, we're friends. Well, that suits me fine. Much better than enemies."

Sophia turned toward the bluff. She knew she was blushing and didn't want Nathan to see.

"You go ahead," he said. "I'll catch up."

Sophia walked part way up the path then turned back toward the pier.

"Be sure to stay on the path. There's quicksand around here. When you get to the top, you can see his house." She waited to see Nathan nod before continuing up the bluff.

"Friends, imagine that," Sophia thought, and there was a little skip to her step as she hurried up the sandy path.

At the top of the dune, Sophia halted. The beauty of the sparkling blue water of Sinnepuxant Bay made her catch her breath in delight. Below, on a sandy point jutting into the bay, she could see Uncle Caleb's weathered gray cottage. Built above ground on thick cypress pilings, the house appeared taller than its one story. Sophia thought it magical. On dark overcast days the pilings seemed to disappear, blending into the gray water and mist. On those days the house looked as if it was floating in the bay. Sometimes, when fog rolled in from the ocean, Sophia had seen the house disappear entirely.

Today, however, the house was fully visible. It was low tide. Small waves chased each other onto the beach to splash against the pilings. At high tide Sophia knew seawater would swirl below the cottage floor.

Uncle Caleb's simple, three-room house had been built to accommodate a waterman's needs. A lengthy pier ran along the north side of the house out to deep water. A short gate opened to a wide porch facing the bay. She had once asked her uncle why he had built such an unusual house.

"I need only to step out onto the porch to get a good view of the entire bay," he had said. "My boat is always near, so I can come and go as I please during any tide."

From her vantage point, today, Sophia saw that Uncle Caleb already had a visitor. A second, slightly larger boat was moored beside her uncle's familiar whaler. Another waterman, she guessed. He was standing next to her uncle on the pier and was pointing south toward the mouth of the bay where large waves crested, then crashed onto the unprotected shoreline. Assuming the man had sought safe harbor in the bay to avoid the rough seas, Sophia didn't hesitate in announcing her arrival.

Putting two fingers to the corners of her mouth, she whistled shrilly the way James had taught her years ago, a skill her mother deplored, saying that whistling girls and cackling hens always come to very bad ends. The two men looked toward the sound. Sophia grinned, pulled off her bonnet, and began waving it in the air like a signal flag before rushing down the path.

As she hurried up the steep wooden stairs that led from the beach to the tall pier, she heard the men laughing.

Uncle Caleb held out his arms to her in welcome. He grinned. "You looked like a schooner under full sail coming down the bluff."

Instead of laughing at the comparison as she normally would, Sophia uttered a low moan. The man standing next to her uncle wasn't a fisherman as she had assumed he was. He was Commodore Decatur. Feeling her cheeks flush with embarrassment, she began smoothing her skirts. He must think me to be a silly little girl, she thought, plopping the sunbonnet back on her head and pulling the brim forward to shade her reddening face.

The commodore doffed his hat. "That's quite a whistle you have, Miss Records."

Wishing she had waited for Nathan, wishing she had worn shoes, wishing she'd heeded her mother's warning, Sophia curtsied, bowing her head so low that when she murmured how pleased she was to see him again, she was speaking more to the cypress planks than to the commodore.

Straightening, she stammered, "Nath . . . I mean Mr. Harkness, the young man helping out at Great House . . ." She gulped and then said, "He's come for some oysters. I am his guide." She gave Uncle Caleb a pleading look. When he suggested she find a seat on the porch out of the wind, she fled without a word.

Sinking into a rocking chair, a twin to Oriole's, she gazed glumly at the bay and the island beyond it. Why must she always appear so awkward, so childish when she met this important man. She wanted him to see her as an accomplished, graceful young woman. She rocked faster, trying to obliterate her humiliation.

Overhead, gulls mewed and, in the distance, large breakers roared. Comforted by these familiar sounds, she looked toward the pier. Nathan had joined her uncle and the commodore and seemed completely at ease. He was raising his right hand in what appeared to be a salute. Sophia cringed, remembering Father's curt correction when James had saluted. "Civilians never salute officers. If you haven't served, you haven't earned the right."

Today, though, both men returned Nathan's salute. How strange, she thought. Men seem to reinvent rules all the time.

She was still puzzling over proper etiquette when Commodore Decatur approached. Sophia rose hastily to her feet, gracefully, she hoped.

"I wanted to wish you and your family a safe journey to Ohio," the commodore said. "Please convey my good wishes. I won't see your family again before you leave. Mr. Harkness has been assigned the task of bringing the famous Pearl to me in Berlin. My wife and I are back here visiting friends." He gave her a curious look. "You seemed surprised. Even though our home is in Philadelphia, we still have friends on the Eastern Shore."

"Oh, no it's not that," Sophia stammered. "I know you have friends. I am surprised. That's all. Father has never allowed anyone to ride Pearl before. I'm glad he has made this exception."

"At least with his knowledge," she added under her breath.

"I won't be riding Pearl. The mare is for my wife. Mrs. Decatur is quite the horsewoman, you know."

"So I have heard."

Sophia glanced down at her hands. Even now the commodore's marriage to Susan Wheeler was considered scandalous to some. She had heard the whispers in Snow Hill. That the commodore, already committed to marry a Philadelphia heiress, had fallen in love with Susan the first time her saw her. Risking damage to his good name, he had broken that engagement and married his true love, who by all accounts was strikingly beautiful.

Sophia sighed, wondering if she could ever love anyone so passionately that she would break all the rules. She looked up. Commodore Decatur was handsome in a dashing sort of way. The two were most likely a perfect match.

"I hope she finds Pearl suitable. She is a wonder, fast and fearless."

Lowering her voice, she added in a conspiratorial tone, "I don't know if my father told you, but I have ridden Pearl on occasion."

"I *have* heard," Commodore Decatur said with a hint of laughter in his voice.

"Not recently," she rushed to say. "Pearl is so responsive. Sometimes I think she knows what you want before you know yourself." Sophia bit her lip, worried that Captain Decatur might think she was bragging.

But he was nodding in agreement. "Those are the very reasons I bought her."

"Bought her!"

The commodore frowned. "I thought you knew. Your father was kind enough to sell her to me before the auction. I am sure the bidding would have been fierce but he worried that the mare could fall into the wrong hands. I assured him that Mrs. Decatur will give Pearl the best of care."

"I am sure that is so," Sophia said softly. Then raising her chin, she held out her hand. "Thank you for your good wishes. I will convey them to my family."

Commodore Decatur took her hand and gave it a gentle squeeze.

"Good day, Miss Records," he said before walking back to rejoin her uncle.

I can't believe I did that, Sophia thought. I dismissed a commodore.

19

Hard Choices

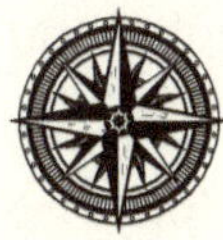

A black-headed gull landed on the porch railing near where Sophia stood. Indifferent to her presence, the bird preened its feathers, then cocked its head and eyed Sophia in such a greedy way that she thought it might peck her.

"Shoo, shoo," she shouted, shaking her sunbonnet at it "I have nothing!"

"Father is making sure I have nothing, she muttered as the gull flew away, leaving behind a downy feather, held fast beneath a splinter on the railing. The feather fluttered there until a stronger puff of wind dislodged it. Sophia leaned forward to catch it as it floated by her, but at the last second the wind moved the feather higher, out of her reach. The only difference between me and that feather, she thought, is that Father determines where I go.

Raising her face to the sun, Sophia closed her eyes, enjoying the warmth. She could hear the gulls and smell the salty ocean breeze. She tried to imagine what scent an Ohio breeze would carry but could not. When she opened her eyes, Uncle Caleb was standing beside her.

"Why didn't Father tell me about Pearl?" she whispered, her uncle's presence weakening her resolve not to cry. He put his arm around her shoulders and pulled her close.

"I can't speak for my brother," he said, "but I believe he was trying to find the right time."

"Father is getting rid of everything." She stepped back. "Now I know why he agreed to Faith's marriage to Mr. Mueller." Sophia held up one finger. "That's one daughter out of the house." She held up a second finger. "Next will be me. He will send me to Baltimore to live with Uncle William and Aunt Polly."

"Only if you decide to," Uncle Caleb said. "Your father told me he is giving you the choice of going to Ohio or staying behind."

"That's a hard choice to make."

"Most important choices are." He fixed her eyes with his. "Don't you think your father has had to make some of his own?"

When Sophia didn't answer, Uncle Caleb said, "I believe he made the right one by selling Pearl to Commodore Decatur. She is a fine mare, a gentleman's horse, bred to run. Your father will have need of a different breed in Ohio. Perhaps he will forgo a horse and buy an ox."

"Never."

"Not to ride, silly." Her uncle gave her a conspiratorial wink and smiled. Sophia had to giggle as she imagined her dignified father astride an ox. Then she scowled.

"No, of course not," she said, miffed that her uncle had tricked her into laughing. She wanted to stay angry with her father. Now, she glared at Uncle Caleb as if he were the enemy.

"Why doesn't Father just buy an ox for pulling stumps and keep Pearl for riding? That's the sensible thing to do."

Uncle Caleb shook his head, no. "Your father can't afford to keep her."

Sophia looked stunned. She had never thought of her father as poor.

"This is all Grandsire's fault," she said. "He willed Records Landing to the wrong son."

"Simmer down, Phee."

"I can't simmer down. Grandsire has purely made a mess of things. Uncle William left Records Landing years ago to live in a fancy house in Baltimore. Still, Grandsire gives him the Landing. And Uncle William promptly sells it to the worst person possible. You should be angry, too."

"Hey, hey, Phee. What's this all about?"

Sophia slumped against the railing. She had half a mind to tell him everything—her concerns about Judith, her fears about Mr. Talcott's threats and the real danger that the folks in Marshtown faced. It would be a relief to turn matters over to Uncle Caleb. Still, she held back. Instead, she told him about finding the will.

"Always the curious cat," he said. "But be careful. You know what they say about curiosity and cats."

"It leads them into serious trouble."

Uncle Caleb nodded. "Or causes them to jump to the wrong conclusions. Before you start spitting fire, blaming people for things you know very little about, you should tell your father that you read the will. Sometimes things are not what they seem."

Sophia shot him a questioning look.

"Your grandsire discussed the will with all of us before making William heir to Records Landing. It is a long-standing tradition—the eldest son inheriting the estate. And your grandsire didn't want to break with that. Only in this case, inheriting Records Landing wasn't some great prize. There was a sizeable debt on the place."

"That's not possible."

"Jefferson's embargo about ruined all the tobacco farms around here. If it weren't for your mother's sheep, there would be meager food in the larder. Even though Congress has lifted the embargo now, it's a little too late for us."

He grimaced. "I probably shouldn't have told you that last part. Your father prefers to keep his problems to himself. Still, you ought to know what this family has been up against."

He gave her a clumsy hug and then a little pat on the back.

"Don't look so glum, Phee. We are sailing around these shoals just fine. Your father's pleased to be shed of this place. No, Grandsire knew what he was doing. In reading that will, did you notice that Grandsire gave his bounty land to your father? The tillable land on Records Landing is useless, good only for grazing. Why do you think your mother started raising sheep? Tobacco had leached everything good from the soil. In Ohio, land is abundant, fertile, and cheap. Plus, out there, I am told that lawyers are as valued as coopers."

Uncle Caleb chuckled.

"I guess," he said, "the thinking is that a man can't go wrong with a good lawyer and a good barrel. Now, how can I coax a smile to your face?"

Sophia eyed him warily, deciding whether or not Uncle Caleb was trying to smear honey over moldy bread. She gave him a little smile.

"That's the spirit, Phee. Now let's you and I get dinner on the table. But first you better scare up that Mr. Harkness."

Looking northward, Sophia saw Nathan walking along the shore nearly a quarter mile away. He had a bucket. Every few feet he would stoop down to dig up a clam. Not wanting to chase after him, she raised her fingers to her lips and let out a shrill whistle. Behind her, she heard her uncle laugh softly.

Dinner was simple, bowls filled to the brim with a creamy fish chowder—pieces of freshly caught haddock, potatoes, carrots, and onions had been simmering in broth since mid-morning. To round out the meal, Sophia at Mother's urging had brought a loaf of Sally's crusty bread and a jar of peach preserves.

"Not bad for a bachelor, eh?" Uncle Caleb said as he seated Sophia at the round pine table he had carried out onto the porch. He looked pleased with himself.

Sophia grinned. "It looks delicious," she said. Then, with a teasing look, she added, "Mother says you are quite the catch, a man who can cook and sew."

Her uncle cocked an eyebrow. "Sew? I can patch sails, but I can't darn socks." He smiled. "Besides, I'm a wily fox, hard to trap."

"Best beware. Aunt Polly will be here tomorrow, and everybody knows she fancies herself a matchmaker."

"Then pray the Good Lord protects me," Uncle Caleb muttered and bowed his head. "Bless this food, Lord, and give us grateful hearts. Amen."

Picking up her spoon, Sophia turned to Nathan. "That's what I like about my uncle, short prayers."

Nathan laughed. He had sat at Father's table enough times to hear many long-winded graces. "Amen to that," he said and began to eat.

Sophia did more talking than eating. As if reporting on a prize pupil, she told her uncle how Nathan had helped Willie make a kite and shown him how to fly it.

"He takes Willie fishing and is teaching him how to ride," she rattled on. "He puts Willie up on Pearl, then leads the mare around the pasture with Willie sitting up there proud as punch."

Glancing over at Nathan, she said, "Willie's taken quite a shine to you."

"Well, I don't know about that but he sure does love that mare."

Sophia bit her lip. Realizing Nathan must have known about the sale, she felt a shiver of jealousy. Why hadn't Father told her first? She scowled at Nathan.

"How could you let Willie get so attached?" she snapped. "It's cruel."

Nathan shrugged. "Didn't see the harm in it." He stared at her as if daring her to say more.

Embarrassed by her outburst, Sophia turned her head to stare at the bay. The accusation was more than bad manners; it was unfair. Everyone knew no one touched Pearl without Father's say-so.

As if he hadn't noticed the beginnings of a quarrel, Uncle Caleb urged Nathan to fill up his bowl from the pot inside on the hearth, telling Nathan that there was more hard work ahead.

As soon as Nathan entered the cottage, Uncle Caleb set his eyes directly on Sophia. "Take it easy on that boy, Phee. He has led a hardscrabble life and not let it sour him or beat him down."

Sophia nodded. "I know," she said under her breath.

When Nathan returned, his bowl brimming, Sophia straightened her shoulders and looked him straight in the eye.

"I'm sorry. You have been kind to Willie. I was wrong to say otherwise."

Taking care not to spill a drop, Nathan placed the bowl on the table and sat down. He smiled at Sophia.

"I understand. It's hard to lose things," he said. "No hard feelings."

Uncle Caleb looked pleased with both of them. Pouring himself another tankard of ale, he offered some to Nathan.

"Well, Mr. Harkness," Uncle Caleb said as he filled Nathan's mug, "Apparently you and my friend Stephen Decatur know each other."

Nathan nodded. "I met him briefly when I was visiting Fort McHenry. A chance encounter but a lucky one. If he hadn't introduced me to Mr. Records, I wouldn't be here today. He's a good man and a great Captain."

"A bit of a hothead, though," Uncle Caleb said. "Still, that's a good trait in the heat of battle."

"Uncle Caleb was with him, fought alongside him during the war with Tripoli," Sophia interjected. "Uncle Caleb was part of the crew who defeated the Barbary pirates."

"Outsmarted them," said Uncle Caleb. He smiled, leaned back in his chair and began patting at his jacket, searching for something.

"Sophia, I seemed to have mislaid my pipe. Would you mind fetching it? It should be on the table beside my chair and please bring the tobacco pouch as well."

She nodded. As a courtesy both Uncle Caleb and Nathan stood as she excused herself and left the table.

As he had resumed his seat, she heard Uncle Caleb say to Nathan, "I suppose you are wondering why the commodore was on my dock. You might say we're mates. Both of us were born here; both started our service in the Navy as midshipmen; both were sons of sea captains. His father was a commodore in the American Navy. Mine was captain of the *Rebel Ann.* The two of us, we grew up loving the sea and the ships that sail there."

He cleared his throat. "Consider The *USS Philadelphia*, the frigate we destroyed that night in the Tripoli harbor."

Smiling, Sophia ducked inside. Uncle Caleb had now launched himself on the telling of a favorite tale. He always began it the same way and Sophia suspected that he loved *The Philadelphia* almost as much as Stephen Decatur. First, he would say that ship was the queen of the American Navy, that Captain Decatur had watched her being built and, in 1799 had seen her launched. Next, he would describe her tonnage, depth of keel, and so on. He liked people to grasp the size and majesty of the three-masted ship. In fact, Sophia believed by now she knew that ship as well as her uncle.

When she returned to the porch, her uncle was deep into the history lesson, explaining the successions of captains and the battles the frigate helped win.

"There were many battles, mostly against the Barbary pirates," he was saying. "Those scoundrels preyed on merchant ships—American, French, or English, it made no difference. After capturing a ship, the pirates either killed or enslaved the crew then sailed their prize and its cargo to Tripoli."

Pausing, he reached for his pipe and the pouch Sophia held out to him. Giving her a smile of thanks, he packed the pipe bowl and tamped down the tobacco.

"Now, Phee, could I trouble you for a light? I've got a story waiting to be told."

Nathan shifted impatiently in his chair. Sophia went back inside, returning quickly with a slender stick. One end glowed red. Uncle Caleb blew the tip into a flame before placing the pipe between his teeth. After several draws, he seemed satisfied and doused the tip in his mug of ale.

"I'll tell you what led up to the burning of that fine ship," he said, withdrawing the pipe from his mouth. "If you have the patience for it, I have time to tell the tale before low tide."

"Please, continue." There was an eagerness in Nathan's voice.

Uncle Caleb cleared his throat, Nathan leaned forward, and Sophia settled into her chair.

"It was 1803," Uncle Caleb began." The *Philadelphia* was sailing near the Barbary coast, when the captain, a man by the name of William Bainbridge, spotted a pirate ship and gave chase. It turned into a cat and mouse game that ended when *The Philadelphia*, lured into the shallows, became grounded on rocks near the mouth of the Tripoli harbor. She tipped to one side; her cannons useless."

Uncle Caleb took another pull on his pipe. Sophia knew her uncle blamed Captain Bainbridge for the loss of the *Philadelphia*, as did Stephen Decatur and Grandsire. She glanced toward Nathan. His eyes were trained on her uncle, the half empty chowder bowl pushed aside.

"Bainbridge," Uncle Caleb said, "tried to lighten the ship by ordering the crew to throw the cannons and ammunition into the sea. When that failed, he told his men to chop down the foremast and dump it along with its sails and rigging overboard. Nothing worked. He ordered his men to scuttle the ship. Bainbridge surrendered. The Bashaw of Tripoli, the worst pirate of them all, now held 309 American sailors hostage."

Nathan groaned.

"Then," Uncle Caleb said. "It rained. Heavy rain for two days. The water in the bay rose high enough so that the pirates were able to refloat the ship. They patched the holes chopped in the hold, retrieved all 44 cannons from the bay, and remounted them. Within weeks, all the *Philadelphia* needed was a new foremast to become the most dangerous ship in the pirate fleet."

Uncle Caleb stood up, walked to the railing, and knocked his pipe ash into the bay before returning to the table.

"And that's where Stephen Decatur comes into the story. He was the captain of his first ship, the *Intrepid,* a beat-up old merchant ship our Navy had captured off the coast of Gibraltar. There were a hundred like it sailing those waters off the Barbary Coast. Captain Decatur convinced his superiors that he could sail his ship into Tripoli's harbor without raising suspicion. With a volunteer crew disguised as harmless Maltese merchants, he would sail close enough to *The Philadelphia* to board her."

"Uncle Caleb was there," Sophia said unable to keep still any longer. "Tell Nathan how you overpowered the pirate crew armed only with a cutlass."

Uncle Caleb chuckled. "There were sixty of us, Sophia. Except even though we defeated the pirates we couldn't save the ship. We had to finish what Bainbridge started. When Decatur discovered *The Philadelphia* wasn't seaworthy yet, he ordered us to burn her."

Nathan shook his head in dismay. "That must have been hard."

"Aye, 'twas a hard choice to make, but a necessary one." Uncle Caleb glanced over at Sophia, who nodded slightly to indicate she understood his meaning."

Finishing his ale in one gulp, Uncle Caleb stood again to look at the bay. Sophia followed his gaze. The water had receded, leaving seashells scattered along the wet sand.

"Low tide," he said. "Let's go scrape up those oysters."

Nathan's Story

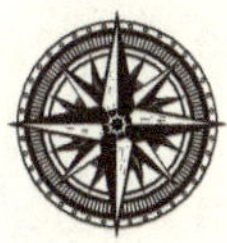

A midafternoon sun reflected brightly off the water. It was surprisingly warm for March. Although Sophia had tied on her sunbonnet, the hat did little to ease the unexpected heat. She lay back, resting her head on the dinghy's bow, and pulled the bonnet's wide brim forward to shade her face. The rocking of the boat was making her drowsy. A nap would be nice, she thought anticipating another long canoe trip before she could sleep in her own bed.

She closed her eyes, only half listening to Uncle Caleb, who was preaching to Nathan about the merits of tonging.

"Harvesting oysters from a boat is better than wading in the shallows and hand picking them from small reefs," he said. "More oysters in less time."

Her uncle sat on one side of the dinghy as he sorted through each catch Nathan brought to the surface with long handled tongs. They looked like a giant pair of scissors; only instead of blades, the tongs had thick iron claws.

"Tonging is slow, hard work," her uncle added, picking up a small hammer to break apart two oysters that had grown together. He threw the smaller one into the bay.

"It's not easy. That's for certain," Nathan said. He was standing on the opposite side of the boat. Facing the bay, he was leaning slightly forward as he scraped the oyster reef six feet below.

Sophia cocked open one eye to look at Nathan. He had rolled up his sleeves and loosened his collar. She could see his arm and neck muscles strain as he pulled open the wooden shafts of the tongs and then pushed the shafts back together to rake oysters from the reef. With a low grunt, he hauled up the catch, spilling it onto the culling board in the center of the boat.

"More than twelve oysters at a time," Nathan said and grinned.

"A few more hauls like this and we'll be done," Uncle Caleb said as he sorted through the catch, once again throwing back a few small oysters and some empty shells.

Nathan nodded, then wiped his brow and plunged the tongs back down.

His hair was tied back at the neck with a black ribbon, but some auburn curls had escaped and kept blowing around his face in the steady breeze. Nathan kept brushing the wisps back. Sophia found the gesture endearing.

He is fine-looking, she thought sleepily. Nevertheless, a puzzle. Could it be he was just a shy person, as Faith had suggested? He never lingered after supper but retired promptly to the barn.

It's not as if he can't carry on a conversation, she mused. He certainly talks to me. And he has a wonderful laugh. If he thinks something is funny, that laugh just bubbles up in his throat and bursts out into the air. It makes a person want to laugh right along with him. Still, there is something unsettling about Nathan Harkness.

Sophia remembered her flash of resentment when Mother had encouraged him to move into James's sleeping chamber and her relief when he said he preferred his quarters in the barn. Nice as he was, he was not family.

Sophia was thinking drowsy thoughts about Nathan when she overheard Uncle Caleb ask him a question. Her eyes snapped wide open.

"So," her uncle had said as casually as if he were asking about the weather, "how did you meet the commodore?"

Nathan hesitated. Sophia saw the worry in his eyes as he opened the tongs and dropped the catch on the culling board.

"Why do you ask?" he said, sitting down and reaching for the canteen. His tone was mild but Sophia thought his demeanor had changed. He looked wary.

Sophia glanced over at her uncle. He had leaned back against the side of the boat and was resting his boots on the culling board.

"Just curious," he said. "I wondered if you had ever been to sea, knew him that way."

Nathan shifted uneasily on the wooden bench. "In a roundabout way," he said. He looked out at the bay then glanced toward Sophia. She lay still, feigning sleep. He began to sort through the oysters.

"Better put these on," Uncle Caleb said and tossed over his pair of canvass gloves. 'Those shells can be sharp."

Nathan nodded, pulled on the gloves and continued to poke through the oysters. He threw an empty shell overboard. There was a soft plop as it hit the water. He cleared his throat.

"I met him at Ft. McHenry. I went there to see if the Navy could clear my name. The commodore offered to help," he said softly.

"Are you in trouble?" Uncle Caleb asked.

"You could say so. I am tired of looking over my shoulder, waiting for someone to turn me into the British Navy for the reward. I'm a deserter in their eyes."

Sophia shook off all pretense of sleep. "No," she said, sitting up so swiftly the little boat rocked. "I don't believe it. You, a rat, a Tory rat!"

Removing her bonnet, she glared at him. In all their supposing, neither she nor Faith had ever dreamed Nathan to be a coward.

Nathan gave her a pleading look. "It's not what you think," he said.

Uncle Caleb said, "If you are British, you hide it well. You sound more Southern."

Nathan shrugged. "Lived in Georgia for a time. Afterwards I signed onto the merchant ship *Pioneer* as a Jack Nasty-Face."

When Sophia gave him a puzzled frown, he grinned. "Cook's helper," he said. "I was a pot scrubber."

"You told me you went to Ohio when you walked away from your so-called uncle's farm. That's nowhere near the ocean."

"I wasn't lying. I did go west, just left out the part about heading east first. Didn't want to bore you with the particulars. "

"I'd like to hear those particulars," Sophia said.

"Why does it matter?"

"It matters to me. It's hard to trust a person who doesn't tell the whole truth."

"Fine," Nathan snapped. "Here are the particulars. After I left that cotton farm, after I'd walked for days with the sun in my face in the morning and at my back in the afternoon, the ocean stopped me. More water than I had ever seen. And I saw ships, big schooners with their white sails bowed out in the wind." He sighed as if remembering how he felt when he first encountered the ocean.

"I'd walked all the way to Savannah,"" he continued. "It's a right pretty town but costly. I had no coin. I had no means of making a living. I'd had no schooling. Couldn't read or write. All I knew was how to tend cotton. No cotton fields in Savannah."

"So, you did what many penniless boys do, you joined the crew of a merchant ship." Uncle Caleb said.

"Yes, Sir," Nathan said. "I thought I'd be safe at sea. Then I got pressed."

"Where?" Uncle Caleb asked, his tone curt.

"Middle of the ocean," Nathan said, as he continued sorting through the oysters, tossing the larger ones into a keg, now nearly full. He picked up a small oyster and threw it far out into the bay, its soft plop barely heard over the mewing of the gulls. He cleared his throat.

"We was halfway to France when this British man-o'-war fires a cannonball over our bow. A press gang comes aboard, demanding our captain turn over any seaman born in England. Someone shoves me forward, maybe to save his own skin. The Brits say my claim to be American is a lie."

He glared at Sophia, who squirmed under the intensity of his gaze.

"I'm no lying Fudge," he said. "When I tell those Limeys I was born in the city of Philadelphia, they laugh. 'Prove it,' they say. Long story short, I end up a swabber on the *HMS Halifax*."

Uncle Caleb snorted. "This impressment has to stop." he said, pounding the culling board with his fist. "Even if it means war. As for that ship, the *Halifax,* I heard five men deserted. That was five years ago. The next year, we almost came to blows with England because of it. We should have. Those Brits attacked and then boarded the *USS Chesapeake* hunting deserters."

Nathan nodded. "'Twas all the talk in Pittsburgh. Folks were calling it the *Leonard - Chesapeake* affair. They were angry."

"Most Americans are still angry," Uncle Caleb said. "England has no right to board an American ship anywhere, let alone in American waters. And for our captain to allow the English to arrest one of his crew, a disgrace!" Uncle Caleb said. "The English hanged the man they took, you know, claiming he was one of the deserters."

"It could have been me. I was with him," Nathan muttered.

"What do you mean?" Sophia asked softly.

"I jumped ship when he jumped ship."

Sophia stifled a gasp.

Uncle Caleb made a clicking sound with his teeth and reached for his pipe.

"Bad business, that."

Sophia drew in her breath. She shot Nathan a questioning look.

"I wasn't planning to desert. Although maybe I was. I know I wanted to get off that ship, away from the English and I knew we were anchored in Hampton Road. But in the end, it was dumb luck. I just happened along when a jolly boat was being lowered into the water for a work detail." He smiled ruefully. "I didn't know those swabbies were planning to mutiny."

Squinting in the late afternoon sun, Nathan turned away, looking beyond the water to the shore. His withdrawn expression made Sophia wonder if he was reliving his escape. Whatever he was thinking, he did not share his thoughts.

After a minute, he turned to look straight at Sophia. "So, I went along with them, disobeyed an officer. As soon as those men beached that jolly boat on American soil, I took off, west. And those are the particulars."

Sophia felt the intensity of his gaze. Slowly retying the ribbons on her sunbonnet, she could feel a flush of embarrassment burn her cheeks. She had been too quick to judge, to speak.

"I am sorry," she said, looking straight at Nathan. "I shouldn't have called you a rat. I can't even imagine the dangers you faced—and with such courage."

"No," he said. "There was nothing courageous about it. I was just lucky."

Sophia started to say that anyone who outfoxed the British was brave when Uncle Caleb interrupted.

"It's better you two debate what constitutes courage another time," he said. "It's time to weigh anchor. You have a long paddle home."

21

Threats and Lies

Sophia and Nathan arrived home after sunset. Navigating the river in the fading light had required her full attention. A thin mist rising from the river made it difficult to see snags or half submerged logs. As soon as they had reached the Pocomoke, Nathan had told Sophia to stow her paddle. He needed her to be on the alert for hazards. As the shadows lengthened, casting wavering shapes on the water, she had lit an oil lantern and held it over the bow. As soon as the canoe pulled alongside the pier, Sophia had scrambled out, secured the bow and with a quick word of thanks left Nathan to deliver the oysters to the spring house. All she wanted was to lie down in her own bed.

As she trudged up the path toward Great House, she saw Mother looking out the front window in Father's office. It reminded Sophia of the time right after James had gone missing. Mother had kept watch at that same window for hours. Eventually, Father had come and gently led her away. "It's in God's hands now, Mary," he had said. She'd nodded, leaned her head against his shoulder, her eyes shiny with unshed tears.

Now Sophia wondered if Mother had been standing watch for her. She waved. Mother waved back and before Sophia could give the knocker its customary pat on the nose, Mother flung open the heavy door.

"You are quite late," she said and hugged Sophia tightly.

Sophia twisted away. "Long day. There is no need to make a fuss. Nathan handles a canoe well."

A little smile flickered across Mother's face. "Oh, so you call him Nathan, now. Not Mr. Harkness."

"Mother, please. He is practically family. You have said so yourself."

"I suppose that is so. It seems you have another new friend as well."

"Who?"

"Judith Talcott. She stopped by today." Mother cocked an eyebrow and gave Sophia an inquisitive look.

"Whatever for?" Sophia asked.

"She told me she had come to look at the furniture and possibly buy a piece or two, but I think she came to talk to you."

"I can't imagine why," Sophia said, her voice tight with alarm. Something must have happened for Judith to return so soon. That was three visits in less than a fortnight.

"Have some compassion, Sophia," Mother said, taking Sophia by the hand and leading her into the parlor where a low fire still burned on the hearth. She pressed Sophia hands between her own.

"You're cold as ice."

Sophia nodded. The warmth of her mother's hands felt good after the cool damp of the river. "And tired," she said as she sank into the sofa.

Sitting down beside her, Mother spoke gently, urging Sophia to make an effort to be kind even if Judith was a Talcott. The poor girl was motherless, practically alone in the world, and soon to wed.

In fact, Mother went on to say, Judith's fiancé, a Mr. Dowling—she never did learn his Christian name—had accompanied Judith, but he had been more interested in the outbuildings. Hadn't even set foot in the house. He had raised his hat in greeting and then scuttled off without so much as a-pleased-to-meet-you. A strange man.

"I don't think there is much love between those two," Mother concluded. "Unlike your sister, who spends every waking moment talking or thinking about Mr. Mueller."

"I think you could call him Zach or Zachariah since he is almost family," Sophia teased.

"I suspect you are right." Mother sighed.

"Don't you like him?"

"No, no. It's not that. It's just I think Faith is too young for marriage vows. Mother took a deep breath. "Anyway," she continued in a more business-like tone, "since you weren't home, Judith wrote you a note. She even sealed it with some candle wax. It's all so very secretive."

Mother handed her a square vellum envelope, one from Father's best stock. Reaching up to the mantel, she removed a candle from its brass holder and held the wick close to the fire until it flamed.

Sophia caught a whiff of bayberry as her mother put the candle back where it belonged. It cast high shadows along the wall but there was enough light to read by. Sophia could see her name scrawled on the envelope. The seal on the back was intact. She shot of look of inquiry at her mother.

"As I said, all so very secretive. I leave you to your reading. Oh, Sally saved you some supper. I am sure you are hungry. And another thing, where did you put the oysters?"

"Nathan put them in the spring house. Two half kegs. That should fill Aunt Polly up."

"Oh, Phee, really. It's not polite to mock your elders," Mother said, sounding more amused than stern. Still, Sophia was surprised when Mother gave her a peck on the check.

"Don't grow up too fast," Mother said and left the room.

Sophia stared down at the envelope in her hand as if it might burst into flames. Judith certainly had no qualms about using the best paper to dash off a note, she thought, breaking the seal. I hope what she has to say is as valuable. As she quickly scanned the letter, Sophia felt a queasy sensation in her stomach.

Dear Miss Records,

The patrollers are arriving by week's end. Pa and Mr. Dowling plan to ride with them to Marshtown to take the woman you call Chloe and her baby and return them to her master. Pa plans to notify the sheriff. The blacksmith, the one who you say is her husband, will be thrown in jail for harboring an escaped slave. If your father or any other member of your family tries to intercede, he or she (meaning you) will be arrested as well. For your own safety, it would be best if the woman left Marshtown now.

Please destroy this letter as I would be severely punished if my pa knew I had confided in you.

Faithfully,

Your friend,

J.T.

Sophia slumped down into one of the chairs. If Father were here, despite what Judith wrote, I would show it to him, she thought. And for a moment she was angry. It didn't seem right for him to leave just when he was truly needed at home.

I could tell Uncle William, she thought. He is coming tomorrow. Except Uncle William owns slaves. He might side with Mr. Talcott. Uncle Caleb would know what to do but there is no time to get to his cabin and back.

Sophia crumpled the letter into a ball and was about to throw it into the fire when she thought better of it. This letter was proof of Mr. Talcott's intentions. Father always said to trust your instincts. Although Judith seemed sincere, she was a Talcott after all. She could deny ever telling Sophia about the plan. Trusting Judith was just too risky.

Sophia smoothed out the letter and walked into the office, where she put it in the secretary's secret compartment. Her mind churned. Preserving the letter, though, wouldn't keep Chloe out of Talcott's clutches. That little family needed to disappear. What better place than Grandsire's hidden room? They could stay there for a while, but not forever.

Sophia walked out of Father's office, closing the door behind her. Supper was secondary now but she headed toward the cookhouse just the same.

Jebbie sat on the bench outside the little log house, swinging his feet forward and back. An oil lamp was beside him. Sophia guessed it was more for comfort than for light.

"Why are you here so late?" Sophia asked.

"Mama doesn't want me walking home alone. She doesn't want to walk alone either. She says folks like us have to be careful these days even on the Marshtown road. So, I have to wait."

"Things could be worse but something tells me that they are. You look like someone just stole your dog," Sophia said.

"I don't have a dog."

"True but that's how you would look if you did and someone took him."

"Someone did take something."

Jebbie scowled. "That skinny white man snatched my gold coin. I was sitting here waiting for Mama to fix my lunch. To pass the time I was tossing my coin up in the air and catching it. It shines so pretty in the sun, sort of winks at you. And that skinny white man, he walks right up to me and grabs it right out of the air."

Jebbie gave Sophia a wounded look.

"That's stealing! That man is a no-account thief," Sophia said.

"I know that. You know that," Jebbie said, "but the man said I was the thief. He said boys like me didn't get paid in gold."

Sophia quickly surmised that the man Jebbie persisted in calling that skinny white man was in fact Judith's fiancé, the strange Mr. Dowling.

Jebbie continued, saying he explained to the skinny white man that a duppie had showed him the gold piece and that Sophia had told him to keep it. Only the man said it was a made-up story, just a thieving darkie's tale, and "duppie" was just a made-up word.

"You know I told the truth," Jebbie said, sounding wounded.

"Of course, you did."

"Except after I told him the truth, then I didn't." Jebbie gave a Sophia sheepish look. A little smile tugged at his mouth.

"I told him that duppies were dangerous ghosts and that Captain Records was a duppie now that he was dead. And that's all true. But then I said the old Captain was guarding a pile of gold coins near here, and he gave me that coin because we were friends. I told that skinny white man if he didn't give me back my gold piece Captain Records would come after him."

"Good for you, Jebbie." Sophia sat down beside him and put her arm around his shoulders and pulled him close. "I hope you scared him into giving the coin back."

"No. He said that if the gold was here, it was his. The plantation would soon belong to him and he would own everything on it. If he hadn't found the stash before then, he would make me show him where I got the coin or else." Jebbie drew his hand across is throat.

"You didn't tell him, did you?" Sophia said. "I wouldn't blame you if you did, but it's important that we keep Grandsire's secret."

"No," Jebbie said flatly. He looked offended that she would even ask.

"Good. When he comes back—and he will because he seems like a man intent on getting rich, be it rightly or wrongly—let's steer him away from the cabin and then scare the stuffing out of him."

"How are you going to do that?"

"I don't know just yet but I'll think of a way," Sophia said.

She was still sitting there beside Jebbie, fretting, when Nathan walked up from the barn.

"I heard a rumor there was Hoppin' John for supper," he said. "I hope I am not too late."

"I haven't eaten yet myself," Sophia said jumping to her feet. "I am sure Sally saved us a bowl or two." She took his arm in a companionable way and walked with him toward the cookhouse door. "In fact," she said, "you are just the person I wanted to see."

"You have been looking at me all day," he said.

Sophia lowered her voice. "This is different. I'll explain later. Jebbie's in trouble and I think you can help."

"I'll do what I can."

"How would you like to be a ghost? A duppie actually." Looking toward Jebbie, Sophia gave the boy a conspiratorial wink.

22

Riddles

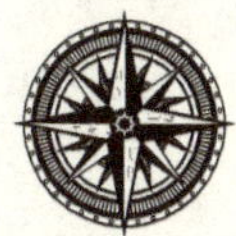

That night Mr. Dowling kept chasing Sophia and Jebbie down the old river road. No matter how fast they ran, Mr. Dowling stayed right behind them until they reached the end where the brambles grew.

Each time the thorny bushes stopped them, Sophia turned to face Mr. Dowling. He was short, not much taller than she, with a thin face, a sharp nose and small, round eyes. He reminded her of the fox that sometimes slunk around the chicken coop.

And in every dream, Mr. Dowling leaned his face toward hers, saying, "Tell me where it's hid." His breath had a sweet, rotten smell, which made her gag.

But she always managed to choke out, "There is no gold. Leave us alone."

But each time, Mr. Dowling shoved her aside and grabbed Jebbie. "The boy will do."

Each time, Sophia tried to scream but failed to make a sound. With a start, she would open her eyes and realize that she was safe in bed, Faith sound asleep beside her. Telling herself that it was just a nightmare, she would flop over on her side and fall back asleep.

Towards morning the dream changed. This time, as she opened her mouth to scream, a shadowy figure stepped out of the brambles. He wore a frock coat and James's hat pulled forward to shade his face so Sophia couldn't tell if he was her twin or Nathan or Grandsire or someone unknown. But whoever it was, he was brandishing a sword, a pirate's cutlass. Without a word, Mr. Dowling scurried away toward the river. Somewhere close by a woman laughed. It sounded like Judith, but when Sophia turned to look, no one was there.

In the morning Sophia stumbled into breakfast late, unrested, and disheveled.

"I don't think I got a wink of sleep," Faith said and frowned at her sister. Sophia shrugged, knowing full well that Faith was exaggerating.

"Sorry. Bad dreams."

Mother gave Sophia a questioning glance. When no answer was forthcoming, she addressed the girls in a no-nonsense tone. "As you know, Uncle William and Aunt Polly should be here by early afternoon. We'll wait dinner on them. The oysters need to be shucked, the table set, and Willie looked after. Sally will have her hands full with the cooking." She turned toward Nathan. "Perhaps, you can help with the shucking to speed things along," She smiled and then added, "After all, tonging is just the beginning when it comes to eating oysters."

By the time the three of them assembled outside the cookhouse, Sally had set out a bucket of water, a brush, and a wide shallow bowl on the plank table. She handed each of them a pair of canvas mitts. "Save your hands from cuts," she said. Those oysters have a way of fightin' back." She tapped the barrel that sat on the ground next to the table before hurrying inside. She returned with a short, thick bladed knife and a gunny sack. Dropping the sack beside the barrel, she said, "For the shells. You'll have to share the knife. It's all I've got."

Nathan pulled his hunting knife out from the leather sheath attached to his belt. "This should work, too."

"It's a little big for the job but I 'spect you know how to use it. Just slide the tip of the knife between the two halves, pry the shell open, and slip the meat into that bowl. The juice too. That's all there is to it," she said, turning toward the cookhouse.

"Where's Jebbie?" Sophia asked quickly, before Sally disappeared inside. It was strange not seeing Jebbie hanging around. He had been coming regularly to help his mother and almost always was around when company was expected.

"With his granny," Sally said. "No need for him to be hanging around here today."

Sophia looked at Nathan and raised her eyebrows. He shrugged. "Probably better he stays out of sight," he said under his breath.

Sitting down on the bench, Sophia selected a large oyster, brushed away the ocean grit, rinsed it and then handed it to Nathan, who was sitting cross-legged on the grass. In one easy twist of his wrist, he pried the shell open.

"Do you think Sally knows what Mr. Dowling said to Jebbie?" Sophia whispered.

"I'd be surprised if she didn't."

Sophia frowned. She was beginning to worry that Sally held her responsible for what happened yesterday. And in a way it was her fault. If she hadn't given Jebbie the gold piece in the first place, Mr. Dowling wouldn't have stolen it from him and then scared him half to death.

Sophia picked up another oyster and brushed the sand off its rough shell with hard strokes.

"I dreamt about that awful man last night," she said under her breath. When Nathan didn't respond, she added, "You know, Mr. Dowling. The dream helped me figure out exactly how and where to scare him. I need to talk to you privately."

"What are you two whispering about?" Faith asked in a teasing way from her side of the bench. "One might think you were sweet on each other." She took a clean oyster from Sophia and pried it open.

"Humph," said Sophia. "That's all you think about, love and kisses."

Nathan laughed good naturedly. "Well, I am sweet on something," he said as he split open an oyster. With a wink at Faith, he raised the shell to his mouth and let the glistening content slide down his throat. "Now that's one fine oyster," he said and smacked his lips appreciatively.

Sophia grinned. "It's March. Everyone knows any month that has an R in its name is a good month for oysters," she said. "Split one for me, please."

"Good idea," Faith, said taking one of the clean oysters from the growing pile on the table. "There are plenty. It won't matter if they all don't make it into the stew."

They looked at each other, nodded in agreement and grinned After slurping down a few, they said in unison, "A good month for oysters," and smacked their lips.

Sophia started to giggle. Faith, apparently forgetting she was too old for such silliness, joined in, then Nathan. Before long Sally stuck her head out of the door to ask what was so funny.

"Oysters," they said in unison as if they had rehearsed their answer.

"Nothing funny about oysters," Sally said crossly but that them set them off again. They were still smiling as they got back to their task.

The barrel was nearly empty when Nathan gave a low whistle.

"Look at this." He held an opened shell toward the girls. There inside lay an elongated pearl.

Sophia let out a low whistle. "It's shaped like a peninsula, like the Eastern Shore."

"Amazing," Faith said. "That would make a beautiful piece of jewelry. You should take it to a silversmith. The pearl might have value."

With the tip of his knife. Nathan lifted the pearl away from the oyster's glistening center and rubbed his prize dry on his sleeve. He held it out to the girls.

"You should have it," he said.

"No, it's yours." Sophia said. "Finders, keepers." Faith nodded in agreement.

'Why, I thank you," he said in a formal way, He pulled a small leather pouch from beneath his shirt. The pouch hung from his neck on a leather cord. Loosening the cord, he dropped the pearl inside.

"What is that?" Sophia asked, staring at pouch. Tiny red and yellow beads, resembling a lightning bolt, zigzagged down the middle.

"My medicine bag."

Sophia gave him a puzzled look.

"A gift from a friend. It holds small things, sacred things that keep me safe," he said in an off-handed way, then reached for another oyster and began to whistle.

Sophia gave him a long hard stare. Just when she thought she was getting to know him, more questions arose. One thing she had learned, however, was that when Nathan wanted to change the subject, he frequently started to whistle. This tune was familiar, a ballad about three ravens, and before long Sophia and Faith were humming along.

As soon as the shucking was done and the shells tossed into the gunny sack, Sally shooed the three of them away, telling the girls that they were needed at Great House and that Nathan needed to chip a bucket of ice to keep the oysters chilling. It was anyone's guess when Uncle William and Aunt Polly would arrive, and she planned to wait until they came before throwing the oysters into the stew.

"Cook oysters too long and they become tough as cowhide," she said. "Now skedaddle."

Nathan was on his way to the springhouse when Sophia caught up to him. "You are a riddle," she said.

"A riddle?"

"Just when I think we are friends, you close up tight like one of those oysters."

"Hum," he said. "You like riddles, don't you?"

"Yes. But . . ."

Nathan doffed his hat and pointed it at her. "Answer me this."

Riddle me, riddle me
What is that?
Over your head
And under your hat?

Sophia hesitated only a moment before answering, "Hair."

"Right!" Nathan grinned at her as though daring her to stump him.

Sophia planted her feet in a challenging stance and tilted her chin up at bit. "Answer me this," she said.

As I was walking by the bay,
I met old, old daddy gray.
I ate his meat and drank his blood,
And threw his bones away.
Now just who was Daddy Gray?

Nathan laughed. "You sound a mite blood thirsty, Sophia. I am hoping you mean an oyster, not a poor old fellow like myself."

"Correct, Mr. Old Fellow. But what is this?" Sophia stood a little taller and gave him an imperious look.

What can run but never walks?
Has a mouth but never talks?
Has a bed but never sleeps?
Has a head but never weeps?

"That's easy," Faith said, coming up to join them. "A river. I hope you don't mind my butting in. I thought I could help chip ice, too. "'Many hands make light work.'" Her imitation of Mother's voice was so close to perfect that both Nathan and Sophia had to laugh.

"Well, Miss Faith, this riddle is for you," Nathan said agreeably.

"What goes round and round the barn and leaves only one track?"

Even though she knew the answer, Sophia kept still. Faith puzzled over it a minute and then said, triumphantly, "Could it be a wheelbarrow?"

Nathan nodded. "Now, here's my last riddle," he said, "Whoever answers first wins my pearl."

"You'll give away your luck," Sophia said, aghast.

"Don't believe in that kind of luck. The offer stands. Answer me this:

"On the outside a stone wall. On the inside a golden lady."

Faith shrugged and looked expectantly at Sophia. "You're the smart one, Phee. You figure it out."

"Give me a minute to think," Sophia said.

"You do that," Nathan said. Then tipping his hat, he gave both girls a knowing smile and walked off toward the springhouse, whistling.

"Wait." Sophia called after him.

Nathan just shook his head and called back, "Later. It only takes one to chip ice. I'll be done in two shakes of a dead lamb's tail. Faster than it will take you to solve that riddle."

That stung her pride. "Suit yourself," Sophia called after him. Then turning to Faith, she asked in an annoyed tone, "Why did you really join us?"

"Thought you needed a chaperone,'" Faith said in a teasing way. When Sophia gave her a look of disgust, she smiled sheepishly. "No, actually Mother asked me to fetch you up to the house. She wants you to look after Willie."

Sophia hurried back to Great House. Even a blind man could see that Mother was in a dither about Uncle William and Aunt Polly coming. "Why today," Mother grumbled. "They could have come sooner," she said, "not now when we're in the throes of packing. And what if they decide to stay to help. Now I ask you, who needs their kind of help?"

Sophia knew there was no need to answer. Mother was in a stew of her own making. Aunt Polly always made her nervous.

With Willie in tow, Sophia escaped to the chicken hut. She wanted to teach Willie the best way to collect eggs without upsetting the hens. Mother's only comment had been, "Make sure he stays clean *and* out of trouble."

There weren't many eggs to collect, so Sophia told him to scatter some grain around while she enticed China Boy inside the coop. He needed to be shut away. It wouldn't do to have the goose chase Uncle William or Aunt Polly around. Although the thought of Aunt Polly scuttling across the lawn made her laugh.

True to her promise of keeping Willie in presentable shape, Sophia headed back to Great house, where she lifted him up to a low, sturdy branch of the giant magnolia that grew near the house, the one James had dubbed the perfect climbing tree.

"Stand watch just like a sailor in the crow's nest on the *Rebel Ann*," Sophia said. "Except you'll be looking for Uncle William and Aunt Polly, not ships."

"Aye, Aye, Captain Phee," Willie said and saluted her smartly.

She saluted him back, thinking this will keep him out of trouble. Walking over to the bench outside the cookhouse, she congratulated herself for coming up with the perfect solution. Willie was in plain view and she could relax. Goodness knows she was tired enough. Sophia closed her eyes, enjoying the warmth of the sun, when she heard a man say, "Miss Records." Her eyes snapped open.

Mr. Dowling stood beside the bench. Another nightmare? No, the real Mr. Dowling was standing there demanding she tell him Jebbie's whereabouts.

"I have no idea where he is," she said crossly.

"You Records should keep better track of your nigras."

"Really, Mr. Dowling. Where Jebbie goes is none of my business. He is free, always has been. And that means he goes where he pleases when he pleases. Why are you looking for him?"

"I told him to meet me here today."

Sophia shook her head. "He must have been called away." She smiled as if in regret.

"Last night," she said, "Jebbie told me you had asked him about buried treasure. I never imagined you were a treasure hunter, Mr. Dowling. Around here, that can be dangerous."

"Whatever do you mean, Miss Records?"

"Surely you have heard people speak about Blackbeard's treasure," Sophia said and smiled up at him, suspecting that he had.

"Miss Talcott once mentioned it," Mr. Dowling replied stiffly. "Like you, she treated it as a joke. But, Miss Records, if you seek out the right people, if you listen to what they have to say carefully, you learn things. Well-guarded secrets."

Here was a fish, hungry for bait, Sophia thought. He has been listening to watermen well into their cups in the local tavern.

She lowered her voice, her expression serious. "The tales about Blackbeard are true. If you have a minute to spare, I will tell you how some men got rich and how some ended up mad or worse. Please sit down."

"I haven't much time for chit chat," Mr. Dowling said as he sat down gingerly as far away from Sophia as the bench allowed.

"You know about Blackbeard, the ruthless pirate who preyed on merchant ships?" Sophia asked. She waited until Mr. Dowling nodded before continuing.

"It is a known fact that Blackbeard buried chests of gold somewhere on the Eastern Shore just before the British captured and killed him."

"I might have heard that," Mr. Dowling said.

Sophia leaned toward him. "It is said that Blackbeard's spirit guards this treasure. Sometimes, perhaps to atone for his evil ways, he gives some of his treasure away. Often a coin or two to little children. Grown men who have met the ghost tell a different tale."

"Miss Records, I have no time for silly ghost stories." Mr. Dowling stood up. "Just tell me where the boy is."

Sophia shrugged. "I told you I don't know. But I do know this." Again, she lowered her voice. "People now say my grandsire haunts this land. Some believe that he acquired a fortune during the War for Independence. He was a privateer for the American Navy. As for those British merchant ships he captured, of course, he turned over their cargos to Washington's army, but some believe he was no better than a pirate himself. There is talk that he kept the ships' coffers for himself and that he hid a strong box here at Records Landing. And like Blackbeard, Grandsire guards his treasure. He gives coins to those he deems worthy. But should a man try to steal his hoard, Grandsire's ghost will drive him mad."

"Nonsense."

"No, Mr. Dowling. There is a man who lives near Berlin that went searching for Grandsire's treasure. My father found him wandering in the woods over by the river. Although young, the man's hair was a ghostly white. He grabbed my father's arm, begging him for protection. The man kept repeating, 'I found the coins. I held them in my hands.' He opened up his palms. 'Gone' he shrieked and then began to mumble incomprehensibly, something about a ghost and a saber and the moon. My father took the poor man back to his wife. But he has never recovered. He drools and mumbles to himself."

"That's nonsense. Now if you will excuse me, Miss Records, I have more important things to do." Mr. Dowling turned abruptly and walked rapidly toward the orchard.

"Ask Mr. Talcott what he thinks of my grandsire," Sophia called after him. That should bait the hook, she thought.

Just then Willie shouted. "They're coming. They're coming. I can see the carriage."

"Don't jump. I'll lift you down."

Standing, Sophia looked toward the low branch where she had left her brother. It was empty.

"Willie, where are you?" Sophia called, half amused. She wasn't worried because she could hear him well enough. He must have jumped down by himself, she thought.

"Willie," she called more sharply. "Where are you?"

"Up here. Phee. Just like the sailor in the crow's nest."

Sophia ran to the base of the tree and looked up. Branch by branch her eyes searched the tree until she found him standing on a limb not far from the roof of Great House.

"Don't move," Sophia ordered, realizing that one misstep could spell disaster. I can't let him fall, she told herself even as she imagined Willie crumpled on the ground. She took a deep breath. I won't let this happen. Not another brother. She took another breath.

With a calm she didn't feel, Sophia called up to Willie. "You should come down now."

"I can see the yellow carriage with a black horse pulling it. It looks like a giant bumblebee." He laughed excitedly. Looping one of his arms around the tree trunk, he began flapping the free one. "I'm a bee. Buzzz!"

"Stop it!" Sophia shouted. "Please come down!" She closed her eyes. "Please, God, don't let him fall," she whispered.

With the grace of a cat, Willie turned to face the tree. Then he peered down at her. With a frightened yelp he threw both arms around the tree trunk.

"I'm too high," he wailed. Sophia could hear the terror in his voice.

"Just hold on. I'll come up."

Fighting her panic, Sophia pulled herself up and onto the first branch with practiced skill. Breathe, she told herself. She had climbed this tree many times just not lately, not after Mother had ordered her down, saying "This will never do, Sophia. It's not proper behavior."

Fiddlesticks to propriety, Sophia thought as the heel of her shoe caught in the hem of her gown. Leaning against the trunk of the magnolia, she fashioned the long skirt's yardage into baggy trousers, tucking the hem behind the waistband of her petticoat.

"Stay where you are, Willie. I'm coming," she shouted. Hand over hand, she began to climb. The branches were perfectly spaced so that it was as easy as climbing a ladder.

"Where are they now?" she shouted, hoping to distract Willie.

"They're coming, just not fast. The horse is walking. I think its Black Jack. Phee, I gotta get down. It's Grandsire's horse, Black Jack."

"Hold on. I'm almost there."

Sophia reached the branch beneath Willie.

"I'm gonna fall!" Willie whimpered.

"No, you're not. Trust me." Sophia forced her voice to sound calm.

"What if I fall? I'll break into pieces just like Humpty Dumpty." Willie began to cry.

"No, you won't. Take a breath. Can you do that?"

As she talked, Sophia studied a higher branch. If she climbed there, she could reach down, hold him steady and guide him down. She looked at the ground. It was about a twenty-five-foot drop. She felt her throat closing and she began to pray: God, just let me do this.

Reaching up, she heard something rip. Fiddlesticks, she thought. Oh well, Mother never said I had to stay tidy.

She stretched a little higher. Almost losing her balance, she steadied herself against the trunk. It wasn't going to work.

"Now, Willie, listen to me carefully. This is what we're going to do." She kept the panic out her voice. "I am going to hold on to your ankle. You are going to crouch down and sit on the branch just like you were riding Pearl."

"No. I'll fall!"

"I won't let you."

Willie scrunched his eyes shut and slowly crouched down.

"Pretend you are riding."

"Good." Sophia guided his foot lower. "Feel the branch with your foot? That's the branch I'm on. I'll hold your foot here. Hold on to the branch. Good. Now bring your other leg over. Pretend you want to get off Pearl."

"I'm afraid."

"You can do it. Hold onto the branch with both hands and swing your leg over. Trust me."

Without a word, Willie did as he was told. Within three thudding beats of her heart, he was next to her. Sophia kissed his teary cheek. "I knew you could do it," she said, realizing that her own legs felt a little wobbly.

Slowly, limb by limb, the two descended, Sophia first so she could guide Willie's feet. When they made it to lowest branch, they sank down on it. The ground looked comfortably close. It was nice just to look at it.

Minutes later, Uncle William and Aunt Polly drove into the yard. Mother came hurrying around the house to greet them. Faith was behind her. She stopped short when she saw the two of them perched in the magnolia.

Willie threw himself into her arms.

"Faith, I was the lookout, and Phee saved me." He seemed to have forgotten his fright. "Look, Black Jack came home. Hello Black Jack, hello everyone," he yelled and trotted away from the tree to pet the horse.

Faith giggled as Sophia jumped down.

"Better straighten your skirts before Mother sees you," Faith said. "And look. you ripped the bodice. Whatever made you climb a tree with Willie?"

Sophia shrugged. "It doesn't matter. But the less said about this affair the better." Faith nodded in an understanding way and gave her a hug. "You'd better change."

Sophia nodded. "One good thing," she said as they slipped into the house by the side door. "While sitting in the tree just now, the answer came to me."

Faith gave her a perplexed look.

"Nathan's riddle," Sophia said. "It's an egg. The shell is the wall and the yolk is the golden lady. I guess there is a solution to every riddle."

23

Plans

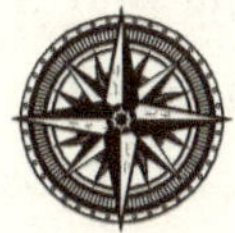

Dinner dragged on. Having eaten her fill of the oyster stew, beaten biscuits, and pickled beets, Sophia fidgeted, waiting for the conversation to end. She asked to be excused but Mother wouldn't hear of it.

Aunt Polly kept going on and on about the President's wife, saying Dolley Madison was the darling of Washington. The soirées she held at the President's Mansion—some newspaper reporters were calling it the White House—were the talk of the town. Congressmen schemed to get an invitation to one of her parties. Foreign diplomats were always in attendance. The British ambassador and his wife came frequently despite the fact that President Madison was urging Congress to declare war on England.

"Mrs. Madison is the finest hostess in America as well as one of the best-dressed women in Washington City," Aunt Polly said. "She imports all her gowns from Paris. Her clothes and those exquisite hats she wears must cost the President a pretty penny." She lowered her voice. "Some Washington merchants told me that she is running the President into serious debt."

"Polly, that is idle talk," Mother said.

"No, I know all this firsthand from the President's grocer. I shop there as well when visiting. Mr. Records and I have journeyed to Washington City on several occasions. We went by carriage once—a dreadful trip through a wilderness on a bumpy road barely wide enough for the buggy. There were only a few cabins, all inhabited by black folk. It took two days. We spent the night in a ramshackle inn. Never again. Now we go by sail."

Sophia sighed. How curious that Aunt Polly never called Uncle William by his first name in public. Her voice was high-pitched and she spoke with a pretentious British accent which Sophia found tedious. She nudged Faith, looking for some commiseration, only to be ignored. Faith was acting as if she was hanging on their aunt's every word. She and Mother were the only ones. Uncle William, now seated in Father's chair, was gazing around the room with a melancholy look on his face. Willie, who had gulped his food and then smacked his lips, was fiddling with the silverware.

Raising her eyebrows in disdain, Aunt Polly glared at Willie. "Stop that," she snapped. Sophia looked across the table at her little brother and wrinkled up her nose. Willie giggled.

"Well!" Aunt Polly said. "Really, Mary, first you serve us a poor man's stew and then you seat Willy next to me. One might think you were trying to annoy me. Young children do not belong at the table."

"How can a boy learn good manners eating alone in the cookhouse? I was hoping you could give him some pointers on proper behavior," Mother said and then smiled at Aunt Polly before continuing. "As for the oyster stew, it is one of our favorites. I thought you would enjoy it, too. I had no idea one had to be destitute in order to enjoy oysters." Mother paused for a moment before adding softly, "But then perhaps we are."

Aunt Polly had just finished her second bowl of stew and was eyeing the tureen on the sideboard. Either she didn't hear or overlooked Mother's comment. "There is no denying your cook can turn any meal into a feast. It is too bad that she won't move to Baltimore after you leave. She could cook for me."

"Sally would never leave Marshtown," Sophia said abruptly. "Her family is here."

There was stunned silence. Faith looked at Sophia in astonishment. It was not polite for children to speak unless spoken too, a rule Sophia knew all too well. Mother tightened her lips into a thin, disapproving line.

"I see, Sophia, that you, too, are in need of a lesson in manners," Aunt Polly said. "As I was saying, Sally and her family will feel right at home in Baltimore. I swear the city has more than its share of free negroes. More come every year. Too many if you want my opinion."

Uncle William looked up. "What your aunt means to say," he said, "is now that the Maryland legislature has eased restrictions on manumission, it is easier for owners to free their slaves. I have even thought of it myself. Still, it is not easy to be a freed man in Baltimore. I am sure Sally agrees."

The front door slammed shut. "Did you save some of that stew for me," Uncle Caleb called out.

Uncle William scraped back his chair in his hurry to rise. Without thinking, Sophia started to stand as well, but a stern look from Mother kept her in her seat.

"Uncle Caleb, sit here," Willie called out, slipping down from his chair. Before he could make good on his escape, however, Mother caught hold of his arm as he sped by.

"Just a minute young man. I think you forgot something." When Willie started to protest, she held her finger to her lips, silencing him. Only when he whispered, "May I be excused?" did she release him and send him off with a request to tell Sally that Uncle Caleb was joining them for dinner.

"Never fear, I told Sally to hold some stew back," she said and smiled up at Uncle Caleb, who had walked over to greet her. "I hoped you would be stopping by."

"As did I," Uncle William said, coming over to clasp his brother's hand.

"I wouldn't miss the opportunity to see you and Mistress Records here," Uncle Caleb said, favoring Aunt Polly with a courtly nod before turning back to Mother. "I thought I'd stay for a few days. That is if you'll have me."

"The more the merrier," Mother said weakly. "I am sure we can find a bed somewhere."

After a few more pleasantries were exchanged, Mother said, "Forgive us, Caleb, if we ladies take our tea in the parlor. I am sure you and William have much to discuss and I suspect Polly has more interesting tidbits to share with me and the girls."

Sophia groaned inwardly. She would rather listen to what her uncles had to say. As she pushed back her chair, Uncle William came to assist her.

"Thank you, uncle," Sophia said with a rush of unexpected sincerity. "I am glad you are here."

He smiled, his expression brightening.

"If I may detain you a minute," Uncle William said as he extracted a creamy envelope from his frock coat. "As you already know, an illness kept Anne at home."

"Nothing serious, I hope," Sophia asked.

"She has a little cough. But your aunt thought Anne's cough would worsen if she traveled. You know how your aunt fusses over her chicks."

He cleared his throat, making Sophia wonder if he might be ill at ease.

"When your father came to Baltimore last week," Uncle William said, "he asked me to consider the possibility of you living with us and attending school with Anne. I want you to know that you are welcome. When I told Anne you might come, she was overjoyed. She said, 'To think my very own cousin might live here. It would be like having a sister.' Those were her very words. But since she couldn't tell you in person, she sent you this letter in her stead."

Uncle William handed Sophia the letter. It was sealed with red sealing wax.

"As for me," he continued, "I think it's a fine idea and a wonderful opportunity for you to continue your studies. It would be a blessing to have another young person in the house. Perhaps we would hear some laughter now and then."

Sophia held the letter close to her chest.

"You are very kind," she said. "And I would truly enjoy being a sister to Anne but I can't give you an answer right now."

"I understand. Remember we would welcome you with open arms." He put his hand on her shoulder and gave it a gentle squeeze.

"Thank you, I will remember." Sophia gave him a quick peck on the cheek before walking away.

The doors to the adjacent room were thrown open. Sophia paused at the threshold. Mother was pouring tea. Faith was sitting primly on the sofa beside her. Aunt Polly was standing by the fireplace, talking. Doesn't the woman ever stop, Sophia wondered.

This time Aunt Polly was going on about fashion. In a few short minutes, Sophia learned that whalebone stays had been replaced with shorter, more comfortable corsets, and that women were wearing a shift and only one petticoat as undergarments. Fashionable women, like Dolley Madison, now wore gowns with a raised waistline, called an empire waist.

To demonstrate, Aunt Polly walked toward the middle of the room and gestured toward the waistline on her gown just below her ample bosom. The beige silk hung straight down from the waist to the tips of her shoes. Perhaps if she were taller and thinner, the dress would be more becoming, Sophia thought. She looks like she is wearing a silk flour sack.

"Really, Mary," Aunt Polly directed, "you and the girls must have gowns made when you are in Baltimore. And start wearing your hair with ringlets like mine. No reason to look like a backwater dowdy when you know better."

"You make me laugh, Polly. I doubt that we will have time for such frippery in Ohio."

"In Baltimore, it is important to keep up appearances."

"In Ohio, it is important to keep one's scalp."

"Humph, all the more reason for Sophia to live with us," Aunt Polly said.

"I trust Elijah will keep us safe. There is a fort nearby."

"I don't mean to sound hard-hearted," Aunt Polly said. "It just that we are eager show Sophia Baltimore. Faith, as well, if only that were possible. Too bad she has already set her cap for that young farmer. The wilderness is no place for young girls. Faith may have found a beau but who is going to court Sophia out there in the woods? After all, it is important to marry well. Our girls need husbands who are established and who can provide for their comfort, not turn them into drudges."

Faith flushed a deep red. "Then you will be pleased, Aunt, to know that Mr. Mueller is a hard-working young man and an excellent farmer."

Mother reached over to pat Faith's hand, "I trust both my girls to determine what makes a good husband. Don't you trust Anne?"

"Of course. Only I believe she should have the opportunity to meet a number of suitable young men. Anne will be introduced to society on her 16th birthday, Sophia, too."

Sophia bristled. Aunt Polly acts as if my living in Baltimore is a foregone conclusion, as if I am eager to be introduced to the suitors that she deems suitable. With a shudder, Sophia imagined herself being trotted out at some elegant ball like a mare being put through its paces at an auction.

Aunt Polly babbled on. "And like Dolley Madison, I plan to have soirees so the girls may converse with a variety of young men."

"My goodness, Polly. You have it all planned out," Mother said, turning toward Sophia who lingered in the doorway. "Don't hang back, Sophia. Join us."

"I am afraid I need to be excused. I must use the necessary."

Keeping Anne's letter hidden in the folds of her dress, Sophia swished through the hallway and out the front door.

Outside, a damp wind carried the scent of the sea. I will miss the smell of the ocean, she thought, as she crossed the lawn and headed toward the outhouse. Except halfway there, she swerved to the right and seated herself on the bench outside the cookhouse. Turning the envelope over, she broke the seal and tugged the letter out. Anne had written in a delicate script, her letters slanting to the right:

My Dear Cousin,

Mother has asked that I encourage you to come live with us here in Baltimore. Of course, you know how your presence would brighten my life. Mother is standing right beside me, nodding her head in agreement.

I think you will find being in the proximity of a busy port exciting. Foreign ships crowd the harbor. Now that the embargo against the French has been lifted many fly the tricolored flag. Father tells me the wharves are teeming with sailors speaking French, English, Spanish, Italian, even Arabic and Chinese. It's a regular Tower of Babel.

Mother has forbidden me to go there, but my brother George has managed to stroll about and comes home with the drollest stories. He often buys me oranges or lemons. Once he even brought home a bolt of silk of the palest blue so that Mother and I could make gowns in the new fashion. Mother took the silk to the dressmaker your mother once worked for. She always enquires about Aunt Mary with great affection. You will have to go there to have a dress made when you come.

Mother says that you could attend my school and that we could study together. I would be so grateful for your help. Baltimore Academy has two departments and two principals, one for young men and one for young ladies. The course of study would please you, I think: Reading, penmanship (we are taught ladies' Spencerian script), arithmetic, English grammar, geography with the use of the globe, rhetoric, natural and moral philosophy, and a general study of history. That's a lot for my poor brain to absorb.

In addition, if you can imagine it, Mother has me taking singing lessons, even though I sound like a crow. How relieved my teacher would be to hear your sweet voice. Anyway, the school is quite popular and is far better than sailing to England to be "finished" there. Finished off would be more like it, considering how the British feel about Americans. Father says President Madison is leaning toward War.

I wouldn't be surprised. Fort McHenry is nearby and, according to George, the troops are on alert. Some girls at the academy talk about their families leaving town this summer as their fathers believe the city will be under attack by year's end. Father says, "Poppycock." The British will never set foot in Baltimore. The fort has sufficient cannon to blow any British warship to smithereens.

I do hope you accept Mother and Father's invitation. Mother has already furbished a room for you where you will have a bird's eye view of our beautiful city.

With my kindest thoughts,

   Anne

Sophia dropped the letter into her lap. Apparently, she thought, no matter what I decide to do, I will make someone unhappy. As she tried to slide the letter back into the envelope, a smaller piece of paper inside got in the way. Frowning, she pulled out a second letter written on a scrap of vellum. This one was scrawled as though written in haste.

Dear Sophia,

Mother was staring over my shoulder when I wrote you, reading every word. I think she wants you here not for me but for herself. She has plans to make you her secretary. So, you will have very little time for studying even though my father promised yours that you would attend the academy with me. The room Mother is readying for you is wretched, on the third floor, with only one window. It will be beastly hot in summer. I would truly welcome your company but I worry about your happiness.

Your loving cousin, Anne

Sophia shivered, feeling the bite of the wind. I should go back inside she told herself, but she stayed on the bench, mulling over Anne's letters. I almost wish Father would tell me what to do, she thought. That way I wouldn't have to disappoint anyone. I could just say that Father put his foot down.

Baltimore is tempting, she thought. Certainly, if Uncle William has promised to send me to the academy, he will not go back on his word. The classes sound wonderful. I have always wanted to attend such a school. Anne is a good companion. I have no doubts that living with Aunt Polly every day would be a trial. But if I did, I could visit the fort. If James made it up the Chesapeake, if he joined the Navy or even if he didn't, he just might show up at Fort McHenry one day. Or he might not. Perhaps moving to Ohio is the better choice. Fiddlesticks! I wish I knew what to do.

Sophia was still sitting on the bench when Nathan strode up from the river.

"We need you," he said. His tone was terse. "I have been out in the canoe, looking along the shoreline for Jebbie. There is no sign of him. We need to search the woods. Go get your uncles."

Sophia scrambled up. "What's happened?"

"Jebbie has disappeared, and Oriole is afraid he may have come to harm. She walked all the way from Marshtown to tell Sally. So, you know she thinks this is serious. I was in the cookhouse when she arrived.

"What did Oriole say exactly?"

Nathan pushed back his hat and gave Sophia an exasperated look.

"Oriole saw a white man peering in her window earlier. Then, when she went out to see what he wanted, the man said he had come for Jebbie, that Jebbie was to show him something. There was something about the man that didn't sit right with Oriole. She told him Jebbie was off fishing. The white man mumbled something under his breath—it sounded like a threat to Oriole—and left."

"Who was he?"

Nathan shrugged. "Oriole said she'd never seen him before. He was a short, rat-faced man with shifty eyes. Her words not mine."

"That's Mr. Dowling, Nathan. He's the man who threatened Jebbie and stole his coin. He is trouble. Was Jebbie fishing?"

"No." Nathan was beginning to pace. "He was in the loft poring over one of those books you lent him. When Oriole climbed up there to tell him a strange man had been asking for him, Jebbie got this worried look on his face and ran off into the woods."

"That Talcott boar is still out there. It is mean."

"That's the least of his worries. Phee. We are wasting time. The shadows are beginning to lengthen. Go get you uncles. We need people to search before we lose the light."

Sophia gathered up the folds of her skirts and ran toward the house.

24

Trust

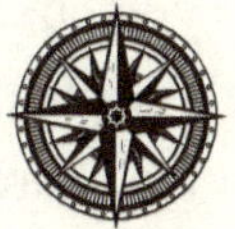

Sophia handed Faith a soapy china cup. "Careful, it's slippery," she warned. "It's a wonder Mother trusts us to wash her precious china."

"I think she's learned some things need to be left to fate." Faith dipped the cup into the rinse bucket. "Anyway, here we are with our hands in dishwater. At least we are helping out by finishing Sally's chores."

Sophia nodded in agreement even though she would rather be out searching. The hearth fire, now reduced to dull red embers, still made the cookhouse hot, stuffy. She opened the door to let in the cooler air. Automatically she looked toward the bench outside, expecting to see Jebbie lounging there. But the yard was empty.

"I can't even imagine what Sally is feeling right now," Sophia said, returning to her task. "It's no secret Mr. Dowling has shown himself to be a thief and a bully. Why Judith has agreed to marry such a man is beyond me. She'd be better off a spinster. He's a scoundrel through and through and if he has taken Jebbie, he is worse than that."

"You mustn't fret, Phee," Faith said, "Jebbie 's not lost forever. He's just off somewhere. He didn't take a boat out. There is no storm brewing. Jebbie will turn up."

"You don't understand," Sophia said. "Yesterday Mr. Dowling threatened Jebbie."

"He has no right to do that."

"Faith, Mr. Dowling doesn't strike me as a being too particular about what's right. I think Jebbie knows this and is hiding from him. I'm pretty sure I know the place."

"Where?"

"That's not important, but if you can finish up the dishes, I'll go get him right now. Please, don't tell anyone I've gone. I'll be back soon."

"I don't understand what all the secrecy is about. Honestly, Sophia. You tend to make mountains out of molehills."

Sophia was about to reply when she heard the sound of horses approaching. Peering out the door, she saw two strangers ride into the yard.

"You there, come out."

The man who shouted had a distinct drawl. He didn't sound like a Marylander.

"Keep out of sight," Sophia whispered to Faith. "Those men must be the patrollers from Virginia. They've come to take Chloe. "

Faith caught hold of Sophia's arm. "What patrollers? How do you know who these men are? Why are they taking Chloe?"

"I'll tell you later. Just trust me for now."

Faith, muttering "mountains out of molehills," stepped back out of sight.

Still clutching her dishrag, Sophia hurried outside.

The riders, one bearded and one clean-shaven, were mounted on thick-legged, dusty horses. One was leading a mule.

"Which way to the darkies' cabins?" the stocky bearded man demanded.

Sophia felt her throat tighten. She felt small and defenseless against men who on horseback appeared gigantic. The beardless one, probably the younger, had a rifle. The other carried a bullwhip, coiled and tied to his saddle.

"What's a matter, girl? Cat got your tongue?"

Sophia felt his eyes taking her measure. He licked his lips.

She wanted to flap the dishrag at the horses. They'd shy, possibly bolt. Instead, she stood tall. With a haughty air she said in her most refined manner, "My name is Miss Records not Girl and this is my father's plantation. There are no darkies' cabins here."

The man pushed his hat back and gave her a puzzled look.

"Excuse me, *Miss Records.* No offence intended. I thought you were the kitchen maid."

"You were mistaken." Her tone was icy.

"So it seems," the bearded one said, pulling his hat forward to shade his face.

"We were told this was the road to a place called Marshtown," the younger one said. "I am afraid we have made a wrong turn."

"Indeed, you have."

"Perhaps, *Miss Records,*" the bearded one said, "you could direct us to the Talcott Plantation. I have a letter here from a Mr. Talcott informing us of a runaway and her whereabouts." He tightened the reins, so his horse backed up, tossing its head.

Sophia smiled but there was no warmth in it.

"Ride back to the Post Road, then turn left," she said. "I think that's the right way. I do get mixed up sometimes. Stay on the Post Road until you come to a small lane. It may be overgrown as I have heard Mr. Talcott discourages visitors. If you get to Snow Hill, you have gone the wrong way."

"Thank you, Miss. Sorry to have troubled you," the younger one said.

Sophia acknowledged the apology with an imperial nod. As the patrollers rode off, she walked casually back to the kitchen house. Once inside, she leaned against the door.

"Were they patrollers?" Faith asked, rushing to Sophia's side.

Sophia nodded. "Now I've time to warn Chloe. She has to disappear."

Faith stepped back and gave Sophia a hard look.

"What are you mixed up in?"

"If I tell you, you must keep it to yourself for now."

Faith frowned. "I don't know, Phee. Those men looked dangerous."

"Can I trust you?"

"Yes," Faith said, giving Sophia another doubtful glance.

Grasping both of her sister's hands, Sophia pulled her closer.

"Judith told me that her father believes he has discovered the whereabouts of a runaway slave. He rode to Marshtown some days ago where he happened to see Chloe. Apparently, he believes she looks like the runaway on a reward poster. He wrote the master, a man in Virginia, telling him what he had seen and asking for the reward money."

"That's wicked!" Faith whispered back.

"Mr. Dowling is no better." Sophia said, dropping Faith's hands.

As she removed her apron, she said, "I have to find Jebbie. Right now. Then get word to Chloe."

Faith shook her head in disapproval. "You can't stop those men. You'll get caught. The sheriff might put you in jail for helping her."

Sophia shrugged. "Then I won't get caught. Please, trust me, just this once. There is a way to help her, if I hurry."

"Well, alright," Faith said, but she didn't sound happy about it.

"Thank you. Stay here. If the men come back, run to Great House as if the Devil is chasing you. Tell Mother what I told you. Ask her to delay the men. She'll do it. I know she will."

Sophia grabbed her shawl. "And pray," she said as she went out the door. "Pray for Jebbie, pray for Chloe, little Abraham, and…" she paused. "And for me."

Walking along the Marshtown road to the orchard, she didn't look back once. Trust goes both ways, she thought. She must trust Faith to do her part.

The March wind had a bite to it. Sophia pulled her shawl close around her shoulders. Stepping off the wagon track, she made her way to the old cabin and its dilapidated porch. This way to Grandsire's secret room was now a familiar route. Lifting the lid to the woodbin, she climbed over the side and dropped to the floor. Then the lid fell shut, leaving her in darkness.

She felt along the floor until her hand closed around the iron ring. Tugging open the hatch, she stepped down onto the first narrow step.

There are seven steps, she told herself. No missteps. No one will find me if I fall.

At the bottom of the stairs, she remembered to breathe. Walking forward, she touched wood and pushed the cupboard away from the wall.

"Jebbie," she whispered. "It's me, Sophia."

He did not answer. The was no sound, only darkness.

Walking with the hesitant step of the blind, Sophia made her way to the table. When she had visited the hideaway earlier, she had left a lantern and a small stack of candles there. She felt around until she found them. Nothing else, no flints, no tinderbox.

Why, she asked herself, didn't I leave the means to strike a flame? Sophia sank to her knees. I am such a fool, she told herself. Thinking I could keep folks safe here was downright prideful. Now Jebbie's is missing. And it's all my fault.

"I am sorry," she whispered, then with mounting remorse, shouted. Her words bounced off the earthen walls before being swallowed into the silence.

In the quiet, she thought she heard someone call her name.

Scrambling to her feet, she made her way to the tunnel door. Maybe, just maybe, it wasn't her imagination. When she tried to open the wood door, it wouldn't budge. Her fingers told her that the bolt had been slid shut. Sliding it back, she opened the door, almost tripping over Jebbie.

She pulled him to his feet. "Oh, you poor boy. I must have locked the door last time I was here. Are you cold? Are you hungry? Come inside. I know it's dark, but there are some blankets in here somewhere."

Sophia would have kept on babbling but Jebbie stopped her with a fierce hug.

"I knew you would come," he said. "What took you so long? My candle burned out."

"Fiddlesticks! We have no way to light a candle."

"I got a tinder box and two flints in here," Jebbie said, thumping the pouch tied around his waist. "Just no candle."

"But I do," she said and led him into the room. She struck a spark into the tinder, which flared in flame. As soon as she lit the lantern, the room filled with a soft yellow light.

"My uncles are combing the woods looking for you and Nathan's searching the shoreline. I have to let them know you are safe. And you have to go back to Marshtown right now. Your mother is there, worried to death about you. But you're not going alone. I am coming with you."

When Jebbie began to protest, saying there was no need, Sophia cut him short. "I must bring Chloe and Abraham here. There are men, patrollers, looking for her."

Jebbie looked at Sophia with alarm.

"What do you mean?"

"There is no time, Jebbie. She's been labeled a runaway. I have to warn her. She needs to hide."

Jebbie shook his head vehemently from side to side. "You are brave, Miss Phee, but I am fast. I can get to Marshtown quicker on my own."

Sophia started to protest until she saw the determined look on his face. "Take the River Trail. It's faster. Bring Chloe and Abraham here."

25

Secrets Revealed

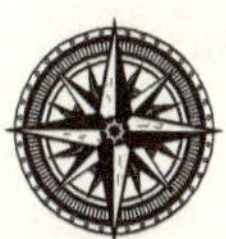

Sophia pushed open the woodbin's heavy lid, praying it wouldn't fall back down again. Third time's the charm, she told herself as the lid thumped all the way open. She was hoisting herself onto the porch when she heard men's voices coming from the road.

"We need dogs," Uncle William was saying. "Someone around here must have bloodhounds. The dogs can find Jebbie."

Sophia hung back until she heard the cookhouse door slam. Then gathering up her skirts, she ran through the orchard and down the road toward Great House. Her uncles were standing in the yard.

"Good news. I found Jebbie!" she hollered.

"Huzzah for you," Uncle Caleb called back, the relief apparent in his voice.

"That little scalawag. Where was he?" Uncle William asked as soon as Sophia joined them.

"In the woods not too far from here. There is a place he likes to go. He fell asleep. I sent him home."

Raising an eyebrow, Uncle William gave her a speculative look. "How did you know how to find him?"

Sophia shrugged. "Just lucky, I suppose. Does it matter?" She thought Uncle William's tone overbearing. Who gave him the right to come here and take over?

"And what's this I hear about patrollers looking for a runaway slave?"

Sophia shot a mean glance toward the cookhouse. Faith was peering out the door. Despite the dwindling light, Sophia was sure Faith wore a guilty expression. "Just a little story to amuse Faith, uncle," Sophia said, crossing her fingers.

"Storytelling is a practice I encourage you to abandon. Making up tales about a fugitive slave hiding in Marshtown could cause trouble for this family. You never know who will believe you."

"I never thought Faith would take it seriously."

Uncle William harrumphed.

"There are laws against harboring runaways," he said. "Some men might accuse your father of complicity by not reporting this fictional woman. He could be arrested. If the court found him guilty, he'd have to pay a fine he can ill afford to pay. It would go worse for the likes of Oriole. Free coloreds can be fined $300 and spend up to a year in prison. If they can't pay, they can be sold into slavery to cover the debt. You don't want that to happen."

"I don't need a lecture, uncle. It was just a silly story." She clenched her fists. He had no right to scold her. He was not her father.

Uncle Caleb took hold of her shoulder, squeezing it hard enough to imply that she should hold her tongue. "We are all glad Jebbie is safe," he said. "Right now, that is the important thing."

"I never said there was a fugitive slave in Marshtown," Sophia told him under her breath.

"Stories often get twisted in the retelling," he muttered. "Faith got flustered. No need to get hot and bothered." He turned her to face Great House. "You best go tell your mother that Jebbie has been found."

Sophia was on her way to the house when Nathan came trudging up the path from the dock.

"No luck," he shouted. He sounded tired.

Sophia whirled back around. "He's found! Sorry, I should have sounded the news." Without another word, she headed toward a large brass bell that was mounted atop a stout post near the cookhouse. Whenever there was news, good or bad, the bell called the family home.

"Save your steps! I'm closer." In a few long strides, Nathan reached the post, took hold of the thick bell rope and pulled and then pulled again.

The deep tolling brought Mother to the side door.

"What's happened?"

"Good news! Jebbie's safe and on his way home," Sophia called out, turning back toward the house.

"Thank the Lord. That scalawag. Wherever has he been?"

"He was nearby, just asleep," Sophia said, approaching her mother. She reached out and grasped her mother's hands. Please," she begged, "don't ask me to go inside. I have things to do."

"Indeed. you do," Mother said. "With Sally back in Marshtown, the supper preparations are up to you and Faith. Put together something simple. I think there are peach preserves in the cellar. None of us can be that hungry."

"But . . ."

"I will brook no arguments tonight, Phee."

Reluctantly, Sophia retraced her steps to the cookhouse, fully determined to ignore Faith as much as possible. She might help Faith by slicing bread and cheese but she would do so in silence. Let Faith do all the talking. Apparently, her sister couldn't keep her big mouth shut.

"I couldn't help it," Faith blurted out as soon as Sophia entered the cookhouse. "You know how relentless Uncle William is. As soon as he heard about the two strange men showing up here, he kept peppering me with questions. Eventually I told him what you said."

"Is that so. Well, I guess you heard Uncle William sermonizing about my storytelling."

"Truly? What you told me was make-believe?"

"That's what Uncle William says."

Later, as the family was finishing supper, Sophia offered to wash up the few dishes. "I'll be late," she said. "I have the milking to do as well."

"No rest for the wicked," Faith said. The smirk on her face said quite plainly, "serves you right for fooling me."

The hall clock chimed the hour. Sophia yawned, being careful to cover her mouth to avoid another lesson on manners from Aunt Polly.

"It's been a tiring day for us all. I imagine everyone will turn in early," Mother said and reminded everyone at the table of the sleeping arrangements. As usual, Sophia and Faith would move to the narrower bed in James's chamber as Aunt Polly and Uncle William will retire to the four-poster in the girls' chamber. Mother would turn the French chaise-lounge in the parlor into a bed for Uncle Caleb.

By the time Sophia got to the barn, twilight was fading into night. Even though she had missed the usual milking time, Ginger wasn't bawling her impatience.

Inside, the barn was bathed in the soft glow of lantern light. Sophia smiled. Ever since Nathan taken up residence here, milking Ginger had become less of a chore. Most times he was off in the tack room, where he had a pallet, whistling and whittling. But since their journey to Uncle Caleb's, he was full of talk.

Tonight, Nathan handed her a half-full bucket of milk. "This is the last of it," he said. "Another bucket is already cooling in the springhouse."

Sophia closed her eyes in relief. One less thing to do.

"Thank you. It's been quite a day."

"Indeed."

Sophia nodded and put the bucket down. Nathan was proving himself to be a friend, a person who could be trusted.

"Could you spare me a minute?" she said. "I have something I want to ask you."

They were standing in the wide aisle of the barn in the circle of light cast by Nathan's oil lantern. He had hung it on a beam near the door, well away from the hay.

"Nathan Harkness," Sophia said, "I need your help."

Her tone was so formal that Nathan laughed outright.

"Shush," Sophia said, looking around nervously. "Someone might be outside. Sounds carry at night."

"Are you about to reveal the time planned for terrifying that fellow who stole Jebbie's coin? What do duppies wear anyway?" Nathan raised his eyebrows and grinned.

Sophia shook her head. "We can deal with Mr. Dowling later. There is a bigger problem. It has to be solved now. Tonight."

As she summed up the dangers Chloe was facing should the patrollers get their hands on her, Sophia kept watching Nathan's expression, worried that he might not be willing to help. Still, she reasoned he had to know the dangers.

"Mr. Talcott tipped them off," she said. "It doesn't matter if he lied. If the patrollers take Chloe back to Virginia, he will have managed to ruin a lot of lives. Anyone involved in helping Chloe remain free runs the risk of arrest."

Nathan took a step backward. "Whoa! You know my predicament."

"Yes. You are brave though. We have to get Chloe and her baby out of sight, away from the patrollers."

"Baby?" Nathan sounded uneasy.

"Abraham, the baby's name is Abraham. Chloe and Abraham are safe right now. At least I think they are. But they can't stay where they are for long. They have to get away from here."

Nathan looked down at the floor, scuffing some straw around in a tentative way.

"You know how terrible slavery is," she said. "Please, help them."

He pursed his lips and gave Sophia a long, searching look.

"I'll do what I can," he said after a minute. "But I can't be gone too long. I promised your father to stay here on the plantation in his absence. I keep my word."

"If you took them upriver in the canoe, you wouldn't be gone long, It's half a day's paddle to the great swamp from here. People hide there."

"A mother and a baby alone in the swamp?" Nathan sounded unconvinced.

"Ulysses will be with them. He'll look out for them."

"Ulysses? Sophia, be reasonable. That little canoe is getting crowded."

"Ulysses has to come. He's Chloe's husband, Abraham's father. You've met him. He a free man who lives in Marshtown and works as a blacksmith in Berlin. He won't be safe here. Besides, he would never leave his family."

Nathan sighed and pushed the straw around with his foot.

"Please."

"Sophia, I will do it but we need to make a watertight plan. I can't just dump this family in the swamp and say goodbye."

"Agreed," Sophia said and reached for his hand. "Thank you. You won't regret this."

"I'll take you to them now, introduce you but I have to stop at the cookhouse first for provisions."

As she turned to walk out the door, Sophia's skirt grazed the milk pail.

"Fiddlesticks. I forgot about the milk."

Nathan reached down and grabbed the handle. "I'll take care of it and meet you at the cookhouse."

"Sounds like we have the beginnings of a plan," she said in a shaky voice.

Inside the cookhouse, Sophia lit a small candle with embers from the dying fire, then pulled open the hatch to the root cellar and walked down the worn wooden steps to the cold earthen room. Placing the candle in a stand on a small table, she searched the shelves for an empty burlap sack. This she filled with some wrinkled apples, two fat onions, and a few potatoes. Back upstairs, she scoured the cupboard for additional provisions.

Thank goodness Sally had baked extra loaves yesterday knowing company was coming, Sophia thought. She inhaled the fresh bread's enticing aroma before adding a loaf to the sack followed by a jar of huckleberry jam, and a small bag of coffee beans.

When Nathan arrived, he handed her two crocks with tight fitting lids.

"Thought you might want these," he said. "Milk and butter."

Sophia shot him an appreciative look.

He grinned. "I am no stranger to scrounging."

"Eggs!" Sophia said, grabbing a small basket. "We'll raid the henhouse on the way."

"On the way where?"

"You'll see."

In the gathering dusk, the henhouse was dark inside. The air was spiced with the aroma of feathers and straw. Sophia moved along the row of nests, murmuring reassurance to the hens as she slipped her hand beneath each one, feeling for a warm egg.

"Six! I found six!" she told Nathan when she reemerged. "We need to smear them with a thin coat of butter. That way they'll keep for a long time."

Nathan uttered a discreet laugh. "You are full of surprises," he said quietly as they walked down the road to the orchard. "I never would have guessed that a girl like you would know that."

"What do you mean a girl like me?" Sophia whispered back.

"Oh, I don't know. You live in a fine house; you dress in fine clothes, although that gown you're wearing looks a little worse for wear."

Sophia snickered. Faith's hasty repairs had pulled apart under her arm.

"I suspect you can read, write, and cypher." Nathan said. He sounded wistful before adding in a teasing way, "I just never suspected you to know about preserving chicken eggs. That's not something a lady needs to know."

"Pish posh. You have some strange ideas."

Leaving the road, they picked their way around the apple trees as they made their way to the abandoned cabin. Here Sophia stopped short.

"This place holds a secret. Not mine, Grandsire's. A secret I promised to keep. And I did until a few days ago. But Jebbie knows, and now so do you. Please don't talk about it, ever. This place is secure because it is unknown."

Nathan nodded.

"You promise?" Sophia's tone was demanding.

"You have my word."

26

Doubts

Sophia led the way to the underground chamber. After shoving the cupboard aside, she tugged on Nathan's sleeve, urging him to enter.

"I'll be blowed!" Nathan said, gazing around in astonishment. He put the oil lantern on the table. "This looks like a smuggler's lair. Your grandsire must have been a sly old fox."

"Muskrat," Sophia corrected. "Oriole always calls him a muskrat."

"Well, he was a wily one."

"No, a patriot. During the Revolution, Grandsire stored everything he took from the British here. Blankets, food, muskets, swords, gunpowder even cannons—all of it was brought here and all of it was passed along to Washington's army."

"This place is a marvel. How did he manage to get all that from his ship to this storeroom? I can't imagine lifting a cannon—even a small one,—into the woodbin."

"Don't be foolish. There's a tunnel. It's how Jebbie will bring Chloe and the baby here." Sophia opened the tunnel door.

Nathan let out a low whistle. "A wily muskrat, indeed."

Sophia didn't respond, just wrinkled up her face in a worried way "Something's wrong," she said. "I can't imagine what's keeping him."

"He'll come."

"What makes you so sure? Maybe Mr. Dowling snatched Jebbie or maybe those patrollers arrested Chloe. "

"Don't go courting trouble."

"It's possible. Those scruffy men may have found Mr. Talcott's place even though I gave them the wrong directions. Mr. Talcott won't invite them in for tea. He will mount up as soon as they arrive and show them the way to Marshtown. Then, no matter what the time of day, he will ride to the magistrate in Snow Hill with a list of names, names of people he claims are guilty of hiding runaways. You know Oriole's and Sally's names will be on that list. Maybe even mine or Father's."

Nathan sighed. "You let worry run away with your thoughts."

"What else can I do?"

"The way I see it, you can wait here and stew in a pot full of grim possibilities or you can walk down that tunnel, walk all the way to Marshtown, if you must, and find out what's holding them back."

Sophia looked away. Nathan is always so cocksure of himself, she thought. Only in this case, he is probably right.

"You'd better come with me," she said.

They left the basket of food and the lantern behind and made their way down the tunnel in the dark. Sophia paused in the small cave at the mouth of the tunnel. "The river is below, the path above," she said. "It's a steep climb to the top of the riverbank. There is an old trail there, a footpath really. Bent trees mark the way."

"I'll be a few steps behind you," Nathan said. Don't look back. I will be close enough."

Sophia felt a great sense of comfort knowing that he would be following, ready to step in if the patrollers or Mr. Dowling came prowling.

Although the moon hid behind sparse clouds, it shed enough light for Sophia to avoid a few downed branches along the way. She moved quickly, always listening. Occasionally there was a scurrying in the leaves or the hoot of an owl, normal sounds not worth dithering about. The woods at night are a peaceful place. Only tonight seemed too quiet, as if even the trees were holding their breath waiting for something to happen. She walked faster.

The thicket stopped her. Getting through the shrubs had been hard even in the daylight. She had forgotten how dense they were. How sharp the thorns were.

Barely a minute later Nathan appeared beside her. Startled, she stifled a frightened little yelp. It's eerie, she thought, the way he can move about without making a sound.

"Grandsire's doings," Sophia said quietly. "I think he planted firethorn bushes here to discourage poachers or other swamp rats. We will tear our clothes to shreds trying to get through."

"Maybe not." Nathan unsheathed the hunting knife that he always kept strapped to his waist. "We'll hack our way to the other side. Chloe has to carry her baby through here. She won't be able to push aside the prickers. Thorns could do a young'un's tender skin great harm."

"The patrollers will see the opening if they come this way. And they will. Men like that don't give up their prize easily."

"Do we have a choice?"

Cautiously, Nathan made his way into the thicket, hacking off branches as he went along. Sophia followed closely behind him.

Once on the other side, she again took the lead. Before long she saw the dark silhouette of Oriole's cabin and through the back window, the flickering light of a fire. She wondered if Oriole and Sally had gone to bed or if they were just sitting by the fire waiting for something to happen. Jebbie must have told them everything.

Resisting the temptation to stop, Sophia kept walking down the narrow lane to the little cabin at the other end of the road. Inside, even though they were keeping their voices low, it sounded as if a woman was pleading with someone.

"No," a man said. "It is safer my way."

Sophia looked back at Nathan, who was keeping to the side of the road. He motioned to her to go on, then stepped off the road and walked to one side of the cabin wall. He seemed to disappear.

Sophia smiled grimly. For someone who had told her that she worried too much, he was acting as if he had a few concerns of his own. Squaring her shoulders, she took a deep breath and walked purposefully up the path to the door. She knocked, timidly at first. When no one answered, she banged her fist against the door. The talking ceased.

She knocked again.

"Open the door, Jebbie," a deep voice said. "Trouble doesn't knock. It barges right in."

The door opened a crack.

"Come in quick," Jebbie whispered. "I can't get Chloe to come along with me. She says I exaggerate."

Sophia peered inside. The blanket wall had been taken down. The cabin now was crowded with people. Oriole and Chloe sat at the table, Sally was leaning against the back wall, Jebbie's brother and Becky were asleep on the bed, and Abraham was in his cradle. Ulysses was standing, a giant who seemed to fill the whole room. He was frowning at her.

Sophia hesitated not knowing whether to stay or to turn and run. Two hours ago, she believed that her plan to help Chloe escape had been the right one. Now, she wasn't sure.

She stood in the doorway, looking at all those familiar dark faces and wishing she was someplace else.

What made me think I had the right to tell Chloe what to do, she thought. Only Chloe and Ulysses can decide the best course. I am no better than Mr. Talcott or Uncle William or any other slave owner, good or bad.

"It seems," Sophia said, her voice quavering. "I have caused an argument. I meant no disrespect. I was only trying to help."

Tilting up her chin, she looked directly at Ulysses. "Jebbie is right. Trouble is coming sooner than you may think," she said, and then told the gathering about the two Virginians riding into the yard at Great House, what they said, and what they were planning.

"I know a place where Chloe can hide," she concluded. "Jebbie will guide you. You'll find food, good spring water and blankets, even clouts for the baby's bottom."

Expecting Ulysses to say that protecting his wife was his business not hers, Sophia gave him a pleading look, fully prepared to argue her case, and was surprised when he walked over to her.

"The Lord will bless you, Miss Phee. Like the Bible says, you provide a stronghold to the needy."

Oriole rose and held out her arms to Sophia, who hurried over.

"You did good, Miss Phee, just like I knew you would," Oriole said softly and hugged her. "Now rest your bones. You look all tuckered out."

Obediently, Sophia sat down on the bench, careful to leave enough space for Oriole.

Chloe looked across the table and tried to smile but her eyes, already puffy from crying, welled up again and spilled over. She dabbed at her face with a sodden handkerchief.

"I am not that person," Chloe said in a halting voice. "You know, the one Mr. Talcott says I am. But that won't make no difference. Will it? So, I thank you kindly for the warning." Once again, she tried to smile but ended up dabbing at her eyes.

Then, taking a deep, jagged breath, Chloe said in a firm tone, "Jebbie, Abraham and I will be leaving shortly." As she spoke, she stared directly at Ulysses. Her look was so full of love and determination and sorrow it made Sophia fumble for the handkerchief she kept tucked in her sleeve.

Ulysses began to pace back and forth across the small cabin. When he stopped, he cleared his throat a couple of times.

"You know I can't go with you," he said looking at Chloe. "You know that."

He spoke with such finality that Sophia knew the disagreement she had overheard was now concluded.

"But you will come soon," Chloe said. "Come to me soon."

Abruptly, as if he could no longer look at his wife without breaking down, he turned to Sally. "I know you've had a bad scare and want to keep your boy home," he said, "but it would be best if Jebbie stay with Chloe and Abraham until I get there."

Sally sighed. "Jebbie can only stay till morning. He needs to be with me at Great House tomorrow, acting as if it's just another day. After all, Chloe is visiting her Mama in Baltimore. Ain't that right, Jebbie?"

"Yes, Mama," Jebbie said, but his eyes were big and round and scared.

"But don't you worry, Miz Chloe. I'll be stopping by from time to time," he added.

One man, Sophia thought, only one, has torn this village apart. She looked up at Oriole. "I feel so ashamed that one man can do such harm."

"Not just one, Honey," Oriole said. "A whole nation of men. Five year ago, Maryland passed a law saying I could no longer sell my corn or anything else I grow in my fields. Now I give it away. Folks give me stuff in return. Like those pesky turkeys. Last year, the government took away Ulysses's right to vote, him and every other free black man in this state. They have no say in the government now."

As if to soften her words, she smiled at Sophia and grasped her hand. "Not all men, though. There is your grandsire's family. With folks like you we'll get along."

Ulysses cleared his throat. "You need to go home, Miss Phee. If those men show up here and see you, well . . ." He didn't need to finish; Sophia knew what he meant and scrambled to her feet.

Oriole patted Sophia's arm in a comforting way. "Now you get along before someone comes here looking for you and starts asking questions."

Sophia nodded then reached over the table to take hold of Chloe's hand before leaving. "You mustn't worry," she said. "You and Abraham will be safe."

"And don't worry about me," Sophia called out to everyone as she walked to the door. "I know my way home. The coast is clear. Mr. Harkness has been outside, keeping watch."

27

Half Truths and Lies

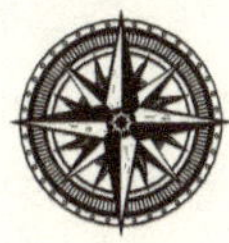

In the moonlight, Marshtown Road appeared to be a black streak drawn across Oriole's pale field of young wheat that disappeared into the dark woods beyond. Sophia shivered and pulled her shawl close around her shoulders.

"The wind has a bite to it," Nathan said, walking over to join her from his post by the cabin. "We should get a move on."

"I am having second thoughts," Sophia said. "You must go back with Chloe along the River Trail. She has much to carry and Jebbie is just a little boy, after all. You can get them to the tunnel safely. I know my way home."

Nathan uttered a soft wry laugh. "Not without me," he muttered.

Suddenly cross and tired, Sophia chose to ignore him. "You must go with Chloe," she repeated.

"No, I would never let a girl walk alone along the Marshtown Road in the dark."

Sophia whirled around to face the wheat field. He had no right to tell her what to do. He was a hired hand after all. "I must insist," she said, directing her remark to the empty field, each word as sharp and hard as a steel blade. There was no reply. She took a deep breath and exhaled loudly before turning back to face him. "You seem to forget, Mr. Harkness, I know that road well. There are no wolves or bears or those big cats you like to talk about. The most dangerous animal around here is a fox. I am perfectly safe, but I thank you for your concern." She tilted up her chin, daring him to disagree.

"What about those feral pigs you talk about?" Nathan said, matching Sophia's prickly tone.

"Pigs don't forage at night."

"And the patrollers? What makes you think they are asleep in their beds? Do you think those men will pass you by with a tip of the hat?"

"I can take care of myself."

"On a wagon path through the woods in the middle of the night?"

"It's not the middle of the night," Sophia said looking skyward. The moon, which was not quite round, hung just above the trees. "I'll be home before eleven."

"I cannot allow it."

"Where I go and what I do is not your concern," Sophia said, raising her voice.

The argument might have escalated to shouting except that Ulysses stepped outside his cabin. He gave a long low whistle. A dark red dog, a hound, appeared almost as if Ulysses had conjured him up from the dirt in the lane. The dog trotted over to him, tail wagging. Ulysses gave it a pat, then walked toward Sophia and Nathan. The dog followed.

"Begging your pardon, Miss Records," he said. "I would be pleased to walk you home. That way no one will accuse Master Harkness here of treating you like a hussy."

Sophia felt her cheeks flame. As much as she didn't want to admit it, Ulysses was right. Her reputation would be compromised if she and Nathan were seen returning together. Mother might overlook the impropriety, but Aunt Polly? Never.

She could just hear her. "It's scandalous," Aunt Polly would declare in that high-pitched voice of hers. "Scandalous! Walking out with a young man, no chaperone, and at this time of night! That simply isn't done. Certainly not in Baltimore." Sophia knew she would never hear the end of it. She felt defeated.

"Thank you, Ulysses," she said. "You are most kind."

Looking at Nathan, though, she grinned in triumph. "This means you will be free to help Chloe," she said.

Nathan leaned down to pat the dog. "Whatever you say, Miss Records, whatever you say," he muttered, making Sophia regret her highhanded tone and worry that the argument may have soured their friendship.

If Ulysses was aware the two were at odds, he chose to ignore it. He clapped Nathan on the shoulder.

"I'd be much obliged for your help," he said. "Oughta be me goin' with my family but that can't be." He shook his clenched his fists. "If those Patrollers come snoopin' around here, I'd be happy to bust open their heads with my bare hands if need be. Problem is more trouble would come. A posse of men. And one way or another, I'd lose my family. Tonight, I play the fox if those patrollers come round. They can chase me to the gates of hell if it'll keep my family safe."

Nathan nodded. "Understood. You have my word I'll protect them."

A few minutes later, Ulysses hugged his wife goodbye then stepped back to let her pass. No words passed between them. Jebbie led, carrying a dim oil lantern. Chloe followed, holding the baby wrapped in a blanket. Nathan brought up the rear, carrying a large basket, the same one Mother had sent the family when Abraham was born.

Sophia watched them walk down the lane and disappear behind Oriole's house. Somewhere in a nearby tree a whip-poor-will sang its repetitive song. Other than the bird, the world seemed empty.

Sophia, Ulysses, and the hound began walking down the Marshtown Road. The wind was blowing steadily from the west, and the familiar scent of the Pokomoke mingled with earthy odors of damp leaves and fertile ground. Even with her shawl wrapped tight, Sophia felt the sting of the wind. She was tired and the long walk home held no promise of comfort. She longed to be in her bed under a warm quilt.

"The woods will block the wind," Ulysses said. Stooping down he gathered up handfuls of straw left beside the road after the fall harvest. He twisted these into a thick bundle.

"Makes a good torch," he said. "I brought fire fixins. We're gonna need a light in the woods. Besides, it'll make a show. Anyone coming down the road tonight is likely up to no good. It's best they see us, see that I've no idea patrollers are comin' to take my wife." He handed her the unlit torch and then began making another.

"You are like the first Ulysses," Sophia said.

"I don't know him."

"In ancient times, on the other side of the ocean there was a king called Ulysses. This Ulysses left his wife behind to right a wrong. He sailed across a dangerous sea to fight the Trojans, whose prince had kidnapped the most beautiful woman in the world."

"Like Mr. Talcott takin' Chloe?"

"Chloe is beautiful, of course, but I was thinking your wife is like the wife of that first Ulysses. She was beautiful and wise as well. Ulysses loved her very much. As soon as he won the war, he set sail for home. Only, he had to fight many monsters along the way before he was reunited with his wife."

"So you're sayin', I have to fight monsters," Ulysses said. "Well, then, let's hope we meet none of them tonight."

The dog pricked up his ears and then took off running. Sophia felt a tremor of fear.

"Probably after a coon," Ulysses said. "He's a good hunter."

Nevertheless, he crouched down to strike a spark to the tinder and light the straw torch. The tinder lit the straw and caught hold, casting a circle of light around them. Ulysses smiled and his teeth gleamed white.

"It's a makeshift torch but it will do," he said. "When this one burns down, we'll light yours."

Sophia nodded, grateful after all she hadn't made this walk by herself. The woods, a friend by day, had become an ominous stranger. She stayed close to Ulysses, who held the torch upright, away from their clothes.

After a while the hound came back. And as they walked along, Ulysses told Sophia how he had come to have the dog.

"A white man in Berlin drove his old tobacco wagon to the forge one day," Ulysses said. "A dog was tied to the back of the rig. The man said his horse, a big dun mare needed new shoes. When I asked about the dog, the man said he was planning on shootin' the dog because he had no voice. 'What good is a hound that can't bay?' the man said. 'Dog's got to earn his keep.'"

"That's not right," Sophia said.

"No, it's not! I told the man I'd save him the trouble of shooting dat dog and shoe his horse for free if he turned dat hound over to me. Quick as a frog jumps, he went to the wagon, untied the dog and handed me the rope. I shod the horse and the man left in a very good mood.

"Later, on the way back to Marshtown, I let the dog loose. It trotted along beside me. When I got to my cabin, the dog sat down by the door. The next morning when I opened the door, the dog was sittin' there, this time with a rabbit in its mouth."

"He brought you dinner," Sophia said and stopped walking in order to stroke the dog's sleek head. "What a fine one you are," she cooed. The dog stood still but kept his eyes on Ulysses.

"It's been goin' on two years now and that hound brings me meat almost every day," Ulysses said. "Oh, he messed with Granny Oriole's turkeys once but she set him straight." He laughed softly, a deep infectious laugh that made Sophia giggle.

"You should have seen him hightail out of her yard with Granny Oriole, her skirts a flappin', chasin' after him with her broom held high. It was a sight. The dog respected her righteous anger though. He has never laid a tooth on another one of them turkeys." He laughed again and leaned down to give the dog a hard pat.

"Does he have a name?"

"What?"

"Does your dog have a name?"

"I mostly call him Hound. Some mornings, though, when we are walkin' to the forge and the sun makes his coat shine, I call him Rust. Because that's his color, the same color as the rust that sometime shows up on forged iron."

"Rust. I like that. Come here, Rust."

But the dog stayed with Ulysses.

They were nearing Records Landing when the dog growled. Halfway between a rumble and a cough, it was the first sound Sophia had heard the dog make. There was no question that the hound was issuing a threat. Then he ran ahead, out of the light.

"The next thing she heard was a man shouting, "Get away, get away." His voice shrill, tight with fear. A horse snorted.

Ulysses whistled that one long, low note and the dog came back. "Now what did you find?" He asked the dog in an amused tone before shouting, "Who's about?"

"Dowling, Abner Dowling from Salisbury. Until recently, that is."

"Don't trust him," Sophia whispered. "He's a dreadful man, a bully and a thief. He stole Jebbie's gold coin."

The two of them walked on until Mr. Dowling came into view. He was standing in the middle of the road, holding a horse by the reins. The horse kept pulling back and shaking his head as if he wanted to shed the bridle and get away.

"You got a good hold on that dog?"

"Yes, Sir."

"He scared my horse."

"He's good around horses. It's people he don't like."

"Why, Mr. Dowling," Sophia interjected, feigning pleasure in the chance encounter. "It's me, Sophia Records. Whatever brings you out this time of night?"

"I might ask the same of you, Miss Records."

"Maybe you haven't heard. But our cook's boy, Jebbie, ran away today. I am happy to report he has been found. I went to tell his mother that he is safe. Mr. Brown here is seeing me home."

"And the boy, where is he?"

"Why, thank you for asking, Mr. Dowling. Jebbie was all tuckered out, poor thing, and my mother thought it best if he stayed with us under the watchful eye of Mr. Harkness." She stepped away from the torch light in case the lie showed on her face. "Perhaps your fiancée Miss Talcott, has spoken of Mr. Harkness," she continued. "He is in my father's employ and is to guide us to Ohio. He is an Indian fighter, you know."

"Your father's servants are of no importance to me," Mr. Dowling barked. Then turning to Ulysses, he said, "You keep that dog in hand, boy. I don't want me or my horse bit by some nigger's dog. It probably would give us the rabies."

Mr. Dowling tried to lead the horse past them, but it kept shaking its head from side to side and stepping backwards, away from the hound, who was growling.

"You ought to put a rope on that dog," Mr. Dowling said.

"He knows what to bite and what not to," Ulysses said.

"Before you leave us," Sophia interjected, "I have a question. I told you why I am walking home in the dark. Now it is your turn. What brings you here tonight?"

"Business," he said.

"And what business would you have on the Marshtown Road this time of night, Mr. Dowling?" Ulysses asked. He spoke in an even tone but like the dog's strange growl, there was an underlying threat.

"Just keeping an eye on things. What did you say your name was? Brown, was it? Sounds like a made-up name to me." He turned toward Sophia. "To answer your question, impertinent as it may be, my fiancée's father asked me to stop by Marshtown, just to see if everything is peaceful there. Mr. Talcott cares about his neighbors, you know."

As Mr. Dowling talked, Ulysses kept opening and closing his fists until Sophia, tugged at his sleeve and ever so slightly shook her head.

"Oh, my goodness, Mr. Dowling," Sophia said taking a step forward. "I am glad we ran into you. Miss Talcott, Judith—we are on a first name basis, you know—would be so worried if she knew you were out on such a chilly night. Why you might develop a serious cough. If I were to tell her that I met you here, she might question your intentions."

As Sophia talked, Ulysses quietly moved back along the road, blocking the way to Marshtown. The dog, who had been sitting, now stood and walked over to Mr. Dowling, sniffing his pant leg. The little man stepped back and the horse backed up, too.

"I have an idea," Sophia said brightly. "Since I have just come from Marshtown, I can assure you all is peaceful there. You can walk me home on your way back to the Talcott place. Mr. Brown and his dog can return to Marshtown and we will all get at least a partial night's sleep."

"Well, I don't know. I'd hate to disappoint Mr. Talcott. He doesn't like to be disappointed."

"Please, Mr. Dowling, I am so weary. I am sure you are too. It's been a very long day."

Sophia didn't know whether it was her argument, Ulysses dark presence blocking the road, or Mr. Dowling's fear of the dog that made him agree. Before she could take two breaths, the two of them were walking side by side along the road, with Mr. Dowling leading the horse.

Sophia did not bring up Grandsire's treasure until Great House was in sight.

"Do you remember what I told you about the man who lived near Berlin finding gold coins last year and how he went mad? He took coins without pleading his case."

"What do you mean?"

"The doubloons he found were Grandsire's. Those coins can only be held by those he deems worthy. How do you think my father got the money to buy land in Ohio? I think my grandsire would give you some coins if you told him how deserving you were, how you are a widower with two young children and how you plan to marry Judith and that you want to keep her in the style she's used to. That would soften his ghostly heart.

"You think so?"

"I do. But you must act quickly, while the moon is early in its third quarter. Tomorrow night. The gold stash is not far from here. I have not set eyes on it but Jebbie says he found his coin just off the Marshtown Road. There is a faint path—pigs use it—that runs past the huge stump of an old pine. The gold is buried there. I know of it. Tomorrow I will mark the way with strips of white cloth."

"Why haven't you been given coins?"

"I am just a girl. I have no need for money. Grandsire gave me something better."

"What could be better than gold?"

"Many things, Mr. Dowling. Perhaps someday you'll find out."

And with that, Sophia took her leave. As she wearily trudged toward the front door, she caught a whiff of familiar pipe smoke. The skin on the back of her neck prickled.

"Grandsire?"

28

A Change in Plans

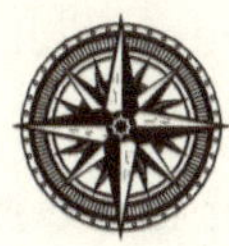

Uncle Caleb stood to greet Sophia. "You keep strange company, Phee." Although his tone was teasing, she detected relief in his voice.

"Come, sit a spell," he said. "It's turned into a beautiful night." He took her arm and guided her to the bench outside the cookhouse, assuring her with a chuckle that he was not a ghost. He didn't scold or ask where she had been. He just seemed pleased for her company. They sat in silence for a while, gazing at the sky and listening to the night sounds, the faint calls of an owl and the rustling of a critter in the leaves.

Maybe it was the hour, her exhaustion, or the worry that her plan might put Chloe and Abraham in greater danger, Sophia began explaining in a halting voice, why she had walked home from Marshtown an hour before midnight. Slowly, most of the story came out, starting with Mr. Talcott's plan to claim Chloe as the runaway slave he had seen on a wanted poster and ending with the steps she had taken to hide Chloe.

"Once our family leaves," Sophia added in a more cutting tone, "Mr. Talcott plans to chase off or burn out all the folks in Marshtown.

Judith Talcott told me he thinks folks like Oriole and Ulysses put ideas in slaves' heads. And that's not all. She came right out and said that her father is ignoring the law. He is importing slaves from Africa on the sly and selling them at a slave market in Virginia."

Uncle Caleb had listened quietly until she got to the last part. "We'll see about that," he had said grimly. Then he put his arm around her shoulders and pulled her close. "Grandsire trusted you with an important secret, and you have not let him down. You have put his hideout to good use."

Sophia gasped. Hearing her uncle say he knew about the hidden room lessened its importance. She had thought she was the only one Grandsire told, that she was the keeper of his secret. Her sharp intake of breath conveyed her bruised feelings.

Uncle Caleb must have understood, because he said gently, "I guess I have some explaining to do as well."

He told her that the tunnel and the hidden cellar were well known to him and his brothers. And like her, they had been sworn to secrecy. During the Revolution, that secret had been critical not only as a place to store weapons but as place of safety. Grandsire had instructed the family to hide there if the British came sniffing around. Uncle Caleb explained that his job, being too young to fight, had been to make sure no one stumbled across the entrance by the river.

"Sophia," he said, "you are one of only a few who know about the tunnel.

Should we fight England again, and that looks likely, the tunnel will be useful." He paused before adding, "You think like your Grandsire. Hiding Chloe and her family there was the right thing to do. As for Talcott, like his father, he is an envious man and prone to treachery. Your mother's sage Ben Franklin may have said it best: *Tricks and treachery are the practice of fools that don't have brains enough to be honest.*"

Again, the pair fell silent. Uncle Caleb clasped his hands behind his head and gazed skyward. It was a pose Sophia knew well: I am thinking, please let me be.

Overhead the sky was crowded with stars. In the quiet moments that followed, Sophia remembered that when she was younger, she had believed stars were tiny windows that let the light of Heaven shine through. How happy we all were then, she thought. We were all together. Now Grandsire and James are gone. If I stay behind, another one of us will be gone.

When Uncle Caleb cleared his throat and began to speak, Sophia could hear the resolve in his voice.

"Your plan to help Chloe escape to the Great Swamp has merit," he said. "There are folks living there who would offer her shelter. Still, it is no place for a newborn child. "

"You don't understand. Innocent or not, Chloe will be arrested."

Uncle Caleb held up his hand. "There is another way. Delay. Keep her and the baby safe in the cellar for a few days, a week at most. Can you manage that?"

Sophia nodded.

"Ulysses is right. He must continue going to the blacksmith shop as normal. Talcott is more likely to believe Chloe is visiting her mother if everything else is routine. In two days, I am picking up the *Rebel Ann* from the boatyard in Snow Hill and sailing her here with only a skeleton crew, trustworthy men. My plan is to carry all of you to Baltimore. Nothing out of the ordinary there. You bring Chloe and the baby on board the night before we sail. I'll make sure she has a comfortable place below deck, away from prying eyes."

"You are putting yourself in danger, uncle."

Uncle Caleb smiled a wolfish smile. "That is a condition I relish."

29

Anything But

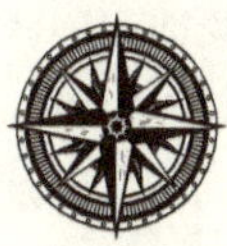

Early the next morning, Sophia was able to waylay Nathan just as he was untying the canoe. "Don't go," she said. "Chloe is staying put for now."

He frowned. "You can't back out now. There is too much at stake here."

"No, I am not backing out. Plans have changed, that's all. Uncle Caleb has offered his help."

After Sophia filled him in on all the details, Nathan nodded his approval. "It makes sense," he said. "Now all we have to do is act as if nothing out of the ordinary is going on around here."

Sneaking out to the old cabin to check on Chloe and Abraham before milking time, slipping out there again to bring Chloe a jar of milk and biscuits hot from the oven, and then going back to the kitchen to ask Sally if she could somehow wash the baby's soiled clouts without Mother knowing—none of these things were ordinary.

Nor was the haunting of Mr. Dowling. Last night, Sophia had omitted telling Uncle Caleb about the theft of Jebbie's coin and her plan to retrieve it, suspecting he would disapprove of her trickery. Now she wondered if that made her as much of a fool as Mr. Dowling.

Whatever the verdict on that, she needed to check the clearing without drawing attention to her whereabouts. Then tonight, assuming Mr. Dowling was still eager to have a ghostly encounter, she needed to keep watch discreetly so that she could slip away to join him if he rode past. The man was such a fortune hunter that Sophia felt certain he would take the bait.

For his part, Nathan seemed keen to play Grandsire's ghost, Sophia thought and chuckled softly. He promised to be in costume and waiting in the barn for her signal, one long whistle and two, short. His ghostly appearance is certain to scare Mr. Dowling into giving Jebbie back his coin. That superstitious little man should be easy to frighten.

She set off after breakfast, saying she was on her way to give the Marshtown children their lessons and she would be happy to take some of the odds and ends set aside for folks there. Mother and Aunt Polly had been sorting through the cutlery and cookware, putting aside duplicates. Some were to go to Faith; the rest were free for the taking.

Mother had laughed when she saw the pile mount and said," I don't believe that there was a time when the peddler came by that I didn't buy something."

Today she asked Sophia to take several of the baskets to Marshtown as well as a handful of the knives, forks and spoons. "I must have a soft spot for baskets," she said. "There are enough here for every man, woman and child in Marshtown. Give them to Oriole. She'll sort it out."

Now, as Sophia pushed a loaded wheelbarrow down the road, she worried about who would teach the children when she was gone. "Worry is like my rocking chair," Oriole had told once her. "You can rock in it all day but it doesn't get you anywhere."

You are right, Sophia thought. She stooped down and picked up a stone. "Your name is worry," she said and threw the stone as far as she could into the woods.

Someone shrieked.

For a moment, Sophia was afraid the stone had struck one of the Marshtown children wandering in the woods, but the shriek turned into a shout, and the shouter sounded a lot like Mr. Dowling.

"Get away! Get away!"

Gathering her skirts, Sophia abandoned the wheelbarrow and set off through the woods toward the sound. Whatever is frightening him, she thought, it couldn't be happening to a better man.

Within minutes she found herself at the edge of the same clearing she had described to Mr. Dowling last night. The slippery little man must have come past Great House when we were at breakfast, she thought. Well, this is what he gets for it. There he was, halfway up a skinny tree peering down at the same feral pig that had challenged Sophia.

"Get him out of here!" Mr. Dowling shouted. "That monster is bent on killing me."

"Oh, he's not so bad," Sophia managed to call as she tried to hide her amusement. As soon as he heard her voice, the pig whirled to face her.

Looking around for something, anything, to intimidate it, Sophia saw a shovel, not something she expected to find out here.

She stared at the pig. "Remember me?" she hissed, holding the shovel sideways, ready to swing. The pig stared back. Sophia thought she saw a spark of recognition in those small black eyes and tightened her grip. "Best be going now," she said in a low threatening tone.

The pig lowered his head, his razor-sharp tusks pointing right at her. Sophia held her ground.

"Go on. Shoo!" Sophia said as if she were talking to China Boy. The pig gave her another hard stare, then turned and trotted off into the woods.

She waited a minute before telling Mr. Dowling it was probably safe to come down. The man shimmied down the tree with amazing alacrity and walked over to her.

"That was a close call," he said. "I'll take that," He reached out for the shovel, acting as if he had been the one to frightened off the pig.

With one quick thrust, Sophia buried the blade halfway into the ground. "Digging for treasure, Mr. Dowling?" she said pleasantly enough. She inclined her head toward a hole dug near the old tree stump in the center of the clearing. "Probably wasn't the wisest thing to do."

"I'll thank you not to advise me, Miss Records." His tone was sharp.

Sophia lowered her gaze in mock contrition. It was obvious to her that besides being shaken by his close encounter, Mr. Dowling resented the fact that a girl had been the one to chase off the pig.

Ungrateful prig, she thought and turned away only to see another hole and then another. Apparently, Mr. Dowling was determined to find Grandsire's rumored treasure on his own. That pig showed up at just the right time, she thought, smiling to herself. Straightening her expression, she turned back to face him.

"I would never presume to tell you what to do, Sir," she said. "I imagine that you have already guessed that the pig is Grandsire's vindictive spirit. He would never hurt me, but he must be very angry with you."

"What do you mean?" Mr. Dowling stepped back a pace. "That was a vicious wild boar. Mr. Talcott told me he'd turned his pigs out last fall to fatten up on acorns. Come butchering time, one eluded capture."

"That may be, Mr. Dowling. Only the creature you saw today was no ordinary pig. I am sure you know that duppies appear as animals sometimes."

"I know nothing about duppies. You said your grandsire was one, I assumed you meant a ghost."

Sophia lowered her voice to a whisper. She spoke earnestly, being careful not to allow herself the slightest smile, not even the twitch of a lip.

"Much worse than a ghost, Mr. Dowling. Ghosts are poor lost souls who wander the earth looking for redemption. Duppies are beyond salvation. If you wrong one, he will harm you. "

"I've done your grandsire no wrong. I never knew the man."

"You took one of his coins, stole it from a boy. Then you come here looking for more coins. Didn't I warn you? You shouldn't have come here without me."

Mr. Dowling seemed to have developed a tic below his right eye. "Here," he said, slipping two fingers into a small pocket just below the waist band of his breaches. He pulled out Jebbie's coin and tossed it toward Sophia, who stepped forward in time to catch the guinea before it hit the ground.

"Do what you wish with it," he said. "I will have no more of this nonsense." He turned on his heel to follow the pig's faint path leading back to the Marshtown Road.

"Shall I meet you here tonight?" Sophia called after him.

"No," he said aloud before muttering under his breath," I am not interested in treasure hunting. I will find another way to wealth."

"You had better take your shovel." Retrieving it, she followed him out to the road.

"Where did you tether your horse? Has he run off?"

"No. I walked. I went for an early morning stroll and happened to end up here."

Sophia again stifled the urge to laugh. "You went for a stroll with *this*," she said, handing him the shovel. "A strange walking stick."

"It is. Very unsuitable. Perhaps you could find a better use for it." He said and handed the shovel back. "I suspect, Miss Records, that you have been toying with me. I am not amused."

Without another word, he began walking briskly away.

Hoisting the shovel over her shoulder, Sophia returned to the place where she had left the wheelbarrow, added the shovel to its load, and continued on her way to Marshtown.

The children were in the yard when Sophia approached Oriole's cabin. Fry got to her first. "Patrollers comed here," was all he said but the way his eyes got big when he said it told Sophia he was frightened.

As the other children clustered around her, she learned more. The men had searched every cabin, thrown things about, even pushed over a privy looking for Auntie Chloe.

"Granny Oriole, she ain't afraid of nothin' or nobody," Summer said. He held his head high and puffed out his chest. "When I am a man, I'm gonna be brave like her. She told those men to get goin', to skedaddle back to where dey come from. And dey skedaddled."

Becky came toddling over to Sophia last. She kept pulling on Sophia's skirt, asking, "Are dey gonna snatch Auntie Chloe?"

Sophia looked at the little girl and shook her head.

Becky whispered, "Miss Phee, are dey gonna snatch me?"

Sophia knelt down and pulled the little girl into her arms. "No, Darling. Don't you worry. You stay close to Granny Oriole. Nobody will snatch you. Not Miss Chloe either. Your Aunt Chloe has gone visiting. She wants her mama to see baby Abraham and she may be there a while."

Becky nodded her head up and down a few slow times then stuck her thumb in her mouth. She didn't seem comforted by the explanation, making Sophia wonder how much the two-year-old really knew. After Sophia stood back up, after she reassured all the children that the patrollers wouldn't be back, she went inside, but she couldn't stop thinking that her comforting words could prove false.

30

Snatched

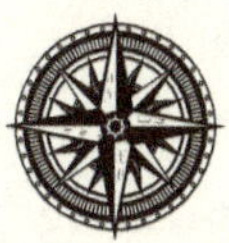

Nobody knew Jebbie had gone missing again until supper. When Sally came into the dining room with more hot biscuits, she whispered to Mother that Jebbie hadn't shown up at the cookhouse. It wasn't like Jebbie to miss a meal. And with the fog rolling in off the river, she was worried.

When Mother asked if anyone had seen Jebbie, Faith said she had no idea where he was. Sophia said she hadn't seen him in Marshtown when she was there and shot Nathan a quizzical glance. He shrugged, saying the last time he saw Jebbie was down by the dock but he didn't know exactly when. It had been in the morning sometime after breakfast.

Uncle William slapped his hand on the table hard enough to make his plate jump. "Not again," he growled. "Doesn't that boy ever stay put?"

Aunt Polly sniffed and said that someone ought to teach that boy a thing two, looking right at Mother when she said it. Mother glared back, saying that Jebbie was very reliable. If he hadn't shown up to help his mother, something must be amiss.

Uncle Caleb didn't say anything. He just left the table then yelled from the doorway for Uncle William and Nathan to get a move on. It's easy to get turned around in such a fog.

Chairs scraped back. Faith excused herself, telling Sally she'd wait with her in the cookhouse. In all likelihood Jebbie would come there first. Mother and Aunt Polly decided to wait in the house in case he came here. As they were walking to the parlor, Sophia heard Aunt Polly say, "Elijah ought to be at home," and heard her mother answer, "You have no argument from me."

Willie stayed at the table, pushing his food around with a spoon. Having been told to stay with him, Sophia fretted. She needed to get to the old cellar. Jebbie must be there with Chloe. The scalawag. He knew he was to follow a normal routine. Resting her elbows on the table, Sophia cradled her chin in her hands and stared at her brother in exasperation.

"Aren't you hungry?"

Willie shook his head, no.

"Cat got your tongue?"

"We don't have a cat," Willie said grudgingly.

"Maybe we should get one."

"I'd rather keep Pebbles. She's my friend but Mother says your friend Miss Talcott bought the chickens, even Pebbles."

"She's not my friend," Sophia said, surprising herself with the sharpness of her tone.

"She is nice to me," Willie said. "But that man who is going to marry her, he's not nice at all."

"Why do you say that?"

Willie gave her a sullen look. "I am not supposed to tell," he muttered and scrambled down from his chair.

"Wait." Sophia reached out and grabbed him by the arm. "Come with me, little man." She led him into Father's office and closed the door. "You don't have to tell me anything. Just nod your head yes or shake it no. Will you do that?"

Willie nodded.

Slowly, softly Sophia began questioning her brother. "This thing that you are not supposed to tell, is it about Jebbie?"

Willie nodded again. Using a patience that she didn't know she had, Sophia continued to ask questions and receive nods until she had pieced together what her brother knew.

Willie was feeding the chickens when he saw Mr. Dowling walking down the road toward Great House. Jebbie was walking the other way toward Marshtown. When they met, Mr. Dowling wouldn't let Jebbie pass. The two talked for a minute. Then Mr. Dowling looked like he got mad.

"Did the man hurt Jebbie?"

Willie nodded one more time, his eyes filling with tears.

Sophia took a deep breath. She could just see Mr. Dowling grabbing Jebbie by the shoulders, shaking him and shoving him down into the dirt.

"Didn't Jebbie try to get away?"

Willie shook his head, no. "He got tied up," he whispered.

It wasn't hard for Sophia to imagine Mr. Dowling pulling a rope from the ditty bag he always carried, tying Jebbie's hands together, and then yanking Jebbie to his feet.

"Did the man force Jebbie to walk with him?"

Willie lowered his head.

"Did the man see you watching?" Willie nodded yet again.

"Did he scare you?" Sophia asked quietly, masking her anger.

Willie's face crumpled into tears. Sophia pulled him to her and hugged him tight.

"The man said," Willie whispered, "if I told anyone, he'd come for me next."

Sophia smoothed Willie's hair away from his face. "Don't worry," she said. "That man can't hurt you. No one in your family will let that happen. It is important you told me about Jebbie. Now I know where to find him."

As soon as Willie was safely tucked in bed, Sophia told her mother she wanted to join the search. "I think he's at Talcotts'."

"Why on earth would he want to go there?" Mother asked.

"Not on purpose."

"What do you mean? Certainly, even the Talcotts wouldn't harm a boy."

"Why don't you believe me?" Sophia cried. "We need to go now!"

"No, you stay put. We'll let the men handle this. They will return before long."

Sophia scowled her disapproval. Grabbing her shawl, she wrapped it around her shoulders and stalked outside to sit on the bench and wait for the men's return. Sitting became a torture and she began to pace. The men were looking in the wrong place. They had to come home now. She had to save Jebbie now. Sophia sprang to her feet and hurried toward the bell.

31

Wayward Behavior

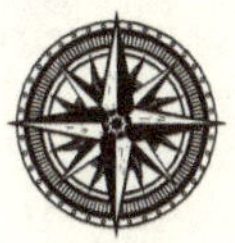

The bell sounded and resounded into the fog until Mother took the bell rope from Sophia's hands.

"You've rung that bell long enough to wake the dead," she said. "Your uncles will be here as soon as they are able. Goodness knows how far away they are. There is nothing left to do but wait."

"Yes, there is," Sophia said. "I can harness King George and drive to Talcott's."

"You will do no such thing. Miss Talcott seems pleasant enough but that father of hers is a schemer. I wouldn't allow you to go there unescorted on a sunny day, let alone now on a foggy night. What sort of mother do you think I am?"

"Hopefully not a mother who would let Mr. Dowling sell a ten-year-old boy."

Sophia's remark must have stung because Mother took hold of Sophia's hands and pulled her close.

"Certainly not," she said in a quiet but determined tone. "I want Jebbie safe just as much as I want you safe. Sally is no different. She is inside with Faith right now crying and praying and threatening to go to Talcott's herself."

Mother's voice hardened. "There is no telling what she might do once she got there. Even if she did nothing, there'd be trouble. Like as not, Mr. Talcott and his so-called partner would cook up some story to have her arrested. What really happened would never be heard in a courtroom."

"It's not fair," Sophia moaned, knowing her mother spoke the truth. She had heard enough of Father's heated criticisms of the justice system to know there were laws barring people of color, or women, for that matter, from testifying in court.

"No, it's not fair," Mother said. "It's not a question of fair. Sally needs to stay here and so do you." Mother dropped one of Sophia's hands but held tightly to the other and began walking, leading Sophia toward the house.

As they approached the front door, Sophia pulled her hand loose.

"I keep making things worse," she said, her voice low and strained.

"What do you mean?"

"As soon as the bell began to toll, Sally came running up from the cookhouse acting all excited and thankful, that is until I told her what Willie saw."

"Nonsense. You had to tell her. It's about her son. It's her right to know. Don't you think I would like to know what happened to James? One minute he is alive, an energetic boy with a head full of dreams, then he is gone. Did the river take him? I don't know. I won't have any peace until I do."

"Again, I'm to blame," Sophia said, her eye smarting with unshed tears.

Mother reclaimed Sophia's hand and gave it a gentle squeeze. "Whatever do you mean?"

"James and Jebbie, they are both gone because of me. I should have told you the minute James left. But I waited because he asked me to. Then the storm came and it was too late."

"Phee, Phee," Mother said, stroking Sophia's now wet cheek. "You are not to blame. James was headstrong. We all know that. He left of his own accord."

"But Jebbie didn't," Sophia said, not willing to be comforted. "Mr. Dowling kidnapped Jebbie because of what I did."

Although Mother's expression was hidden by the dwindling light and the fog, Sophia could feel the familiar stare, the one demanding more of an explanation.

"It's a long story," Sophia began and proceeded to relate the theft of the gold coin Jebbie found and how she had confronted the thief this morning, leaving out the part about telling Mr. Dowling that Grandsire was a duppie who would haunt him to the end of his days if he didn't give the coin back. Some things were best left unsaid, Sophia thought, especially where Mother was concerned. She didn't need to know about the pig, either.

"Mr. Dowling is an avaricious man," Sophia said. "Yesterday, I told him Grandsire had buried a chest of gold in a clearing near the Marshtown Road. He actually believed me because this morning I saw him searching for that imaginary treasure on my way to Marshtown."

"I can't believe you did that, Sophia," Mother said. "Or that he believed you."

Certain she heard a hint of amusement in Mother's tone, Sophia grimaced. Her hoax was no longer laughable.

"When I showed up in that clearing this morning," she continued, "I think he suspected my story was false. He was angry. When I demanded that he return Jebbie's coin, he threw the gold piece at me, saying he had no use for a dead man's money. He stomped off, hopping mad, along the Marshtown Road toward Great House. I went the other way, to Oriole's. He must have encountered Jebbie minutes after we parted company."

"You think he took Jebbie to spite you?"

"No, I think Mr. Dowling snatched Jebbie as another way to make money. After all, he and Mr. Talcott are slavers. Apparently, they have a list of traders who are just as shady as they are. At least that is what Judith told me."

"I had no idea," Mother said, sounding shocked. "No question, the man has few moral scruples, Phee." She sighed deeply before continuing. "Even if you made him feel foolish, the fact he kidnapped Jebbie is not your fault. You mustn't think that. Your uncles will get Jebbie back."

"They're not here. Nathan's not here. They are all looking in the wrong places."

"Patience, Sophia, patience. No one is going anywhere on a night like this. We just have to wait," Mother said and shepherded Sophia into the house.

The women had gathered in the parlor. Sally and Faith sat on the sofa. Aunt Polly had claimed the wing chair by the fire. No one was speaking. Mother seated herself beside Sally and gave her shoulder a gentle squeeze. Sally looked down at her hands, one of which held a balled-up handkerchief.

"Ain't no use," she said. "I can't keep from cryin'." She dabbed at her eyes with the soggy square of calico. "I must go to the Talcott place. And bring my boy home."

Mother patted Sally's hand in a comforting way. "As hard as it is," she said, "it is best to wait. The men will confront the kidnapper."

Sophia stood in the doorway, unwilling to enter. The fear and hopelessness in the room seemed palpable. Waiting here is wasting time, she thought and then leaned against the door frame, feigning exhaustion.

"You go on to bed," Mother said. "You must be all tuckered out. I'll wake you when Jebbie's back home."

"Don't you worry," Aunt Polly said. She was seated as a proper matron should be, with her feet together and her hands folded in her lap. Now she stood to position her chair so that she could have a clear view of the hallway and the front door. "I'll see the men the minute they open the door," she said, "and let them know what has happened."

Her aunt's self-righteous tone made Sophia bristle. *You'd think you were the mistress here,* she thought, realizing that any hope of slipping out the front door was now dashed.

"Rest if you can," Mother said. "And," she added, "don't get any fancy ideas. You stay put."

With a quick nod, Sophia turned to leave, took the lighted candle from the hall table, and hurried up the stairs to the bedchamber she shared with Faith. Placing the candle on the small writing desk beneath the window, she tore a page from her diary and hastily penned a note— *Please don't tell on me. I will be back soon. Love, Phee.* She placed the paper on Faith's pillow. That was the easy part.

Pushing the desk to one side, she raised the window. Even though the magnolia grew close to the house, the fog made judging the distance to the tree difficult. Sophia knew she would have to rely on memory to grab hold of the nearest thick branch which, if she remembered correctly, was about an arm's length away. Once she took hold of it, the climb down to the ground would be easier. James had used this route to freedom numerous times, but not Sophia, not once. Now she wished she had paid better attention. She also wished she wore britches.

Sometimes a girl has to put modesty aside, she thought as she bunched up her skirt and tucked the hem into her bodice. Now able to move her legs more freely, she straddled the sill. Clutching the window frame with both hands, she carefully pulled her other leg over the sill so that she was seated facing the tree.

So far so good, she thought. Letting go of the frame with one hand, she leaned slightly forward and reached out toward the tree limb. *Please, please don't let me fall,* she prayed. Her fingers touched the smooth bark. She leaned forward another inch to grasp the branch, first with the one hand and then, loosening her grip on the window frame with the other. With another quick prayer, she swung free of the window. Hanging on to tree limb with both hands, she told herself, if James can do it, so can I.

Hand over hand she moved along the branch until her feet touched a lower one. Branch by branch, she lowered herself. When she thought she was near enough to the ground, Sophia jumped. She landed with a jolt, lost her balance and sat down hard. Glad that no one was around to witness her inelegant landing or her bare legs for that matter, she shook out her skirt and headed toward the barn.

Once inside, there was another problem—harnessing King George. Sophia had never harnessed the mule. She had watched, of course, but never tried it. In Ohio, she thought, I, most likely, would have to do lots of chores unthinkable here in Maryland.

Sophia knew her way around the dark barn, having milked Ginger before sunrise a few times. She found the oil lantern on its peg near the door and lit the wick with the small flame she sparked into life in her tinder box. The harness hung on a peg near the mule's empty stall.

"Oh, Fiddlesticks," she said aloud. Nathan had turned King George out to pasture. Now she would have to fetch the mule. More time lost, she thought as she filled his feed bucket with a handful oats, made her way to the pasture, and coaxed the mule back to the barn.

"We are going to get Jebbie," she whispered into one of his long ears as she bridled him. Not knowing what to do with the yards and yards of reins, she knotted them together and draped them over his neck. This is not so hard, she thought, as she pulled the leather collar off its peg. The rest of the harness straps fell into a jumbled heap on the floor. "Rats," she muttered. Figuring out which strap went where would be harder now.

Getting the heavy collar over King George's head soon turned into a battle of wills. Every time she tried to slip the collar on, the mule threw up his head. I can do this, she thought and glared at King George.

"I am the smarter one here," she said aloud only to be answered by a muffled laugh.

Nathan was standing just inside the barn door.

"You're going about it all wrong," he said. Walking over to her, he took the collar and gave the mule a reassuring pat on the neck.

Sophia scowled at him. "You!"

"And a good evening to you, too," he said and smiled. "I guess it is a good evening now that Jebbie's been found safe. I heard you ring out the good news."

"Jebbie's not safe. Willie saw Mr. Dowling tie Jebbie up and pull him down the road like a dog. I rang the bell to bring you all home. No one came."

Nathan was staring at her in what Sophia took to mean disbelief.

"Willie's telling the truth," she said, annoyed that he would think otherwise. "Even worse, I have every reason to believe that horrible man plans to sell Jebbie into slavery."

"Not if I can help it," Nathan said. "I came back as quick as I could. I was halfway down the river trail when I heard the bell. As for your uncles, they are probably all the way to Marshtown and out of earshot."

"Be that as it may, I can't wait," Sophia said. "I have to go get him now."

"I am here. I'll go. I can't imagine your mother allowing you to undertake such a risk."

"Don't you think I have the wits to get Jebbie away from those Talcotts?"

"I didn't say that. What I said was I didn't think your mother would allow you to even try."

"Well, that's the truth! She told me to wait for my uncles. Well, I can't wait. Jebbie is in real danger. I managed to leave the house unnoticed."

"What do you plan on doing once you get to the Talcott place?"

Sophia shrugged. "I don't know. I'll figure that out as soon as I get the lay of the land. It's just a matter of saying the right things."

"Oh," Nathan said. "Apparently you have the wits to face the Talcotts, argue for Jebbie's release, and bring him safely home. Too bad you don't have the wits to harness the mule."

Sophia clenched her fists. "You think I am a know-nothing! Well, I have read my father's law books. I know a thing or two about the law and I can put the fear of God into Mr. Talcott and Mr. Dowling. They wouldn't dare hurt me. Reading gives you knowledge and knowledge gives you authority. You ought to try reading sometime, Mr. Harkness."

Nathan took a step back. "Whoa. There is one thing you know how to do well."

"What?"

"How to put this know-nothing in his place."

"I am sorry," she said, wishing she could take back the hurtful words. "I was angry. You made me feel ignorant. I remembered what you said about having no schooling and I wanted you to feel ignorant, too."

"I guess that makes us even," Nathan said. "Still friends?"

Sophia nodded and leaned against the barn wall, relieved. Nathan smiled. Without further comment, he began untangling the jumble she had made of the harness. As he worked, Sophia studied the contours of his face highlighted by the soft lantern light and thought him handsome.

Apparently unaware of her scrutiny, Nathan hummed as he unknotted King George's reins and pulled off the bridle. Setting those aside, he picked up the horse collar, sliding his hands along the worn leather as if searching for a flaw.

After a minute or two he said, "Look, it's not my place to tell you not to go. For one thing, you'd never listen. You are as headstrong as this mule. But neither can I let you go alone. Let's make a pact. You teach me how to read and I'll teach you to harness a mule."

Sophia took hold of his right hand. "Agreed."

Nathan returned her firm handshake with a smile.

"The collar goes on first," he said, slipping it over the mule's head in one easy motion. Step by step, he named each piece as he harnessed King George. When he led the mule outside to hitch him to the wagon, Sophia followed with the oil lantern. Nathan took it from her and put it on the wagon seat.

"We'll need to take this along," he said. "King George may be able to see where he's going at night but we can't." Sophia nodded and was gathering her skirts to climb up to the board seat when Nathan put his hands around her waist. He turned her toward him. Pulling her close, he kissed her square on the mouth then lifted her up to the wagon seat.

"Mr. Harkness!" Sophia sputtered, at a loss to say more.

"You are the bravest girl I have ever known," Nathan said as if that explained everything. Sophia touched her fingers to her lips. She had never thought about kissing him but now that he had, she couldn't stop thinking about it.

Going around to the other side of the wagon, Nathan untied the reins and sprang up to sit beside her. With a soft, "Gee haw," he urged the mule forward.

King George walked slowly out of the yard. The wagon wheels crunched softly over the crushed oyster shells. And, just for a moment, all those thoughts about the Talcotts, Mr. Dowling, the patrollers, Chloe, and poor frightened Jebbie disappeared. Sophia thought about the kiss and about traveling to Ohio with Nathan.

32

Returns

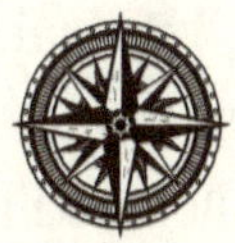

As the wagon moved away from the river, the fog began to lift. The familiar landscape began to reappear. Only a wispy veil covered the neglected field beside the carriage way and hid in the dark trees beyond. Overhead the moon shone brightly in a sky dotted with stars.

Halfway to the main road, Sophia took hold of Nathan's arm. "There used to be a shortcut near here, a wagon track leading to Talcotts'. It's probably overgrown. No one will be watching a forgotten lane."

Nathan pulled back on the reins. He had been keeping the mule at a slow steady trot despite Sophia's urging to go faster, telling her that although the mule might be surefooted, the wagon was not. They couldn't risk breaking an axle.

When the wagon stopped, Sophia jumped down and reached for the lantern. "It's up ahead," she said. "James and I came this way a few times to scout out Talcotts' place. There wasn't much to see. A long skinny house, a stable, and a few old pigsties with pens next to them. My guess is that Jebbie's in one of those."

"Is it passable for a wagon?"

"Used to be."

Both were speaking in terse whispers, their voices fading into the prevailing silence. No night birds called; no frogs peeped. Sophia felt as if she and Nathan were the only two people in a solitary land.

Walking ahead, Sophia spotted a grey cedar gate post, the single reminder that there had once been a fence here. The rails had been sold years ago. Swinging the lantern back and forth, Sophia signaled Nathan to bring up the wagon.

"This is where it all started," she said as she climbed back into the seat. "Early on, before the Revolution, Grandsire grew tobacco here. This is where he killed and butchered a Talcott hog. Old Mr. Talcott saw to it that Grandsire got hauled before the British magistrate. He fined Grandsire 900 pounds of tobacco for no good reason. By all rights, Grandsire had every right to shoot that pig. It was trespassing, rooting up his cash crop. And not for the first time."

"So, the two families had a falling out over pigs?" Nathan sounded incredulous.

Sophia nodded. "That and the war. Grandsire was a Patriot. He was one of the first to sign's Maryland's Oath of Fidelity. Mr. Talcott was a King's man."

She drew her brows together and stared down at her hands, remembering Grandsire's stern warning when she and James had gone exploring, saying that they were putting their noses where they didn't belong. "Don't you go roaming on Talcott land. You'll only find trouble there," he had growled.

"No," she said looking back at Nathan. "The Recordses and the Talcotts never have seen eye to eye—not on free roaming pigs, independence, or slavery. Mr. Talcott has a different view of things, that's for certain. Father says the man has no respect for American law when it doesn't suit his purpose. And if Judith speaks the truth, her father is importing slaves from Africa, something our Congress passed a law against four years ago."

"All slavery should be against the law," Nathan said and with a slap of the reins and a soft "Haw," he told the mule to turn left into the lane. The stiff, tall grass which grew between deeply grooved wagon tracks was matted down. Nathan let out a soft whistle.

"Looks like this lane has not been forgotten."

"It's easy to deduce who is using it. You can add trespass to Mr. Talcott's list of crimes," Sophia muttered. "I wager he is using this old wagon track so as not to draw attention to his illicit comings and goings. He can follow the road to an old river landing and then transport his slaves by boat to a grab-and-go auction in Virginia. Father says no one asks questions there. Men merely pay the trader a set price up front, select a negro from the holding pen, and leave."

Nathan pushed his hat back and looked straight at Sophia. "It's time then that we draw attention to Mr. Talcott's business."

Sophia looked at him in disbelief. "How can we do that? We've got to get Jebbie home safe."

"Two birds, one stone," Nathan said and once more slapped the reins to urge the mule into a trot. "Kidnapping a free black child is against the law, as well."

The track wound through a stand of trees before crossing over into Talcott land. The mule was entering the woods when Sophia thought she saw a figure in the lane. Almost as soon as she saw it, it was gone. Grabbing Nathan's arm, she whispered into his ear. "I saw something, someone."

"Duck down," Nathan whispered. "Mr. Talcott may have posted a guard."

Slowly, Nathan got down from the wagon, bringing the lantern with him. All the while he kept talking to the mule.

"Did you pick up a stone, George? Well, now, let me take a look." He set the lantern down next to the wagon and stepped out of the light. Unsheathing his knife, he made his way forward.

"Careful," Sophia whispered, slipping down from the wagon. Creeping forward, she picked up a jagged stone from the road, ready to do battle, when a boy dashed from the brush. He threw himself at Nathan, grabbing him around the knees.

"Don't kill me, don't kill me," he kept sobbing.

"It's Jebbie," Sophia cried, dropping the stone and rushing forward.

Nathan clapped Jebbie on the shoulder with a reassuring squeeze and helped him to his feet.

"It's not you I meant to stick," he said, sheathing the knife. "Just those pesky Talcotts."

As Jebbie started to speak, Sophia enfolded him in tight hug. "Thank the dear Lord, you are safe. Are you alright?"

He nodded. "I am now. Back there, in the shed, I was so scared. I kept calling for my mama."

"You'll be with your mama soon," Sophia said, giving him another hug before picking up the lantern. "Now, let me take a good look at you. You're sure you are not hurt?"

"Yes, Miss Phee. I surely want to go home, but you can't take me without Miss Judith." He gave Nathan's sheathed weapon a baleful look. "Even if she is a pesky Talcott."

"Judith?"

As if conjured from the fog, a figure stepped from the trees and onto the road. "I was bringing him to you."

Sophia could only stare. It was Judith, standing in the middle of the road, without her veil or her haughty manner. Out of place and, judging from the slump of her shoulders, strangely forlorn.

Handing the lantern to Jebbie, Sophia took a few hurried steps toward her, tripped over a clump of weeds, and would have fallen if Judith hadn't caught her by the arms to hold her upright. The two girls stood there facing each other in uncomfortable silence until Sophia gave a nervous little giggle.

"Sorry to be so clumsy," she said.

"I am the one who is sorry," Judith said, taking a step back.

"No," Sophia said. "You have nothing to be sorry for." Her voice wavered with uncertainty. "We are so grateful to you—me, Sally, my whole family—for bringing Jebbie home."

Judith looked back toward the woods. "What Mr. Dowling did was wrong. I am trying to right things."

"How did you convince him to release Jebbie?"

"I didn't convince anybody. I merely searched the sheds until I found Jebbie. He was with the Africans. I untied him. Then we both ran."

"And the Africans?" Sophia asked.

"They were in chains. There was nothing I could do for them." Judith said, shrugging her shoulders in a helpless sort of way. "I can't go back there ever. I know that."

Sophia frowned. "You can't go home?"

"I am afraid I have burned my bridges." Judith looked over at Jebbie and gave him a timid, sad smile. "When I learned what Mr. Dowling had done, I made a scene. I called him despicable, nothing more than a money-grubbing thief. Certainly not someone I would marry. I went to Papa's desk, picked up the marriage contract Mr. Dowling and Papa had drawn up and tore it into tiny pieces."

"You did that?" Sophia said, sounding incredulous. Judith had seemed so, so—she searched for the word—so biddable, so obedient. "Good for you!"

"Good for me? Not really. Father sided with Mr. Dowling. He disowned me on the spot. Told me to pack my things and leave his house."

"No," Sophia said, "Fathers are supposed to protect their children."

Judith sighed, a sound mixed with exasperation and sorrow. "No one crosses my father, certainly not me."

Drawing herself up to her full height, she said with an imperial lift of her chin, "Now, please excuse me. Since Jebbie is safe, I must be on my way." She turned toward Records Road.

"On your way to where?"

"I don't know. To the church in Snow Hill, I guess. Throw myself on their mercy."

"You can't walk all that way. Come home with us. We will help you sort things out," Sophia said, surprising herself. It was something her mother would say.

"Your family will never have me. After all I am a Talcott."

"Fiddlesticks. It's already settled. You are coming with us."

Sophia took Judith by the hand and led her to the wagon where Nathan and Jebbie were waiting.

Nathan touched his hat. "We are obliged," he said. "Does your father know what you have done?"

Judith shook her head. "No. I made sure no one followed me when I left."

"Even so, we need to go," Nathan urged.

Neither girl argued.

Clucking softly to the nervous mule, Nathan convinced King George to circle back through the grass and onto the track. As soon as he knew where he was headed, the mule pawed the ground, anxious to get started.

Sophia boosted Jebbie into the back of the wagon, then crawled up next to him, motioning to Judith to sit beside her.

As soon as the wagon began to move Jebbie leaned against Sophia. "I am all tuckered out," he said, closing his eyes. "I knew you'd come." Before falling asleep, he murmured, "All that time, I kept praying you would."

Sophia eased the boy down onto the wagon floor, cushioning his head on her shawl.

"Tell me," she whispered to Judith, "tell me everything."

"They were arguing, Papa and Mr. Dowling," Judith began. "I didn't know they were arguing about Jebbie. I thought, well it doesn't matter what I thought." She pulled her knees close to her chest and talked into the folds of her skirt as if the story might get trapped there and she could shake it out later like so many crumbs to feed to chickens. And bit by bit her story unfolded.

She was walking past the parlor when she overheard her father and Mr. Dowling in a heated dispute. She had nudged the door open a crack so as not to miss a word. Mr. Dowling was saying that since he has risked taking the boy, it was his right to receive the entire sum from the sale. Her father—Judith called him Papa—disagreed, pounding the desk with his fist and saying Mr. Dowling should only get a portion of the sale.

"We have an agreement," Papa had shouted. "You will get a percentage of all our transactions, nothing more."

"It was what Mr. Dowling said next that caused me to come bursting into the room," Judith said.

"He said, 'And your pockmarked daughter. What percentage do I get from that transaction? I agreed to take her off your hands for the dowry. Do I only get a percentage of Records Landing?'"

Judith raised her head to look directly at Sophia. "It was as if I were packaged goods, damaged goods at best," she said. "With two men bickering over my price."

"Despicable," Sophia whispered, aghast at the avaricious plan.

"Papa told me Records Landing was my dowry. But don't think he put the title in my name because he was overly generous or because he wanted to secure my happiness."

Judith picked at the folds of her dress. "It was all about money. Papa did it to avoid paying the triple tax. Did you know that the government charges him three times what your family pays in property taxes because he refused to sign a fidelity oath thirty years ago? With me named as the owner, no triple tax. I wasn't alive thirty years ago. No, Papa wants Records Landing for himself. He wants easy access to the river. And he stooped to trickery to get it."

Judith rested her forehead on her knees. "You probably despise me now."

"Fiddlesticks. I think you are brave."

The girls fell silent as the mule clopped along. Judith remained tense, attentive to every sound. It's possible, Sophia realized, that by inviting Judith into the wagon, I may have invited trouble right along with her.

"Listen," Judith said, gripping Sophia's hand. "Do you hear that?"

"Horses. I hear horses on the road."

"Maybe the Patrollers are coming for Jebbie and me."

"I don't know," Sophia said as she reached up to the wagon seat and tugged on Nathan's jacket.

"I think trouble's coming. Judith and Jebbie need to hide."

Nathan looked back at her. "No, listen carefully. Riders are coming from the direction of Great House not the Post Road."

Minutes later, two riders appeared in the distance.

Shifting the reins to one hand, Nathan removed his hat and began waving it from side to side. The men slowed their mounts to a walk.

Standing to get a better look, Sophia rested her hand on Nathan's shoulder for balance. "There's only one horse in our stable," she said, "and that's Black Jack. Who's on the other horse?"

She stared at the oncoming riders, one on a dark horse, Black Jack for sure, the other on a misty white one.

"Pearl! I can't believe it. Father's back. Stop. Please, I want to get out. I need to explain the situation."

Halting the mule, Nathan leaped down to help Sophia off the back of the wagon, then handed her the lantern.

"Watch your step. The road is uneven. You've already tripped once tonight."

Good advice, she thought even as she ignored it, hurrying along one of wagon tracks, holding her mob cap in place with one hand and the lantern in the other. She wanted to tell Father about Judith before he found her in the wagon.

Suddenly shy, Sophia paused as she neared the riders. The last thing she wanted was to make Father cross. He was always insisting she and Faith behave with decorum, saying that respectability and good manners were important characteristics. Sneaking out of the house, being in the company of a young man after dark unchaperoned—these were serious breaches of decorum.

"Phee!" Father said, dismounting in one easy motion and handing Pearl's reins to his brother. With the briefest of nods, Uncle William rode on.

"This is a happy surprise! I thought you were at home asleep in your bed." By his wry tone, Sophia knew Father was wise to her absence.

"You are the better surprise. I am so glad you are home."

"It's good to be here," he said, opening his arms wide and Sophia walked into them, finding comfort in his tight hug.

After a moment, Father released his hold, stepped back, and directed her to hold up the lantern. "Let me take a good look at you. I must say your disappearance left the household in an uproar. As for what happened to Jebbie, unconscionable! William and I are on our way to right that wrong."

"He's safe, asleep in the wagon. I should have told you the minute I saw you. Judith Talcott was bringing him home when Nathan—I mean Mr. Harkness—and I found them. She is with us."

"Jebbie's with you? That is good news, indeed." Then Father frowned. "Did I hear you right? Miss Judith Talcott is sitting in our wagon?" He sounded incredulous.

"I can explain . . ."

"As you will," Father interrupted, "but for now I am grateful everyone—you, Jebbie, and Mr. Harkness—is safe." He sighed deeply. "I know your actions were well intentioned, Sophia, but you acted on impulse. You put yourself and the others at risk. When are you going to begin acting like a lady not some harem-scarum child?"

"Soon, just not tonight."

"Well, then it better be tomorrow." He smiled and offered her his arm. "Shall we join the others?"

As they walked back side by side, Sophia told him about Judith. Father listened, occasionally clicking his tongue against his teeth, his habit when working out the details of a troublesome court case.

As they approached, Sophia saw Uncle William had dismounted. He was holding both horses and talking with Nathan. Judith, apparently unwilling to wait in the wagon, was standing nearby. Sophia, sensing that Judith was feeling apprehensive, hurried ahead to reassure her that she was welcome.

As soon as Father reached the wagon, Uncle William said he wanted to leave.

"Agreed," Father said. "You should ride on ahead. Let everyone know Jebbie is safe, Sophia found, and that we are bringing a guest. Take Pearl with you. I'll come back in the wagon. I've had enough riding for one day."

Uncle William clapped his brother on the shoulder. "Indeed. It's been an extraordinary day. I am glad it has had a good end."

Tipping his hat to Judith, Uncle William mounted Black Jack and, leading Pearl, set off at a trot back to Great House.

After a quick word with Nathan, Father walked over to greet Judith. Although she returned the greeting politely, she turned her face away from the glow of the lantern. Sophia lowered the light and stepped back. It was obvious that Judith was ill at ease without a veil to hide behind. Still, as Father continued talking, she seemed to regain her poise. At one point she smiled.

As soon as their conversation ended, Father beckoned to Sophia. "Miss Talcott will be staying with our family until her father's current situation is clarified."

"That's wonderful news."

"And," Father added, "we will do everything in our power to make sure she is safely settled into her new home at Records Landing before we leave even if we must delay our departure."

Looking directly at Judith he said, "It is important for you to remember that your father has no claim to Records Landing. You are the rightful owner. You are not responsible for his debts unless you choose to be."

Judith nodded. "I understand. And thank you for your advice."

"Now, wouldn't you be more comfortable sitting up front? We'll sort things out at Great House."

She nodded and walked over to Nathan, who helped her up onto the wagon seat.

Father turned to Sophia. "Now, young lady, let's get you home." He boosted her into the back and then climbed in himself. Nathan clicked to the mule, signaling him to move on.

Sophia nestled against her father. "You weren't expected so soon," she said. "I am so glad you are here."

"As am I. Although not soon enough. I heard about the kidnapping the moment I walked into the parlor. I didn't learn about your absence until your mother went to wake you."

Father cleared his throat. Sophia squirmed, expecting a scolding.

"I've had news," he continued, his voice barely audible above the rumble of the wagon wheels. "News of your brother. It's the reason I came home early, to let you all know. I wanted to tell you all together. When you couldn't be found, I told the others. It's news that couldn't wait."

Sophia grabbed hold of Father's arm.

"Tell me he's alive," she said.

Father nodded. He took her hand, enfolding it between his large square ones. Sophia held her breath.

"James is alive, at least for now. Apparently, he managed to walk to Norfolk after losing the shallop in the storm. Once there, he signed on as a deckhand on a merchant vessel. Off the coast in international waters, Royal Navy officers boarded the ship and pressed James and three others into service. He is now on a British warship somewhere in the Atlantic."

Sophia exhaled and turned her head upward to look at Nathan. He seemed at ease, his hat cocked slightly forward, the way he like to wear it. The British couldn't hold Nathan, she thought. They won't be able to hold my brother either.

"Certainly, James will be released," she said. "He is an American."

"I have appealed to the British consulate in Washington and to our Secretary of the Navy asking for his release. But right now, all I know is he may be aboard the frigate *Gruerrie*. I do not know the exact date of his impressment. Commodore Decatur has been alerted. He will help in any way he can. For now, Phee, we must wait.

"But there is hope, right?"

"Yes," Father said. "There is hope."

33

Last Days

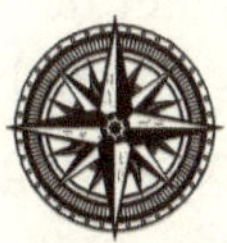

The next morning everything was in turmoil. At Mother's urging, Sally was staying in Marshtown with her family for the day, which left Mother to manage meals on her own. Breakfast was simple fare, to be sure. Cornbread, fatback, and weak coffee. After a disdainful sniff from Aunt Polly, Mother said she intended to brush up on her cooking skills and suggested Aunt Polly do the same.

"It's never too late to learn," Mother said and smiled. "If the rumors prove true and we go to war with England again, cooking skills might prove to be necessary."

Soon after breakfast, Father and Uncle Caleb rode off to Snow Hill. Father intended to report Mr. Dowling to the sheriff, saying Jebbie's kidnapping should not go unpunished. He would also inform the authorities that Mr. Talcott was conducting illegal slave trades. Uncle William stayed behind to ward off the patrollers should the men dare to threaten Marshtown inhabitants again.

While Sophia fretted that Chloe and Abraham might be discovered, Mother, Faith, and Willie swarmed around Judith like bees to honey. She was the heroine in Jebbie's story. Sophia and Nathan, they were footnotes. No one congratulated them. Judith seemed to glow with the praise.

Aunt Polly wandered in and out of the parlor saying she had no idea why she and Uncle William should stay. There was barely any room, the bed was uncomfortable, and she worried that Anne might have taken a turn for the worse. "What did Mr. Franklin remark about fish and guests after three days?" she asked.

"They stink," Sophia said under her breath, and continued packing Mother's china between layers of wool batting.

Father returned midafternoon, riding Pearl and leading Black Jack. Now worried something else had gone wrong, Sophia ran out to meet him and learned that Uncle Caleb had stayed behind to inspect the *Rebel Ann.* Not all the seams had been re-caulked even though the schooner had been in the shipyard for nearly a month.

"He wants to hurry things along," Father said. "That and to scare up three of his crew. He plans on sailing the *Ann* here as soon as she's seaworthy."

"And the sheriff?" Sophia asked, worried Father's complaint had not been taken seriously. The Talcott and Records feud was no secret.

"I will speak about that matter once, in the parlor, to whomever is there to listen. There will be no need for gossip or speculation."

He turned away, his signal that he would hear no more questions. Worse, as far as Sophia was concerned, Father didn't seem to be in any hurry to get to the parlor. First, he asked Nathan to cool down the horses before letting them drink their fill and turning them out. While Sophia cooled her heels in the parlor, Father rummaged in the cookhouse for something to eat, had a whispered conversation with Mother on the porch, and spoke briefly to Judith in his office.

Only then, did he walk into the room where the family, including Nathan and Judith, waited.

His demeanor was grave. When Mother motioned to Judith to sit beside her, Sophia realized something serious had happened and that it involved Mr. Talcott.

Choosing to stand near the hearth, Father got right to the point, recounting the events of the past twelve hours in the impassive voice he used in the courtroom. "Mr. Talcott was arrested early this morning. Two Virginians, patrollers, spoke to the sheriff in Snow Hill late yesterday afternoon, claiming that Mr. Robert Talcott had summoned them on a false pretense—saying he knew the whereabouts of a runaway slave. No such slave could be found."

Sophia felt relief surge through her. She wanted Chloe to know her tormentors were gone that she and the baby could return to Marshtown. She was halfway to her feet when Father cocked a questioning eyebrow in her direction. Sophia sat back into her chair.

With a loud harrumph, Father continued with his account. According to the sheriff, the Virginians had come to complain that Mr. Talcott, after summoning them here, had refused to pay them for their time and travel costs. Angry and out the money, they asked the sheriff if he paid for information on illegal trafficking. When the sheriff said he might, they informed him that Mr. Talcott and his partner, a Mr. Elias Dowling, were bringing Africans into the United States and selling them here in violation of federal law. Acting on that information, the sheriff and a deputy rode out to the Talcott plantation early this morning where they discovered six African men chained together and housed in a former pigsty. The sheriff arrested Mr. Talcott on the spot and escorted him to the jail in Snow Hill.

Sophia looked over at Judith. Expressionless, the older girl sat straight, staring into the hearth.

"It is unusual for a man of Mr. Talcott's stature to be jailed," Father said, "but the sheriff thought he might flee, just as his partner had. When the sheriff arrived at the plantation, he said that the man called Mr. Dowling was nowhere to be found. Apparently, he had slipped away during the night—taken his children along with Talcott's finest horse, and simply vanished. There is a warrant out for his arrest. Mr. Talcott has been charged with importing slaves. It's a serious offence.

If convicted, he faces a hefty fine plus up to five years in prison. The Africans are being held as contraband and most likely will be sold by the state. That's all I know for now."

Oriole was right, Sophia thought remembering Oriole's earlier words—"De higher de monkey climb, de more exposed de monkey be."

Father walked over to Judith and put his hand on her shoulder. "It is important you all realize that Miss Talcott is in no way implicated in her father's or her fiancé's wrongdoing."

"That engagement is dissolved," Judith said under her breath.

"I don't know about Mr. Dowling but your father will survive this," Mother said, squeezing Judith's hand.

"But will I ever survive the disgrace? "Judith said, sounding as if it wasn't a question.

"Of course," Mother answered briskly. "Energy and persistence conquer all things."

Judith sighed. "I might as well be an orphan. I have no family now."

"Fiddlesticks," Sophia said. "You have us."

At the time she said it, Sophia meant it; but after three days, she had had enough of Judith Talcott. It seemed like every time Sophia turned around Judith was there, watching her. The only saving grace was now that Chloe and Abraham were reunited with Ulysses in Marshtown, Judith would not be able to sniff out Grandsire's secret. Whenever Sophia walked to the barn, Judith followed. If Sophia went to the cookhouse, Judith was there. No matter what chore Sophia performed, Judith came along. Except for trips to the necessary, there was no escaping her. Sophia and Faith even had to share their bed with her.

"Now, I can't wait to leave this place," Sophia whispered to her mother. "At least I'll be shed of her."

"Be generous. Show Miss Talcott some gratitude," Mother told her as she dismantled the loom. "That poor child is all alone in the world. Be a sister to her. She will have to cope with loneliness soon enough."

"She is not a poor child. She owns this planation now and is probably eager for us to leave." Sophia gave her mother a petulant stare.

"Don't twist my words. Judith needs extra care right now."

Sophia knew Mother had been going out of her way to be pleasant. She seated Judith beside her at meals, spoke softly about household matters, never about Judith's father or his arrest.

"You are too kind!" Sophia grumbled. She flounced out of the wool room and into the parlor where Judith sat in one of the wing chairs by the hearth, her hands folded in her lap. Judith was wearing the same dress she had worn every day since she came. Faith sat near the window, taking advantage of the strong sunlight to make the final fancy stiches on her embroidery.

Judith straightened when Sophia entered, as though preparing to stand.

"Don't you have something better to do than follow me around?" Sophia demanded, glaring at Judith.

Judith gave Sophia a baleful look. "I don't know what to do." She took in a great gulp of air, which sounded very much like a sob. "At home there are slaves. My girl, Kisha, helps me dress and does up my hair. I don't know how to cook a meal, let alone run a plantation. I am trying to learn by watching you."

Sophia sat down in the chair opposite her. Judith did look unkempt. The hem of her skirt was stained with mud, the leather soles of her brocade shoes had pulled away at the tips, and under her cap her hair was pulled tight into a severe bun on top of her head. Sophia couldn't remember ever seeing her loosen the bun, not even to brush her hair. No, Judith was not the haughty young woman who had sat in this parlor two weeks ago to warn Sophia about Mr. Talcott's plans for Chloe.

"I don't know why you are being so unpleasant," Judith said fretfully. "I thought we were friends."

Sophia gave her a speculative glance but held her tongue.

"James and I were friends," Judith continued. "True friends. Now I hear snatches of conversations about him. I was relieved to learn he is alive, but that is all I know. Please, Sophia, tell me what has happened to James."

Sophia looked at Judith, saw the pleading in her eyes, and lowered her gaze. Thinking about Mother's advice—be a sister to her—Sophia realized that by ignoring Judith, she had been acting as snooty as Judith Talcott had when they first met.

"I am sorry," Sophia said. "My parents mostly talk about James behind closed doors. There is so much uncertainty. All I know is James is a seaman, impressed into service on a British warship, maybe the frigate *Gruerrie*. The Secretary of the Navy is attempting to procure his release. These requests generally don't go well."

"I see," Judith said. "Nothing more can be done?"

Sophia shook her head. "Wait and pray. Pray we do not go to war. According to Father, impressed seamen are nothing more than cannon fodder. He and my uncles believe President Madison will ask Congress to declare war on England before the year is out."

"Enough of war talk," Faith said, holding up her needlework. "See I have finished. This piece goes in my trunk. Zach will make a frame for it so we can display it once we build our house in Ohio."

Sophia had to smile. Faith managed to work Zachariah's name into almost every other sentence she uttered.

"As for you, Miss Talcott," Faith said with a determined look on her face, "it's time you learned to do up your hair."

And when Judith shrugged, as if to say why bother, Faith grabbed her by the hand, led her upstairs with Sophia following, and stood her in front of the looking glass.

Removing Judith's cap and releasing her dark brown hair from its tight bun, Faith said, "You have beautiful curls. Make the most of them. It never hurts to put your best foot forward. Now sit down and let me get to work."

As Faith brushed and rearranged, she told Judith that a flawless complexion was highly overrated. "Your face has character," she said.

Judith listened, complacent with Faith's attempts until Faith pulled scissors out from the top drawer of the chest.

"No, no," Judith cried out, holding her hands to her head. "Don't cut off my hair."

"You just have to trust me," Faith said, gently pushing Judith's hands away.   Turning Judith's head first to one side and then the other, Faith snipped away at the curls nearest to Judith's face, shaping them into short ringlets that fell across Judith's forehead and along her checks, hiding some of the pock marks. Next Faith brushed the rest of Judith's hair into a long tail, asking Sophia to fetch some brown yarn from her sewing basket downstairs. "I'll need it to hold the hair in place," she explained.

Sophia left and returned with the yarn.

With the tail firmly held together, Faith coiled it into a loose bun at the nape of Judith's neck, securing the bun with long hairpins.

"Finished?" Judith asked. She seemed eager to see the results.

"Just one more thing," Faith said, pulling a brown ribbon from top drawer of the bureau. She tied the silken strip around Judith's head so that it covered the tips of her ears and held the ringlets in place. "Now," she said. "Take a look."

Judith stood and walked slowly toward the looking glass. She turned her head from side to side.

"What do you think?" Faith and Sophia asked in unison.

Judith smiled and Sophia realized this was the first time she had ever seen Judith genuinely happy. "I look almost presentable," she said. "But I will never be able to do this myself."

"Of course, you will," Faith said. "I will teach you. The ringlets are cut. Now, a few simple steps every morning and you're done."

"You are lucky, you two," Judith said. "Lucky to have each other. I never had a sister."

"Well, you have two now," Sophia said, wondering why she had waited so long to welcome Judith's friendship. Without question, she had proved herself to be a true friend to this family.

Walking toward the stairs, Sophia poked Faith in the ribs. "How did you learn to do that?" she whispered.

"You are not the only one who reads," Faith whispered back. "You read Father's books. I read magazines. *The Lady's Magazine* to be precise. Aunt Polly brought a couple with her. One issue, I think it was March, had detailed illustrations of different hair styles with step-by-step instructions."

As the days passed, Mother and Father did what they could to help Judith settle in at Great House. Even though all of the Talcott property had been seized, Father arranged with the judge in Snow Hill to release Judith's belongings. These included her clothes, a few pieces of jewelry, and her horse. Mr. Talcott's slaves, including Kisha, were counted as part of his estate. Judith's maid would not be coming to Great House.

"You are better off not owning slaves," Sophia told Judith. "The folks in Marshtown probably wouldn't work for you if you owned a slave."

"They probably won't work for me anyway," Judith said. "I can't pay them." She took a deep breath. "This is all so overwhelming. Sally has offered to stay on without a wage until I get on my feet. But she can't do that forever. Then there is the livestock. I don't know how to milk a cow or plow a field."

With that she burst into tears.

"There might be a way to solve your problems," Sophia said, suggesting that Chloe's husband, Ulysses, was looking for a way to repay Judith for her timely warning.

"You know that ramshackle cabin in the orchard?" Sophia continued. "He could fix it up, make it a home again. He and his family could live there rent free. In exchange, he and Chloe would help out around Records Landing. It's called bartering."

She held back the fact that Ulysses already had agreed to keep Grandsire's hideout secret, promising that neither he nor Chloe would speak of it or go down there unless there was dire need. Living in the cabin would make him the perfect guardian.

As Sophia talked, Judith began to look more cheerful. "I'd be agreeable to that," she said and gave Sophia a quick unexpected peck on the cheek.

Together, they went to Father, who put aside assembling his papers to listen. "Would such an arrangement be possible?" Judith asked.

"Not only possible but ideal," Father said with a rush of enthusiasm as he pushed back his chair. "We must go to Marshtown, ask Ulysses if he is agreeable."

When Sophia hung back, Father offered her his arm. "You are the author of the plan," he said. "You must see it through."

The three were waiting for Ulysses when he returned from work. But instead of accepting the plan, he hemmed and hawed, his eyes darting around the room until they rested on Chloe and their son.

While looking down at his hands now pressed together as if in prayer, he said to Father, "I mean no disrespect, but there's no telling if Miss Talcott might change her mind. She could turn my family out. If she marries, her husband might turn us out. Right now, I have a cabin here in Marshtown and a job blacksmithing. If I agree to this plan, I might end up with nothing."

Sophia saw Judith send her a disappointed sideways glance. Answering with an almost imperceptible shake of her head, Sophia pleaded with Ulysses, saying that would never happen, that a person had to have faith. Ulysses rubbed his hand across his closely cropped hair, saying that sometimes people meant well, but . . ." He didn't finish the sentence.

Saying that he understood Ulysses's concerns, Father suggested a written agreement that stipulated that the cabin and half of the orchard belonged to Ulysses and his heirs as a payment for overseeing the work on the plantation until the plantation became profitable. As soon as the Landing generated income, Ulysses would draw a fair wage.

Ulysses's face brightened and glanced toward Chloe, who nodded.

The very next morning, Father drew up the agreement and a bill of sale, which Judith and Ulysses both signed, Judith with her full name, Judith Abigail Talcott; Ulysses with his mark. The cabin in the orchard now belonged to him in perpetuity. Nathan served as a witness, and for the first time signed his name. Sophia couldn't have been prouder. It had been less than a week since, true to her promise, she showed up at milking time with her dog-eared copy of one of the McGuffey Readers, a slate, and chalk. It was hard to tell who was enjoying lesson time more.

That night at supper, Father proposed a toast, "To the new mistress of Records Landing."

Judith blushed and stammered her thanks for all their help. She hesitated. "I have one last indulgence to ask of you, a request really. I think since you will be moving on, building a new home, I would like to shorten this plantation's name to The Landing. I know I am happy to have landed here."

There was a murmur of surprise around the table until Uncle William stood and raised his glass. "Here! Here! I propose a toast to The Landing."

All, even Willie, raised a glass of cider. "Here! Here!"

"And," Uncle William continued, raising his glass again, "a toast to the young Sophia, who will be joining my family in Baltimore."

"No, you misunderstood," Sophia gasped. For her uncle to make such an announcement was not only out of order, but it also wasn't correct. She twisted her napkin around and around, tighter and tighter as she thought how to explain herself. She had planned to tell her parents her decision in private, not at supper in front of everyone. She just hadn't found the right moment.

Uncle William had spoiled it. Mother was looking disappointed; Aunt Polly triumphant. Faith and Willie both looked as if they were going to cry. As for Nathan, when she glanced his way he gave a little shrug, as if to say, I should have guessed you would stay behind. It stung. He thinks I am deserting, she thought.

Pushing her chair back, she stood up and squared her shoulders.

"I truly appreciate you and Aunt Polly opening your home to me but . . ." Sophia looked around the table, at all the expectant faces before continuing. "I am afraid you misunderstood me. When I said I was thinking of staying here, I meant here at Great House with Judith. I . . ."

"Well!" Aunt Polly broke in, her tone icy. "You have such promise. Now you are throwing your future away." Turning to Father, she said, "Her reputation will be ruined, Elijah. Do not allow it."

Father's expression was stormy. "Sophia, please sit down before all the men at the table feel obliged to stand. We will discuss your plans after our meal."

Sophia sank down on her chair, realizing that her knees were a little wobbly.

There was no more happy chatter at the table.

34

True North

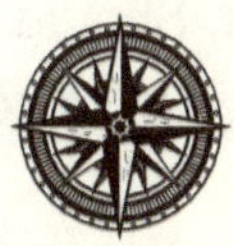

Sophia walked into Father's office after supper with her head held high because she knew her decision was the right one. She wanted to explain herself. To her surprise, Father was not alone. He was standing by the window. Mother was sitting in the wing chair. The tension in the room was unmistakable. Stopping in the center of the room, Sophia looked at them with apprehension.

"I think you have the wrong impression," she began. "When I talked to Uncle William, I was just thinking out loud. He mistook what I said."

"That's the trouble, Sophia. You rarely think before you speak. Words just spill out of your mouth," Father said, not unkindly.

"But . . ."

"No 'buts.' Your rashness only demonstrates your youth," Mother added.

Father walked over to stand beside Mother's chair. He placed a comforting hand on her shoulder before addressing Sophia. His tone was stern. "You agreed to either living in Baltimore under the protection of my brother's family or coming with us to Ohio. There is no other alternative."

"I never would have considered a third if Judith hadn't proven herself to be a friend. When I discussed remaining here with her, she seemed amenable."

Mother pressed a handkerchief to her mouth as if to hold back angry words. When she lowered the lacy cloth, she gave Sophia a steely-eyed look. "Under no circumstances can you remain here at Great House. It is unseemly, unthinkable. With Ulysses and Chloe living here, Judith will manage. Should her father be released, there is no accounting what would happen to you. The possibilities make my blood run cold."

Father cleared his throat, a well-known habit of his when emphasizing the importance what he was about to say.

"I cannot promise life will be easy in Ohio," he said, "Any more than I can promise that perusing your studies in Baltimore will make you happy. But those remain your choices."

Clenching her fists, Sophia turned away, half tempted to walk out of the office. Her parents' unwillingness to hear her out was unfair. But walking out on them would be just as unfair. Instead, she walked over to Mother's chair, sat down on the floor and reached for Mother's hand.

"You don't understand," she said wearily. "Please, hear me out."

Father, who still stood behind the chair, took a deep breath. "Proceed," he said.

Now it was Sophia's turn to take a deep breath. It was important that there be no more misunderstandings. "Having given both my choices considerable thought," she began, "I know for certain that I have no interest in staying in Baltimore. I don't want to live in a city where smoke and squalor perfume the air or where I would be compelled to live a dull, ordinary life. I want to see the world from the top of a mountain and to hear a wolf howl at night. I want to do important things, to live an extraordinary life." She paused to take a breath. "But when I found out James was alive, I thought I should stay here at Great House with Judith so that when he comes back, we can make the journey to Ohio together."

"Is it wise to make such a decision for your brother?" Father said. "I have learned not to assume that what you want others want, too."

Hearing the remorse in his voice, Sophia realized that his regret in demanding that James study law was the reason Father had given her a choice.

"Waiting for me to decide must have tried your patience," Sophia said, looking at her father with a new understanding, "and I appreciate your giving me a choice. What I have been trying to explain is that waiting here for James was only a consideration, not a decision. When he comes home, James has the right to make up his own mind. As for me, I want to go to Ohio."

Mother must have been holding her breath because Sophia heard her exhale before whispering, "Thank you, Lord."

Father cleared his throat before asking "What changed your mind?"

"Something Grandsire said," Sophia replied. "I remembered the night he pointed out the North Star. He said that it was the only constant point of light in the night sky. The other stars moved across the sky just as the sun and the moon do. When a sailor sets his compass by the North Star, the compass will point to the Earth's True North, the North Pole. He said anyone can find his True North in life by setting his spiritual compass to what he values most. I thought about what I hold most dear and realized my North Star is pulling me to Ohio."

Sophia stood and straightened her skirt. She wanted to hug her parents, to tell them that they were her True North, but, suddenly self-conscious, she just smiled and left the room before her parents could utter a word. After all, there were others, one person in particular, who needed to learn the truth.

Now that she knew where she was headed, the days flew by. Uncle William and Aunt Polly left for Baltimore in their shiny carriage, promising to collect everything being shipped to them on the *Rebel Ann* as soon as Caleb sent word the schooner had docked.

On the night before Father packed up his books, stationery, and pens, Sophia lay on her side of the bed, staring out the window at the stars above the magnolia tree when she remembered a promise. She and James must have been ten or eleven years old. Sophia wasn't sure. They had been outside, beneath the magnolia. It must have been winter as the tree branches were bare. Overhead thousands of stars decorated the night sky.

It was the night James told her that as soon as he was old enough to qualify, he was going to join the Navy. She said she would join, too.

"Girls can't be sailors. Don't you know it's bad luck to have women aboard on a man-of-war?" He had shot her an annoyed look implying she was a bother, a tag-a-long. "You don't have to do everything I do."

Sophia had called him a dunce and declared that someday she, too, would have a grand adventure.

James grinned. "I have no doubt of that, Phee," he said. "Just be sure to let me know." He gave her a thoughtful look. "You know it won't always be like this. We won't always be together. When I am away, write to me."

"Where will you be?"

"At sea, of course."

"Where will I be?"

"Here, probably married."

"Let's make a promise then," Sophia said.

"A promise?" James sounded skeptical.

"Yes. Look at the sky." She pointed to two bright stars high in the sky. "Those are the star twins. Grandsire showed then to me. They are part of a constellation named Gemini. The two bright stars are the heads of twins. The other, fainter stars make up the twins' bodies. It's harder to see those stars without Grandsire's spyglass."

James stared up at the sky and after some searching found the two bright stars. "Which one is me?" he asked.

"Does it matter? What matters is that those twins are there, together in the sky. So, promise me," Sophia said. "Wherever you are, if you are lonesome, look for Gemini and think about me. And when I look at those stars, I will think about you. That way we will always be together."

James laughed and called her silly but in the end he promised.

Now, wondering if Gemini was visible, Sophia slipped out of bed and walked to the window. Clouds hid the stars from view. Quietly, she left the room and padded downstairs. She lit a candle from embers in the hearth, walked into Father's office, and sat down at the secretary. Sheets of vellum were still stacked on the desktop. She uncapped the brass inkwell, inked a quill, and began to write.

Dear James,

I always knew you would come back. What I did not know is that we would be gone. Miss Judith Talcott, your friend first and now mine as well, is mistress of Great House now. I will leave it to Judith to relate all that transpired prior to our departure.

Our family has a new home in Ohio. Imagine we have to cross the Allegheny Mountains to get there. Father has inherited Grandsire's bounty land in Adams County. He goes on and on about the good black soil and the tall trees. He believes that the future of our country lies in the West.

Although I imagine you are tired of traveling, I hope you will continue on to Aberdeen, that's the name of our town. It's just off the Zane trace near the Ohio River. Apparently, the town's not much to look at right now but Father says it will grow. He also says the Indians have moved further west. Even so, during the winter, we will live in a nearby stockade.

Our family is not quite the same as when you left. Faith is engaged to be married to Zachariah Mueller. His parents own a parcel of land next to ours, and Zach (that's what Faith calls him) plans to build his own cabin there, so we will be neighbors. Willie is wearing britches and has learned to ride, thanks to Mr. Nathan Harkness. Mr. Harkness has been helping out here and will accompany us to Ohio. I think you will find him to be a stalwart friend, as have I. Willie was brokenhearted when he learned Father had sold Pearl. After he begged Father not to send Pearl away, Father promised him a dog, a Newfoundland just like the one that traveled west with the Lewis and Clark expedition. Yes, you read correctly. Father's beautiful mare now belongs to Commodore Decatur. Father said she wasn't suitable for frontier life.

I hope I am. Imagine me living in a log house on the frontier! Surely this is my grand adventure. It can be yours, too.

We all miss you and hope to see you very soon.

With great affection,

Phee

As soon as the ink dried, Sophia folded the letter. Sliding it into an envelope, she sealed the top flap with candle drippings then pressed her thumb into the hot wax. The hall clock chimed the hour before striking one mellow note. It echoed throughout the sleeping household. Blowing out the candle, Sophia tiptoed back upstairs. She slid the letter into the drawer with her spare clothing.

A week later, Sophia stood in front of the long wooden pier, saying goodbye. As her Marshtown friends gathered around her, she was tempted to change her mind again. Leaving Great House was proving to be the hardest thing she had ever done. How could the folks in Marshtown go on without her? Who would teach the children to read?

Oriole must have understood because she patted Sophia gently on the cheek.

"Never you mind about us," Oriole told her. "We'll be fine. You go on." Then she handed Sophia a wooden box with small packets of seed inside, each one labeled in Oriole's careful hand.

"Plant these herbs next spring," Oriole said. "In time, your garden will be as beautiful as the Widow's."

Sally stepped forward, handing Sophia a tin of biscuits. "I copied my recipe and put it inside. You'll bake the best biscuits in Ohio with that recipe. Now these chillens have something for you to remember them by as well."

Fry, Summer, and Becky each had drawn Sophia a picture. Fry had turned an A into a teepee. Summer chose the letter S, making it look like a Snake, while Becky, with Oriole's help, had scribbled wavy lines. "Ocean," she said proudly. Sophia hugged each child, saying she would always remember her very first students.

"And me," Jebbie said. "Don't forget me." He handed her a muslin bag, insisting she look inside. "Nathan helped me carve it," he said, suddenly shy. "I made it from a sycamore branch. Try it."

Sophia held the whistle to her mouth and blew. The loud, high-pitched sound made everyone on board turn to look.

"Doesn't it make a mighty sound?" Jebbie said, clearly delighted. "Blow hard if you need help. If I was closer, I'd come right away."

Sophia felt her throat tighten as she reached down to hug him. "I am sorry we will be so far apart," she said. "Your mama needs you now, but when you're older, maybe you will come to Ohio."

"I will. Soon as I'm grown," he said and then abruptly walked away.

"Until then," Sophia called, tears standing in her eyes.

Judith was the last to step forward. She had hung back until all the Marshtown families had left the pier.

"A month ago, I never thought I'd be saying this to a Talcott, but I will miss you," Sophia said and laughed lightly to make sure Judith knew she was joking.

Judith smiled. No longer hiding her face behind a hat and veil, she now wore her hair in the manner Faith had taught her.

"It won't be the same here without you," she said. "Stay safe."

Sophia nodded. Feeling her eyes begin to smart again, she looked away. Goodbyes were hard. Reaching into the small linen bag that hung from her wrist, she pulled out her letter to James. "Please," she said. "Give this to James when he comes. Even before you give him Father's instructions."

"Of course."

Sophia turned and walked up the gangplank. She stood on deck as the crew unfurled the sails and raised the anchor. After the rest of the family had waved their final goodbyes to the small crowd on the shore, she lingered, watching the long wooden pier grow smaller.

As the schooner sailed around the bend in the Pocomoke, she felt a tap on her shoulder. Nathan stood beside her.

"Come ahead," he said. "Everyone is forward at the bow."

Sophia smiled. The journey had begun. The Chesapeake lay ahead, then Baltimore. Beyond the city, lay the distant Alleghenies and beyond the mountains a whole new land.

"I am coming," she said, taking hold of Nathan's arm. "I can't wait to see what will happen next."